SIN

K. LORAINE
USA TODAY BESTSELLING AUTHORS
MEG ANNE

This book is a work of fiction. The names, characters, places, and incidents are products of the author's imagination or have been used fictitiously and are not to be construed as real. Any resemblance to persons, living or dead, actual events, locales, or organizations is entirely coincidental.

Copyright 2025 © Ravenscroft Press

All rights reserved.

ISBN:

978-1-961742-44-4 (Paperback Edition)

978-1-961742-45-1 (Hardback Edition)

No artificial intelligence was used in the creation of this work of fiction.

You may not copy, distribute, transmit, reproduce, or otherwise make available this publication (or any part of it) in any form, or by any means (including without limitation electronic, digital, optical, mechanical, photocopying, printing, recording, or otherwise), without the prior written permission of the author.

NO AI TRAINING: Without in any way limiting the authors' [and publisher's] exclusive rights under copyright, any use of this publication to "train" generative artificial intelligence (AI) technologies to generate text is expressly prohibited. The author reserves all rights to license uses of this work for generative AI training and development of machine learning language models.

Permission requests can be sent via email to: authors@themategames.com

Edited by Mo Sytsma of Comma Sutra Editorial

Cover Design by CReya-tive Book Design

Photographer: Wander Aguiar

Model: Mattheus M.

Breeder Readers (aka anyone who enjoys some sexual Russian roulette, better known as a breeding kink) we see you, we love you, this one—this whole series really—is for you!

"This is the way the world ends, not with a bang, but a whimper."

— T.S. ELIOT

SIN

K. LORAINE
USA Today BESTSELLING AUTHORS
MEG ANNE

AUTHORS' NOTE

Sin contains mature and graphic content that is not suitable for all audiences. Such content includes scenes of dubious consent, sex work, kidnapping, captivity and more. **Reader discretion is advised.**

As always, a detailed list of content and trigger warnings is available on our website.

OPERATION PFFN SUPER SECRET VIDEO CORRESPONDENCE: #1

Static screen blinks to life. Asher Henry appears in camera shot. Reaches out and taps microphone. Frowns into the camera.

<<static>>
<<clothes rustling>>
<<finger tapping mic>>

Asher: Is this thing on?

<<door opens>>

Remi: Asher, I told you not to start filming your weird porn stuff without me.

Asher throws a pillow at Remi.

Asher: Do you see my dick? This isn't porn, assface. It's the first official Operation Protect the Future From Non-existence video correspondence.

Remi: *laughs* Operation PUFFIN. Come on, Asher, are you serious?

Asher: It's a fucking apocalypse, Remington Mercer. Of course I'm serious. I'm a little busy here. If you're not going to help, can you get the fuck out?

Remi enters the frame and takes a seat next to Asher. Preens for the camera.

Remi: God, I look good. I see why you couldn't resist me.

Asher rolls his eyes.

Asher: You're as bad as a bottlenose dolphin.

Remi: Don't tell me you have a new aquatic mammal to obsess over. What will the puffins think?

Asher: Technically, puffins aren't mammals.

Remi: Not the point.

Asher: If you're going to insist on being here, at least do us both a favor and keep your mouth shut.

Remi: But you love my mouth.

Asher: Only when it's on my dick. Now shut up. Daddy's got to work.

Remi: Oh, kinky.

Remi waggles his brows at the camera then sits back and spreads his arms out across the back of the sofa.

<<couch rustling or squeaking>>

Remi: Continue . . . Daddy.

Asher: *heavy sigh* Thank you. Now, where was I?

Remi: *snorts in laughter*

Asher cuts Remi a withering stare.

Remi: Sorry. Sorry. Go on.

Asher: If you're watching this, you've been indoctrinated into a very elite group. Either you've already helped stave off one apocalypse, or you're somehow tied to those who have. Either way, we need your help.

Remi: Save the cheerleader, save the world.

Asher: For fuck's sake, Remi.

Remi: It had to be said.

Asher: Did it, though?

Remi: You're making it all doom and gloom, man. I had to lighten the mood. Everyone knows the best apocalyptic stories have a heavy dose of humor. Or romance.

Remi waggles his brows for the camera and proceeds to make kissy noises.

Remi: *kissy noises*

<<clothes rustling>>

<<couch rustling or squeaking>>

Remi leans his face close to Asher's with his lips puckered for a kiss. Asher uses his palm to push Remi away.

Remi: Ice cold. I'll remember that.

Asher: Now's not the time. I'll romance you so hard you won't be able to walk for a week if you just let me finish this.

Remi: You heard him, folks. If he doesn't deliver, your next message will be from me.

Asher: God help us.

Remi: Don't you mean Grandpa?

Asher glares at Remi. Remi mimes locking his lips.

Asher: As I was saying. We need your help. Before I can get to that, I figured it might be best to get everyone up to speed. While some of you have ties to each other and know a few of the pertinent details, others are new to our merry little band of delinquents.

Remi: Introduction time! Previously on The Mate Games...

Asher: I'm sorry, The what games?

Remi: The Mate Games. Because, you know, we've all come together and found our mates while also fighting off the psycho bitch horse-women and staving off the apocalypse... Apocalypses... Apocalypsies?

Asher: *sighs* I'm sorry I asked. Sure. We'll go with that.

Asher leans forward and rests his elbows on his knees, looking earnestly into the camera.

Remi: Oh, you're hitting them with the Zoolander. Good move, babe. You're sure to win them over now.

Asher shakes his head, sighs, and looks back at the camera.

Asher: It all started with Sunday Fallon and her mother, the horsewoman War.

Remi: But she didn't know War was her mom.

Asher: I was getting to that. Stop backseat storytelling.

Remi: I can't help it if I have a certain flair for it that you lack.

Asher: I will fucking gag you, I swear to God, Remi.

Remi: If that was supposed to motivate me, I think you picked the wrong threat, handsome.

Asher: Later. Sunday was sent to Ravenscroft University and met her four mates under the super sneaky manipulation of War, who'd been posing as an ally.

Remi: Tell them about the baby. That's the most important part.

Asher: Oh my God. Yes, War brought all four mates together and ensured Sunday got pregnant to break the seven seals.

Remi: Don't forget the hot priest. He was the one who saved everything.

Asher: Kind of.

Remi: The dude died so everyone else could live. He's basically Jesus with an Irish accent.

Asher: By that logic, so is Pan.

Remi: *snorts* He wishes.

Asher: The baby was the harbinger of the apocalypse, but Sunday and her men were able to stop War before she took the final step to start the end times. They sent her packing and thought it was over.

Remi leans forward and stares intently into the camera.

<<clothes rustling>>
<<couch rustling or squeaking>>

Remi: Us next, right? This is the best of the stories.

Asher: Narcissistic much? *heavy breath* War might have been dealt with, but that only opened the field up for her sister Pestilence.

Remi: a.k.a. Mommy Dearest. Wait . . . Do all the horsewomen have kids that are involved in this? What in the weird pregnancy pacts . . .

Asher: It looks like that's the way this is shaping up. Except while War had a daughter, our Rosie isn't connected to Pestilence. I am. I'm the weird byproduct of a horsewoman and a fallen angel's wild night.

Remi: Don't forget the part where you were possessed by your demonic half brother.

Asher: I wish I could. Pan was in league with Pestilence until he accidentally fell in love with Rosie and mated her. Once Rosie found us all and accepted our marks, she became a vampire Queen. Capital Q. They're kind of a big deal. Super rare. You get the idea.

Remi: After that bitch Aisling killed her, forcing her to turn. Otherwise, she might never have been a vampire at all.

Asher: As much as I'm glad I didn't have to see Rosie die, I wish I'd been there to kill that bitch Aisling.

Remi: Ben took care of that for all of us. My twin is nothing if not fierce. And if it hadn't been Ben, Gavin would've done the job.

Asher: Yeah. The Count is good for something, I guess.

Remi: Don't you mean the Duke?

Asher: It was a joke. You know what, never mind. Continuing on. Pesty was masquerading as the mayor, spreading her plague right under our noses. We almost didn't stop her in time.

Remi: Tell me about it. I was patient zero. Until the power of true love saved me.

Remi gazes adoringly at Asher, batting his eyelashes. Asher scowls but takes Remi's hand in a tight grip.

Asher: Stop looking at me like that. You would have done the same for me.

Remi: I mean, we had a whole moment on my deathbed.

Asher: Okay, yes, we get it. I love you. Happy?

Remi: Yes.

Asher: Anyway, we took down Pestilence but nearly died doing it when she brought her bitch sisters to help in her attack. Pan was the real hero, though he never needs to know I said that.

Remi: Too bad he has a front-row seat to your thoughts.

Asher: We've gotten better at keeping each other out.

Remi looks to the camera.

Remi: The six of us have a little telepathic group chat. Perks of Rosie's whole vampire Queen thing.

Asher: And that brings us to the most recent crew. Dahlia and her mates.

Remi: *cough* losers *cough*

Asher: They were all housed at Blackwood Asylum, where the most dangerous supernatural creatures have been locked up for the 'good of the world.' Dahlia thought she was human but soon realized she could see ghosts and control the dead.

Remi: She's Death's daughter.

Asher: Thank you, Remi.

Remi: Just pointing out another connection. If Gavin was here, he'd be hanging up red strings all over the place.

Asher pats Remi's knee.

<<sound of hand patting leg>>

Asher: I'm sure he would be.

Asher rolls his eyes and makes a face at the camera.

Asher: Death turned out to be the biggest cunt of them all. Whereas War and Pesty were making moves in plain sight, Death was much more underhanded than her sisters. Her moves were so subtle, no one saw the writing on the wall until a literal army of the dead was unleashed on Blackwood's grounds.

Remi: That's Death for you. Sneaking around, snatching you when you least expect it.

Asher: Inevitable.

Remi nods, looking uncharacteristically somber.

Asher: Just like War, Death had a series of tasks she needed completed. Instead of seals, she was working on a different sort of ritual. One that required the assistance of the other horsepeople.

Remi: *neighs*

Asher: Seriously?

Remi: Had to be done.

Asher: If you say so. So anyway, unlike War, Death was successful with her ritual. Not only did she capture the four horsemen—

Remi: Yeah, about that . . . Do we need to worry about these fuckers? We've got enough on our plates just trying to survive over here.

Asher flicks an annoyed gaze at Remi and takes a deep, centering breath.

Asher: Hard to say. We have to assume that those guys were already in play to some extent.

Remi: Yeah, but now their beehive got smacked, you know? They're probably out for blood.

Asher: That might work in our favor if it means they're against the women. The enemy of my enemy and all that.

Remi: True. True. Maybe we could recruit them to the puffin cause. How *does* one go about hunting down a horseman?

Asher: Right now we need to be focused on the aftereffects of Death's win. She didn't just capture the horsemen and complete her ritual. She also managed to unlock the cage that was keeping Lucifer in check. So now, you know, the devil's loose. The apocalypse has started—

Remi: To be clear, it's still in the early stages, at least according to Pan. It hasn't fully taken root yet. Maybe there's still time to cut it down to size?

Asher: You done?

Remi: With the plant metaphors? Totally. But I have a question.

Asher: Of course you do.

Remi: Who's the new sibling?

Asher: What do you mean?

Remi: Well, like . . . think about it. Noah and Rosie, related. Me and Ben, twins. You and Pan, halfsies. Tor and Alek, also twins but less good-looking. We're all tied to each other somehow, outside of the bitches of the end times. So who else is there?

Asher: I don't know.

Remi: You think Famine had a kid? Is that the connection?

Asher: Seems likely.

Remi shudders and makes a face, shifting uncomfortably on the couch.

<<couch rustling or squeaking>>
<<clothes rustling>>

Remi: Ugh, Pamela.

Asher: Pamela?

Remi: That's what I named her after she gave me that stupid soul-sucking kiss.

Asher: I still don't get it.

Remi: Poor Man's American Lilith.

Asher: And yet, you gave me shit about Operation PFFN.

Remi shoves Asher playfully.

<<sound of bodies making impact>>
<<couch rustling or squeaking>>
<<clothes rustling>>

Asher: *soft Oof* Careful with the goods man.

Remi: Don't worry, I'll kiss it better as soon as we're done here.

Asher: Why'd you shove me?

Remi: I was having an epiphany.

Asher: Do I even want to know?

Remi: I think I figured out what Operation PFFN is. A way we can try to stop all of this, right? Because from the sound of things, the world is ending, and there's nothing we can do. We're not the heroes here. Someone else has the reins.

Asher: That's not what Gabriel said. And we might not be the heroes, but we still have an important part to play. Consider yourself assembled, fellow Avenger.

Remi: Dude. No. Just no.

Asher: Guess we're crossing off the Captain America, Winter Soldier role play.

Remi: Dibs on playing America's ass! I was born for that role.

Asher: Can confirm.

Remi: Back to the topic at hand—

Asher: Since when are you the one to get us *back* on track?

Remi rolls his eyes and scowls.

Remi: The question you *should* be asking is, since when are we still listening to Leather Feathers?

Asher: Not like we have any other angels out there willing to talk to us. But regardless, we've got to try, right? We didn't all come this far and sacrifice everything we have just to let it all go to shit now.

Remi: Careful, you're starting to sound like a hero. It's hot.

Asher: Anyway, if you're still watching this shit show, a text message will be coming through from an encrypted number containing coordinates and a date. I hope you'll show up so we can meet face-to-face and figure out our next steps.

Remi: This message will self-destruct in 5 ... 4 ...

Asher: *world weary sigh* It won't, but that would be cool. Maybe next time. You might want to delete it, though, just to be safe. Never can be too careful.

Remi gives the camera a shit-eating grin and an obnoxious salute.

Remi: Operation PFFN out!

<<static>>

End of transmission.

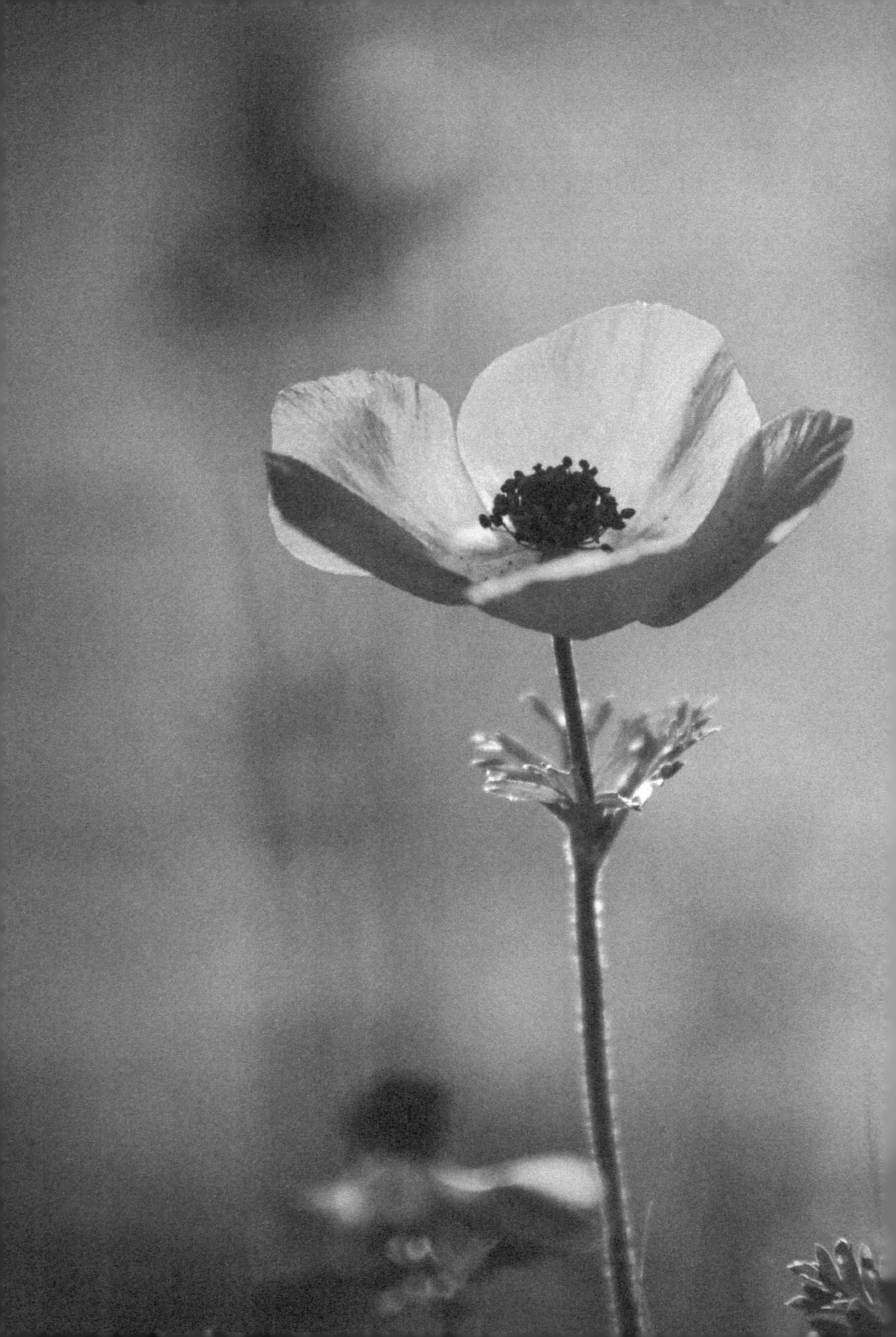

Chapter One

GRIM

I hadn't been to a sex club in over fifty years. Not exactly my scene, not even one as posh as *Iniquity*. Then again, it's not like I exactly had a choice in the matter. I'd been summoned, or rather, we'd been summoned by Lilith, the first demon.

Without conscious thought, I fingered the edges of the smooth black card in my pocket, recalling the words on the back with perfect clarity.

I'm calling in that favor you owe me, Grim darling.
Iniquity. Midnight.
Don't be late.
L

One by one, my brothers popped into existence behind me until the four of us stood shoulder-to-shoulder staring up at the tasteful neon sign emblazoned with the establishment's moniker. I said stood, but what I really meant was swayed.

It had only been a handful of hours since we escaped the clutches of my counterpart and former paramour, Hel. She was more commonly known as Death herself, and now, the architect of the end times.

Damn her.

If anyone deserved the honor of that title, it was me. I was the oldest of our kind. The original, you might say. When the horsewomen were created centuries later, we'd thought they were made to help us in our task of bringing about the apocalypse. One for each of us.

They had other ideas, or perhaps ambitions is more accurate. Whatever the word, those four had no intention of playing second fiddle to anyone, let alone us. So instead of allies, we became competitors, all working toward the same endgame.

Hel was the first to ever reach the finish line.

At our expense, no less.

A low growl escaped, my fury at not only being bested but humiliated making me lose my grip on my ironclad self-control.

The wave of discomfort that washed over me had me gritting my teeth and taking a steadying breath. I had never before felt this way. Weak. Damaged. Mortal. Hel had nearly drained us dry of our power, and she'd done it so easily. If I was being honest, I don't think we ever stood a chance. The second she sprung her trap, it was over. Inevitable.

Death always was.

"Did we come all this way just to stare up at some pretty lights, Grimsby? Or are we actually going inside the place?" Malice's droll voice dragged me from my spiraling thoughts.

"No one gets inside without a membership," the mountain of a man standing guard at the door grumbled.

Sin huffed out an incredulous laugh. "We're the horsemen of the apocalypse. Lilith grandfathered us in. I can guarantee it."

The doorman checked his list and shook his head. "No, mate. No horsemen on the list. Better luck next time."

Chaos bristled beside me, his body seeming to swell in size as he took a step forward and demanded, "Check again."

He crossed his arms over the wide expanse of his chest. The move appeared threatening due to the way it made his muscles bunch and flex, but I clocked it for what it truly was. A way to hide the trembling in his fingers. It was taking everything he had to appear outwardly unaffected. Same as me.

Still using the same bitten-off growl, he slowly and purposefully gave the doorman our names. "Grimsby, Chaos, Malice, and Sinclair. Or perhaps you'd prefer our aliases. Death, War, Pestilence, and Famine."

The cocky Australian raised one brow. "Get in line. There's always someone who thinks they're the most important creature in the world trying to get in. You're not on the list, and that's final."

Pulling the notecard from my pocket, I stepped forward and presented it. The stupid fucker clearly didn't believe in or understand the power we wielded because as he took the note, his bare fingertip brushed mine. The light left his eyes instantly, his soul absorbed by my power. A chill covered my body as it happened, almost like his energy blanketed me before becoming part of my being.

The doorman crumpled to the ground in an ungraceful heap just as the door behind him swung open, revealing the woman we were here to see.

"Did you really have to kill him? I liked that one. Such a delicious accent."

Lilith Duval stood in the doorway, dressed head to toe in shiny red vinyl. All she needed was a pair of devil horns and she'd look the part of a university girl playing sexpot for Halloween.

"At least you know I've still got it," I muttered.

"You're lucky that happened outside the actual walls of the club, or you'd find yourself on the receiving end of one of my punishments, if not outright banishment."

I rolled my eyes, not remotely in the mood for all this posturing.

"Let us in, would you? We're dead on our feet, and your doorman was a real tosser."

"What's with inviting us to your place and not making sure our names were on the list?" Sin asked, using the wall to keep himself propped up. He looked marginally better than he had in my penthouse, the sweat merely beading his hairline and no longer dripping down his face. Maybe it was the proximity to all the lust pouring out of *Iniquity's* door. I certainly felt a bit perkier after draining that nuisance.

"Forgive me for assuming the four of you could manage to simply transport yourselves to my office. You're the horsemen, after all. If a bloody angel can do it, I thought surely you could as well."

Chaos coughed. "We've been weakened by Helene. Her ritual took almost everything we had."

Lilith's gaze traversed his form slowly, soaking in every detail. "Mmm, yes, you are looking a tad peaky." She shot a sly glance at Malice, lips quirking as she took him in. "If it isn't the deadbeat to end all deadbeats."

Mal's upper lip curled in what could only be labeled as loathing. "I am not one of your puppets, Lilith. Do not confuse me with one. You will not like how it ends."

"It's shocking how alike you and your son sound. Have you ever met him? He's much changed now that he saved the world."

Mal, the only one of us to successfully sire a child, stiffened. He rarely spoke of Pan and his tryst with the horsewoman Pestilence, Odette. I'd gotten him outrageously pissed once, and he'd spent the night spilling his secrets, but we never spoke of it again. I very well might be the only creature in existence who knew just how deep her betrayal where their progeny was concerned cut him. Or that the wound never fully healed.

"I haven't had the pleasure," Mal said through gritted teeth.

I forced myself not to flick my gaze his way. I knew that was a bald-faced lie. Mal practically had a tracker on his son; he'd been watching every move Pan made for decades as soon as technology allowed. Before then, he had his spies. Lilith could accuse Malice of being an absent father all she wanted, but that didn't make it the truth. If given the chance, Mal never would have let that child out of his sight.

"Well, perhaps I'll arrange a little introduction soon. He has become like a son to me. Such an asset to my . . . lifestyle." Lilith crooked her finger and smirked. "Come along, boys. We have much to discuss, but this is a conversation best held behind closed doors."

Exchanging glances with each of my brothers, a wordless warning to be on guard passed between us. Outwardly, no one would guess that unease coursed through each of us. It was only the centuries of familiarity that allowed me to sense what they were really feeling. What was harder to say was whether that unease resulted from Hel's ritual or just the rather ironic position we'd found ourselves in. For while we were arguably the four most powerful creatures in the room, Lilith currently had us by the metaphorical balls.

Once in the hallway, we were met with a dashing fae man who leaned against the wall, impatience written all over his face.

"Finally, Lilypad. I know you expect me to be at your beck and call, but waiting on you to bring back four men is a bit much."

"Who's this idiot?" Sin asked before the rest of us could.

As Lilith opened her mouth to respond, a current raced along my arms and I would have sworn I heard an echo of thunder in the distance.

"I'm hers. That's all you need to know."

Lilith pulled on the thin chain connecting her wrist to the collar around his throat. The golden strand between them was so thin I nearly missed it, save the slight glint when the links hit light. She tugged harder, pulling him toward her before leaning in as if she would kiss him. Then, when he closed his eyes, ready to accept, she licked his lips and a faint giggle escaped her.

"He *is* mine. Crombie, meet the horsemen. Boys, this is my pet,

Drystan Abercrombie Nightshade. My captive fae prince. Isn't he delightful?"

This time it was Chaos who spoke. "Nightshade . . . If memory serves, that would make you the heir to the Night Court, would it not? So how did you find yourself here, chained to this one?" He tilted his head to indicate he was speaking about Lilith.

"That's a long story, and frankly, none of your fucking business," Crombie replied silkily. There was another ripple in the air, as if a storm was just about to break, and I realized it was coming from him.

As one of the fae royals, he was power personified, same as we were. That much was obvious. But it had nothing to do with why the word *dangerous* danced through my mind as I studied him. No, that was thanks to the slightly unhinged look in his quicksilver eyes. The look that didn't quite abate until Lilith's fingers caressed the length of his chest.

"Now, now, poppet. You're making my hair frizz with all this bluster, and that just won't do." Lilith began walking, her prince trailing behind her as we followed.

"What the fuck does this succubus want with us, Grim?" Chaos asked in a low voice. "I'd much rather be recovering and then plotting our revenge than wasting time at a sex club."

"I love it here. I don't know about you guys, but I feel ten times better than I did earlier. This place is feeding me by just existing." Sin took a deep breath. "Mmm, lust in every corner."

"Careful," Lilith warned. "No one likes a thief, and you're poaching my evening meal, incubus."

"Aw, come on, Lil. Sharing is caring."

"I'm going to remind you that you said that, Sinclair. Sooner than you think."

I was able to ignore the impulse to roll my eyes yet again, but only just. The constant bickering and one-upping were just a few of the many reasons I despised interacting with demonkind. Everything was a fucking competition. I wasn't any better, far from. I'd just long ago learned that Death always won in the end, and that took most of the fun out of it.

The deeper we went down the darkened hallway, the louder the pulse of house music became. Sin stopped at the side-by-side doorways, each one with staircases going in opposing directions.

"Mmm, you've created quite a smorgasbord for yourself here, Lilith. The energy coming from either of these could feed me for a week."

Lilith stopped and cast a glare over her shoulder. "It will feed *me*. Don't get any ideas, Sinclair. I've already told you." Her gaze flitted to me. "It's a little different than it was the last time you were here, isn't it, Daddy Death?"

I bristled and offered her a grunt in response.

Those shrewd eyes trailed my body, stopping at my bare hands. "Where are your gloves? Don't tell me you've forgotten the rules. It's not like you to miss such an important detail."

The rule she referred to she'd set in place the first time I'd been invited to a, let's call it a business meeting, at her sanctuary. Fair enough, I supposed. Sitting around a table with Death could hardly inspire comfort. The only way she could get the others to agree to attend was if I promised to wear gloves. The fact that they believed that would stop me from reaping their souls if I so chose was laughable, but it made them feel safe. The important detail to note was the gloves would prevent me from *accidentally* killing someone who might be stupid enough to brush up against me.

"I'll be on my best behavior." My hands wouldn't leave my pockets the rest of this visit.

"What's downstairs?" Chaos asked, peering into the stairwell, its red-hued ambience making it clear exactly what we'd find.

"Sex," I muttered. "More than you'd know what to do with."

"And my special rooms."

"Special rooms?" Malice asked. "Like torture chambers?"

Lilith's blood-red lips quirked into a wicked grin. "If required by the user, yes. My rooms give their occupants every fantasy they can dream up."

"I'm in the wrong line of work," Sin said, closing the distance between himself and the staircase. "You guys can handle this without me, right? I just want to see—"

"No," I barked. "Keep going. We need to get this meeting over with."

Lilith's throaty laugh carried through the hall as she continued forward, stopping when she reached a nondescript door. Turning to Crombie, she said, "Now, you wait out here while I tend to business. We are not to be disturbed, pet. Not even by you."

"Aren't you going to give me a kiss before you abandon me yet again?"

"Aw, is my poor prince feeling neglected?"

"Regularly."

Lilith's laugh was like the tinkle of a bell. Instead of giving him the kiss he'd asked for, she brushed her knuckles down the side of his cheek. "Need looks good on you, pet." Then she sashayed into her office, leaving him pouting in her wake.

"I feel like I should be taking notes," Sin murmured as we filed into the room after her, the door whispering closed without anyone touching it.

"Of course you should, darling. Everything I do is noteworthy."

Lilith fell gracefully into the chair behind her desk, kicking her stiletto-clad feet up onto the polished wood top. The golden chain connecting her to the man outside glittered in the light, and I wondered about the magic binding them.

Apparently Malice did as well because he asked, "Why is it you have a chain instead of a regular demon mark to represent your deal?"

"What makes you think we made a deal at all?" she countered with a lift of one perfectly sculpted brow.

"Because I know you. Deals are your forte."

She lifted one shoulder in an elegant shrug. "I can only assume it has something to do with his fae nature."

"You didn't think to press the issue?" Chaos asked.

"Why bother?" Lilith replied. "What's done is done, and I have much bigger fish to fry."

"Speaking of," I chimed in, my body one never-ending ache and my patience long past waning, "Why did you summon us?"

"Because the end is here."

Chaos let out a disbelieving snort. "Do you think we don't know that?"

"And I need you to help me stop it."

"There it is . . . the other shoe." Malice plopped heavily onto a nearby velvet chair, looking a little worse for wear. "We don't stop the apocalypse, Lilith. We herald it."

"Not this time, I'm afraid. As I told Grim, I'm calling in my favor. You don't get a choice."

Three sets of eyes swung my way, but my gaze was locked on Lilith and her smirk. "Regardless of our interference on your behalf, it might be too late."

"You know as well as I that it's not. The Princes are currently still locked away, and there's that *other* matter."

My skin crawled at the thought of the final piece required to crown Lucifer the king of Earth and hell. "How are we supposed to stop the antichrist from being born? We don't even know who its mother will be."

"Yes we do."

"We do?" Sin asked, leaning forward from his perch on the arm of Malice's chair. "Mmm, the plot thickens."

Lilith trailed a finger over her desk, her sharp black nail causing a deep scratch. "Lucifer won't be successful if he can't find her. That's where the four of you come in. Who better to protect her than the horsemen?"

"Let me get this straight," Chaos said, ever the stickler for details.

"You want us to directly oppose Lucifer by standing between him and the one woman in existence that can—"

"Say what she really means, War. She wants us to cockblock him."

Chaos shot Sin an annoyed glare and kept speaking. "Give him what he wants."

"Yes," Lilith said simply, though it was unclear which of the horsemen she was agreeing with.

"It won't stop him," I said.

"It will if you beat him to the punch," Lilith announced, looking like the cat who ate the fucking canary.

So that's what she was *really* after.

"Knock her up?" Sin asked, perking up considerably. "Really?"

"If he can't impregnate her, this little apocalypse of his will fizzle out. The antichrist is the key to clinching the deal. The oh-so-important cherry on top of the sundae. The countdown began the moment Hel released him from his prison. It must be his vessel, and it must be her firstborn."

"So he can do this any time he likes if we don't get to her first?" Malice asked, almost conversationally.

"Why not let him breed her and then we *take care of it*? Wouldn't that be the easier course of action?" Chaos asked.

Lilith sprang to her feet, eyes blazing with power. "You will not harm a hair on her head. If you do, all hopes of future procreation or even practicing it will be gone because I'll have your cocks strung up like garland on my mantel."

Sin winced and protectively cupped his crotch. "No thank you. I'm much more interested in the plan that allows for all the fucking."

As usual, we ignored Sin and carried on as if he hadn't spoken.

"Friend of yours, is she?" I asked, sensing what Lilith hadn't said.

"Not a friend. Merri is more of a daughter, not by blood, of course, but she might as well be."

"You have her here?"

"I've been keeping her safe. She's working in her room as we speak."

Turning her computer around to face us, she pointed to the video feed where a breathtaking redhead sat on the edge of a bed clad in nothing but a soft pink babydoll nightgown. The way she leaned forward and pressed her hands between shapely thighs as she focused on the laptop positioned on her desk was so sexual I had to suck in a tight breath.

"We'll take her," Sin breathed, clearly enamored.

"What is she doing?" Chaos asked, his voice tight.

"Working." Lilith turned the monitor around and broke the spell. "And feeding."

"She's a succubus?" Malice's question was filled with suspicion. "Doing cam work?"

"Not just any succubus. An extremely powerful one with a dangerous appetite. Exactly why it won't be a hardship for any of you to impregnate her before Lucifer gets a chance."

I stiffened, knowing exactly what would happen if I attempted to even graze her with the tip of my finger, let alone my dick.

"Count me out," Malice said. "I refuse to father another child that will be used for someone else's gain. Once was more than enough."

"Your loss," Lilith said breezily before turning her gaze to Chaos and Sin. "Surely you two don't have any complaints."

Chaos remained silent, his expression impossible to read. Sin, however, was like a child in a candy store. "I couldn't be more in. This is more gift than favor."

"You say that now," I warned. "What if the girl isn't interested in being bred by you?"

"You're joking, right? Have you seen me? I'm the walking epitome of seduction. If it was possible to impregnate women with a glance, I would have at least a million kids by now."

Malice shoved him off the couch. "Oops. Sorry. My arm slipped."

Sin grumbled something under his breath that sounded suspiciously like "corpse fucker" as he stood and straightened his clothes.

"You're forgetting something vital by assigning us this task, Lilith," Chaos said.

"Oh?"

"By design, we are unlikely to breed."

Lilith tutted. "False. Each of the four horsewomen has birthed a child. Twice over for Odette." Under her breath, she added, "How appropriate for Pestilence. Replicating just like a virus."

"Death is not supposed to create life," I said, the depth of my conflicted feelings about the matter completely absent from my tone.

"And yet Helene did just that. Gives me hope for the rest of you. Especially you, dear Grim. If your counterpart found a way to bear a child, surely you must be able to participate in the process as well."

In theory, that was true, but I'd yet to discover a way to touch any mortal without them immediately dropping dead at my feet. Sort of put a damper on one having a love life.

"I can't make any promises."

Chaos grunted, nodding in assent. "Then it's settled. We have to try. Lucifer can't be allowed to take over this world. He'd lock us away if given half the chance."

"Lock us up? What need does he have to keep the horsemen around once his apocalypse is complete and he gains all that power? We'll be lucky if he doesn't kill us outright," Malice said.

Sin's lips spread in a wide smile as he clapped his hands together. "Right. So when do we start?"

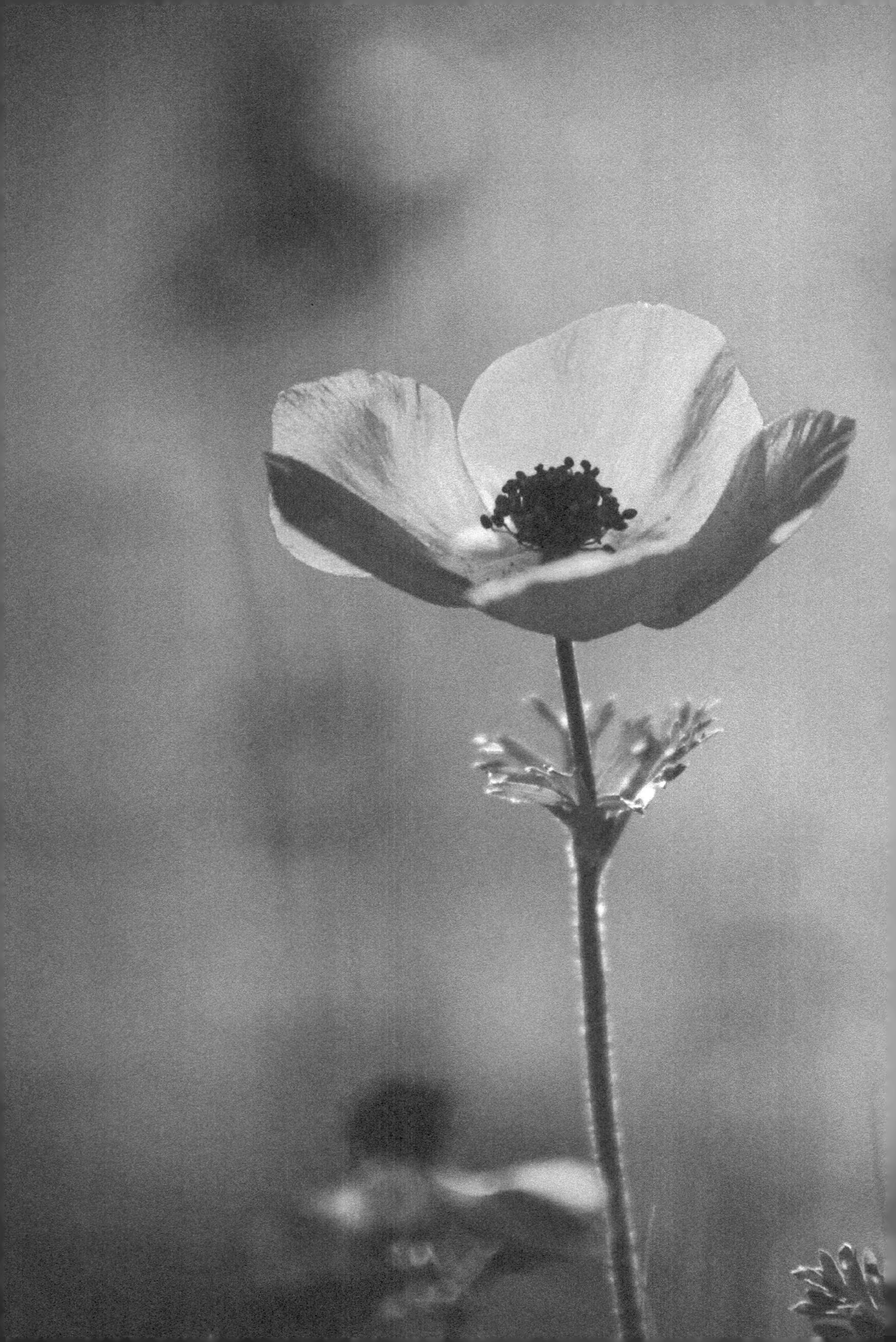

CHAPTER TWO

MERRI

It was hard to believe that only a handful of hours ago, Auntie Lilith broke me out of an asylum. Was I relieved? Yes, absolutely.

Blackwood Asylum wasn't supposed to be my permanent home like it had been for so many others. Lilith had sent me there on a fact-finding mission under the very true guise of me being an out-of-control succubus. It had been touch and go for a while when we realized the wards at the asylum prevented any resident from leaving for longer than a few hours. Thankfully, that hadn't ended up being an issue since some sort of ancient ritual broke through the wards that were locking us in there. I'm not sure what my aunt would have done otherwise.

A shudder worked its way down my spine at the thought of an eternity spent behind those stone walls. Shaking the cloak of unease off my shoulders, I continued unpacking my suitcase, desperate to settle back into what had become my normal life. I was where I belonged, here in the secret wing at *Iniquity*, where no one could be hurt by my ravenous appetite, but I could still live in relative peace.

This was a lonely existence: my bedroom, a few hallways, a very luxurious bathroom, a stocked kitchenette, and a little sitting room/library. It was almost like an apartment—until I remembered the literal sex dungeon a few floors above. That had been an eye-opening experience for a young succubus, let me tell you. I'd fed until I was something akin to drugged, and everyone in the dungeon was on the floor unconscious. To say Auntie Lilith had been displeased was an understatement.

In my defense, it wasn't my fault. I'd been sent back to Lilith specifically because I couldn't seem to get a handle on my power. I hadn't even known what I was until she put a name to it. Imagine my surprise when I finally decided to give Jimmy Harris my virginity and he dropped dead on top of me. I thought the poor boy had a heart attack, but no. It had been my newly awakened succubus draining him dry.

RIP Jimmy.

My foster parents hadn't wanted anything to do with me from that moment on. I couldn't really blame them. I'm sure it was terrifying, not knowing if I was going to murder them in their sleep. It wasn't until later, when I was safely tucked away at *Iniquity*, that Lilith explained to me what I was. And that my birth mother had dropped me off on her doorstep when I'd only been days old. Not wanting anything to do with raising an infant, Lilith had placed me with a human family, thinking that would be the end of it.

And maybe it would have been if Jimmy kept it in his pants.

Realizing exactly what happened, Lilith swept back into my life and took me under her wing. A child may not have been her cup of tea, but a budding succubus. That she could handle.

Looking back now, it all makes sense—how every time we made out I felt so good, but he was exhausted after. And that one time, when we'd dry humped on the couch and he came in his pants, then got a nosebleed and had to go home. It was me. I was the problem.

I'd never touched another partner again.

Which brings me back here. In my room, safely hidden from anyone I might accidentally harm. You'd think a girl would have learned how to control herself by now, but you'd be wrong. My power lashed out at the most inconvenient times. Do you have any idea how embarrassing that is? To be reading a sexy book and realize you made the entire subway car burst out into an orgy? Or daydreaming about your tutor only to realize she'd slumped into a drooling mess on the floor while you'd been twirling your hair around your finger?

Messy. That's what it was. Not to mention dangerous.

Consent was what separated us from other demons. Lilith had taught me that on my first day with her. But I still needed to feed in order to survive. That meant we needed to find a workaround since I couldn't be trusted not to murder everyone in *Iniquity* with my insatiable appetite.

Enter camming.

It was the answer to my prayers, really. A way for me to feed on the lust and sexual energy of consenting individuals without fear of them suffering any of the side effects. There was something incredibly freeing about the process. Knowing that I could give in to that part of myself without worrying that someone else would suffer for it. Camming was the only time I felt in control of my life and my body.

It also gave me a steady income stream and a way to pay Lilith back for some of what she gave me. I wasn't helpless or a freeloader. I needed to be able to stand on my own two feet, even if that was within the confines of her domain.

A wave of dizziness hit me, causing me to reach out and steady myself on the dresser.

"Well, you're not going to be standing on your own two feet if you don't freaking feed yourself, Meredith Anne Devereaux," I muttered to myself.

Pulling my laptop free of its travel case, I plugged it in and powered it on. The second I logged on to TwoLips—my preferred camming site—an electronic chime sounded, notifying me of an incoming message.

"Keep your pants on. I just got here."

The message wasn't one of my regulars, though. It was from Andi, my bestie, fellow cam girl, and sole connection to the outside world. I clicked on the picture of her with two blonde pigtails and a schoolgirl outfit, laughing as I always did at her chosen pseudonym.

PRETTYPENNY:

Where have you been?!?!?!

MERRI-GO-ROUND:

Did you run out of exclamation points?

PRETTYPENNY:

No.

PRETTYPENNY:

!

PRETTYPENNY:

!

PRETTYPENNY:

!

PRETTYPENNY:

I could do this all day.

MERRI-GO-ROUND:

Okay, okay. Point taken. Stop blowing up my DMs. I was on a vacation.

PRETTYPENNY:

And you didn't tell me? I thought you were dead.

MERRI-GO-ROUND:

So dramatic. I didn't have cell reception, and it just kind of happened.

PRETTYPENNY:

Oh, so when you say vacation, you mean vacation. I hope it paid well.

> MERRI-GO-ROUND:
> It wasn't a job.

> PRETTYPENNY:
> Sure. Sure. That's what I would say too. 😉

It had been a while since I used this room for camming, so I took my time setting up my ring light and adjusting my webcam for the perfect shot. Just enough cleavage, the ideal frame for my face, and of course, the goods. The goods being right between my legs.

> PRETTYPENNY:
> Getting back to work now?

> MERRI-GO-ROUND:
> Exactly. Gotta eat.

I chuckled at my little joke. Andi didn't know I was a succubus and meant that literally. For as close as we were, that secret would never be one I'd share. Andi was human and didn't know about the supernatural world. And just like Fight Club, the first rule of the supernatural world is we didn't talk about it with outsiders.

> PRETTYPENNY:
> Get it, girl! Wear that little pink number. You know the johns love that sweet, innocent look.

> MERRI-GO-ROUND:
> Babe. You've seen me. This body does not say innocent.

> PRETTYPENNY:
> True. It sort of screams fuck me and pay me for the privilege.

> MERRI-GO-ROUND:
> Guess I'm in the right line of work, then.

> PRETTYPENNY:
> One-hundo.

My head swam again, this time accompanied by a cold sweat on my lower back. It was showtime. I didn't have a choice. If I didn't feed soon, my body would force the issue, and I'd start sucking the lust out of the club above me. Auntie Lilith wouldn't like that. Not one bit.

MERRI-GO-ROUND:
GTG. Time to go live. I'll talk to you after if you're around.

PRETTYPENNY:
Knock 'em dead, babes.

Oh, if only she knew that was exactly what I was trying to avoid.

With a shake of my head and a little self-deprecating chuckle, I clicked out of our chat and into my online room: Merri's Playground. Taking a deep breath, I clicked the green camera icon that would take me live.

In a matter of seconds, my followers started popping in.

"Hi there!" I said in my seductive croon. "Did you miss me? I know it's only been a few days, but I missed all of you so much."

I was dressed in a robe, a deep purple velvet number that set off my hair, and I toyed with the collar, trailing a finger down the v between my breasts.

"I'm just getting ready for bed. Do you want to help me?"

Immediately, the replies started swarming in, each one punctuated with their monetary gifts.

JohnBoy27: You know it, baby doll.

TheRealMan: Only if I can get in with you.

BigMan69: Take off the robe and sleep naked.

ShyGuy25: Dibs on big spoon!

Bob1212: Show us your tits.

> CallMeMommy: You look so beautiful tonight. I love when you take your hair down.

> OnMyKnees4U: I missed your sweet voice. I wish I was that robe.

I blew a kiss into the camera. "You are so sweet."

Pulling the robe open a little more, I gave them a tease of my breasts before closing it again.

"What should I wear to bed tonight?"

I popped a poll in the chat, with pink babydoll and black lace teddy as the only two options. I knew this crowd, though. They'd pick the babydoll. Andi was right; they liked me innocent.

I was no psychologist, but I think it had something to do with being such a notable difference from my extreme hourglass curves. They loved the juxtaposition between something sweet and pure and carnal pleasure. Who was I to judge? To me, they were all basically one giant hamburger.

The money kept rolling in as they reacted to the poll, choosing exactly as I predicted. So, with deliberate slowness, I stood, turning my back to them as I dropped the robe. I had on a minuscule nude thong, but nothing else, and I could hear the notifications blowing up my computer.

Casting a glance over my shoulder, I said, "Oops, how clumsy of me. I dropped my robe."

The second I bent over, a flood of power swam through my veins. My followers might be predictable, but it just made the job easier. I spent an extra second or two playing with the fabric at my feet, letting them get their fill of my fabric-clad pussy and round ass. Selecting the pink babydoll from the two options I'd laid on my bed, I slipped the garment over my head. Their energy continued to wash over me, rejuvenating every cell and helping me return to my normal self.

I moaned and rolled my head from side to side before turning around to face the camera.

"What do you think?" I asked, striking a couple of cutesy poses before sitting back down and scrolling through some of the comments I'd missed.

At least ten newcomers were lurking, but my regulars were chatty as hell.

> EverySteve: Yeah, baby, just like that. Fuck, you make me so hard.

> BigMan69: Spread your legs for me. Pull that thong to the side so I can see what I really want.

> Bob1212: You're such a good girl.

> JohnBoy27: Touch yourself. Show us how wet you are.

> OnMyKnees4U: Fuck. Those nipples were made for my mouth. I'd worship you for hours.

> Tls4Tony: I can't wait to leave my handprint on that ass, beauty.

> TheRealMan: If I was there, you'd be the one begging me.

> ShyGuy25: I can't believe you're real.

> CallMeMommy: Me-ow! You have the prettiest kitty. 😺

"Some of you are getting very demanding. You know what to do if you want more. Book a private and I'll show you what you want to see." My mouth watered at the thought of how much more energy I received when I was in a private session.

> EverySteve: 🍆 💦 💦 😋

> Tls4Tony: Show me how you'd suck this dick.

"Book me and I will," I said, winking.

> BigMan69: Such a tease. Begging for a spanking.

> Bob1212: I want to see you make yourself come.

> TheRealMan: At least show us your tits. We're paying you to be here, give us something.

That sent a flash of anger through me, but I tamped it down, instead leaning forward, hands on my parted thighs and letting them get a good look at my breasts through the sheer material I was wearing.

"That's all you get in the playground. You want more, you have to book time in the tree house."

Almost on cue, a notification flashed in the upper right corner of my screen, showing me someone had done just that. I had to fight a smile when I saw the name of the requester.

ShyGuy25. Or as he'd recently asked me to call him, Cole.

"Looks like someone is taking me up on my offer," I told the others with a flirty wave. "Be back in a while."

I popped into the private room and waited for the notification that he'd joined. As usual, his portion of the screen remained black. Most of my clients preferred to remain anonymous, but every now and then, one would opt to get on the screen with me. Others liked to join the audio channel so we could directly interact and their hands could be free for . . . whatever. But for the most part, they liked to keep it text only. That was fine with me. As long as they participated, I got what I needed.

"Hi, Cole. How are you?"

"I'm glad you're back. The chat was really raunchy today. Are you okay?"

I'd never tell him, but Cole's voice was beautiful. Smooth and deep, soothing and addictive. I always looked forward to it when he booked time with me.

"Aw, it's sweet of you to ask. I'm fine. Sort of comes with the territory, but I don't want to waste our time talking about them. Tell me about your day."

Usually Cole spent our sessions just wanting to talk. Sometimes we'd get a little R-rated, but he struck me as exactly what his moniker suggested, a shy guy. I got the feeling he didn't interact with people out in the real world very often. Just like with the rest of my most loyal clients, Cole was interested in what Andi referred to as the "girlfriend experience." With me he was able to experience the kind of intimacy his real life denied him. And I had zero problem with playing girlfriend/therapist/real-life fantasy. So long as he kept me fed, I'd be anything he wanted.

"I'm fine. I spent most of the day plotting. Had a few deliveries arrive. Worked out, but I don't know why I care about keeping fit. It's not like anyone is going to see me."

"Well, just because you don't leave your house, that doesn't mean no one will see you. If you turn on your camera, I'll be able to look at you right now."

His husky laugh filled the line. "Tempting, but I'd hate to disappoint you."

"Cole, you could never disappoint me."

I knew it sounded like a line, but it was true. I didn't care one iota what Cole looked like. He'd proven himself to be a sweet soul more than once, and the gentle intimacy of our conversation kept me fed. What more could a starving succubus ask for?

"Maybe another time. I'd much rather focus on you."

"Okay then, tell me what you want tonight."

"What book are you reading right now? Tell me about it so I can get a copy and read along. Then after, I want to watch you make yourself feel good."

This was one of the things I enjoyed most about my time with Cole. He somehow made our transaction feel like a date. He made me feel respected, even when telling me he wanted to watch me get myself off. What a gentleman.

I lay across the bed, my body facing the camera. "Well, the book I just started is a historical romance about a wild viscount who has to hang up his rakish ways and settle down in a marriage of convenience."

"Mmm, and does she end up taming him?"

Giggling, I nodded. "Over and over."

"Show me how she did it," he whispered, his voice wrapping me in a sensual haze.

The high I got from his pleasure was nearly better than what I'd feel from my own. Closing my eyes, I rolled onto my back and pressed my ass into the bed. This move was a favorite. It arched my spine and popped my tits up so they could see them before my hand began moving toward the juncture of my thighs.

"Fucking beautiful," he said on a sigh.

"Will you touch yourself too?" I asked.

"No. This is all you, Merri."

I pouted a little, not actually faking my disappointment. I'd get way more out of this exchange if he participated. Lust was great, but nothing filled me up quite like a partner's climax.

My fingers were nearly to the waistband of my thong, my nipples hard, pussy wet from the sound of Cole's voice.

"Tell me what to do, C—"

The door burst open and the lights went out, casting the room in near-perfect darkness.

"Grab her," a gruff British voice snapped.

"Wha—" Strong hands hauled me off the bed before I could get the word out.

Something soft and sweetly scented covered my mouth and nose, making me instantly woozy. My eyes closed, and sleep began to overtake me, but not before warm lips at my ear whispered, "Sorry, Red. You're coming with us."

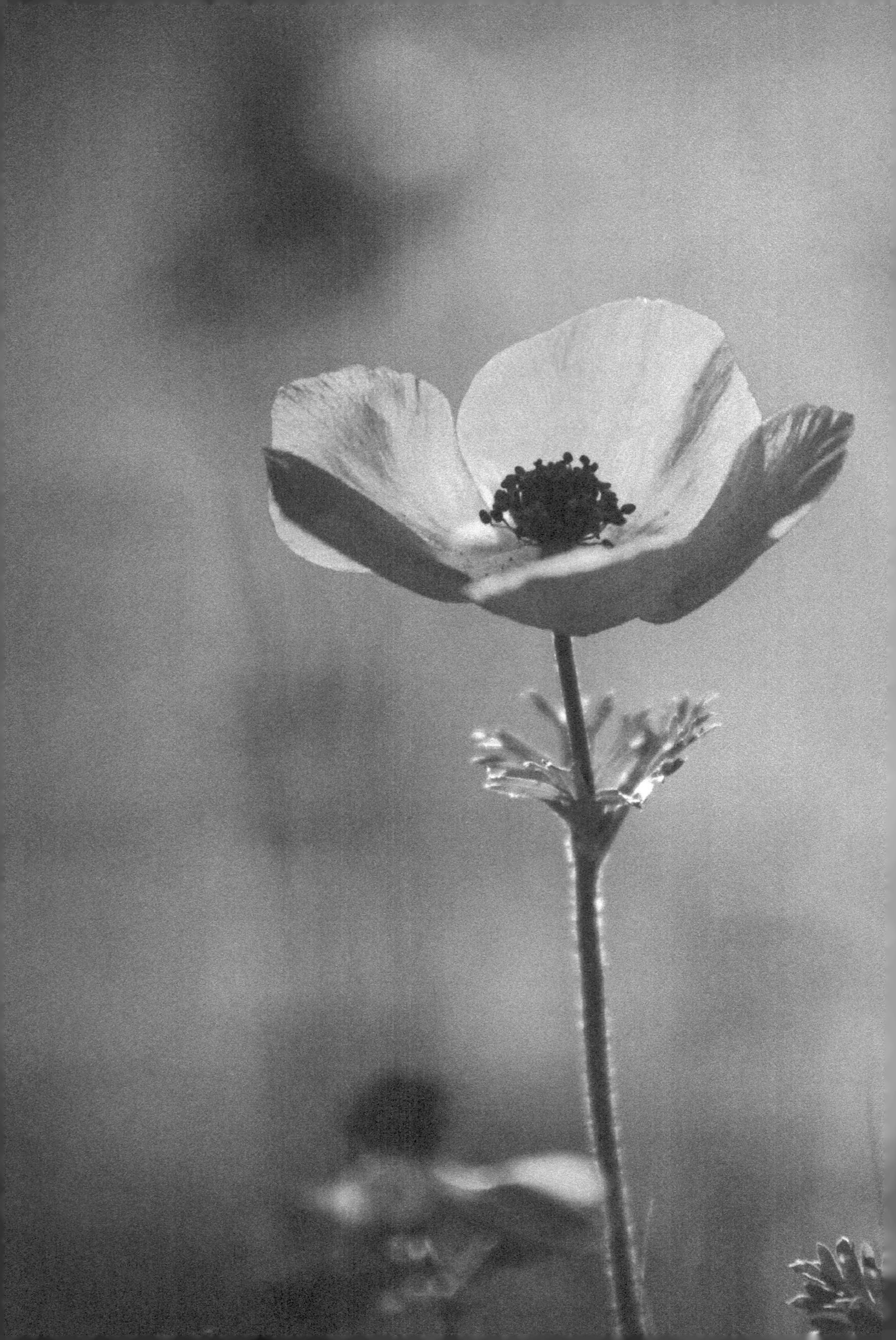

CHAPTER THREE

MERRI

"Did I tell you how beautiful you look tonight?" Jimmy murmured as he nuzzled my neck in the hotel elevator.

I giggled and turned my body into his embrace. "You've said it like a hundred times, James Harris. But you can tell me again, at least one more time."

He cupped my face and pulled me in for a sweet kiss before the elevator stopped and another passenger joined us. Now that we weren't alone, my handsome boyfriend adjusted our position so I was in front of him, his hands around my waist. The walls of the elevator were mirrored because Jimmy had pulled out all the stops for us on prom night. This was special. Monumental really.

"Look at us," he murmured in my ear as the other passenger exited and the doors slid closed again. "The perfect couple."

My God, he was handsome in that black tux. His blond hair was slicked back and parted to one side, bright blue eyes shining with adoration for me. Jimmy was about as boy-next-door as you could get. Kind, good-looking, with dimples in both cheeks when he smiled really wide. I was good at getting him to do that. My favorite part, though? The way his two front teeth were just slightly crooked. Something about that small imperfection made him real.

"Perfect? Speak for yourself," I murmured, my attention fully on him.

I knew what I looked like and the way people—men especially—looked at me. But I found my own beauty boring and generic. Stick straight red hair, blue eyes, some freckles. Meh. I was also too short at only five-five, which brought me up to Jimmy's armpit without heels—and what the heck was cute about that?—and these tits made shopping impossible. I could never find anything that fit both my boobs and around my waist correctly. And I hated my stupid freckles. I'd give anything to be built like Taylor Griffin, the captain of our school's volleyball team. She was tall and athletic. Everyone knew she was strong. They didn't assume she was a bimbo because of her curves.

But when Jimmy looked at me, everything changed. I actually felt like I might be something special. He didn't see me like the rest of them did. He saw *me*. Merri.

"That dress is gorgeous on you. You remind me of a princess."

"Does that make you my prince charming?" I simpered with an uncontained smile.

"Only if you agree to live happily ever after with me."

Swoon.

The car finally reached our floor, and Jimmy led me to the room he'd reserved.

Nervous butterflies took off in my stomach. I couldn't believe that we were standing here, that tonight was *the night*. We'd been dating for almost a year, ever since Suzi's pool party at the start of last summer. And even though things had gotten steamy, we both promised that we would wait to go all the way with each other until prom.

Jimmy opened the door to our hotel room, and I let out a startled gasp at the enormous suite. My handsome boyfriend smirked, tugging me inside.

"My dad might be a dick, but being the mayor's son has some perks."

"I'll be sure to never mention this to him."

He chuckled. "Please don't. At least not until we've been married at least ten years, okay?"

My heart skipped a beat as my gaze left his and went to the beautiful promise ring he'd given me at the beginning of the night. I could already imagine it nestled against an engagement ring and wedding band in a few years. After I graduated from college and he got into law school. I wasn't sure what I wanted to do with my life yet, but I'd figure it out. As long as we were together, nothing else mattered to me. I'd marry him tonight if I was old enough. Unfortunately, at seventeen, that wasn't the case.

"I love you, Merri. You know that, right?"

The way his voice shook had me reaching up to stroke his cheek. "I know. I love you too. So much."

"Are you sure you want to do this? We can wait if you're not ready. I want you to be comfortable. We have forever to spend together. We don't have to rush."

Reaching behind me, I unzipped my gown and let it fall to the floor in a puddle of tulle and sparkles. "I've been waiting for you my whole life, Prince Charming."

"Come here," he whispered, reaching for me.

Our lips collided in the most perfect kiss.

I woke with a start, a heavy, oppressive weight on my chest and the ghost of Jimmy's touch still on my skin. I hated these dreams. They seemed so real that when I woke, I always had to sit in the pain of the memory of what I'd done. Even four years later, it felt like yesterday.

We never got our happily ever after because shortly after, the night took a hard turn from fairy tale to horror story. What should have been the single most romantic night of my life ended in tears, sirens, and a body bag.

Jimmy never got to be a lawyer. Or my husband.

Thanks to a cruel twist of fate—and the manifestation of my succubus nature—when he gave me his body, I drained him dry.

I'd made a vow then and there that I would never be that intimate with a man again, and I would never, *ever* allow myself to fall in love.

⁓

"Is she still supposed to be out? How much did you give her?"

"She's fine. She should wake up at any moment. I am not an idiot, Sin."

"Maybe not, but kidnapping isn't exactly part of your usual skill set. Or is it, Chaos? You have some skeletons in your closet you need to bring to light?"

The deep, rumbling voices filtered into my brain as the dream finally released me from its grasp. I was almost thankful for the distraction. Chaos? Sin? What kind of names were those? Neither was the gruff British man who'd burst into my room before I'd been taken.

Taken.

Fuck.

Lilith was going to be so angry when she realized I was gone. There would be literal hell to pay.

Not knowing who these men were or what they wanted with me, I decided to play dead a while longer. Maybe I'd learn something to help me escape.

Almost as quickly as the plan formed, it was ruined.

"She's awake, you numpties. She can hear everything you're saying."

The smooth, posh drawl sent the picture of an upper-class Brit who fancied himself royalty through my mind. Handsome, snobby, and bored with everything. Definitely not the British voice I'd heard in my room, which meant a fourth man was lurking around somewhere.

My odds were growing worse by the second. Four on one? Sexy in the bedroom, but not in my current situation.

"Come on, little succubus," one of them crooned, his voice strangely alluring. It felt almost like he was a magnet, and I was being pulled right to him.

I blamed that for why I blinked open my eyes instead of jumping to my feet and bolting for the nearest exit. I was far from calm, but my curiosity was overriding all reason.

That's not curiosity you're feeling, you shameless hussy. That's lust. You want to know if the face matches the voice.

The room was dark, but not the pitch black I'd been stolen from. I could make out simple shapes. A fireplace on the wall directly across from the couch I was lying on, a chair in the corner, sheer curtains spanning the large floor-to-ceiling windows to my right. A luxurious cage. Seemed an odd choice for kidnappers. Shouldn't I be locked up in a cell or something? Getting to my feet on shaky legs, I took a deep breath and ran my hands over the tops of my bare thighs. Great, I was still in my camming outfit.

I found that oddly comforting. If they'd wanted to take advantage of me, they certainly could have. But I hadn't been bound or stripped, and my body didn't feel abused in any noticeable way. That had to count for something.

"We're not going to wait all day, Red," the man with the deepest voice of them all growled, pulling my focus from my surroundings to what really should matter. My captors. He didn't scare me at the moment, though. No, they'd interrupted me when I was feeding. His voice, the dominance in the tone, the energy and power, only served to bring my hunger to the forefront once again.

I turned toward his voice and found two men sitting in club chairs, softly illuminated by a single lamp on a table between them. Both were devastatingly gorgeous in their own way. One was large with enormous shoulders, dark hair, a thick beard, and a slightly crooked nose that made me wonder if he was a fighter. The other smirked at me, his entire being exuding sex. From top to toe, he was every inch the quintessential rock star, with his messy and overly long blond hair and a lean but sculpted build. He was also very clearly an incubus. One wasn't raised by Lilith without learning how to recognize our kind.

I swayed on my feet in response to him, then closed my eyes and took a deep breath, steadying myself by siphoning some of the incubus's power.

"Mmm," he groaned, his eyes falling closed as he bit into his full lower lip. "She really *is* powerful."

"Didn't anyone ever tell you it's rude to feed without permission?"

My head snapped to the right, my eyes locking on the man half-hidden in shadow in the far corner. He was the Brit, the posh one. His voice conjured images of billionaires in boardrooms, but he looked like someone who'd be more at home playing lumberjack. He wasn't as muscular as the guy at the table, but he was obviously well built in his dark denim jeans and deep blue flannel. It was hard to spot any other details cast in darkness as he was, but I could just make out the hint of a dark blond beard along his jaw.

"Really?" I snapped. "A lecture on consent from one of the men who just kidnapped me? A little hypocritical, don't you think?"

"Ooh, our new kitten has claws." This from the rockstar. Sin, I realized, matching the voice to the speaker. What an appropriate name.

That made the man sitting next to him Chaos, the one who drugged me.

"I might sound sweet, but I'll use these claws if I need to."

He smirked, getting to his feet. "We don't feed without permission, kitten. Rule one. That's how we end up locked up and starving with our powers bound."

"You don't understand," I protested.

"We understand plenty," Chaos bit out. "You're a fucking liability, and we're saddled with you."

"Excuse me? What's with the attitude, buddy? You kidnapped

me. If anyone gets to be pissed off here, it's me." I pointed to myself for added emphasis.

"We did not kidnap you," he said with a sneer.

My eyebrows flew up. "Do you have a memory problem or something? I was minding my own business—"

"Fuck yeah, you were," Sin agreed, his eyes heavy lidded and a sexy smirk curling his lips.

"—and you all just barged in and hauled me to wherever the fuck this is. What is that if not kidnapping?"

"Nope, guess again, Red. We were charged with your care."

"Really? That's what we're calling this?"

He just stared me down.

"Okay, fine. I'll bite. By whom?"

"Lilith herself. God knows why she trusts us with you. Maybe she's trying to weaken us. You clearly don't understand boundaries."

I took a step toward the hulk of a man but stopped when he stood to his considerable height. "She wouldn't have me snatched out of my bed like this. Lilith would talk to me first, tell me what was going on."

When I'd been sent to Blackwood, Lilith had kept me informed, sharing every pertinent detail with me so I could do what needed to be done. Why would she leave me in the dark like this? Had I made a misstep and become, exactly as they'd said, a liability? Our flight from Blackwood had been chaotic, to say the least. A war had broken out on the grounds, but before I could wrap my head around it, Lilith appeared in my room and told me it was time to go. Not one to question my benefactress, I grabbed the bags I'd kept packed and left without a second's hesitation. After a brief reunion that mostly comprised her depositing me in my room with a hug and perfunctory kiss to my cheek, she'd assured me we'd talk later and left.

Sin shook his head, his voice helping to anchor me to the present. "Not if she needed plausible deniability. Or if she was in the middle of creating a distraction so we could leave with you with no one being the wiser."

There was an unmistakable ring of truth to his words. And yet, there was also an uncomfortable niggling in my belly.

"But she only just got me back. Why bother bringing me to *Iniquity* if she was never planning on letting me stay?"

"This was likely one of many contingency plans. You're so much more important than you think you are. Now it's up to us to keep you safe."

The man in the shadows snorted but didn't say anything.

"Have something to add, Malice?" Sin asked.

"You mean other than the laundry list of objections I've already raised? No."

This guy was a real piece of work. Every time he spoke, my feathers got more and more ruffled. "Oh, I'm sorry. Is it inconvenient for you? Stealing me from my room and sneaking off into the night with me? Did I ruin all your big plans? Poor wittle baby. How hard your life must be."

"Careful," Sin warned as Malice pushed away from the wall and into the light.

I had to swallow a gasp at the sheer masculine beauty of him. Even with his face twisted in fury, he was stunning to look at.

"You have no idea what the fuck you're talking about. None. I'd suggest you show some fucking respect before you learn the hard way who you're dealing with."

That should have shut me up, but I'd spent the last few months around men and women far scarier than him. "What are you gonna do? Spank me?"

"If he doesn't, I will," Sin interjected as Malice nearly burned a hole through me with his gaze.

"Take me back." It was a demand, not a request.

"No," Chaos said with such finality my throat tightened.

"We can't," Sin offered. "You're ours now. Like it or not."

Realizing I wasn't going to get anywhere with these three, I cast my gaze around the room. "Where's the other guy? The grumpy one. Maybe he will listen to reason."

"Not bloody likely," Malice muttered while Sin snickered.

"Clocked without even being in the room. Grim will love that."

His name was Grim. How fitting.

"Wait, you said you're keeping me safe? Safe from what? Myself? Because Lilith was doing that with no problems."

The three of them glanced at each other in turn.

"What aren't you telling me? Is someone after me? Am I in danger?"

Chaos sighed. "Listen, Red. I don't make a habit of answering stupid questions. We already told you that Lilith assigned us as your bodyguards. You do the math. Just stay out of our way and don't make waves. It'll go easier on all of us that way."

He stalked out of the room, leaving me with the two others.

"What the hell is that supposed to mean?" I asked.

Malice chuckled, but it was completely devoid of humor. "If you need an explanation, then you're even more helpless than I feared."

Malice followed in Chaos's wake, echoes of their energy leaving the room charged as I turned all of my attention to Sin.

"So what, I'm just supposed to blindly accept that I'm your prisoner now?"

Sin walked toward me, wrapping an arm around my shoulders and tucking me into his side. I had half a mind to shrug him off, but the physical contact was like food for my starving soul.

"Think of it more like a princess trapped in a tower with four very scary ogres guarding the door. You're our ward. Our responsibility."

I snorted at the comparison but wasn't satisfied. "And you swear Lilith set this up?"

There was no way to know he'd tell me the truth, but he stopped and drew an X over the center of his chest. "Cross my heart."

I stared at him for a moment, chewing on the inside of my cheek as I considered his words. Since the day I'd been born, Lilith had done everything in her considerable power to keep me safe. I had to believe she wouldn't stop now. And these men had all but walked out the doors of *Iniquity* with me in tow. That never would have happened without Lilith's knowledge or permission. *Iniquity* was a sanctuary, its rules strictly enforced. No one would risk doing anything that would incur her wrath.

Which led me to one unfortunate conclusion. They weren't lying.

"Fine. If my life is truly in danger, then you owe me the truth. Tell me everything."

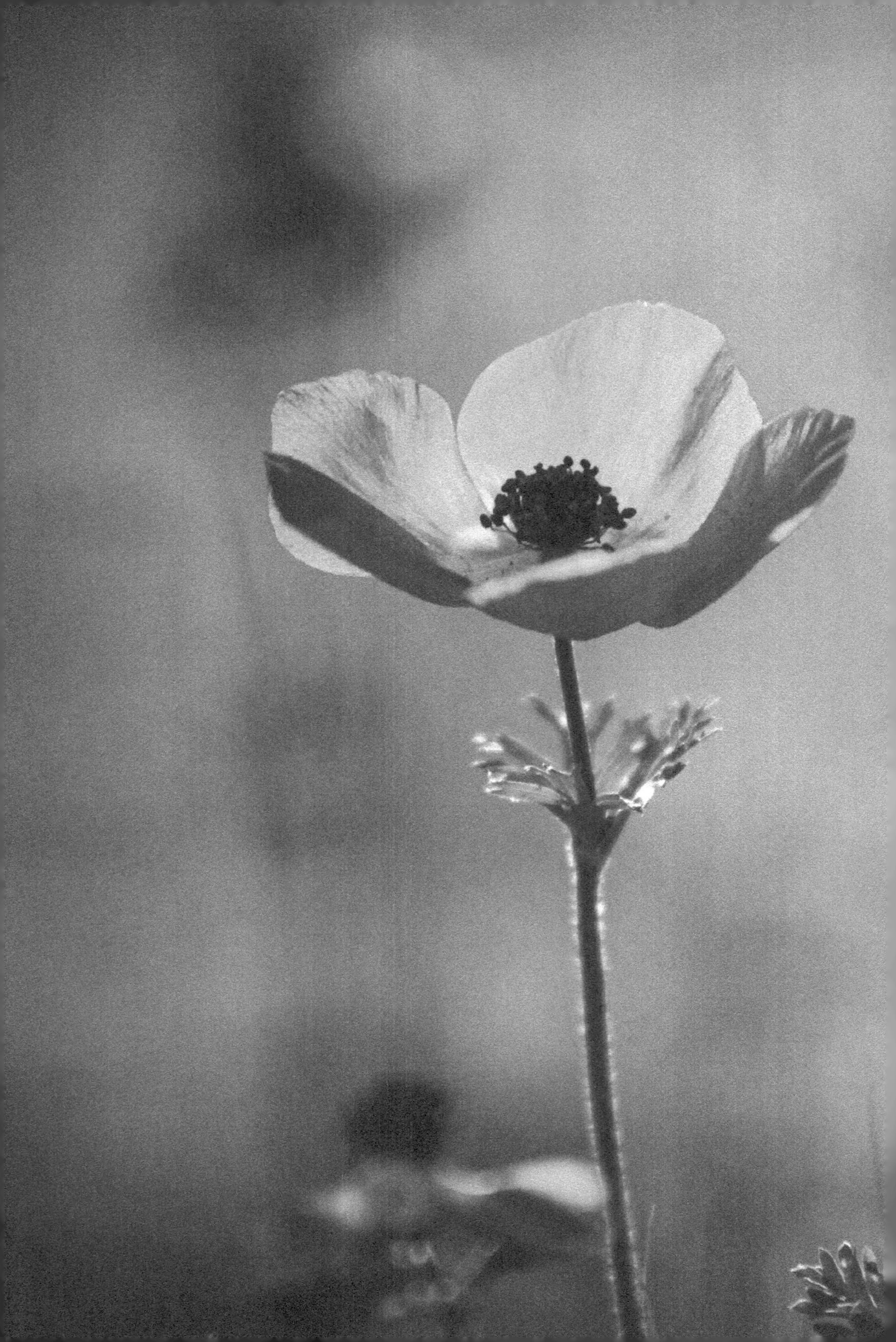

CHAPTER
FOUR
SIN

I fought the urge to let my grin slip as Merri stared me down, arms crossed under her ample breasts, challenge blazing in her eyes.

"You're cute."

She huffed. "Stop deflecting. Tell me, Sin. I deserve to know what's going on. Unless you're lying and I really am your captive."

The weight of my exhaustion still sat on my shoulders, even after feeding in Lilith's lair. Sips weren't enough to replenish what Hel had taken from us. I needed more. Cocking one brow, I let my focus trail down Merri's body, soaking up the sensuality she radiated. Fuck, she was made for me. A luscious hourglass, plenty to hold on to, and I hadn't even gotten to her face yet. Angelic was the word that came to mind. Plump lips, pink cheeks, brilliant blue eyes. A smattering of freckles that were somehow both innocent and alluring. She was a delightful contradiction. The perfect blend of sinful and sweet. I wanted to devour her.

A furrow formed between her brows. "Are you okay? Are you having a seizure or something? I had this friend once who had absent seizures. They looked a lot like whatever you've got going on right now."

I cleared my throat and turned away from her, adjusting the rapidly growing erection in my jeans as I did. "I'm fine. Just... I need a fucking drink. You thirsty?"

"Uh, sure."

I made my way over to Grim's bar cart, snagging the decanter of Brimstone whiskey and liberally pouring us both a glass.

Her eyes widened when I turned with the nearly full highball glasses in hand.

"I thought you meant water."

I snickered. "There's some ice in there."

She rolled her lips between her teeth and mutely shook her head.

When Lilith had mentioned her ward, my curiosity had been piqued. What sort of creature could tempt someone as innately selfish as the original demon to take her under her protection? I was sure there was some element of blackmail involved, but after seeing Merri, I got it.

There was just *something* about her.

She's a succubus, you dumbass. You know exactly what it is. She's literally made to give you a hard-on so she can feed.

"So, you want to know why you're here," I said before knocking back a swallow of whiskey.

"We've established that."

"I'm surprised you don't already know after your time at Blackwood."

She flinched in surprise. "What does any of this have to do with Blackwood? Also, how the hell do you know I was there?"

I reclaimed my seat from earlier, falling into a comfortable sprawl and draining the remaining contents of my glass. The burn of liquor was welcome as I held her stare with a pointed lift of my brow.

She waved her hand dismissively. "Okay, so Lilith told you. That still doesn't answer my first question. What does Blackwood have to do with me being in enough danger to warrant four dickhead kidnappers as bodyguards?"

I couldn't help but laugh at her description. It wasn't that far off, and kidnapping was the very least of our collective sins. "Do you have any idea the number of women who'd eagerly take your place?"

Her lip curled back in a sneer. "I'll go ahead and add delusional to the list. No woman in her right mind wants to be taken hostage."

"My observation stands. You're cute." Leaning forward, I rested my elbows on my thighs and focused on her. "We didn't kidnap you. We're keeping you protected."

"You've said that. But from whom? Barely anyone knows I exist."

"The legions of hell are hunting for you, Meredith Deveraux."

Her expression blanked before she threw her head back and laughed. "Say I believe you. What could possibly make the four of you qualified to protect me from the 'legions of hell'?" The latter she said in an obnoxious imitation of my voice with over-exaggerated air quotes as emphasis.

Standing to my full height, I closed the distance between us and took her by the hand, sending a pulse of my power into her. The way my head immediately swam told me it was power I couldn't afford to waste, but I had a point to make.

Her eyes flared and locked on mine.

"Because we're the fucking horsemen of the apocalypse, kitten. No one starts the end of the world without us."

Her lips parted on a silent gasp. Whatever she'd expected me to say, it definitely hadn't been that.

"The four . . ." Her tongue darted out to wet her lips, and I couldn't help but envision that little pink tip doing the same to mine. She swallowed and tried again. "You're the four horsemen?"

Still holding her hand, I dipped into a courtly bow. "At your service, sweetheart."

Any surprise she'd initially felt was carefully hidden as she studied me. I had to admit she was handling her current situation much better than I'd expected. Though I suppose having Lilith as a de facto mother would tend to put things in a much different perspective.

"So which one are you then? Ringo?"

I feigned offense. "Excuse me? I'm a lead singer, baby. Not a fucking drummer. We'll leave that to Malice."

"The four horsemen are my bodyguards," she mused, not really speaking to me at all. "What did I do to deserve this much attention? I've barely even lived."

"Hell needs you to finalize the apocalypse. We're going to make sure that doesn't happen." Fuck, I was stretching the truth here, but I couldn't tell her we planned to fuck her until she was knocked up in order to keep that from happening. Something told me this little succubus needed seducing before that happened.

"Hell needs me to finalize the apocalypse," she repeated slowly, drawing the statement out like she was testing each word and searching for hidden meaning. Then she blinked and held her palm up. "Wait, you're trying to *stop* the apocalypse? Isn't that like . . . your shtick? Your sole reason for existing? Why would you want to stop it?"

"Because we weren't the ones to start it."

Confusion flickered in her eyes. "If not you, then who?"

I sighed. "It's complicated. But for now, do you believe me when I say you're not a prisoner here? We want you safe. The world *needs* you safe."

The cutest little furrow appeared between her brows as she processed my explanation. "But why? Does it really matter that much to you that you get credit for ending the world?"

"This isn't about credit."

Though, it sort of was, because had it been us doing the heralding, we wouldn't be here. And after the way Hel had used us, there was certainly an element of revenge that was fueling our intervention.

"So what then? Is there like a prophecy or something?"

I latched on to the excuse and nodded. "Yup. Exactly. You're the chosen one."

The way she rolled her eyes had me itching to put her in her place. Under me, with my hand around her throat while I made her come and we both fed.

"I don't want to be chosen. I've seen Buffy. I know what happens to the chosen one. She dies in the end. Twice."

"That's why we're here, kitten. To ensure the only kind of deaths you experience are the little ones," I said with a wink.

The flush creeping across her cheeks betrayed how my words affected her, but she held my stare, refusing to look away.

"If you want, anyway." I shrugged and turned away, taking a few steps toward the hall. She'd follow. There was no doubt in my mind. I was the king of the long game and with women like her, playing hard to get was the only way to get her interested.

"Well," she breathed from behind me.

Like clockwork.

"Yes, kitten?"

"A girl has to eat."

Now I was the one trying to disguise the effect her words had on my body. "I should warn you, the others get a little testy about being on the menu. But I'm sure if you play your cards right, you'll find a couple takers."

"No need. That's what camming is for." She stopped short. "I'm going to need my computer. And Wi-Fi."

"That's Malice's territory. You'll have to take it up with him."

She cocked her head. "A hacker horseman? I don't remember that from the book of Revelations."

"You'd be surprised how . . . adaptable we are."

There was a lot more to the story than that, but I wasn't about to get into it with her. She had enough to worry about, and there were some secrets one didn't divulge on the first date. Or ever.

"Would I?"

"Yes." I couldn't come up with any other retort. She'd knocked me off my game. Fuck.

"Where are you taking me? Is there a point to this little stroll?" Impatience bled from every word.

"I figured you'd want to see your room. Unless you'd like to stay in mine. I'm sure we could entertain each other."

"No, thank you. I'll stick to my own space."

"Your loss," I said, tossing a little wink over my shoulder. "If you change your mind, I'm just a next door, and I'm a world-class cuddler."

"I won't. Thanks."

Opening the bedroom door, I gestured for her to enter before me and waited until she was fully inside before joining her.

"Welcome to Grim's guest suite. You should have everything you need to keep you comfortable. Egyptian cotton sheets, a bathtub built for two, a walk-in closet fully stocked with designer clothes in your size, every beauty product you could ask for, and unlimited streaming on every service available. You shouldn't be bored."

She took in the room before turning to face me with an unimpressed look. "If you don't set me up with my computer, boredom will be the least of my worries. I refuse to starve myself, Sin. I have to be able to work."

Now this was an opening I could work with.

Not that I'd ever met one I couldn't, if you know what I mean.

"No one said you have to starve, kitten. If you're hungry, I'm right here. I don't mind lending a helping hand."

I reached behind me and tugged my shirt off in the way the ladies loved, then went for my belt.

"What the hell are you doing? I don't even know you."

"I'm gonna feed you, obviously. How do you want it? You on top? Me on top? A little light choking? I can work with pretty much anything."

"None of the above, thanks."

I blinked at her. "I don't understand. You just said you need to feed." I pointed to myself. "I'm a guaranteed five-course meal, darling. I dare you to find better."

What the fuck was happening? Everyone wanted me. Always. No one rejected me. Ever.

"I'm ... uh ... sex is off the table, Sin. I don't feed that way."

"What do you mean? Of course you feed that way. That's how we feed."

"Not me. I'm celibate."

I started laughing, great heaving guffaws that had tears streaming from my eyes. "Fuck, you really had me going there, kitten. That's fucking hilarious."

She wasn't laughing with me. "I don't see what's so funny."

I sobered and blinked at her. "Sorry, I don't think we're speaking the same language. You're a succubus. You can't be celibate."

Her eyes narrowed in challenge. "Yeah, I can. And I assure you, I am. Your dick isn't getting anywhere near me. Now if you could please get dressed and get out of my room, I'd appreciate it. Tell Malice I need my stuff set up sooner rather than later. You don't want me to lose control and accidentally drain you all."

Stunned, I picked up my shirt and sort of staggered out of the room, barely paying attention as I shut the door behind me.

What the fuck just happened?

Celibate? That was a damn plot twist.

How the hell were we supposed to knock her up if her lady garden was locked up tighter than the pearly gates?

"Well, you look like day-old rubbish," Malice said as he slipped out of the shadows and into the hallway. "Did she already take you for a ride?"

I shook my head. "Um, about that. We've got a problem."

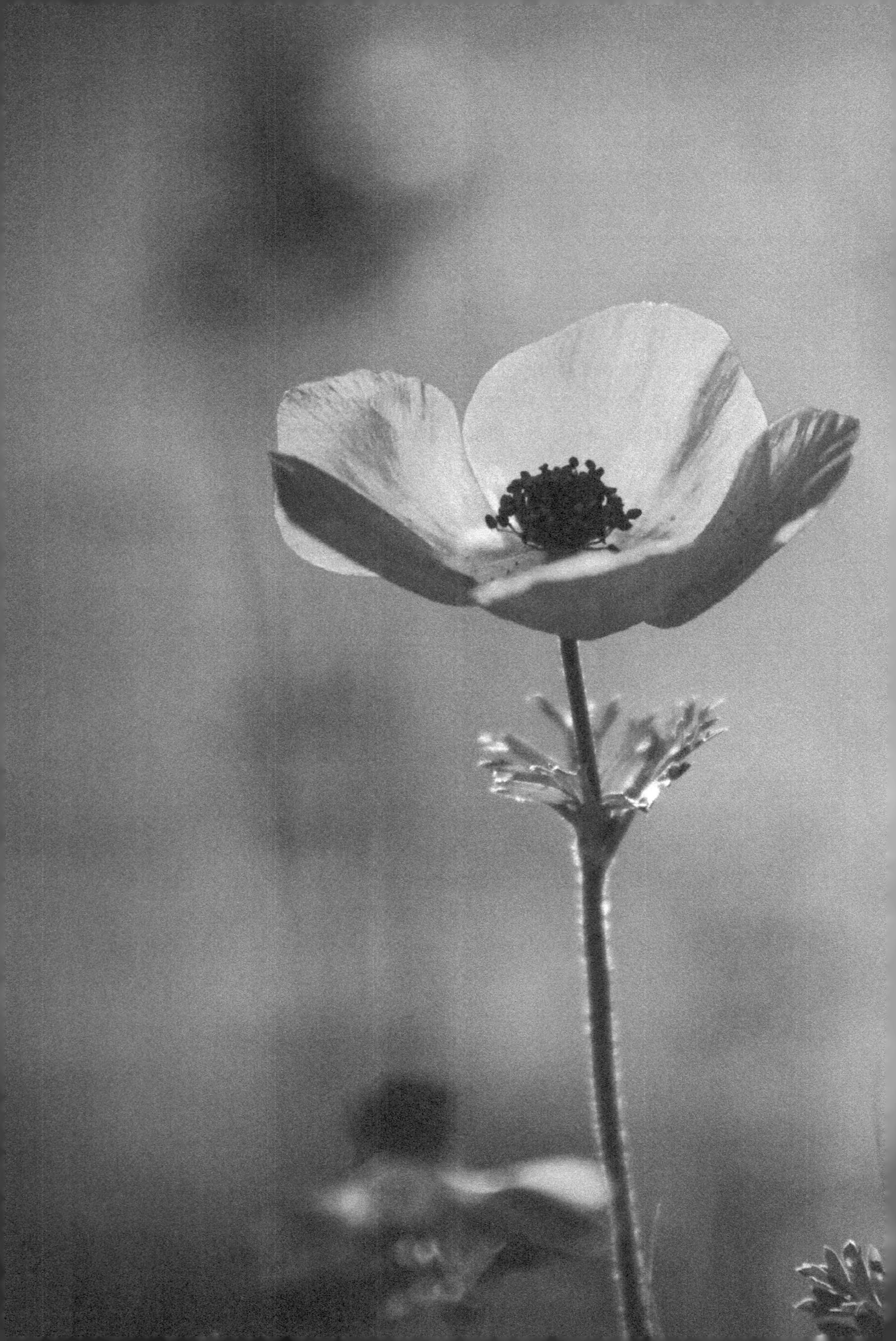

CHAPTER FIVE
MALICE

"Celibate? Well, isn't that interesting?" I murmured as Sin's words finally registered in my overstimulated brain.

He narrowed his eyes. "Interesting? That's the word you're going with? Try in-fucking-convenient. Or even giant hurdle. Big problem works too if you want to keep it simple."

"Plot twist?" I offered, amused at his mounting ire even as my temples throbbed from my lingering migraine.

I wasn't one for social gatherings on a good day, but take me prisoner and drain my power, and I could barely handle a conversation with one being, let alone four. Add in the constant competing noises of *Iniquity's* dance club and sex dungeon, plus Lilith's yammering, and I was in a downward spiral akin to a whirlpool in the ocean.

"That's what I said. Helluva plot twist. The succubus who won't fuck. That's like . . . an eating disorder. How are we supposed to do our duty now?" He stared off into space for a moment, then flicked his gaze back to me. "Turkey baster?"

I raised a brow. "And how do you propose to talk her into that? 'Come over here, love, and spread your legs for me, will you? I need to leave a deposit.' Or were you planning on a more gynecological approach? Do we need to purchase one of those tables with the stirrups?"

"Pretty much."

Sighing, I shook my head. "And this is why I'm the only one who procreated."

"I don't see you coming up with any ideas."

"That's because this isn't my show. I've already done the accidental pregnancy thing. Not interested this time around."

"Yeah, but it's not going to be an accident. We're doing it on purpose. You've never had an on-purpose before."

I could barely check the impulse to snarl at him. My son was off-limits, and this fucker damn well knew it. I didn't talk about him or any of the events surrounding his birth and subsequent excommunication from my life. To say it was a sore subject would be like referring to a global pandemic as flu season.

"Are you done?" I drawled.

"I guess so. I just don't know how we're going to do this if she's not interested in making the beast with two backs. I mean, I'm sex personified, and she's not the least bit interested."

I pinched the bridge of my nose in an attempt to counter the tiny sledgehammers working at my temples. "Did you ever consider that you might have to help spark her interest?"

He stared at me. "What?"

"Seduction, Sinclair. I'm talking about fucking seduction. You know, foreplay?" He continued to stare at me blankly. "Jesus. It's a wonder you've ever gotten laid."

The look on his face was priceless. It was as though I'd told him Father Christmas and the Easter Bunny weren't real. "Well, yeah, but I *am* the foreplay. I don't have to work for it. I have to turn them away in droves. They come to me, not the other way around."

"Those poor, unsatisfied women. Do you even know how to tell if they're faking it?"

This garnered a reaction. "How very fucking dare you. I feed on their sexual energy, you putrid, festering herpe. Of course I know what a real orgasm feels like." Then he paused, his expression going inward, and I could practically hear him thinking back through his conquests.

"Sounds like something someone who hasn't felt a woman come around his cock would say."

Sin's expression turned stormy. "I hate you."

"You'd better go write down your best chat-up lines and work on your seduction techniques, Famine. This one looks like she's going to be a challenge." I held out my hand, palm up, and made a beckoning gesture with my two middle fingers. "Might I recommend the come hither? Emphasis on the *come*."

"Go fuck yourself, Malice."

"Sounds like you're going to be doing enough of that for the both of us, Sin. Unless you start studying."

He flipped me off.

"Now you're just being redundant," I taunted.

His scowl would have withered a weaker man. Alas, while I might currently be weakened, I wasn't a man. Not a mortal one, anyway.

"I hope you sit on a cactus, dill hole. Or you have a rampant case of anal leakage."

"Ah yes, one of my better side effects."

Sin left me, his grumbles audible as he made his way down the hall before he stopped and called over his shoulder, "She needs you to set her up to feed. Work your computer wizardry, will ya? Since she won't ride my dick, she's gonna have to get off strangers on the internet."

I chuckled under my breath and muttered, "Ouch. So it's clear she'd choose a bear over a man in the woods, then."

"I heard that!"

"I meant for you to, you walking wankstain."

I spun on my heel and headed to my room before he could come back with some other insult. I had no desire to spend time in anyone else's company, but a starving succubus would be bad news for all of us, so I needed to get that sorted immediately. I didn't have access to most of my usual supplies, but I should be able to scrounge up the basics.

I really missed my fucking lake house. Not just for the stockpile of electronics but also the solitude. I'd chosen the remote location in northern Europe for a reason. After centuries of wandering among the suffering masses, I was done with them all. I was sick of phlegm, bodily fluids, fevers, and the like. So when the twentieth century came around, along with technology, I let Odette take the reins when it came to physical pestilence, leaving me to focus on greener, unexplored pastures. The types of viruses I could spread now didn't just kill bodies; they destroyed spirits and brought down entire countries. The latest one I created shut down a hospital's server for a twenty-four-hour period. It was beautiful. The panic, the chaos, the sheer terror. All with one little string of code.

Since the dawn of time, it was the microscopic, sometimes invisible menaces that were the most prolific killers. Chaos may revel in his body count, but mine trumped his by millions. Take that, War.

Not that I was stupid enough to say so to his face. I'd leave that to Sin.

The others may have felt as though their specialties made them the most fearsome, but the truth was, in a world reliant upon technology for survival, I was king. I could destroy empires, make planes fall from the sky, and fire nuclear weapons, all with a few keystrokes. I simply chose not to.

The man with the biggest dick in the room never had to announce it to anyone. That was a game for the lesser men who had something to prove.

∼

ARMS LADEN with the supplies needed to set up Merri's new computer system, I had to resort to kicking her door to get her to come open it.

"Thank fuck, I'm starving," came the somewhat grumbled and muffled response.

I wasn't prepared for the wave of lust that slammed into me when the door swung open.

"Oh, Grumpy Brit Number Two. I didn't expect to see you again," she said, her eyes dropping to take in me and the equipment in my arms.

"You can simply call me Malice. Mal, if you'd like."

"I don't know, Mal. That makes it seem like we're friends. Pretty sure captors can't be caught palling around with their prisoners."

I must have made a face because she tilted her head to the side and mused, "Do you *want* to be my pal, Mal? Ha! Pal Mal. You're a Brit. Damn, I'm a comedian, and I didn't even know it. The jokes write themselves."

Frowning, I grunted. "Where am I setting this up?"

I pushed past her, a rush of desire chasing across my skin when my arm brushed hers.

"Come on in, I guess. God, I thought you were supposed to be polite, at least."

"That's Canadians."

"Noted." She gestured to the empty desk across from the bed. "There's fine. I don't need much to make it work. They're not booking me for the ambience."

No, they're booking you for your fucking fit body and bountiful . . . Motherfucker.

I gritted my teeth against the onslaught of thoughts about exactly what her body was made for.

"Do you mind?" I all but growled.

"Mind what?"

Dumping the contents of my arms unceremoniously onto the table, I gestured to her body. "Tamping down the allure. I can't focus with all these *pheromones*."

Her cheeks went delightfully pink, and she lowered her gaze to her perfectly manicured toes as she curled them into the carpet. "I'm sorry. I said I was hungry. I can't help it."

What the devil was Lilith thinking, having such a precious creature in her midst? She was little more than a bunny in a den of wolves. Or perhaps I was seeing what she wanted me to see, and she was actually a vixen lurking behind an innocent facade, waiting for her moment to strike. So which was she, truly? Harmless fluffy bunny or cunning little fox?

Why did the idea of finding out make my mouth water?

"Tamp. It. Down."

She flinched. "I'm trying. It's not as easy as that."

"If you can't control yourself, at least give me some breathing room," I snarled.

She obeyed with a huff, moving as far away as she could and primly sitting on the edge of her bed.

After setting up everything she needed, I discreetly adjusted myself before turning to face her again. My whole body felt alive, my blood singing with unsatisfied hunger. It took every ounce of control I had not to imagine the things I could do to her in that bed. Things I hadn't done with any partner since my son was conceived.

Fuck.

My cock throbbed as though reminding me of exactly how long it had been since I'd had a release. Centuries. I hadn't touched myself or anyone else in literal centuries. I'm pretty sure that made me some kind of born-again virgin, without the religious fanfare of it all.

"This would be easier if you weren't so on edge," Merri said as she repositioned herself in the camera view from the desk.

"I'm not on edge."

"Liar."

"Don't," I warned. "You won't like what happens if you keep poking at us. We're not made of stone. We will snap."

"Right, because you're the horsemen." She tapped her lower lip. "Which one are you, I wonder?"

When I didn't provide an answer, she shrugged and said, "Anyway, the big guy seems like he might be made of stone."

"Chaos. He has a very short fuse."

She plopped down on the bed and sighed. "So I can't poke at you, I'm assuming I'm not allowed to leave, and I probably can't touch anything. What *can* I do?"

"I suppose you could leave, but not alone. You need one of us with you at all times. That's not up for discussion. Also, this is Grim's penthouse, so I'm not at liberty to tell you what you can and cannot touch, but he's very . . . fussy about his things. I definitely wouldn't go after his whiskey if I were you."

She wrinkled her nose. "What would I want with his whiskey? Do you think I'm just going to get drunk in my room by myself?"

"I certainly would."

"Because you're a million years old."

"Not quite."

"Close enough."

"Grim is older than me."

"And?"

I frowned, not sure why I'd felt the need to point it out. "Seemed like it was worth mentioning," I mumbled.

Oh fuck, her little nipples were hard and pressing against the sheer fabric of that damned lingerie she was still wearing. Tearing my gaze away from her, I took a few deep breaths, which was a mistake of epic proportions. She smelled too fucking good.

"Merri, this is important," I bit out as I made my way toward escape.

"Go on. Lay it on me, Malice. I can see you want to. What is it?"

My cock twitched.

She doesn't mean like that.

"I've installed a number of firewalls and other protective measures on your computer. That will only do so much, however, unless you are also careful."

"I'm not an idiot, Mal. I've been camming for years now. I know how to keep myself safe."

"Still, it would be irresponsible of me not to remind you that under absolutely no circumstances are you to share the details of your whereabouts with anyone. I don't care if it's your mother. No one means no one."

"Well, seeing as I don't know my birth mother and have absolutely no idea where I am anyway, pretty sure that won't be a problem."

"Peachy."

She stood, stretching her arms and rolling her shoulders before settling in at the desk. Without a glance back at me, she began typing, pulling up her camming website as I stood there.

I recognized a dismissal when I saw one.

And if I happened to linger just long enough to memorize the site and her username, well . . . that was just a matter of security, wasn't it?

Someone needed to make sure she followed the rules.

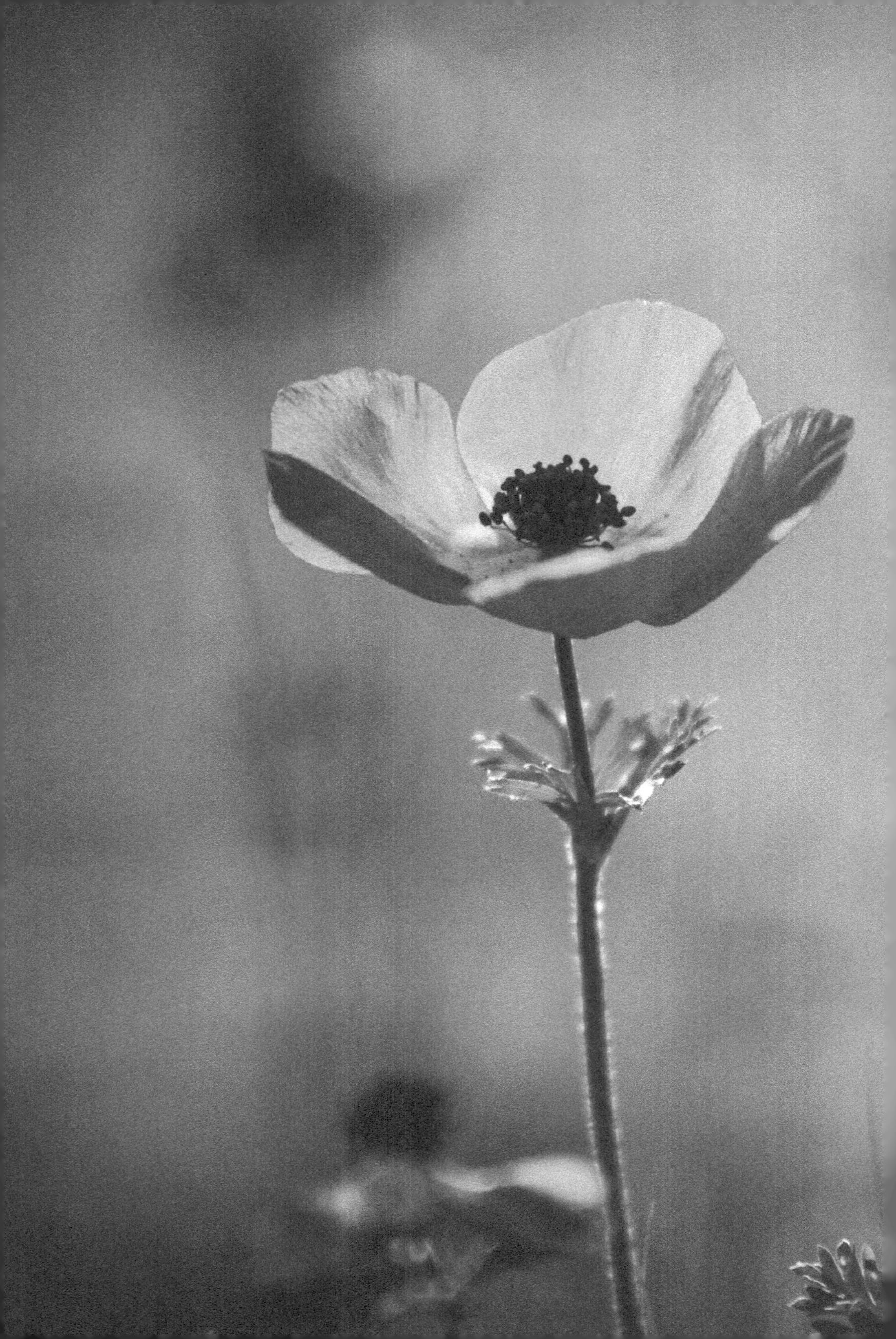

CHAPTER SIX
CHAOS

The sight of Sin's back as he stormed into his bedroom greeted me as I rounded the corner in search of Grim. Before I had the chance to utter a single word, the incubus slammed the door behind him. Looks like Red had him wound up already.

I chuckled to myself as I continued past his room, shaking my head as the distorted scream of Sin's guitar filtered down the hall. He was more affected by her than I thought he'd be. He'd been so confident earlier, but she'd obviously thrown him for a loop. Served him right.

For as long as I'd known him, Sinclair had been annoyingly arrogant. Anything that took him down a peg or two was a win in my book. Not that I was about to tell *her* that. My plan was to stay as far away from Lilith's ward as possible. Though I supposed she was technically our ward now. And I had to . . . breed her. Unless Sin was successful first.

Fucking Grim. This was all his fault. And in typical fashion, after tossing us headfirst into this disaster, he fucked off and left the rest of us to deal with the fallout.

He wasn't going to run from this. I wouldn't fucking let him.

"Grim!" I bellowed as I barged into his office, the door swinging so hard the knob embedded into the plaster wall. "Grimsby! I know you're in there."

As expected, I found the avatar of Death behind his desk. The only indication I'd startled him was a slight flinch of his eyes before he quickly clicked something on his keyboard. For Grim, that was the equivalent of a teenage boy caught jerking off to his daddy's porn.

"What are you doing?" I asked, immediately closing the distance between us.

"Nothing you should be concerned about."

"Really?" I mused, peeking around the desk at his computer screen. His screensaver was up, the 3D line art swirling around and changing colors. "You won't mind if I do this then," I added, shooting forward and clicking the button that would bring his desktop to life.

"Motherfucker," Grim growled, settling back in his chair in what could only be called defeat as the surveillance feed we'd installed in Merri's room came up.

"Well, well, well. Espionage is supposed to be my forte. I didn't expect Death to be so conniving. Usually you just waltz in and take what you want."

He cut a deadly glare my way and scoffed. "Espionage? Spare me. You barge in like a bull in a china shop. There's a reason your name is Chaos."

"I'm strategic when I need to be. Brute force usually gets the job done."

"Mmm," he hummed noncommittally, telling me without using words that he thought I was full of shit.

Chaos hadn't always been my name, though it was as appropriate as my first. A long time ago, I'd been known as Ariston. My mother had visited a seer prior to my birth. She'd been told that I was destined for greatness and that I required a name deserving of my future legacy. I couldn't help but wonder, knowing how things played out, how much of my name ended up being a self-fulfilling prophecy. Because surely one whose name meant 'the best' had placed a target on their back not only for their enemies, but the gods as well.

Not that any of it mattered. I'd set that life aside when I'd taken up the horseman's mantle. As had Sin when his time came centuries later. Out of the four of us, only Grim and Malice were the originals, at least as far as I knew. We didn't really talk about who or what came before. Those versions of ourselves were long gone. Dead and buried.

"She's a pretty little thing, I'll give her that," Grim muttered. "Already giving them hell."

"Pretty things have a way of getting people into trouble."

"They aren't the problem."

"Oh?"

"It's the ones who want to possess them."

"Speaking of . . ." I drawled, settling myself on the corner of his desk with my arms folded across my chest. "What do you think he's going to do when he finds out we're hiding her?"

There was no need to say his name. There was only one 'he' I could be referring to.

"Nothing good."

"Are we prepared to handle that? We're weakened, drained, and vulnerable. Not in fighting shape."

One silver brow raised as he assessed me. "Afraid, Chaos? That's not like you."

"Concerned. Our enemy is much more powerful than we are as it stands right now."

"How do you know that? He's been locked away for decades. He could've been drained just as we have."

"The Morningstar has a reputation for a reason. I would never underestimate his ability."

"But you're happy to underestimate mine?"

My eyes narrowed slightly at Grim's tone. He might consider

himself the leader of our little warband, but I'd long ago stopped bowing to any man.

"Show me your shadows. Then maybe my faith will be restored."

It was a gamble to challenge him, but if I'd been considerably weakened by Helene's game, there was no doubt in my mind he was too.

"No."

"Because you can't?"

"Because I have nothing to prove. No matter my current state, I am Death, same as I've always been."

I waved a hand. "Yes, yes. You're inevitable. Blah, blah, blah. I've heard this speech before, Grim. But you're failing to consider one very key fact. You've never been weakened before. None of us have. And none of us have ever been stupid enough to face off against Lucifer and his Princes either. How exactly do you see this playing out? Did you even stop to think what this meant for the rest of us when you accepted Lilith's proposition?"

Grim sighed and dragged a hand through his thick, pewter-colored hair. "It takes time."

"What does?"

"Releasing the Princes. We will regain our strength, of that I'm sure. You'll succeed in breeding the girl, so Lucifer won't get a chance, and then he won't want to fight. He'll slink back to where he came from like he always does."

"If you think it will be that easy, you're an even bigger fool than I imagined."

It was ludicrous to think this would go off without a hitch. Something would get in the way, and relying on Sin or me to successfully impregnate her was a long shot at best. There were so many other factors at play, not the least of which was the dawn of the apocalypse. Just because it hadn't fully taken hold didn't mean it wasn't a threat. The veil between the mortal realm and hell had lifted. That was cosmic interference on the very highest level. There was no telling what sort of hell—no pun intended—that would unleash.

And that didn't even take into consideration the four of us all cohabitating for the foreseeable future. There was a reason we'd all gone our separate ways. Needs we each had to fulfill and manage. Needs that, if left unmet, would become . . . problematic.

I balled my hands into fists to hide the tremor in my fingers. The urge for violence surged to the surface, clawing at me as I contemplated the potential enemies that lurked in every metaphorical shadow.

"We are the only thing standing in the way of Lucifer claiming his throne. If you think he doesn't already know we're not on his side, you haven't been paying attention."

Grim drummed his fingers on his desk before shoving his chair back and rising to his full height. "Of course he knows. The girls have already aligned themselves with him if they're smart, and we know they are."

"Smarter than us?"

He leveled me with a weighted stare. "They've done what we never could. They beat us at our own game."

The echo of my earlier thoughts added fuel to my inner fire. Around me, Grim's desk rattled, and books fell from the floor-to-ceiling shelves lining the wall.

Grim's eyes clocked the movement and slowly dragged his silver gaze back to mine. "Chaos," he warned.

"I'm trying. My control is threadbare after Hel's game."

"Fix it."

"Don't you think I would if I knew how?"

"What do you usually do to let off steam when you're not out waging war?"

I knew the question was more reminder than bid for information. Grim already knew the answer. When I couldn't actively participate in war—mortals tended to notice when you didn't age after a couple of decades—I usually moved on to other violent outlets. Anything that would allow me to siphon off bits of the violence simmering within me. Most recently, I'd been an underground fighter with a perfect record. Or at least I had been before Hel captured me and took me off the scene.

"Your punching bag is still in the gym."

My surprise helped ground me. "We haven't been together in decades. Yet you kept this place as though we'd return at any moment."

Grim shrugged, silver irises flashing in the pre-dawn light. "This is your home. It always will be."

I grunted in response. I wouldn't go so far as to say I was touched by his sentiment; that implied a depth of emotion I didn't think either of us could lay claim to. But it was as close to brotherly as any of us got.

"I'll work it out of my system."

"Good. See that you do."

⁓

"Motherfucker!" I slammed my fist into the punching bag hard enough to burst its seams, but not without a shockwave of pain accompanying the blow.

The agony radiated through my bones, up my arm, and into my shoulder. I wasn't mortal, hadn't been for longer than most could comprehend, but I remembered this feeling. Overexertion. Weakness. Fatigue.

The last time I'd been this wrung out, I'd just completed the Crypteia. I'd nearly died during the rite of passage, but I proved myself worthy of the title of Spartan warrior. So while the sensation was one that certainly left an imprint, it was also one I had never anticipated experiencing again.

With each minor defeat, my frustration mounted, and with it, my rage.

It began when I couldn't successfully bench press my usual weight and then grew when I had to not only slow down but cut short my run on the treadmill. But the final insult was this fucking wheezing in my lungs as I threw punch after punch at the bag. My godsdamned muscles trembled and threatened to give out.

If I ever got my hands on Hel, I'd make her wish she was never created.

Snagging a towel, I wiped the sweat from my brow before storming out of the gym and toward the kitchen. At this rate, I'd need to ensure I had a pre-workout shake along with my usual smoothie after. Just like a fucking mortal gym bro.

The disgust I felt at my current situation had my stomach churning.

Yeah. Disgust. That's the reason I currently felt like puking, and not because I'd just spent the last three hours running my body into the ground.

Some male specimen I was. Even if I wanted to breed our little troublesome ward, I had little to offer at the moment.

I'd just thrown everything into the blender when the elevator emitted a soft chime and none other than the menace herself tumbled out of the doors. I had to admit, she looked better than when we'd taken her. Cheeks rosy, lips plump, hair somehow glossier than before. Thankfully, she'd changed clothes, but even in sweatpants and an oversized T-shirt, she was somehow the most alluring creature I'd laid my eyes on. I hated how she could draw my attention with so little effort.

I didn't want to desire her in any way. There were so many more important things to focus on. She was an inconvenience I didn't want or need.

"What the hell are you doing?" I snapped, annoyed that out of everyone here, she was the one who caught me in my moment of weakness.

"Oh, it's you," she said, tossing her hair over one shoulder. "I was just looking for the kitchen."

"Well, you found it," I muttered, pressing the button on the blender and drowning out whatever else she was about to say.

When I couldn't keep the blender going any longer, I shut it off and kept my gaze focused on the task at hand. Pour the ugly green drink into a cup. Don't spill. Don't look at her.

She let out a musing huff as I started chugging my smoothie. "I think I'm going to call you Grumpy. Oh wait, that might be confusing with the Brits. Hmm. Oh, I know. I'll call you Moody!"

"Great. And I'll call you Annoying Pest. Glad we've established our roles. If you'll excuse me."

"I thought you'd settled on Red," she called after me.

I would have smiled at her sass if I didn't find her mouthing off so fucking annoying. There were clearly better uses for that mouth. Ones that didn't involve her uttering a word.

"Wait!" she cried just before I could slip out of the living area and back into the wellness half of the penthouse's bottom floor.

"What?" I grumbled, irritated for many reasons, the least of which was the erection her proximity was causing.

Succubi were as notorious as sirens for the way they preyed on lesser men. I was not a lesser man. I was one of the strongest beings in existence. And still, her power called to me. I would not be bested by lust magic. I was the master of my domain, even if I was weakened at the moment.

"Where's the refrigerator?"

She gestured to the cabinets all around her, not realizing that the fridge was camouflaged behind one of the many doors.

I let out a heavy sigh, wishing I was callous enough to walk away, but there was something about those doe eyes that made me feel like leaving her to her own devices would be akin to kicking a puppy.

"Sonofabitch," I hissed to myself as I stalked back over to where she stood. The way her gaze trailed up my body as I stepped directly in front of her filled me with irrefutable male pride. She liked what she saw. Of course she did. Why wouldn't she?

"Um . . ."

Unable to help myself, I leaned down and breathed in her intoxicating scent. Immediately irritated with myself, I couldn't help but put my lips to her ear and growl, "Take a picture, Red. It'll last longer." Then I opened up the door directly behind her, blasting us both with cool air.

I stepped away, needing the space more than I wanted to admit. I had to get out of here before I hate-fucked her on the kitchen island. The last thing I needed was to get that close to her.

A soft clearing of her throat stopped me in my tracks. "The fuck is it now?" I bit out.

Turning around, I saw her bewildered expression and sighed in resignation as she pointed to the elaborate espresso machine on the counter. "Make go, please?"

"You don't know how to make a cup of fucking coffee?"

The sweet little doll was replaced with a brat as she popped her hands on her hips and met my glare with one of her own. "No, Moody, I don't. Not when the machine looks like an alien spaceship."

"Then maybe you don't deserve any," I muttered, shocked to find myself once again stomping back over to her to flick the buttons necessary to get the machine percolating.

Five minutes later, I'd frothed milk, added syrup and espresso, and all but created latte art for this thorn in my side. Handing her the mug, I took a deep breath and stared her down, jaw clenched tight before I asked. "Anything else, princess?"

"Nope." She brought the drink to her lips and took a slow sip, her eyes never leaving mine. "Mmm. You know, if this horseman gig doesn't pan out, you'd make a really hot barista."

My irate growl was met with a soft giggle as she took another sip.

I was almost clear of her when her voice rang out a final time, stopping me in my tracks. "Thank you, Moody!"

My dick jerked in my pants, begging for attention. I stared down at my crotch, frustration coursing through me.

"Absolutely not."

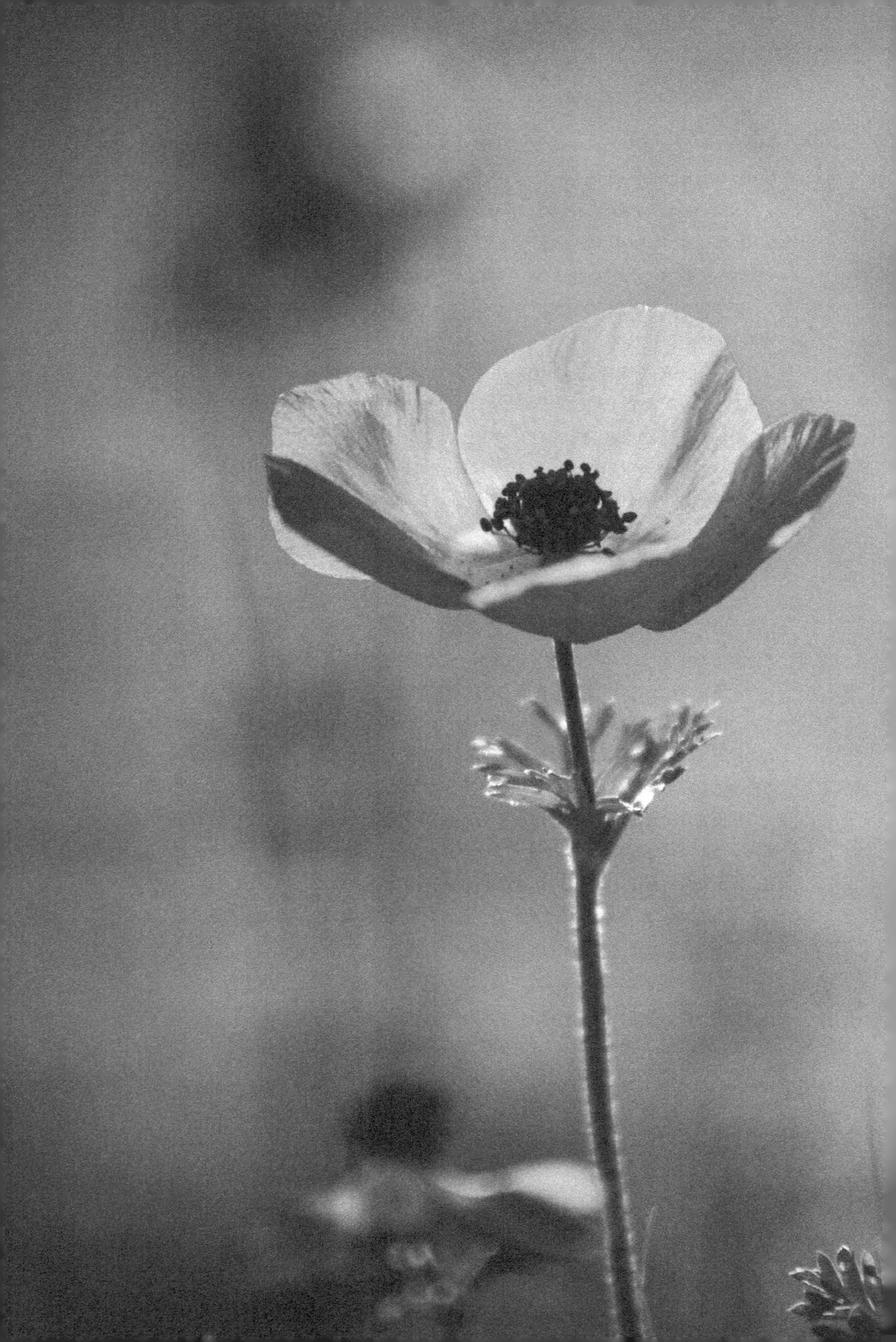

CHAPTER SEVEN

MERRI

I thought the constant sexual energy pulsing through *Iniquity* was tempting, but being trapped in this extravagant penthouse with the four horsemen of the apocalypse was far worse. Well, I had to assume all four of them were here. I still hadn't come across the older Brit—Grim, they'd called him—since he'd overseen my kidnapping.

Regardless, there was something about them, their power, the way they moved through a room, that had my mouth watering and my body on high alert. Thank fuck Malice was able to get me up and running so I could at least cam. Unfortunately, that kind of feeding seemed even less satisfying than usual. It had me snacking far more than I'd ever needed to before, just to try to appease the gnawing hunger that never seemed to be fully sated.

And by snacking, I meant posting and reading the comments in my private feed. It was yet another page on my site, but instead of going live, it was more akin to a traditional social media platform where I could post photos or short videos and all my followers could comment and interact with each other. Like Instagram. No one had to pay for access, but there was enough sexual energy threaded through the thirsty comments to give me a bit of a top-up between camming sessions. Thus, snacking.

I'd already *snacked* twice since my last session, and still, my appetite wasn't satisfied.

I was starting to fear that it never would be unless I gave in and reconsidered my hard stance on physical encounters. But that was a line I didn't want to cross. A gateway to far more dangerous territory. You know, like murder.

Even if Sin's stupid face and perfect body made it sound like it might be worth it.

Or Malice and his dangerously bad attitude.

And then there was Chaos. The sexiest grump who ever grumped. Goddess help me, he was straight out of the cast of *300*. I'd never wanted to climb a man like a tree more in my life.

Did somebody turn off the AC? I had to fan my face as I clicked on my latest post to take a peek at what the snack pack had to say about it.

I scrolled past the photo of me in a white athleisure set, with a tight crop top with a crisscross that went under my tits and tied in the back. It really showcased the girls in a teasingly demure way. The pants were simple leggings, nipped in at the waist, fit like a glove, and accented my round ass. I'd pulled my long hair up into a sleek high pony, a cute little bow giving the illusion of innocence even as my wickedly sharp cat-eye liner hinted that maybe she wasn't a total Goody Two-shoes. Had to cast that net wide and satisfy all kinds in this business.

The caption simply said: Yoga fit.

Apparently, they liked it. Comment after comment, reaction after reaction, came from my regulars and newcomers alike.

> JohnBoy27: Damn, baby girl. Looking absolutely edible today.

> MarlaCakes: Get it, girl. You look gorgeous.

> EverySteve: I'll help you work up a sweat! 😈

> CallMeMommy: How's your downward-facing dog?
>
> Tls4Tony: Do you need me to help stretch you?
>
> ShyGuy25: You're so beautiful.
>
> TheSingularity: Fuck.
>
> TheRealMan: Now show us the view from the back.
>
> Bob1212: Fit is right! 😁
>
> PrettyPenny: That's my girl!!! 😍 Slay, baby!
>
> Only1Leesh: Who is the designer? I need to send a gift basket.
>
> OnMyKnees4U: 😍 🍆 💦 💀
>
> BigMan69: I have a plank you can sit on.
>
> CoffeeandSmut: Link please.

I grinned and replied to CoffeeandSmut with the link to my outfit before typing out a quick good morning/day message to Andi. She was a hard one to pin down sometimes, so it might be a few hours before she got it. I never knew which time zone she was in, and it could be days sometimes before I'd hear back from her.

Taking time to like each and every comment, I stopped when I reached Cole's. Even his screen name made me smile these days. He was the only client I had who didn't make me feel like I was his dirty little secret. If anything, it felt like he was courting me. He was sweet, whereas everyone else was raunchy. In a lot of ways, he reminded me of Jimmy.

My heart gave a little pang as I clicked on his name and opened up our DMs. I wasn't planning on messaging him. From our prior chats, I knew he was on the West Coast of the US, and it was something like two in the morning there. Instead, I settled for scrolling back through our prior chats.

SHYGUY25:
I'm glad you posted today. I was thinking about you.

MERRI-GO-ROUND:
You were? Good things, I hope.

SHYGUY25:
Always good things.

MERRI-GO-ROUND:
Such as . . .

SHYGUY25:
That's for me to know.

MERRI-GO-ROUND:
And I thought I was the tease.

SHYGUY25:
Oh, you are. Definitely.

SHYGUY25:
Are you okay? You've been quiet on the site for longer than usual.

This conversation must've been when I was in Blackwood Asylum. They'd kept me offline for over a week. Big mistake.

MERRI-GO-ROUND:
Yup! All good. I've just been traveling with family. It's hard to sneak away.

SHYGUY25:
Where did you go? Anywhere fun?

MERRI-GO-ROUND:
Let's just say it's very cold and dreary. Not my definition of fun at all.

SHYGUY25:
So what is your definition of fun?

MERRI-GO-ROUND:

Ideally, I'd be laid out on the beach with a cocktail in one hand and a good book in the other. Although my fair skin doesn't love the sun as much as I do.

SHYGUY25:

Do you burn?

MERRI-GO-ROUND:

No. I freckle. LOL

SHYGUY25:

Freckles are adorable. If I was there with you, I'd count each one.

MERRI-GO-ROUND:

So long as you don't try to play connect-the-dots, I suppose I'll allow it.

Before I could keep reading, a notification popped up with a new incoming message. From Cole.

SHYGUY25:

Morning, beautiful!

MERRI-GO-ROUND:

Good morning. But what are you doing up so late, mister? Don't you have dragons to slay or something?

SHYGUY25:

Not just yet. I'll save the world conquering for another day.

SHYGUY25:

I couldn't sleep. Figured I'd check in on my favorite redhead.

I blushed and found myself grinning down at the screen like a smitten tween.

MERRI-GO-ROUND:

Does that mean you have favorite blondes and brunettes, then?

SHYGUY25:

I should have clarified. You're my favorite everything.

A giggle escaped as my tummy gave a happy little twist.

MERRI-GO-ROUND:

Do you practice these lines in the mirror? You're very smooth.

SHYGUY25:

It's easy because it's true.

MERRI-GO-ROUND:

Mmmhmm, I bet you tell that to all the girls.

SHYGUY25:

There are no other girls. I'm shy, remember?

MERRI-GO-ROUND:

Doesn't seem like it.

SHYGUY25:

That's because I'm comfortable with you.

MERRI-GO-ROUND:

I'm glad. You make me comfortable too.

I was really skirting the line with Cole these days. Honestly, I liked him. Our relationship had evolved from simply cam work to something deeper, and I knew I shouldn't keep opening up to him. As a rule, I never DMed with any of my clients. They had to pay for access to me. End of story. But then there was Cole. Sweet, caring Cole who made it easy to forget there should be rules, a paywall, and emotional distance dividing us.

The reminder that he was still a paying client, even if not at this exact moment, dimmed most of the excitement I felt at his text. I needed to restore the dynamic between us.

> MERRI-GO-ROUND:
> Gotta go! That yoga won't do itself.

> SHYGUY25:
> Talk to you later?

> MERRI-GO-ROUND:
> Book a session, and we can do more than talk. 😉

> SHYGUY25:
> You got it, beautiful. XOXO

Closing out of the chat, I let out a sigh.

"What now?" I asked myself, looking around the room as if it contained an answer.

I'd only been here a few days, and I was already bored with my captivity. At least at Blackwood, there were grounds to explore and people to talk to if I was brave enough to risk it. I'd also had a purpose to keep me company. But here, I felt stuck.

Standing, I roamed the bedroom, eventually making my way to the closet. Whoever had done the shopping for me definitely understood the assignment. I'd bet the farm it had been Auntie Lilith. She knew my size, my preferences, and what I'd need for camming. After opening one of the drawers, I pulled out a hot pink and white striped one-piece with cutouts on the sides. It fit like a dream while still supporting the girls. Thank the goddess Lilith didn't send me nothing but sexy bathing suits.

When I spotted a robe and some cute slides, my decision was made for me.

"Looks like I'm going swimming."

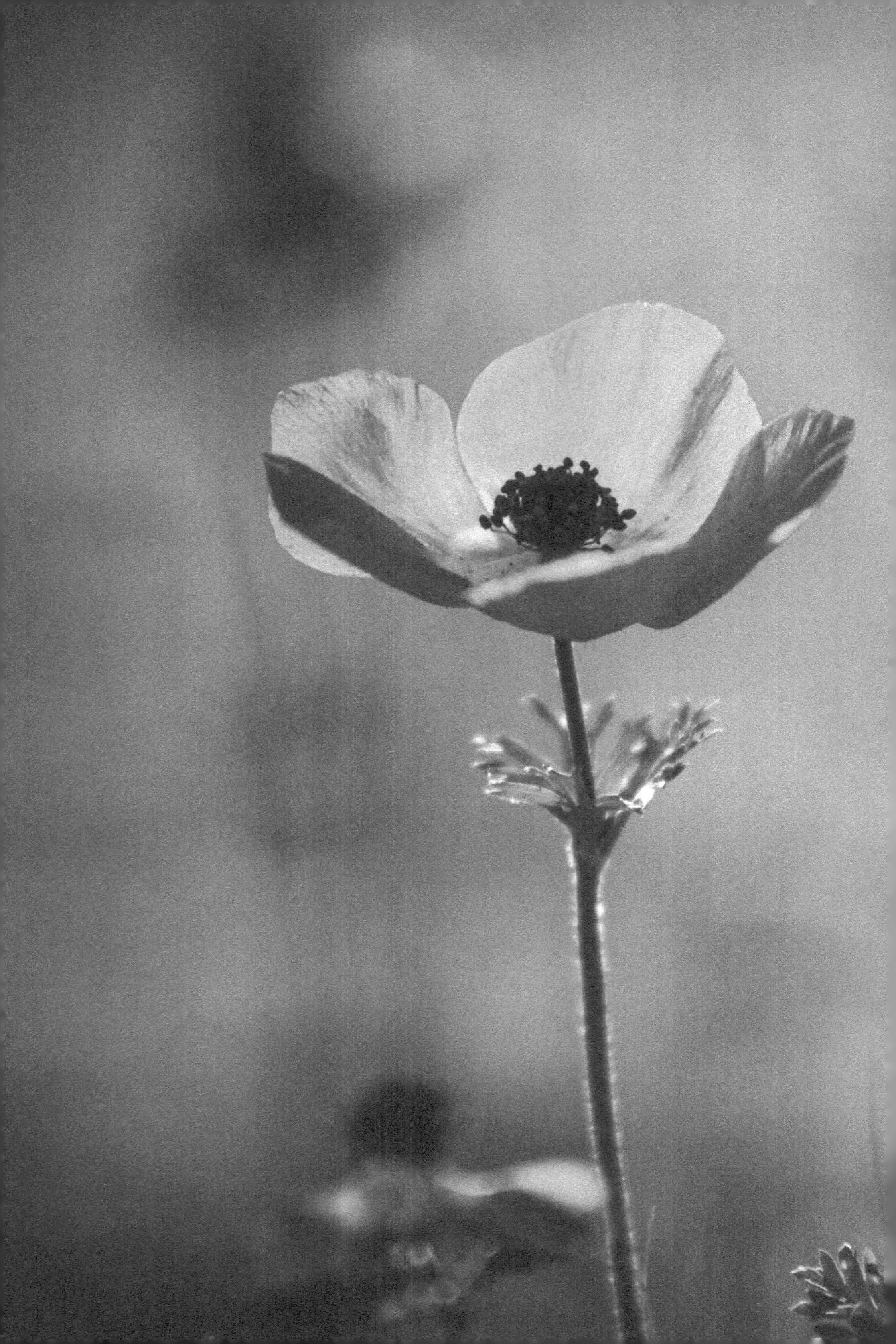

CHAPTER
EIGHT
GRIM

"You're late," I rumbled from my place behind my desk as all three of my brothers filed into my office. "I summoned you here ten minutes ago."

Sinclair rolled his eyes. "Okay, Dad."

"Remind me why we're in this dark cave of an office again? There's an entire penthouse at our disposal." Malice pulled open the curtains, revealing the London skyline in all its glory.

"Says the man who lived in a shack for the past few decades," Chaos said under his breath.

"It was a lake house, thank you very much."

"He's afraid of the little succubus wandering the house," Sin said in a bored drawl as he studied his cuticles.

"I am not," I said, immediately bristling. The thought of me being afraid of anything, let alone that mere slip of a girl, was hilarious. And offensive.

"What was it Shakespeare said?" Sin stage-whispered. "Thou doth protest too much."

Shadows slipped out from under me, threatening to wrap around his throat so they could silence him for me.

"Oops. Looks like somebody made Daddy angry."

"Call me Daddy one more time, I fucking dare you."

Sin winked at me. "Sure, you hate when I do it, but I bet you'd fucking nut yourself if *she* said it."

The tingles that raced down my spine betrayed exactly how his suggestion affected me. He was closer to correct than I wanted to admit.

"And then he'd kill her, and we'd have to start from scratch figuring out who Lucifer's new incubator is," Chaos grumbled.

Mal nodded his agreement.

Sin flicked his gaze between them. "Why go through all this trouble of keeping her safe if he's just planning to kill her?"

"Not because he plans to. Because he quite literally kills every living being he touches," Chaos explained with a pointed stare.

"Oh right. That." Sin shrugged. "So he wears his cute little gloves. Problem solved."

"On his dick?" Malice asked with a lift of his brow.

"Not conducive to reproduction," Chaos chimed in.

Sin's shoulders drooped. "You're right. But you know, he doesn't have to be the one to knock her up. That's what I'm here for. I can take care of putting a baby in her. You three can warm her up. The more aroused she is, the better, right?"

"If it's that simple, Sinclair, why haven't you gotten the job done yet?" I asked, leaning against my desk as I stared at him sprawled in one of my good chairs.

"You didn't tell him?" Malice asked.

"Tell me what?"

Mal waved a hand, opening the floor for Sin to proceed.

"So . . . our girl Merri is celibate," he said after a second, his expression shifting as if he was confused by the words coming out of his mouth.

"A celibate succubus?" Chaos's words sounded as if he'd just asked "Are you fucking kidding me?"

Sin nodded. "Stupidest thing you ever heard, right?"

"You have to be joking."

Fucking Lilith. She couldn't have shared this tidbit of information with us *before* saddling us with the girl?

"She'll come around," I said, rising from my chair and walking to the windows.

London had always been one of my favorite cities, but it was especially stunning at night as the lights of modern-day buildings accentuated the contrast between old and new. There was a reason I'd made it my primary residence. I'd roamed these streets an uncountable number of times, taking souls, sparing others, a wraith playing at being alive. Now if I wanted to continue existence as I knew it, I'd have to help ensure one of us created life rather than snuff it out.

The irony.

Death tasked with the continuance of life.

Somewhere, God was having one hell of a laugh.

If he was even paying attention. Something told me it had been a long time since he peered in on the first of his creations.

"She won't if you all keep being pricks to her." This from Sin, the accusation clear in both his tone and expression.

"I've had minimal contact with her. Surely you can't mean me."

And by minimal, I meant none. I hadn't seen the girl since we collected her.

He leveled a stare at me. "She calls you Grumpy Brit Number One. Yes, it means you. Chaos, you storm around the place like you're ready to toss her over the balcony at any moment. Mal, you're . . . well, you."

"Grumpy Brit Number Two?" he supplied.

"You said it, buddy."

Chaos chuckled. "And here she just calls me Moody."

"Well, she's accurate, if not particularly creative," Sin mused.

He seemed to have forgotten that the rest of us weren't built to exist on seduction and lust. I hadn't been with a partner since my disastrous relationship with Helene. I'd thought, stupidly, that

Death was the only one meant for me because of her nature. I realized now the whole thing was a stroke of madness on my part. We'd been doomed from the start, both of us far too selfish to ever make us good partners. But oh, how I'd craved the ability to touch another being aside from my brothers. To know firsthand what they'd been talking about when sharing their various exploits.

I shoved the thoughts away, along with the frisson of loneliness that always accompanied them.

Death did not get lonely.

Death did not have emotions.

Death did not need anybody.

I repeated these mantras, wrapping them around me like armor until my control slipped firmly back into place.

"So, what do you think, Grim?" Sin asked, pulling me from my thoughts. I'd clearly missed some asinine plan.

"Whatever gets her pregnant fastest."

Malice's narrowed gaze met mine. "How does Sin leaving to feed get Merri pregnant?"

"Wait, what?"

"Told you he wasn't listening," Sin muttered.

Fuck. Merri's presence had me spun up in ways I wasn't prepared for. It was best I keep my distance for everyone's sake. I was a liability. The biggest kink in our plan. If I slipped up and touched her, all hell would literally break loose.

Well, technically, it would be a couple decades later, once the next vessel was located and inseminated. But what were a few decades when you'd walked the earth since it was first formed?

"You can't leave. None of us can. The last thing we need is one of Lucifer's lackeys following you here."

"Because hiding in the penthouse you've owned for just under a century isn't an obvious place to look," Chaos muttered.

Sin groaned. "C'mon, man. I'm starving."

"Feed from her."

He rolled his eyes, his favorite response. Then he spoke slowly, as though I were a child. "She is cel-i-bate. I can't."

"I never thought I'd live to see the day these words left my lips, but . . . Sin has a point."

Sin's mouth dropped open as his attention snapped to Chaos. "Say that again. More slowly this time."

Chaos snorted but sat up straighter in his chair, looking to me. "He needs to feed. I need to fight. We are in a pressure cooker here. If I don't release my mounting violence, you know what will happen."

The memory of what had happened in my office just the other day was the mere tip of the iceberg when it came to what Chaos could do. He had to siphon off his violence regularly, or he was liable to bury us all beneath this entire tower and the city block it stood on.

"Fine. You make a good point, but drawing attention to ourselves is a risk. You and I both know this." It would be naive to think War wouldn't already have considered this. He was a brilliant tactician. "We will all spar with you between fights. Keep your encounters to the absolute minimum. Both of you." I shot a pointed glare at Sin, who loved to be in the spotlight.

"You and Malice will have to step up if we're gone. You understand that, right? You two can't ignore her. She'll leave."

Chaos wasn't wrong. I nodded in response, adjusting my gloves out of habit.

"I'll do what must be done."

Malice muttered something unintelligible under his breath, but I could only assume it was also some form of begrudging assent.

"That's all well and good for Chaos, but I have to feed frequently and intentionally. It's a hunger that's never sated. You know this." Sin shook out his shoulders as though he was ridding himself of an unwanted bit of clothing. The incubus was struggling even as he tried to disguise it with bravado. "My minimum is still more than you're going to approve of. Especially when none of you are willing to help me out and the buffet-de-Merri is closed."

Malice cleared his throat, distracting me from my rapidly growing ire as my shadows began spreading across the floor.

"She feeds by camming. Why can't you?"

Sin opened his mouth, likely to protest, but closed it as his expression turned considering. "I've never needed to, but there might be something to it. All those adoring fans of mine are going to need to turn somewhere now that the tour's ruined."

So that's why Sin kept muttering, *"This is going to ruin the tour,"* when he arrived in Hel's prison. The fucker was still living out his rock star dreams.

Malice checked his watch. "Merri's about to start one of her daily sessions. Why don't you test it out? Your room is next to hers, so if nothing else, maybe the proximity alone will benefit you."

The way Sin lit up reminded me of a fireworks display.

"Say no more. OriginalSin reporting for duty."

"How... original," Malice teased.

Sin cocked a brow. "Oh, and you think TheSingularity is any better? I saw you trolling her page, creeper. You can deny it until you're blue in the face, but you're just as interested in her as I am."

Malice shrugged, entirely unfazed. "She's a succubus. My interest in her is about as controllable as flatulence."

"Cute. Make sure you tell her that. It will definitely get her to spread her legs for you. Wait, weren't you the one claiming to know all about seduction?" Sin laughed and rolled his eyes. "Man, if that's the best you can do, the world is seriously in trouble. Thank God for me."

"She doesn't want to fuck you either," Malice all but growled.

I found it interesting he went with that rebuttal instead of his usual insistence that he wasn't going to participate at all so it didn't matter what she thought of him.

Sin stood, sauntering toward the door, his incubus hunger already radiating from him as he turned and looked at the three of us.

"She wants me. She just doesn't know it yet."

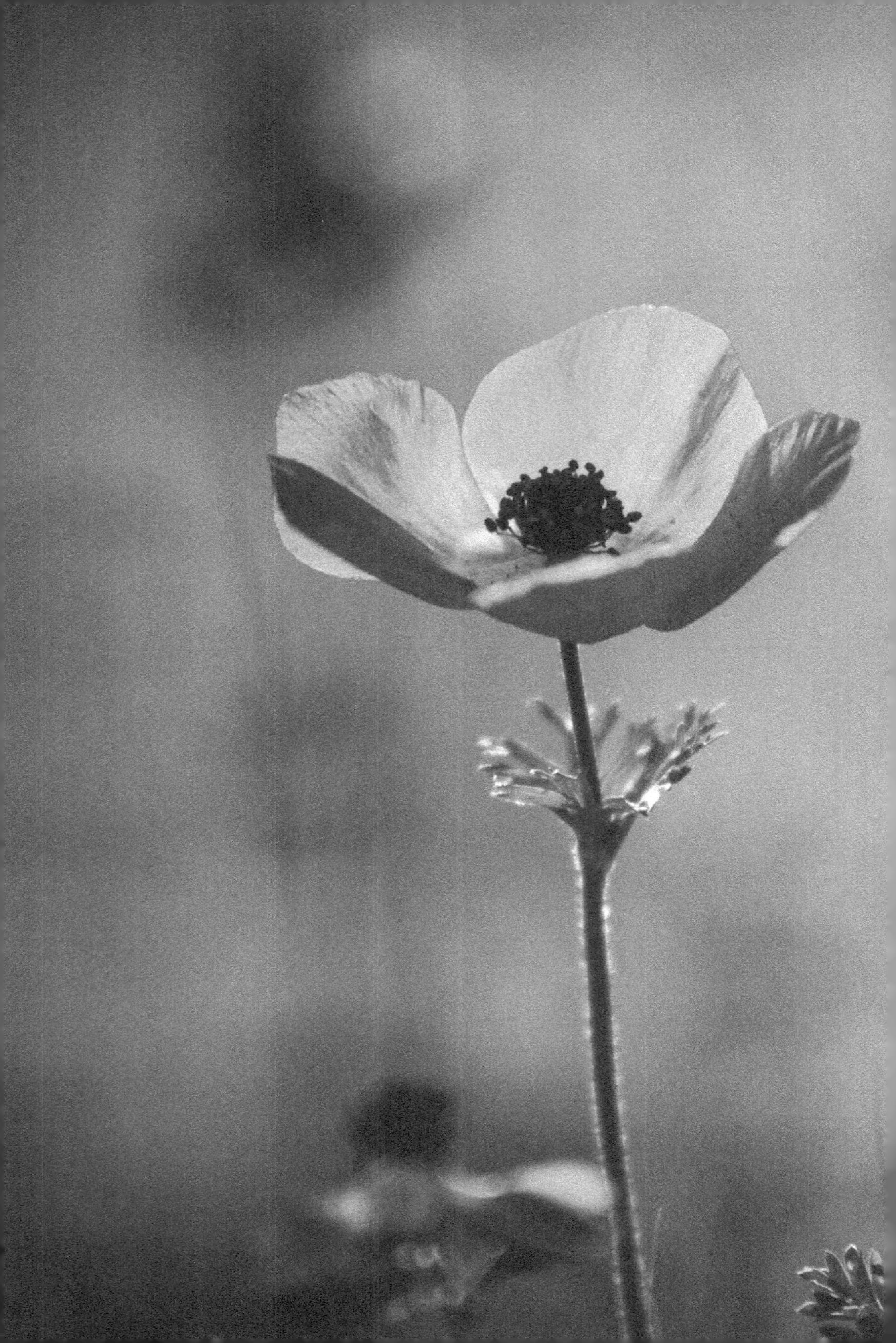

CHAPTER NINE

MERRI

I hummed as I contemplated which outfits to offer as options for tonight's "Get Ready For Bed With Me" session. The pink babydoll I'd worn last time hit the "no" pile first. They enjoyed that one, but a repeat so soon wouldn't get me as much interaction.

"Red?" I murmured as I held up a lacy crimson number with hearts embroidered over the nipples. My favorite part of this set was the matching undies with a heart-shaped cutout across the ass. "Definite maybe."

I kept flipping through options, impressed with the selection Lilith had sent over. These sexy little outfits had her name all over them. I snickered when I found the black leather dominatrix outfit. That was much more her style than mine, so it was an absolute no for tonight, but I filed it away for future possibilities. Maybe it was my succubus intuition, but I had a feeling Cole would be *really* into that kind of roleplay.

"Black *is* good, though. I haven't done black in a while. Maybe I could paint my toenails too."

The toenails would go over really well if a few of my foot fetish regulars showed up. They went wild when I brought out the nail polish. My stomach growled just thinking about how much more I could feed if they were present.

Pulling out a combination of pieces, I laid them on my bed.

"Hmm, this as the base," I said to myself, looking down at the bodysuit that was more straps than anything. It covered the important bits, but had a real air of bondage about it. "Then the sheer black robe over top. Open, of course." Biting my lower lip, I scurried back to the closet and snagged a pair of thigh-high black stockings with the seam up the back and sexy lace at the top and my favorite kitten-heeled feather slippers, à la our iconic 1950s housewives.

"If my foot lovers show, no stockings. If they don't, I'll make a show of putting them on."

One thing I'd learned pretty early on was that it was important to have backup plans. With a live show, you never knew who would be present and if they were going to be an active participant or a lurker, so you had to have enough material planned to keep the ball rolling on your own. Or be ready to improv if the crowd went in an unexpected direction. Camming sessions were a minefield to navigate and way more complicated than anybody would think.

Before I logged on, I draped scarves over the two lamps in the room, effectively giving the space a softer and warmer ambience. The mood was important. This session was all about seduction. When I did sessions where they got to watch me exercise, everything was brighter. When it was my once-per-month "Watch Me Eat" session, I went with soft pinks and purples to make the setting cozy.

What? You thought it was all dirty talk and playing with toys? That's just one element. The easy part, if I'm being honest. Thinking out of the box and creating content with mass appeal was a lot of work. But a girl had to eat, and I couldn't afford to drop the ball.

For the final touch before go time, I selected some soft jazz to play while I streamed. A little sultry, a lot sexy, and we were good to go.

As soon as I went live, they began popping into the chat. Pings announced arrival after arrival even before I was settled in my chair fully.

"Hello, friends! I'm so glad you're here," I said, batting my eyelashes and putting on an exaggerated pout. "I was worried I'd have to get ready for bed all alone."

Gesturing to my plain white shirt and pink shorts, I gave them my most charming smile. "Can you help me pick out what I should wear tonight? I have two choices."

> OnMyKnees4U: Yes, baby. The answer is nothing. Not. A. Stitch.
>
> JohnBoy27: Can I peel it off you with my teeth?
>
> ShyGuy25: You'd look beautiful in anything. Wear what you like the most.
>
> Toto_the_dog: Woof! 🐶
>
> Cerberus: Watch it, Toto. There's only one top dog in here, and it's me.
>
> CallMeMommy: Sounds like these two need to go to the dog park. Don't worry, beautiful, I'll take it from here. Show us what you've picked.

I made a show of getting up from my seat and making my way to the bed. "Mommy always takes good care of me." I tossed a wink over my shoulder for good measure, grinning to myself at the flood of messages and sexual energy that sent my way.

> Cerberus: Call her mommy all you want, but you know I'm your daddy. Now rub my belly and tell me I'm your goodest boy, please.
>
> OriginalSin: Daddy? You wish, pup. That's a title you've got to earn and I doubt you know the first thing about topping.

I could only just make out the screen as I headed back with my options in hand. It was harder than usual to keep my face schooled in a neutral expression as I caught up on the drama in the chat. Their banter wasn't uncommon, and I typically enjoyed it because it kept things moving without me needing to be engaged. But sometimes they got out of hand. These two might be the latter.

> ThisLilPiggy: Is that nail polish on your nightstand?
>
> BigMan69: Show me your tits!
>
> Tls4Tony: Bend over and let me see if you're wearing panties.
>
> OnMyKnees4U: The stockings! Ohmygod please say you're wearing the stockings. 🥒
>
> TheRealMan: Dude's cumming in his pants and she hasn't even done anything yet.
>
> OriginalSin: As if you aren't already rubbing one out. 👀
>
> TheRealMan: . . . okay, bud. 🤏

And with that, I realized this was going to be one of those moments where I had to step in and take back control. OriginalSin was a bit of a troll.

"If you're going to be naughty, then I guess I'll just have to choose for you."

Spinning around, I placed the black option on the bed and dropped the red one on the floor. With a glance over my shoulder, I winked and wiggled my ass before pulling my top off and letting the white cotton float to the carpet. All they saw was my bare back and shoulders, but the way the closet door was positioned offered them a teasing side view in the mirror. The curve of one breast, the dip of my waist, the swell of my hip. Enough to keep them focused on me, but not enough to give away the goods yet.

I was nearly there, though. The tension radiating from my chat room was thick, like a delicious chocolate syrup dripping from a spoon over the ice cream I was about to eat. Time to put the cherry on top.

Hooking my thumbs in the waistband of my shorts, I wiggled my hips as I pushed the fabric down my legs. My ass was in full view, tight, toned, round. Exactly what they wanted.

> OriginalSin: Fuuuuck.
>
> Bob1212: Oh fuck yes, beautiful. Now turn around and show us the rest.
>
> ShyGuy25: Where's the biting my knuckles emoji?
>
> OnMyKnees4U: I know exactly what to do with that 🍑
>
> CallMeMommy: That ass would look even better with my handprint on it.
>
> EverySteve: Let me take a bite, baby.
>
> Tls4Tony: Fuck, your ass is juicy.

Taking a long, slow breath, I pulled as much sexual energy from the chat as I could. They were already feeding me better than my session earlier this week. Thank fuck. There was something about being in this penthouse that had me feeling ravenous. No matter what, I couldn't seem to assuage my hunger.

CallMeMommy had some excellent suggestions tonight. She always did. I reached behind me and smacked my butt, the pain burning over my skin, but their reactions filling me even more.

A thud from the room next to mine pulled me out of the moment as I was reminded I wasn't alone here. This wasn't *Iniquity*, where every room was spelled to be soundproof.

Turning my attention to the camera with my hands strategically hiding anything I didn't want them to see, I giggled. "I need to be more quiet. I forgot I have roommates."

Little heart bubbles floated across the screen. Oh, they really liked that I had roommates. I bet they wouldn't if they knew the people in question were three of the hottest men I'd ever seen, plus one surly Brit I was sure wouldn't disappoint if I ever got to meet him.

> ShyGuy25: Where can I sign up for the waitlist? 😊 I'm super neat and make one hell of a grilled cheese sammich.

> BigMan69: Tell them to join you. The more the MERRI-er.

> JohnBoy27: How many are there?

> OnMyKnees4U: Do they all look like you? I'd pay good money to see you have a pillow fight with them.

> Tls4Tony: How'd you know my fantasy was a night at a sorority house?

> ThisLilPiggy: But back to the nail polish . . . 😏

> OriginalSin: Invite me in, sweet girl. I'll put your roommates to shame.

Something about OriginalSin's comment had my body tingling. It almost sounded like a threat. A sexy threat.

My computer dinged twice in a row with private session requests. One from Cole and the other from OriginalSin. For a heartbeat, I was torn, my cursor hovering over the green accept button on Cole's request, but then I remembered the blurred lines and boundaries I needed to reestablish. I moved my cursor from Cole to OriginalSin, opting for the one-on-one to begin in two minutes.

Sorry, ShyGuy. Next time.

With frenetic energy stirring my blood, I shimmied into my black lingerie, the robe sliding over my skin like a caress before I turned around.

As I sat on the bed and slowly pulled on one stocking after the other, I broke the news to my followers.

"Sorry, loves, I've been booked for a private session. I hope you stay around."

Leaning forward, I blew them a kiss, watching as the protests filled the chat.

> Toto_the_dog: Growl.
>
> CallMeMommy: Such a perfect tease. As always.
>
> EverySteve: Fuck. Of course. When are we gonna get to see your pretty pussy?
>
> ThisLilPiggy: Wait! You didn't paint your toes yet!
>
> BigMan69: Come back and make yourself cum. 🧁💦

They were still going as I opened the private chat room, a little timer counting down in the corner.

4...

3...

2...

1...

OriginalSin has entered the chat.

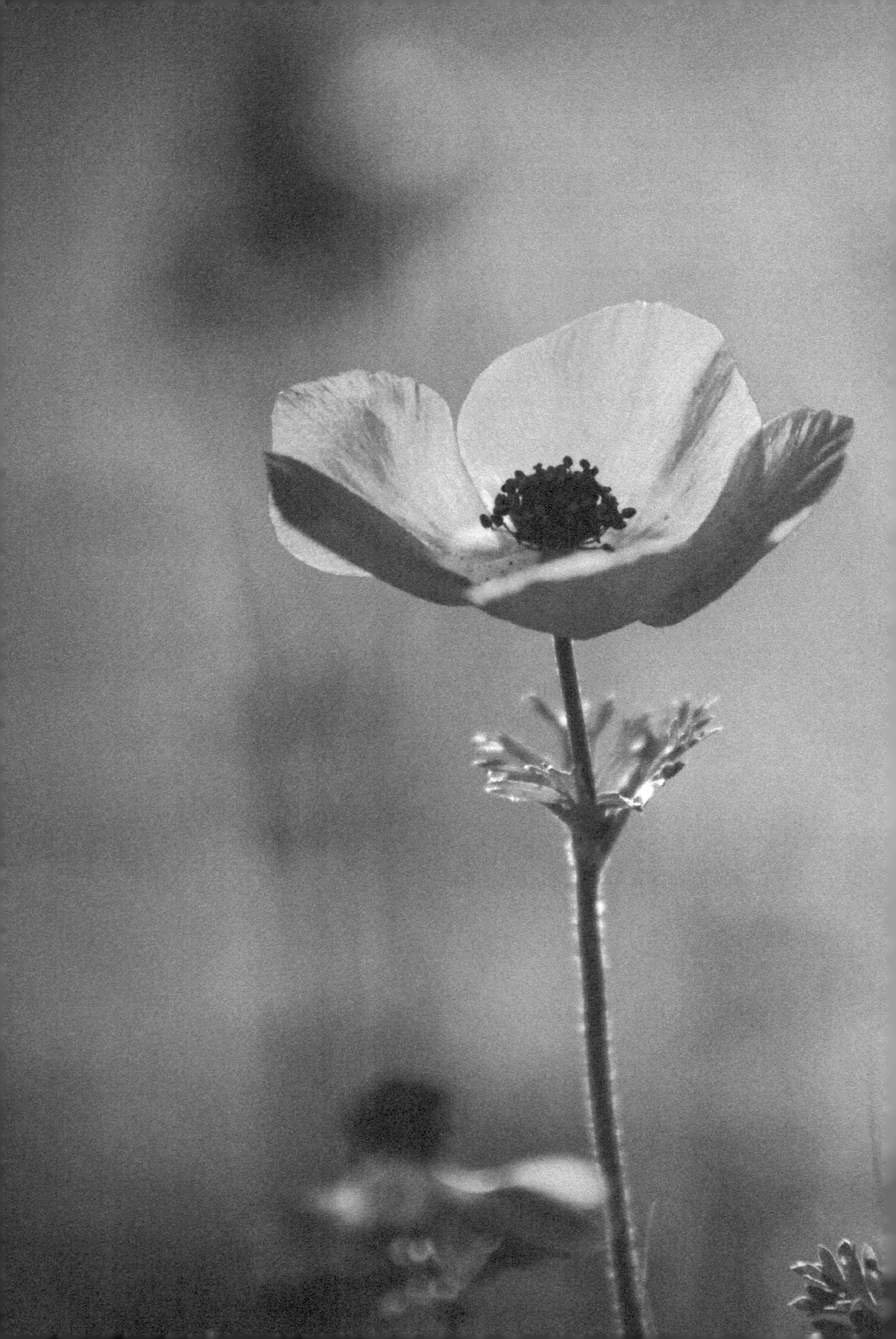

CHAPTER
TEN
SIN

Fuck me, Merri was the prettiest thing I'd ever seen. The moment I entered the private chat room, my dick went from mostly hard to straining behind my fly. The little succubus sat on her bed, blinking those big doe eyes at the camera, fawning for me as she toyed with the sash of her robe.

"Hi," she purred, lifting a hand and wiggling her fingers at me. "Are you comfortable sharing your name with me?"

I had to swallow back a groan at the thought of her whimpering, moaning, or screaming my name. Not that I could give it to her. I was incognito. But the thought of hearing her doing that with any other fucker's name pissed me off. What a quandary.

Sitting back in my chair, I watched her wait patiently for my reply. What could I use that benefited me as well?

Then it came to me. A name I hadn't heard in far too long. One I'd given up in exchange for immortality.

Emmett St. James

Disgraced film star.

The man I'd been. The one I buried so Sinclair St. James could rise from his ashes.

Emmett, I typed after what I hoped wasn't too long of a pause.

Merri's smile stretched as she read my reply. "Pleasure to meet you, Emmett."

> ORIGINALSIN:
> Not yet, but it will be.

I knew I'd made the right call with my response when she giggled, "Cocky. I like it."

> ORIGINALSIN:
> Confident. Not cocky.

She leaned forward, giving me a view of her full breasts as they strained behind the strips of fabric barely covering them. "What are you here for, Emmett? What do you like?"

The tent in my pants said I liked every fucking thing she had to offer, but I couldn't feed on my own lust. I needed hers.

> ORIGINALSIN:
> This isn't about what I like, baby. I want you to feel good.

In what was clearly a practiced move, Merri let her long hair fall over one shoulder and gave me a look from beneath her thick lashes. "I feel good when you feel good."

> ORIGINALSIN:
> Trust me, beautiful. Looking at you makes me feel really fucking good.

"Is that so?" she crooned, her fingers trailing over the full swell of her breasts.

Closing my eyes, I attempted to take in her energy, to sip from the lust she should be sending my way. Nothing. It was like trying to drink through a broken straw. This was never going to work if she wasn't genuinely enjoying herself. I had to pivot. Fast.

I rapidly drummed my fingers on my desk, thoughts racing a mile a minute as I came up with and discarded a dozen possibilities.

"No, dumbass. You need to set yourself apart from the other horny fuckers who pay for her time."

I couldn't seduce her properly from behind this screen. Words in a chat bubble only went so far. But a voice? *My* voice? That could make women wet and men hard from fifty paces when I put power behind it. The only problem was, she'd know who I was the instant she heard me. We'd had enough conversations for the jig to be up with the first sentence.

Unless I put my acting skills to good use.

I'd won a few major awards in my day. I could do this. Accents were—mostly—my forte. And as an incubus, I was basically a walking chameleon. There was no part I couldn't play to perfection. But the part I was interested in right now was becoming Merri's dream lover.

Who the fuck was that?

The sexy Australian ready to take her on a journey down under?

"Are you ready for me to give you the ride of your life?"

I frowned. The accent was solid but lacking something. I didn't think the Aussie rugby player I had in mind was going to do it for my sex kitten.

"What about a sexy Russian prince?" My frown deepened. "Emmett is not a Russian name," I continued in the accent before switching to a posh British one. "He could be a Brit, though. A royal in disguise, ready to bend her over for a proper fuck?"

I tossed that idea in the bin too. We were overflowing with Brits in this penthouse, and she hated them at present. That would annoy her, not seduce her. I needed something that would stand out.

I ran through my arsenal of accents. "Something tells me she won't trust a German professor. But maybe an Italian vintner with a villa in Tuscany? Or a French pastry chef who is an artist on the weekends." I shook my head, wincing as my French accent came out more Lumiere from *Beauty and the Beast* than I'd intended. "Maybe we stay away from France. I've got to find a surefire panty dropper. Something that drips sex."

A ghost of a memory flickered to life in my mind. A remnant from a conversation held years ago.

"Everything sounds good when I say it."

Hades. That cocksure motherfucker. He wasn't wrong, though. His accent would be perfect. Every lady melted when you called her darlin'.

Southern gentleman, it was.

"Emmett? Are you still there? You didn't get started without me, did you?" Merri bit her lower lip and slid her fingers between her thighs, not touching herself, but hinting at the possibility.

I wanted her to bring those fingers up and show me how wet I could make her.

Unmuting my microphone, I rolled my shoulders and got into character.

"Sorry, darlin'. I was just getting set up to go hands-free for the rest of our time together. You're too pretty to waste time typing."

Her eyes widened, and a pulse of lust came through from her. I'm not ashamed to admit a sharp stab of jealousy hit me that she reacted so viscerally to my Hades-inspired persona. But this was what I needed. She couldn't know it was me. Not yet. Not until she brought down some of those walls.

"Your voice . . ." she murmured, rubbing her thighs together.

"What about it?"

"I like it."

"Glad to hear it, sweet girl. Now open your thighs for me and tease me with what I want to see."

"Like this?" she asked, falling back on the bed, her shoulders and head propped up on a conveniently placed pillow so she could still look into the screen.

"Wider," I practically growled, hand dropping to my zipper. "That's my good girl," I praised as she spread those shapely legs for me.

Every command I gave her pumped up the lust radiating between us. Now we were talking. I could feel her taking little tastes of me, and I did the same, desperately hoping she wasn't experienced enough to know that's what I was doing.

Fuck, my dick was hard as stone. Painfully swollen and dripping for her as I pulled it free of my pants.

"Are you touching yourself?" she asked, showing me that she wasn't too far gone to forget about her *client*. My mouth curled with distaste. I didn't want to be just one of her johns, but beggars can't be choosers.

This is a temporary measure, I reassured myself. *Baby steps.*

"Yeah," I gritted out, squeezing my needy cock and giving it a taste of the attention it craved. "You make me so hard, baby. I have been since the moment I first saw you."

Not a lie.

Not one little bit.

"Do I? Really?"

"Yes. Now stop fishing for compliments and take off that ridiculous bodysuit. I want to see you when I make you come."

Merri pushed herself up and immediately started stripping. I couldn't help but wonder if she'd be that compliant in person or if she'd be more of a brat and make me work for every inch of her obedience. Given what a firecracker she'd been up until now, I felt like it might be the latter. But right now, she wanted to please me so she could feed.

Her nipples were tight, a deep pink so tantalizing I couldn't help but lick my lips as I imagined pinching them and making her moan before taking each one in my mouth.

"Fuck, darlin'. Pretty as a picture." I was really laying on the cowboy right now, but she seemed to like it a whole hell of a lot. "Are you wet for me?"

She nodded, the little hitch in her breath telling me she wasn't lying.

"Show me."

I stroked myself, my hand replaced by the fantasy of her mouth, or fuck, her soaked cunt. Her eyes flashed with the glimmer of power as she took from me what I willingly gave. I'd get it all back when she came with my name on her lips. When we were done, we'd both be sated, filled in ways we couldn't get from others. One might think an incubus and succubus feeding together would be a never-ending cycle, leaving the two constantly fighting for sustenance. Not the case. Her sexual energy filled my power reservoir, and mine did the same for hers. We charged each other up better than anyone else ever could.

"Fuck, baby. Spread those swollen lips for me."

Merri let out a little whimper, her pupils flaring wide at the command. When her fingers slipped back between her legs, she let out a soft gasp, as if surprised by how wet she was.

There was no stopping my grin. I might be using a fake voice, but that reaction was all mine. I was earning every drop of her pleasure.

"Show me," I demanded, not elaborating.

Merri held her glistening fingers up, her chest rising and falling in rapid pants.

My strokes became more deliberate, the pleasure of the rhythmic motion forcing me to grit my teeth as I held tight to my control.

"Suck them clean, baby. Tell me how good you taste. I want to see if I'm right about you."

Merri leaned forward, making a show out of sucking and licking her fingers.

"You're such a good fucking girl for me."

Her cheeks turned an even deeper pink at the compliment. And I tucked that little nugget away along with the others I'd been collecting in my mental dossier.

"Mmm, oh God," she whispered.

"What was that for?" I asked, my voice rough as I continued working myself.

"I can hear you," she breathed.

It took a second for her meaning to click. She wasn't talking about my voice. She meant what I was doing to myself.

"You're making a mess of me over here. My cock is leaking at the sight of you."

Her sharp inhale made me wish I was there with her, smelling her arousal, able to pin her to the bed and fuck her deep and long.

"Want to feel me?"

Her eyes widened. "What do you mean?"

"Go grab a toy. Make sure it's nice and thick." I groaned at the thought. "God, baby, hurry. I want to see you stretched around my cock."

Merri seemed to be on the same page as me because she was quick to return to the screen, an impressive pink dildo in hand. "Will this work?"

"Oh, fuck yeah. Lay back and slide it in, baby. Then I want you to time your thrusts with mine. And while you do, I want you to remember that it's my cock inside you. That I'm the one fucking you and making you feel good."

My cock twitched as she did what I told her, the urge to come knocking at the door stronger with every little moan and gasp that escaped her.

"Yeah, baby. Just like that. Fuck, you're taking my cock like such a good girl."

Slowly, she fed the dildo inside herself, wriggling as her pussy stretched wide around its girth. I was bigger, but she'd find that out soon enough. I imagined her doing the same around me, her eyes locked on mine, staring into my soul as we joined.

My groan was ragged as it spilled out of me unbidden. I was no longer sure who this fantasy was for.

"You feel so good," she panted, hips rolling as she kept timing with me.

The dildo glistened with proof of how aroused she was. Even if I couldn't feel it coming from her, I'd know based on the way her slick dripped down her ass. Motherfucker. I was going to blow before long.

"Use your other hand, pretend it's me, and rub that clit, darlin'. I need you to come all over my cock."

I wasn't sure what word to use to describe the sound that left her at my words. It was part growl, part mewled moan. But with a little bit of shock and awe thrown in. I was rocking her fucking world with just my voice.

Wait until I get my hands on you, kitten.

Her thighs shook uncontrollably as an orgasm barreled toward her. I could feel the shift in the energy between us. The mounting tension echoed in me, and I barked out her name in warning.

"Yes, Emmett. Come. Please. I can't until you do."

"Together," I ground out, my hand shuttling furiously as I finally gave into the climax that I'd been holding at bay.

"O-okay," she panted.

One stroke.

Two.

"Now!" I demanded, damn near blacking out as her pleasure crashed into me. I wasn't sure if it was from the screen or through the walls, but I was utterly lost to it as I fed.

Her cries of pure euphoria filled my headphones as my release pulsed in nearly painful bursts across my chest. I had to bite my fist to keep myself from shouting loud enough to make her realize it was me in the next room and not some handsome stranger on the internet.

We panted in unison, each still feasting on our sexual afterglow.

I'd just opened my mouth to ask when we could do it again when I got unceremoniously booted out of the chat room.

"Well then," I muttered, reaching for a tissue—then thinking better of it and grabbing a handful—so I could clean myself up.

Not a second after I tucked my dick back into my pants, my bedroom door swung open, a distraught Chaos standing there, eyes blazing, chest heaving.

Shit. Were we under attack already? I really needed Lucifer to give us some breathing room.

"What's wrong?"

"What the fuck was that?" he demanded.

"What do you mean? I've been . . . oooohhhh," I said, clocking the raging erection his sweats were doing nothing to hide. He must have felt the same sexual shockwave I just had. "*That* is what happens when a succubus comes."

Chaos dragged a shaking hand through his hair. "Fuck."

I couldn't help but snicker. "Consider yourself supernaturally Viagra'd. You're welcome."

War shot me a dirty glare, not the least bit grateful as he flipped me off and slammed my door shut.

"At least make good use of it!" I shouted after him, already knowing that surly bastard would head straight for the nearest cold shower.

Leaning back in my chair, I threaded my fingers behind my head and sighed. "Well, Emmett St. James, I'm gonna go on record and say that was a very successful experiment."

I was fed, sated, and by all accounts, feeling more like myself than I had since before Lady Death took us all captive. But why did the thought of pretending to be someone I wasn't in order to get close to her leave a bitter taste in its wake?

I knew exactly why.

I wanted Merri to crave me—the real me—the same way I craved her.

Taking a page from Chaos's book, I let out a soft, fervent, "Fuck."

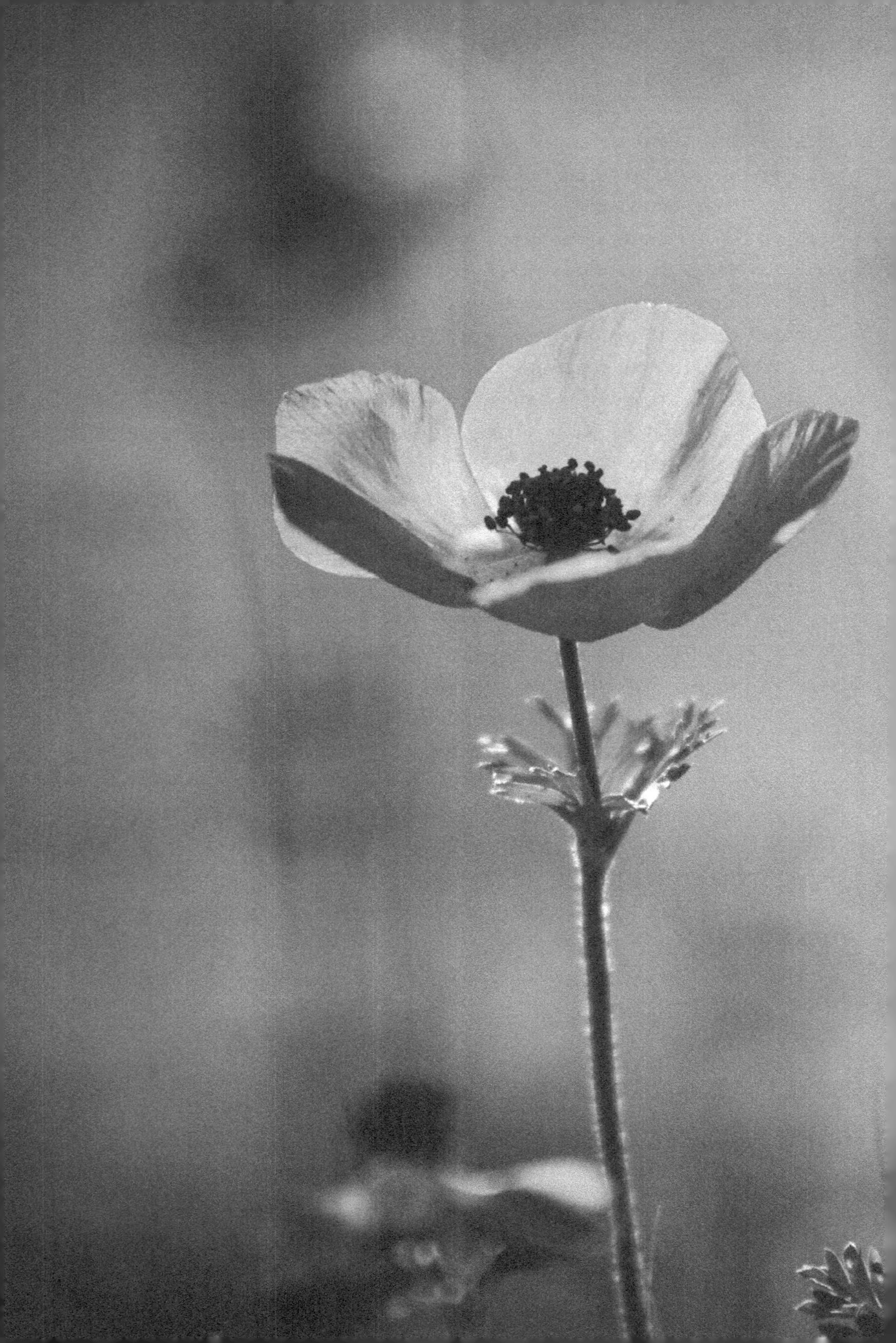

Chapter
Eleven
Lucifer

"Bloody light pollution. That's the first thing I'll get rid of," I grumbled as the sky darkened and the cityscape beyond began to blaze to life.

I sighed and gathered my shoulder-length locks into a knot at the base of my skull, fighting the wind coming from the south. The bustle of Los Angeles had gotten even worse since my imprisonment in hell. This used to be one of my favorite views on Earth. Now it was nothing but smog and neon. Oh well, more souls for me to corrupt, I supposed.

That was the point of all this, wasn't it?

Arms crossed over my chest, I stared down at my future kingdom. "And the wicked shall inherit the Earth," I mused, a small, vindictive smile curling my lips.

Oh, how my siblings will hang their heads in sorrow when they finally come to understand that they should've fallen right along with me so long ago. Michael, so virtuous, so self-righteous, would be the first to surrender his wings before I took his grace. And then Gabriel. My plans for him were too great to name. But all of them involved eternal suffering. No one locks me up and gets away with it. A gilded cage is still a cage.

"My, what a frightful scowl you have, grandmother," a sultry feminine voice crooned from my left.

I turned slowly to face Famine, taking in her disguised appearance as she did the same with mine. "The better to show off my teeth, little horsewoman," I replied, flashing her a grin.

She closed the distance between us with a slow, sensual walk, her curves on full display in the ensemble she'd chosen. The black cocktail dress she wore stood out and made her pale skin nearly glow in the light of the rising moon. The last time I'd seen her, she hadn't boasted dark, penetrating irises framed by thick black lashes. She'd been all demon, with milky eyes and a tail.

"Look at you all dressed up. I hadn't realized this was a formal occasion."

She did a small twirl. "What else is your return topside if not a reason to celebrate?"

If only that were true. There were still far too many obstacles in my path to celebration. Not the least of which was the reason I'd summoned her tonight.

"You disappoint me, Sabine. As usual, you are the failure of your sisters."

Her face fell. "What do you mean by that?"

"Death released me. War broke all the seals. Pestilence delivered me so many souls. You arrive empty-handed."

"How can you say that? I'm the one who ensured you'd have a vessel." Her scowl tightened, rage burning in the depth of her gaze. "The second I saw that Death would have her turn before me, I knew I needed to take the steps to ensure my place in your regime. All of this is for nothing if you don't have the appropriate womb to bear your child."

I held out my hands, gesturing at the open space around us. "And where is my vessel, Sabine?"

Her teeth clenched together hard enough that I could hear them grinding.

"Exactly my point. If she's not in my fucking bed, she may as well not exist. Where. Is. She?"

"I . . . I don't know, my lord."

"Your lord? Try again, Famine."

"My king," she bit out as she choked back her fury.

Sabine and her sisters weren't weak or subservient to anyone, usually. But this bargain, made so long ago, had been one of pure desperation. She knew down to her core she didn't stand a chance to win against Death. A wise assumption. And like a scrambling cockroach, she found a way to keep herself relevant. Make me a vessel—one from Eve's bloodline, the only bloodline capable of creating an antichrist. Maintain her status and power.

I had children scattered across the world. Generations of them. Honestly, how do you think politicians got so charismatic? Luck? Nope. Deals? Too easy. They've all got a little of the devil in them. But none of them were firstborns from Eve's line.

My gut twisted with disdain at the ridiculous stipulation set forth by my father. Eve was a sore subject. Literally.

"So quiet, little horsewoman. Where's all that bravado and swagger you had when you showed up and vowed to help me bring about the end of times?"

Her expression tightened, but she didn't offer an explanation. Which proved that she wasn't as stupid as she looked.

"I may not know where she is, but I know how you can find her."

I raised a brow, silently demanding she get to the point.

"Her name is Meredith, Merri. She's a succubus—"

"You'd better be on the verge of some new groundbreaking revelation, Sabine, because that's all information I already know." Nothing angered me more than people wasting my time.

My hands balled into fists, wings sprouting from my back and spreading in irritation. I was certain my eyes were glowing with the promise of violence if she disappointed me.

"She's a *succubus*, my lo—my king. That means she can dreamwalk."

"And?" I drawled, impatience dripping from the word.

"*And* that means you can call her to your dreams. Once she's in your clutches, you'll be able to draw out any information you need. Like, say, her current location."

Taking in a long breath, I turned away from her and stared out at my dominion once more, the wind caressing my wings, begging me to fly. A dreamwalker. Of course. Honestly, I was a teensy bit ashamed I hadn't thought of that, but I'd been busy plotting the rest of my coup. There was just one glaring issue.

"How am I meant to call her to me when I have nothing to connect us?"

"You're irresistible, my king. Now that you've been released, your power is unmatched. I'm sure she won't be able to help herself. Moths and flames and all that."

"I'd rather not leave it to chance," I murmured, eyeing her like she was some rare specimen beneath my microscope. "Let's at least bait the trap."

She blinked, likely following my train of thought.

"For something like this, blood magic is the only surefire way to connect the two of us."

"You require her blood."

I smirked, lengthening one of my nails into a sharp claw. "Or yours."

With a precise slashing motion, I opened her throat, dark red blood pouring down her front like a macabre waterfall. She gaped, wet gurgles all she could manage as I summoned a chalice and held it beneath her flowing life force.

"What was that? I can't quite hear you."

Ah, it was good to be me.

Once my cup was full, I let her fall. She continued to gasp and flop around like a dying fish beside me. "Oh, don't be so dramatic. You'll live."

With a final appreciative glance at the world I'd claimed, I grinned and brought the cup to my lips. "To us, my sweet vessel. May our union be fruitful."

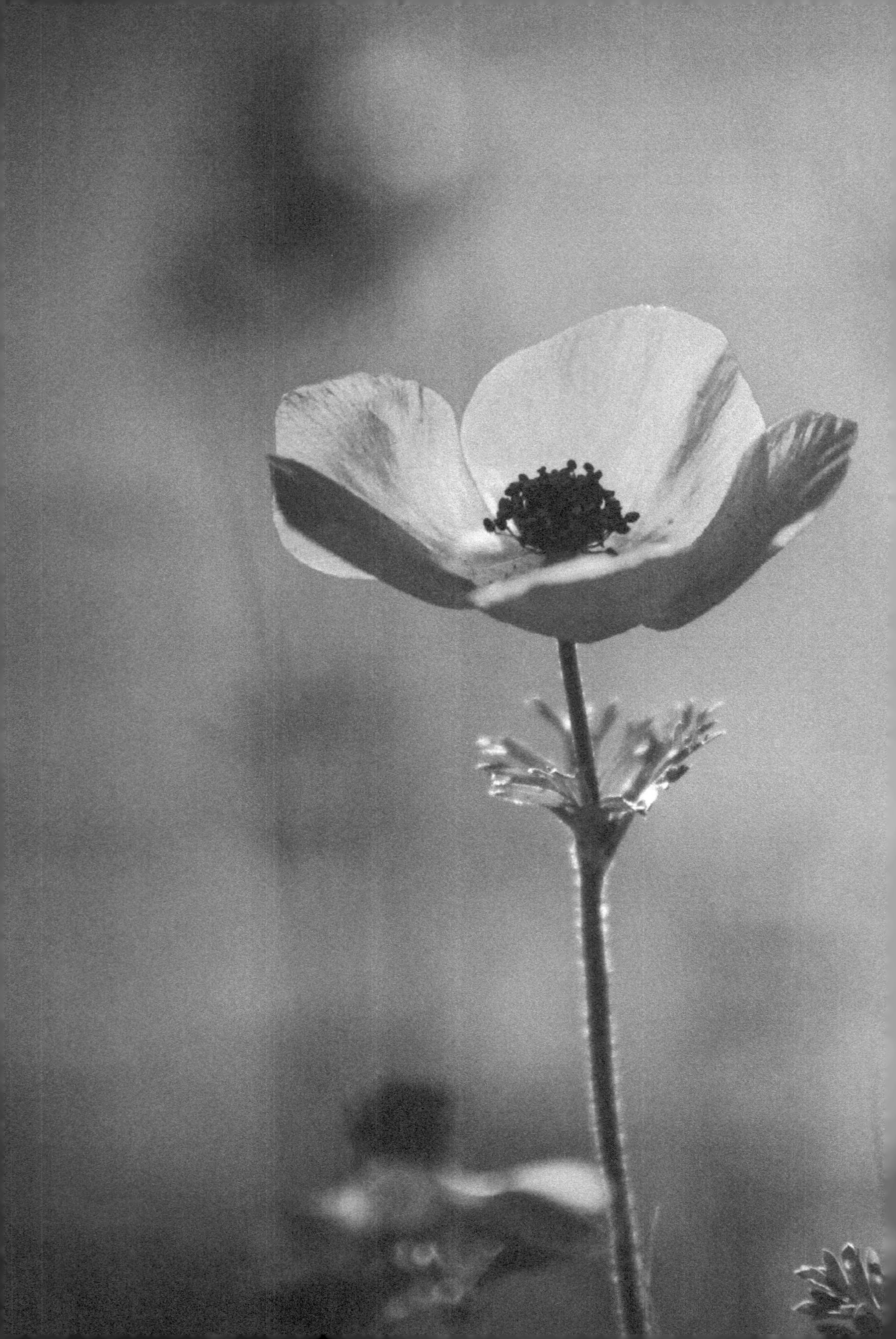

CHAPTER
TWELVE
MERRI

"This place is romance novel enormous," I muttered as I roamed the hallways of the penthouse. Any minute now, I expected to run into the broody billionaire who owned it.

I hadn't been able to settle my mind or my body all evening, no matter what I tried. Exercise, meditation, reading, counting sheep, binging trashy reality shows, nothing worked for me tonight. So, exploration it was. It was coming up on one week since my little staycation began, and I still hadn't seen the entirety of this place. Or its owner.

It was well past time to change that.

A glance at the clock had me hesitating, but only for a second. It might be after midnight, but these men weren't exactly human. It wasn't like I'd interrupt precious sleep they needed for survival. They were immortals. Sleep was an indulgence. A habit. Not a necessity. Right? Besides, they said I wasn't a prisoner, that I was free to move around the apartment.

So why did I feel like I was mid-burgle as I tippy-toed my way to the elevator? I'd limited myself to the main and second floors thus far, but I had my sights set on the elusive third floor tonight. What skeletons would I discover? Dead exes like that Bluebeard guy? Some monstrous but totally hunky beast in ripped trousers? A hidden wife who'd gone mad? My money was on the last one, and my heart raced as the elevator ascended.

I winced when a ding announced my arrival, my pulse ratcheting up another notch at the fear of discovery before I was even able to snoop. I'd get in trouble. I was sure of it. Punished for my sneaky ways.

Hmm. That could work to my advantage if whoever found me enjoyed doling out discipline. I could feed.

I held my breath as the door soundlessly slid open.

I have to admit I was a little disappointed when no stern brunch daddy was waiting for me on the other side. Nor psychotic wife or Tor-like beast.

Le sigh.

Some other bitches got all the fun.

Where was my fun? I deserved fun.

Instead I killed anyone who tried to give that to me.

Again, le sigh.

Having a proper pity party now, I crept out of the elevator and took in the expensive but understated furnishings. Every wall was floor-to-ceiling glass, offering unimpeded views of the city lights.

"Wow," I breathed, walking forward on instinct, my feet sinking into plush carpet so soft I was surely leaving footprints. I noted the grand leather sectional that seemed to dominate this den—living room didn't seem like the right word for the space. The cushions were so deep they could fit at least two of me comfortably.

"You and I totally have a date later," I whispered, giving the sofa a little finger gun before starting toward what looked like it could be an epic rooftop balcony. Before I made it more than a couple of steps, the whisper of two voices met my ears.

I dropped like a sack of potatoes.

Fuck.

I wasn't so good at the sleuthing thing. I think I was much more of a Scooby than a Velma. Or maybe I was more Bumblebee. You know from that one movie where the giant robot car guy tried to hide himself behind a tiny boulder? That was me right now with this ottoman.

"This can't happen again," a smooth, deep British voice said, the timbre skating over my skin and leaving goosebumps in its wake.

"It won't. I've reinforced the firewalls on every one of your servers. I also hacked into the cyber-pirate's accounts and returned every cent they stole from you, and a little off the top for me. Their systems will be fried the moment they attempt to access any of their banks." That was a voice I knew much better. Malice.

That must mean the other smooth-as-butter Brit must be the infamous Grim. Why did that excite me so?

Rising to my feet, I padded closer to the sound of their voices, most definitely eavesdropping with zero shame.

"Good. We can't afford any distractions right now. Not even some petulant wankers who think they can steal from me."

"Are we sure they're not working for someone else?" Malice drawled.

"You think they might be *his* minions?"

There was a slight pause where I could only make out the rustle of clothes and the sound of fingers moving quickly over a keyboard. Then Malice sighed. "I think it would be foolish of us not to consider the possibility. He is a problem we have to solve."

"He? He who?" I blurted, stepping through the open doorway and crossing my arms over my ample chest.

I had the briefest of moments to take in the surroundings. A dark and moody office, walls of books, another of windows just like in the den, and more importantly, a stunner of a silver fox standing there, only adding to the view. Malice was seated at the desk, half-hidden by the sleek computer monitor.

"How did you get up here?" the man, who could only be Grim, snarled. His silver hair was artfully tousled, the thick locks holding just a hint of curl. His face was beautifully sculpted, the sharp angles of his cheeks matched by his bearded jaw. And then there were those eyes. Whew. A dangerous liquid silver, framed by ridiculously long black lashes.

"I scaled the windows, obviously," I said with a roll of my eyes, annoyed with myself for drinking him in like a fine wine while he was being an absolute prick.

A snorted laugh came from Malice, but he didn't say anything.

Grim narrowed his eyes at me, his jaw setting in a harsh line.

"Uh, the elevator. No one said this floor was off-limits."

"Well, it is."

I raised both of my brows, meeting him glare for glare. I grew up with Lilith Duvall. I was not easily intimidated by silent dick-measuring contests.

"Seems to me like you need to bust out your label maker, then. A sign or something would really help if you want privacy up here."

He took two steps forward, his aura heavy with the power that came along with his title.

"Stay out of my rooms, little girl. For your own safety."

"Damn, you are a grump. I was right. Snow White at least had different personalities to go by with her seven roommates. I got stuck with the grump brigade." I glanced from him to Malice. "Is it just a Brit thing? Bred to be annoyed all the time? Well, that's not right because Chaos is"—the word Greek god came to mind, but I wasn't about to compliment any of these assholes—"in a pretty bad mood most of the time too."

"You need to leave, Meredith," Grim said through gritted teeth.

"Oooh, Meredith, huh? Sounds like I'm in trouble. Too bad you don't know my middle name. You could have really driven the point home, *Daddy*." I drew the name out, really laying on the saccharine sweetness.

Did his palm just flex?

Heat suffused my cheeks. I think it fucking did. Well, looks like we found our brat tamer. Honestly? I loved getting to play the brat and didn't get to do it enough.

"Malice, get her out of here."

I locked gazes with Grim, my body reacting to the molten pewter of his irises. Oh, sweet agony, this one was just as hot as the others. My lower belly gave a warning clench as arousal sang in my veins.

Dammit, I couldn't be hungry again.

Power flared in Grim's eyes, making them glow in a way I wasn't prepared for. Then, I swear the shadows cast by the light on his tall frame darkened, spreading impossibly.

"Right, let's get this naughty little succubus tucked into bed before she ends up six feet under," Malice grumbled, heaving himself out of his chair. "I swear, you're more trouble than you're worth," he continued under his breath as he approached.

I could feel the weight of Grim's gaze tracking my every move as Malice not-so-gently took me by the arm and hauled me out of the office.

The second we were clear of him, it felt like an entire house fell off my chest. "Wow. So that was Grim, huh? I see why you guys keep him hidden."

Malice chose not to answer my question. Instead he gave me a gentle shove toward the elevator and asked one of his own, "Do you have a death wish?"

"He's not going to kill me."

"Don't be so sure. He has claimed countless lives. Yours isn't special."

"That makes no sense. You four are *protecting* me," I said, using air quotes to accentuate my point. "Why would he agree to guard me if he's just going to kill me?"

"Maybe because being around you has the rather unpleasant side effect of making one murderous."

"Please," I said with a huff as we stepped inside. "You're barely around me long enough for that to possibly be true." I ran my gaze down Malice's body, pausing on the obvious bulge behind his fly. "Besides, I don't think murderous is the word you're looking for."

It was his turn to make a sound of amused annoyance. "Don't think you've accomplished anything, hellcat. You're a succubus. This is just an involuntary reaction to being in your presence."

Did I have a whole involuntary reaction of my own to the nickname he just gave me? Yes. Yes, I certainly did.

"Hiss," I teased, making like I was going to scratch him.

He caught my wrist, his expression stormy as he leaned in close. "You don't want to pick a fight with me, I promise you."

If I'd been in my right mind, I might have thought twice about poking at one of the four horsemen of the apocalypse. But I was bored, starved for companionship, and insanely horny—I mean hungry. So can you really blame me?

"Oh, I dunno. Seems like it might be fun."

"It won't be. I'm far more than a girl like you could ever handle."

The elevator door opened and he ushered me out of the car, down the hall, and to my room without another word. As soon as we reached my doorway, he released me but didn't step back.

"Go to sleep, Merri," he growled.

"I don't want to."

"That's unfortunate."

"Why?"

He closed the distance between us until we were nearly nose to nose. "Because you don't have a choice."

Then, with a brush of his lips over my forehead, a wave of fatigue hit me so hard my knees buckled.

I had the brief sensation of weightlessness as I was carried to my bed, and then nothing but darkness followed in its wake.

∽

THE WARM PULSE of lust permeated the air as I stepped out of my room and into the familiar halls of *Iniquity*. It was so good to be back. This was my home—or had been for the last few years. My safe place. Auntie Lilith took care to make sure I had what I needed and loved me in her own way. She was the closest thing I had to a mother.

I moved through the club, noting the writhing bodies on the dance floor, their faces all cast in shadow. Red lights moved over them, painting them in a warm, sensual glow. I kept walking, not sure yet where I was heading, but knowing whatever I needed wasn't waiting for me out there.

A tugging sensation began in my middle, like someone had a rope tied to me and was reining me in. Pulling me to them. But who was it? Anticipation bloomed deep in my belly at the thrill of not knowing, and the feeling only grew as I was led to the bottom floor.

Lilith never allowed me down here. Too dangerous.

Not for me, of course. But for all the couples hidden in the secret alcoves acting out their most depraved fantasies. For them, it was a haven. For me, it would be a hunting ground.

A fleeting thought that I wasn't hungry for once came to the surface, then was gone as quickly as it had arrived. I moved past all the shadow figures, letting their energy wash over me, careful not to sip any of it. I wasn't here for them.

I didn't know where the certainty came from. Only that it was true.

I continued past the main room, down a long hall flanked on either side by a row of closed doors. My pace was steady, focused, and confident. I knew none of these doors would take me where I was supposed to end up. The truth of it sat in my bones, growing stronger with each step until my breath caught and the door to my right swung open, the energy within beckoning me over the threshold.

A thrill danced down my spine as I stood, transfixed, beside the open door. I couldn't make out what awaited me inside, but it was like my body already knew. My pulse quickened. My thighs clenched. My lower belly warmed with liquid desire.

I'd only ever heard of Lilith's special rooms, but what I knew made this even more thrilling. Her magic gave the occupant of this small nondescript box carte blanche and transformed it into their ultimate fantasy or their heart's greatest desire.

As I finally stepped into the room, I learned what that was for me. Freedom.

Everywhere I looked, glittering white sand and turquoise water met the eye. A bit in the distance, I could make out a short pier with a hut on the end. Paradise.

The sun was low in the sky, but the air was still warm as it washed over my mostly naked skin. A quick glance down showed that I was now in a black string bikini with a sarong knotted around my waist. Closing my eyes, I lifted my face toward the sky and let the peaceful environment sink in.

"Can I just stay here forever?" I whispered as I returned my gaze to the crystal-blue water and began a slow stroll down the beach.

Curious about the door, I peeked over my shoulder, finding only more white sandy beach stretching indefinitely behind me. I wasn't worried about the disappearing door or that I was, for all intents and purposes, stranded in some deserted tropical paradise. Nothing here would harm me. This was a gift from Lilith's magic room. All I would find here was happiness.

The warm grains of sand tickled my feet as I walked along the beach, letting water lap at my toes now and then on my way to the pier. I wanted to see what was in the structure. What I'd assumed to be a hut seemed much larger now, and it reminded me of pictures of a resort I'd seen in Bora Bora. Rooms over the water, private, beautiful, and romantic.

That had to be for me. This was my ultimate heart's desire, after all.

Letting out a little squeal of pleasure, I began running toward the dock. I had a soaking tub with my name on it waiting. The sound of splashing water brought me up short when I was within touching distance of the wood.

My breath caught as a figure of pure perfection walked out of the waves. Whether he was my fantasy man brought to life, dreams made flesh, or just my subconscious pulling from years of reading romance novels, I didn't care. He was giving merman meets Baywatch as he ran his hand through his wet hair, drops of water glinting in the fading sun as they dragged down his gloriously sculpted body.

My mouth ran dry as my gaze followed one of those droplets through the chiseled line between his abs and further until it met the trail of golden hair that led to his dangerously low-slung swim . . . What were those? Not trunks. Not a Speedo. We'll call them shorts. Skintight swim shorts.

I was incapable of speech—and grateful for it, certain I'd have embarrassed myself—when a whimper left me.

Gray-blue eyes snapped open and locked on me. Instead of surprise, or annoyance, an intrigued smile curled those full, fuckable lips.

"Hand me that towel, would you, love?" he murmured, gesturing with a nod of his head to the white towel on the sand at my feet.

I scooped it up and took a few steps closer as he exited the water fully, all six-foot-two of him. His fingers brushed mine as he took the scrap of fabric from me, and I couldn't help but stare into his eyes, the sun setting behind him casting his form in a golden glow. Mesmerizing. Beautiful. Captivating. Angelic. Any of the above fit him to a T.

"Cat got your tongue?" he teased when I still hadn't said anything.

"H-hi," I stuttered, having been rendered absolutely stupid by his presence.

"Ah, so she's a shy beauty. Noted. I'll have my work cut out for me if I'm going to get you to come out of your shell."

"I hear treats work."

I could have kicked myself for my blurted words. But any embarrassment was soon forgotten as he took me under his spell once more.

"And what is your favorite treat, pet?"

The way he smirked at me sent a very different kind of hunger through me.

"Right now, you."

I couldn't believe that escaped my mouth, but then I remembered this guy wasn't real. He was my fantasy. It didn't matter what I said or did, he was going to eat it up.

And then, hopefully, he'd eat *me* up.

His eyes narrowed, his smile quizzical as he studied me. "You're thinking something naughty."

"Am not."

"Are too. And I should warn you, it's rude not to share your secrets with your friends."

"Well, you're certainly feeling sure of yourself. Stranger to friend in mere seconds."

He winked, and my insides went molten. "I'm not a stranger. Not anymore."

I fucking tittered when he took my hand in his and brought his lips to my knuckles. "I don't even know your name."

"Luc." He said it with a slight French affectation, but his accent was British.

Interesting shit my brain came up with.

"Nice to meet you, Luc. I'm Merri."

"Like the virgin, how appropriate."

I blushed to the tips of my toes. He couldn't have been more wrong.

"I'm not that innocent, I'm afraid."

"By all accounts, neither was she," he said with a chuckle.

He threaded our fingers and tugged me gently down the beach, the two of us strolling in the perpetually setting sunlight. Fantasies were fun. I'd spend all my time here if I could.

"What has your brow furrowing like that, my sweet, not so innocent Merri?"

I sighed. "I was just thinking I'd like nothing more than to never leave this beach."

"You don't like the rest of your life?"

"Not currently. This is beautiful, warm, peaceful. When I leave, I have to go back to dreary, cold, oppressive, and then there's... them."

It felt good to unburden myself to another person. Even if he was a fictional dream man.

"Them?" He cocked a brow as he pounced on the word.

I snorted. "My prison guards."

He stopped walking and turned me to face him. "Do you need me to arrange a prison break? Exactly how many of them are there? You know, so I can plan."

A wan smile spread across my lips and I opened my mouth to tell him how much I wished he was real so it would be possible for him to rescue me. Instead, he and the paradise beach vanished, leaving me sitting up in the darkness of my room at the penthouse prison.

"Sonofabitch," I hissed under my breath, smacking the little lamp beside my bed to turn it on. "Cockblocked by my own brain."

My eyes fell to the cover of the book I'd been working through, now illuminated by a pool of golden light. I picked it up, chuckling at the image featuring a hot blond surfer on a very familiar beach.

"Well, I guess that answers that question."

Flopping back onto my pillows, I sighed and tried to go back to sleep, hoping to conjure up a vision of Luc once more. As much as I'd loved lusting over his body, it was actually the conversation I wanted more of. I'd gotten used to being alone, my interactions with others mostly conducted through a computer screen. At least they had been until Blackwood. I hadn't even realized how much I missed that daily dose of socialization until I'd gotten stuck here and it was withheld from me once more.

I craved it, even if my safety required this level of isolation. Lilith would never have arranged this for me if it wasn't necessary, but that didn't mean I wasn't suffering from debilitating loneliness. I'd seen the possibility of a full life with friends and love and everything in between. Then it was snatched away from me.

I wriggled on my pillow, attempting to get comfortable as I let out another sigh. Looked like my dream lover and I had a lot of time to kill. Especially if the grumps holding me hostage got their way and kept me indefinitely.

What they didn't know wouldn't hurt them.

Right?

OPERATION PFFN SUPER SECRET VIDEO CORRESPONDENCE: #2

Static screen blinks to life. Asher Henry appears in camera shot, looking worse for wear. Adjusts camera to get a better angle. Asher sits and leans closer to the camera.

<<static>>
<<clothes rustling>>
<<chair creak>>

Asher: Uh, hey out there. Wherever this message finds you, I hope you are safe and doing well. *sighs* I wish I was coming to you with good news today, but I'm not. As you might have guessed, the world is *still* ending. So you know . . . not ideal. And if you've been living under a rock or off visiting some other realm and my first message hasn't reached you yet, welcome to the apocalypse. We've got fun and games. Actually, no, we don't.

Asher scrubs a hand over his face.

Asher: *groans* I've officially spent too much time with Remi and Kingston. *heavy exhale* Sorry about that.

Asher sits back in his chair and takes a deep breath.

Asher: Okay, listen, I'm not going to beat around the bush. Shit is going down. We're not just under a looming threat of the end times. We're living the events now. As of this morning, Victoria Falls, one of the seven natural wonders of the world, mysteriously went dry. I'm talking bone dry. Nothing but cracked earth and dusty silt to remember her by. I'm sure you'll see reports on the news if you haven't already. There's no explanation. At least, not one any scientist will be able to provide.

<<Drums fingers on the desk>>

Asher: I wish I knew more about what this means, if there are going to be more events like this one, and how much time we have before, you know, everything goes tits up for good. But I don't. I am one hundred percent confident this is a direct result of the apocalypse. That's why I've called you all in. Some of you have already arrived, but there are a lot more to our ragtag Scooby gang, and we need all hands on deck.

<<door opening and closing>>

Remi: Excuuuuse me, ASH-hole. I told you to tell me the next time you were doing one of these. Every news anchor worth his salt has a sexy co-host. That's me. I'm the sexy co-host.

Asher: *sighs* Did you ever stop and consider that I don't want a co-host?

Remi: Too bad. I don't make the rules. Scoot over.

<<footsteps coming closer>>

Remi comes into frame, hoisting a chair. Asher begrudgingly moves to make room.

<<chair scrapes the floor>>
<<clothes rustling>>

Remi: *clears throat*

Asher: *sighs* Are you ready?

Remi: Not just yet. You didn't tell me this was happening and I need to warm up. Lubricate the vocal cords.

<<clothes rustling>>

Asher: *sighs louder*

Asher gives the screen a pointed look and mouths I'm sorry.

Remi: Betty botter bought some butter. Betty botter bought some butter. A proper copper coffee p—

Asher: You have *got* to be kidding me.

Remi: Shh. You're messing with my flow. *deep breath* Six slippery snails slid silently. Six slippery sn—

<<door opens>>
<<footsteps coming closer>>

Caleb Gallagher enters the room, and Remi's mouth drops open in awe.

Remi: Oh God, it's the hot priest.

Caleb cuts him a disapproving glare and then turns his attention to Asher.

Caleb: I take it you've heard.

Asher gestures to the screen.

Asher: I was just updating folks about the latest developments. The media will try and brush off the falls running dry as a fluke, but we know it's not.

Remi: Poor Victoria. I bet she never thought there'd be a time she was dry.

Remi mugs for the camera before winking.

Caleb: *groans* I see you haven't changed a bit.

Remi: You're welcome.

Asher: Not a compliment, babe.

Remi: Of course it was.

Caleb slams an old black book onto the table.

<<book crashing onto tabletop>>

Remi: Do you always have thick books in your pocket, or are you just happy to see me?

Caleb: I'm afraid we've got bigger problems. The falls running dry is just a side effect.

Asher: Side effect of what?

Caleb: The first prince has been released.

Remi sits up straighter, eyes wide.

Remi: There's a prince? What prince? No one said there would be a prince.

Caleb: Not that kind of prince. One of the seven Princes of hell.

Remi takes the book from Caleb and riffles through the pages.

<<pages turning>>

Remi: What bible are you reading? I don't remember learning anything about princes during Sunday school. I definitely would have remembered princes.

Caleb: *sighs heavily* It's not a bible.

Remi holds the book sideways and tilts his head with a confused scowl.

Remi: What language is this written in?

Caleb: It's an ancient demonic text. I've only been able to decipher a little of it. This dialect hasn't been used for millennia.

Asher: Well, don't keep us in suspense. What does it say?

Caleb: As I said, I haven't managed to decipher much. Only that there are seven Princes, and each is required for the apocalypse to take hold.

Caleb reclaims the book from Remi and sets it down before rubbing his temples.

Caleb: I fear the secrets hidden within these pages may never be discovered in time. The first prince is only the beginning.

Remi: How do you know he's been released? Did he send out a press release? I haven't seen anything.

Caleb: Because I felt it.

Remi cocks a brow.

Remi: Like . . . in your bones?

Caleb: No, Remington. Here.

Caleb opens his shirt and shows a seven-ringed scar on his chest. Remi's arm shoots out and clutches Asher's sleeve. Asher rolls his eyes and shoves Remi's hand off him.

<<clothes rustling>>

Remi: *gasps* I wasn't prepared for a show.

Caleb: Each one of these rings was linked to the seven seals War opened during her attempt.

Asher: So what do they have to do with what's going on now?

Caleb: I'm not sure, but I felt the same searing pain last night. So I can only assume the magic that created them is linked to the arrival of the Princes.

Remi and Asher exchange a look.

Remi: *speaking under his breath* He's our own personal sexy supernatural disaster warning system.

Asher: How long do we have until the next one?

Caleb: I don't know. I haven't been able to identify anything resembling a timeline.

Asher: Why don't you ask my brother? You know, the ex-demon?

Remi jumps up and runs out of frame.

<<footsteps rushing away>>

Remi: Hey! Purple people eater! Get your ass down here!

<<footsteps coming closer>>
<<rustle of clothes>>

Pan steps into the room, annoyance on his face.

Pan: I am no longer purple, and I have never feasted on human flesh. That moniker is misleading and frankly, you can do better, dog.

Pan looks around at the others.

Pan: What is this? Your monthly book club?

Remi: Pfft. More like secret society.

Remi thrusts his fist in the air.

Remi: Go go Team Puffin!

Caleb: Jesus.

Asher: *sighs* It's *Operation* Puffin.

Pan: How does any of this involve me?

Remi slides the book toward Pan.

<<book sliding across the table>>

Remi: You're a former bad guy. Maybe you can read this? It's demonish.

Pan: Demonish?

Remi: You know, your native tongue.

Pan: My native tongue is French, you wankstain.

Remi: But . . . you're British.

Pan ignores Remi as he takes the book.

Caleb: I've translated what I could, but most of this language is too foreign for me. It's not rooted in anything I know.

Pan: And it will come to pass the end of days shall commence. Seven seals broken, seven Princes released, seven wonders destroyed. Lucifer shall possess the chalice, and with it, inherit the crown. And the world will forever kneel before his glory.

<<stunned silence>>

Asher: Well, fuck.

Remi: What does it mean?

Pan: I thought it quite obvious. The hourglass has been tipped.

Remi: Well, duh. We already knew that. You're a video behind, buddy.

Pan: *snarls* You're lucky I no longer have my tail. I'd gag you with it.

Remi: Kinky.

Caleb: How long do we have? Until the arrival of the next prince?

Pan flips through the book, brow furrowed as his eyes quickly scan the pages. He snaps the book shut.

<<pages turning>>
<<book slamming shut>>

Caleb: Well?

Pan: It doesn't say. But they are coming, and Lucifer grows stronger with every one who joins his ranks.

Asher: Great. So we know as much now as we did before. We're up shit creek.

Remi: This really changes the meaning of that song "Some Day My Prince Will Come."

Caleb: Do you know what this says?

Caleb points to the markings on the cover.

Pan: *hums musingly* It says: The Book of . . . somebody. I'm not familiar with that sigil.

Remi: So it could be like The Book of Ted?

Everyone shoots him a glare.

Asher: Not the time, Rem.

Remi: What? If we're all about to die, it's absolutely the time. This could be one of my last chances to share an epic joke. Humor is the spice of life. It's my defense mechanism.

Caleb: We're not going to die.

Pan: Mmm . . . I wouldn't be so sure of that if I were you. My brethren are notoriously crafty, and the dominos certainly seem to be falling quickly.

Caleb: Abandon your mate if you want, demon—

Pan: Ex-demon.

Asher: Ex-demon.

Brothers share a look when they speak in tandem.

Caleb: —but I, for one, am not going quietly into the night when I have a pregnant wife to care for and children to protect. No one, not the Princes of hell or Lucifer himself, will harm a hair on my family's heads. I'll die first.

Remi: So will I. No one hurts Rosie or our pups.

Asher blinks, his head snapping back to the camera.

Asher: Shit, I forgot we were filming. But, uh, guess it was good for you to hear all that. *clears throat* So, it looks like we're fighting. Again. And we could really use your help. I'll include the coordinates in a separate encrypted message. See you soon. I hope.

Remi: Ca-caw!

Asher: What the fuck was that?

Remi: The puffin battle cry. Obviously.

Pan: I can't believe you haven't suffocated him in his sleep yet. I volunteer my services if assistance is required.

Caleb: Fecking children. All of you.

The bickering continues as Asher reaches out for the camera. The screen goes dark.

<<static>>

End of transmission.

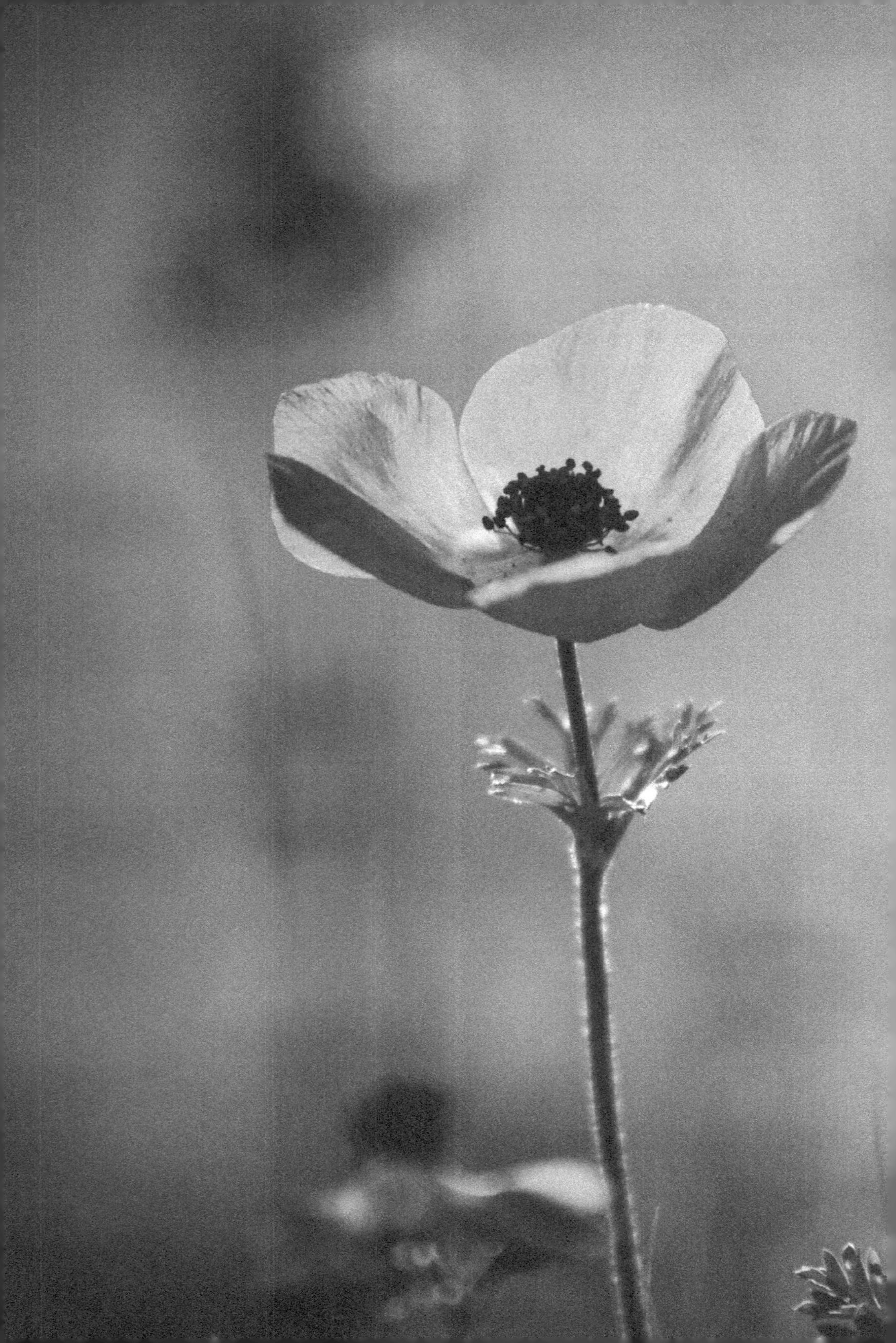

CHAPTER
THIRTEEN
MERRI

I ended my live stream and plopped back into my chair with a satisfied sigh. That was the most fulfilling "Get Ready With Me" session I'd had in a long time without adding on a private breakout with a client. As I wrapped a soft robe around my shoulders, I let myself scroll through the comments I'd missed. It was important to interact with every one of them, even if they didn't see it until after the show was over. Andi taught me this trick when I first started. She'd been such a great help, like a big sister, really.

A pang hit me when I realized how long it'd been since we'd talked properly. She was off on some all-inclusive vacay with one of her clients. I was looking forward to hearing about all the trouble she'd gotten into as soon as she got home.

"Let's see how you all felt about the pedicure."

I grinned as the comments filled my screen, most of them from the usual suspects, but there were more than a few newbies this time too. Like . . . way more.

> EverySteve: I'd suck the shit out of those.

> Shyguy25: Please let me paint your nails for you next time, beautiful girl.
>
> Magic_Fingie_Dingies: Can you do your fingers next time too? 😂
>
> PimpinAintCheezy: Daaaaayum girl. Sit on my face.
>
> LongWalksOnTheB: Spread those toes, and your thighs. 😉
>
> OriginalSin: You should let me pick out the color, darlin 😈

I smirked at the comment Emmett left. I hadn't realized he'd been in the chat this time. My reaction to him was close to the same as how I felt every time I saw Cole's handle pop up. Comforted, aroused, seen. Honestly, I was a little put out that neither of them tried to book any solo time. But I'd made it clear I wasn't open for those kinds of sessions tonight, so I supposed they were upholding and honoring my boundaries, unlike a couple of the others.

> ThisLilPiggy: 🐽🐽🐽
>
> Trash4Toes: I've never seen more perfect feet. 🥒🐽🔥
>
> GaryRunsFast: I know what you could do with those little babies.
>
> Mayor_Poundtown: We can start with the feet, but I want to eat your 😼
>
> DILF79: Looking for a daddy? How do you feel about an age gap?
>
> BigRichard: 💸 Make $200,000 without leaving home. Click here to find out more!!! 💸

I rolled my eyes at the spammer. Usually the mods were pretty good about keeping those jackholes out of here. I appreciated the hustle, but they really fucked with the vibe. Especially since I didn't care how much cash my members brought in. I needed lust-filled engagement, not bots who got past my paywall.

With a swift click, I blocked his ass, then continued reading and loving each of their horny as fuck comments. Seriously, the high I got reading through these thirsty posts was better than any joint.

> Bob1212: I vote we do the lipstick-smearing contest next time.
>
> CreamPieLover: Take off your panties and let us look while you work on those nails. 👀 🙈 🐱
>
> Tls4Tony: I know what I'll be dreaming about tonight. 👅🐷🐮
>
> PeeperBPeepin: Boo! 👻
>
> MakeItClap22: I'd paint them white, then lick them clean.
>
> BigMan69: You've got me over here like the Kool-Aid man. Oooh yeaaaah.

That one made me snicker. I could picture the Kool-Aid man in all his glory bursting through my wall. I did *not* want to fuck him, though. BigMan69 would be so disappointed.

> Tittiesinmyfayce: 👅 🙈 👻
>
> CumGutters11: Anyone else dehydrated? Fuck me.
>
> URDreamLover: Tell me what your pussy smells like.
>
> JohnBoy27: 🍆💦 I just made a mess of myself.
>
> ThisIsSparta: What the fuck did I join?

The snort that escaped me was loud and undignified, which set off a full belly laugh. Oh, that last one. I had to catch my breath before I could like his comment. Sorry, Greek boy, you stumbled in on the wrong night. I couldn't help but wonder if he'd come back. If he did, I made a mental note to make it up to him.

Caught up on the comments, I also noted the explosion of new members. They were all from tonight, i.e., people who joined the stream but didn't necessarily comment. Close to a hundred new names were listed, all at the minimum membership pledge and all with generic handles that made me think these might be bots, but one stood out in sharp relief, both because of the name and the dollar amount pledged.

1N3V1T@BL3 has joined the Prince Charming tier

My mouth fell open. Wow. He must have *really* enjoyed the show. That was my highest tier and only had one other member: Mr. Shy Guy himself. It was $500 a month and included one private session plus a personalized video message for each month they were an active subscriber. I'd limited it to only five spots to ensure it didn't get too unwieldy fulfilling their rewards.

I shot him a quick direct message.

Dear 1N3V1T@BL3,

Thank you so much for your support. I see you identify as male on your profile. Does that mean I can call you Daddy?
Keep an eye out for more from me soon.

Kisses,
Merri

All in all, a good night's work.

So why was I still feeling a little restless? I'd fed better than I had since arriving at this pretty little prison of mine. I should be sated.

Calm. Content. Instead I was like a tiger in a cage, pacing in my own mind.

Okay, so maybe it wasn't that much of a mystery. A pretty prison was still a prison.

I'd occupied one form of cage or another since Lilith took me in, but this was the first time I really felt the walls. I needed something to ground me.

Drumming my fingers on the desk, I let my mind stumble toward a solution. Sometimes, you really just had to get out of your own way. Lilith had taught me that long ago. *Let your gut guide you, darling.*

Lilith's voice glided through my mind as clearly as if she were sitting on the bed beside me. How many times had she said that exact thing to me?

The memory had a small smile curling my lips. Auntie Lilith always had the best advice. Maybe that's what I needed. A little dose of her magic. I could call her. Tell her everything and ask for her help.

My shoulders slumped almost as soon as the idea percolated, however, because *Malice* confiscated my phone. He'd been so smug when I asked for it. Motherfucker.

Just as I was about to accept defeat and fling myself back onto the bed in a full sulk, I realized that an actual phone was no longer the only means of making a call. Tapping my computer back on, I navigated my way to Lilith's contact information and hit the video call button.

There. Problem solved.

Take that Grumpy Brit Number Two.

The call connected after two rings, and Lilith's perfectly made-up face came into view. Her hair was done in a pinup style with a red silk scarf tied in a neat little bow at the crown of her head. She looked ready to pose for a rockabilly photo shoot. Shoulders bare, black corset, cleavage cleaving, lips painted crimson to match the scarf. Damn, she was good.

"Merri, darling. What a surprise. I thought the boys would've had you under lock and key."

"They do. That's why I'm calling."

One of her perfectly sculpted brows arched. "Oh? Do tell. You know I love a piping hot tea break during a session."

As if it had been timed, Crombie's voice rang out from somewhere off-screen. "Oh bloody hell, Lilypad. Not again."

Lilith's lips twisted into a faint smirk. "Quiet, Drystan. Or I'll make it last even longer."

Her submissive—though, in truth, there wasn't much submissive about the fae prince—let out a low grumble before she turned her attention back to me.

"What's got you looking so down, sweet girl? Are your guards mistreating you?"

"Mistreating?" I repeated, mulling over the word. "No. Not exactly. Ignoring, more like."

"Ignoring you? I find that hard to believe."

"You wouldn't if you could see how they act around me. Seriously, they barely speak to me. One has exchanged all of five words with me. Two of them would rather watch paint dry than even look at me. And then there's Sin, who just wants to fuck me."

She grinned. "Of course he does, my love. You're exactly what he needs."

Examining her manicure as though this wasn't my entire life we were discussing, she hummed.

"Auntie Lilith, please. I need to get out of here. I can't live like this. I have no one to talk to. No one to keep me company."

At this, my aunt frowned. "I'm sorry, darling girl, but you must start considering your new lodgings as your home for the foreseeable future."

"What?" I all but screeched. "Auntie Lilith, no. I can't stay here indefinitely. Surely you'll handle whatever threat is out there like you always do, and then I can come home."

"You are home, darling. Best make peace with it. This isn't the sort of threat one can *handle* easily. It could be . . . a while before it's safe for you again."

Once again, Crombie's derisive snort met her words, but my aunt silenced whatever he might have said with a warning glare.

Panic and frustration warred inside me. Stuck here with four men who hated me, feeding off of nothing but my clients. That wasn't sustainable. Not if my appetite had anything to say about it. And the truth was, I didn't do well in pure isolation. I never had. I was like a flower denied sunlight, and I'd wilt until there was nothing left. Being around others, even if I didn't engage with them, filled me with energy.

Iniquity had offered that in spades. And even Blackwood, to a degree, had provided me with the buzz of overwhelming emotions to siphon as needed. By comparison, being locked in Grim's penthouse was a bit like being on an unwilling hunger strike. These four had all the emotions of a fucking rock garden.

"She has four cocks at the ready. Explain to me why she's whinging." Crombie came into the frame, fully nude, save the cage Lilith had put around his package.

"Ugh," I cringed, shielding my eyes. It wasn't the nudity, mind you. But Crombie was practically my uncle. No one wanted to see a family member under these conditions.

"Go back to your corner, pet. I'll see to you soon enough." Lilith's voice was a steely purr that told me he was in a lot of trouble. Then she returned her attention to me. "He's right, though. You must win them over. Make them your allies."

"Were you not listening to the part where three of the four refuse to engage with me?"

She waved a hand as if that was no big deal. "Use the charm you were born with and gain the devotion of each and every one of them. That will make your life much easier."

"Lilith—"

But she cut off my protest with a tight smile. "You know what you need to do, darling. So do it." Then she clapped her hands and blew me a kiss. "Right, well. It was lovely to see you, but I must go. Brats to punish." She winked. "Ciao, sweet girl. I can't wait to hear how you bring these men to their knees."

As the screen went dark, I let her words tumble in my head, knowing she wouldn't have given that advice if it wasn't exactly the right thing to do. Auntie Lilith was the wisest creature I knew. She was also ancient. The original demon. If anyone knew how to get shit done, it was absolutely her. I simply had to use some of the tactics she always kept in her pocket.

Charm.

Manipulate.

Outsmart.

She was a master of her craft. If she could build an entire empire because of it, surely I could handle a few grumpy immortals. But how?

"Hmm," I mused, tapping my index finger to my chin. "What would Lilith do?"

Releasing a determined breath, I stood and popped my hands on my hips. I wasn't going to get anywhere allowing these men to continue thinking they were the ones in charge. I might have to live in their house, but they were going to start playing by my rules.

Out of sight, out of mind seemed to be the name of their game. So I'd simply have to flip the script. I was about to be all up in their business every moment possible.

I adjusted my tits so they were at their most perky and tempting, then opened my door with one particular silver fox in mind. Or should I say crosshairs.

Operation Make The Horsemen My Bitches was about to begin.

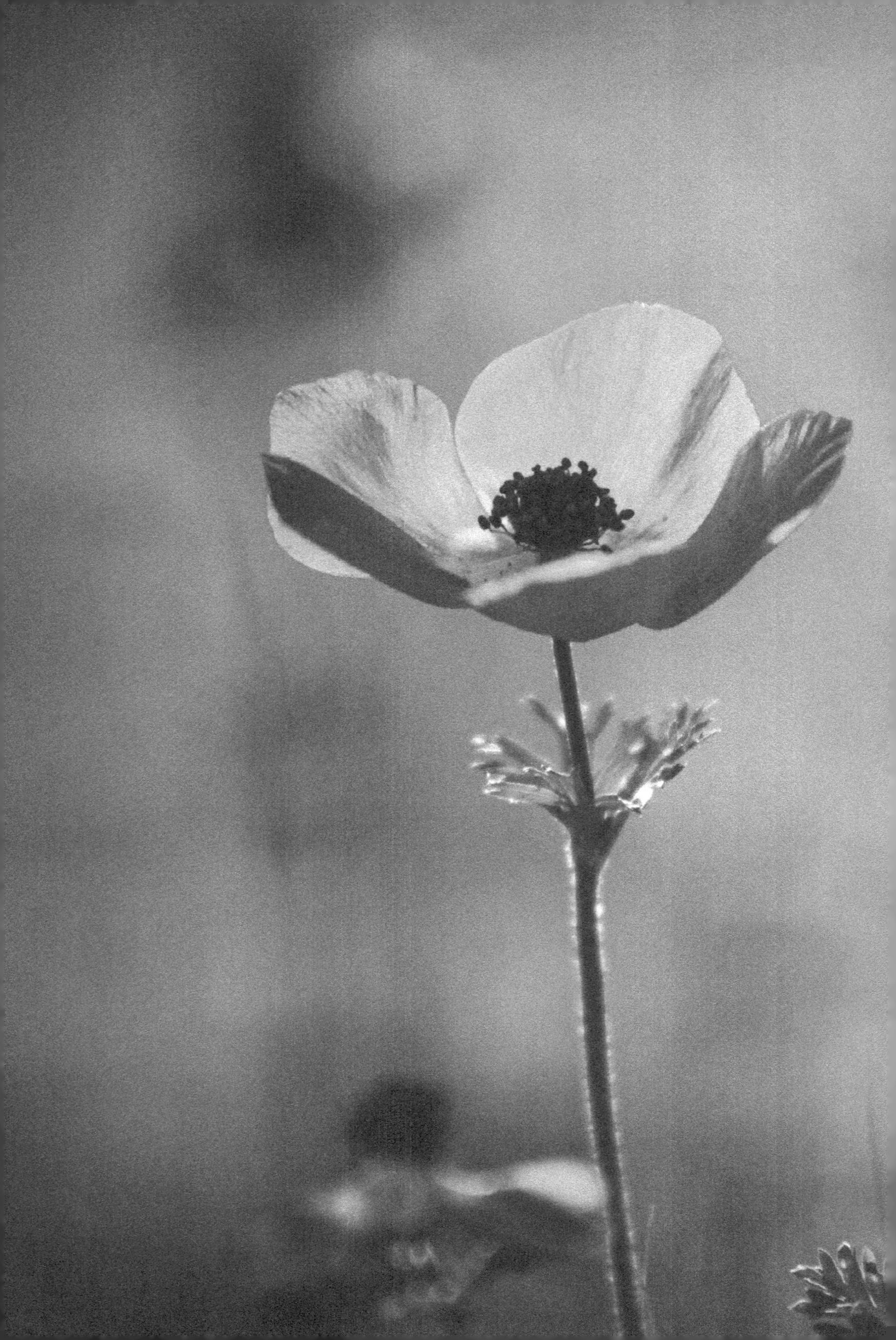

CHAPTER
FOURTEEN
GRIM

"There we are, my beauties. A bit of water, and you'll be right as rain," I murmured as I misted liquid sunshine onto the last of my sadly neglected plants. "Hel and her nefarious plans nearly killed you all."

Anger burned through my veins at yet another reminder of what that bitch had stolen from me. My rooftop garden, and more specifically the blooms in this greenhouse, were one of the few things I'd ever truly cared about. Here, I didn't have to be a threat to living things. Quite the opposite. So long as I kept my gloves on, I could experience what it was to help something thrive. Watching these plants grow from seedlings, their stalks unfurling with each passing day, bright blooms opening under my care, gave me the one thing I never had in any other facet of my existence.

Hope.

Satisfied with my night's work, I'd just set my mister back in its rack when I heard the whisper of the balcony door sliding open.

If Malice thought he was going to come in here and send disease through my plants like he had the last time he was in my penthouse, he was about to learn a very painful lesson. I'd toss him over the side of the building with nary a single thread of remorse. Sure enough, the greenhouse door opened, letting in a burst of winter air. Readying myself for conflict, I tensed, but every ounce of defensive energy vanished at the very soft, very *feminine* gasp that filled the air.

Merri.

She couldn't be here.

This floor, these flowers, were my sanctuary. I didn't want her to sully any of it with her presence.

Filthy liar.

I ignored the voice crooning in my ear, choosing instead to wrap myself in shadow and spy on my own would-be voyeur. What's good for the goose...

"Oh my God, Daddy has a green thumb. Who would've thought?" she murmured, moving deeper into the small space.

Her fingers trailed across leaves I'd just taken care to wipe down, and I hated the rush of jealousy I felt as the plants were gifted her touch.

She was a vision in moonlight, the silvery glow lending her an ethereal quality that was as sensual as it was innocent. But I was coming to learn that dichotomy was inherently Merri. She was both temptress and ingenue. A walking contradiction that left me aching for reasons I couldn't begin to explain. I'd felt the stirrings of lust few times in my long years, but nothing compared with my reaction to this little succubus.

Or, as I'd started silently referring to her, this little wildflower.

She was beauty amidst chaos. Untamed. Stubborn. Resilient.

My hands balled into fists at my sides as I immediately scolded myself for thinking of her in such a way.

She was a job. Nothing more.

My ward.

My responsibility.

Quite literally untouchable and forbidden. At least to me. For my brothers, she was a bloom made for plucking, but all she would know at my hand was rot.

The closer she got, the darker I made my shadows.

Before I could stop her, Merri reached for my rare orchid, the prize of my collection. She couldn't touch it. They were notoriously finicky and temperamental.

"Don't touch it!" I blurted, jumping out of the shadows and startling Merri so badly that she fell into the orchid and sent it toppling over. "No! Bloody hell, look what you've done."

I knelt down and carefully extracted the plant from the shards of broken pottery, heaving a sigh of relief when I realized none of the stem had broken. "This is one of the most rare varieties of orchid on the planet. It blooms one night per year if we're lucky. You could've killed it."

"I-I'm sorry," she stammered, eyes wide, one hand covering her lips.

I glared at her. "You should be. What are you even doing out here? I recall expressly forbidding you from wandering about my floor."

She was coming back to herself the longer I spoke, her fear and remorse swiftly replaced by annoyance. "Expressly forbidding? Okay, Mr. Rochester," she said with a roll of her eyes. "Anyone ever tell you you're a bit of a drama queen?"

I gritted my teeth. "If they have, they certainly didn't live to tell the tale."

Without allowing myself so much as a glance at her beauty, I snagged an empty pot and rehomed the orchid as delicately as possible.

A gentle pressure alighted on my forearm, stopping me in my tracks and sending pure panic through my bloodstream. She was touching me. By the grace of the fabric between us, Merri was still breathing, but if there'd been so much as a sliver of my skin showing, she would be nothing more than a corpse.

Yanking my arm from her, I narrowed my eyes, my voice barely more than a snarl, "It would behoove you to stop touching things that *do not* belong to you."

"Behoove? Lordy, I'm going to need to walk around with a notebook so I can keep track of all these antiquated phrases of yours. What's next? Constult?"

I frowned. "Why would I use that word? We are not speaking in pure frivolity."

"Aren't we?"

An irritated huff escaped me as I pushed past her. "Do not touch me or my plants again."

She held her hands up in surrender.

"I solemnly vow to never accidentally molest your plants again, okay? God, you really are taking the grump thing to the next level."

All I could do was grumble. I had no interest in gaining her affection or attentions, not when a single touch would end her life. What was the point in getting close to her if I'd only lose her? She was for Sin and Chaos. Not me.

"Come. Let's get you back to where you belong."

"So you're taking me to *Iniquity*?"

The absolute cheek of this girl. Though she was raised by Lilith, so could I really expect anything else?

"You know that's not an option."

She crossed her arms and made a soft hum in her throat.

"So help me, Merri, if you force my hand right now, you will not enjoy the outcome."

"Your hand, huh? What are you going to do with it? Spank me? Because I should probably warn you, I'm sorta into that."

My teeth ground together as I worked through my frustration. I couldn't get the picture out of my mind. The things I'd seen from her video feed alone were far too tempting.

I grabbed her bicep. Even through my leather glove, the contact sent tingles up my forearm.

"What happened to not touching things that don't belong to you?" she mocked, her steps awkward as I towed her behind me.

"Who said you don't belong to me?"

She scoffed. "Everything about you."

"Then you must not be paying very close attention," I growled, tugging on her arm until she was standing directly in front of me. I leaned down until our noses were less than an inch apart. Risky? Yes. But she was spirited in a way that made me forget myself. "You became mine the second Lilith forced you into my custody." I turned her around and gave her bottom a slap. "Go."

Her shoulders stiffened momentarily before she stepped forward, heading for the elevator. There was no way I could be trapped in a steel box with her for any length of time right now. I'd give in and show her who was in charge, then when the doors opened, have to explain to the boys why I had her corpse in my arms.

"Stairs. Right there," I said, gesturing to the staircase on the right.

Her brows lifted at the demand, but shockingly, she didn't fight me. "You first," she said with a wide sweep of her arm. "I wouldn't want to accidentally stop short and have you run into me or something."

It was a special kind of torture, having her behind me, her gaze pinning my back with every step as we descended into the main floor. The murmur of masculine voices and music that sounded more like cats in heat than the kind of melodies I preferred grew louder with every passing moment.

"Someone is having a party," Merri said as she took up her place at my side in the hall.

"It would seem Sin found his record collection."

She glanced up at my tall frame with an arched brow. "Did you hide it from him?"

"I did."

"That wasn't very nice."

"As a rule, neither am I."

"Was that supposed to be a surprise or something? You're certainly not telling me anything I haven't already figured out,

Grim." Then, lowering her voice as if sharing a secret, she added, "The name sort of gives it away, you know."

"It's Grimsby," I corrected on principle.

The music continued, Jimi Hendrix wailing on guitar as I heard Sin call out, "Fuck yeah, man. That's the reason he's immortal right there. Do you hear that?"

I snorted. Immortal? I'd been there when he died. No human was immortal. I was proof positive.

"Oh, I'm sorry, *Grimsby*. Would you like me to stand on ceremony every time I see you, my lord Grumpypants? I can start practicing my curtsy now."

"You do that," I muttered, trying my best to ignore her as I stalked into the salon. It took every ounce of control I had not to let my face showcase the disgust I'd felt at what Sin had reduced the once pristine and peaceful room to. The bar cart had been moved, my expensive collection of liquor pilfered and absolutely wasted on his rubbish bin of a palate.

"What do you wankers think you're doing?" I shouted, rousing Sin from his blissed-out stupor, where he lay sprawled on the floor amongst piles of vinyl records.

Chaos was sat on the sofa, arms spread across the back, but the moment my booming voice rattled the walls, he flinched. The record stopped playing with an ugly scratching sound a second before glass shattered upstairs.

Sin stumbled to the record player, face stricken. "Come on, man, that's vintage. You fucking scratched it."

I leveled an accusing glare at Chaos. "I thought you had a handle on your flares. That's why you've been leaving us in the first place."

"That wasn't me," Chaos said, expression tense as his focus lifted to the ceiling, as though he could somehow see beyond it. He launched to his feet, muscles tensed and eyes wide as he homed in on whatever it was he sensed. A low snarl built in his chest and he shot his gaze to Merri. "Get behind me."

True to her brat nature, the succubus crossed her arms under her ample chest, then lifted her chin defiantly. "I'm really fucking sick of you guys thinking you can boss me around. You could try asking once in a while. I'm not just some spineless plaything for you to contr—"

Malice skidded into the room, eyes flashing with lavender fire, laptop open in his hands. "There's been a breach."

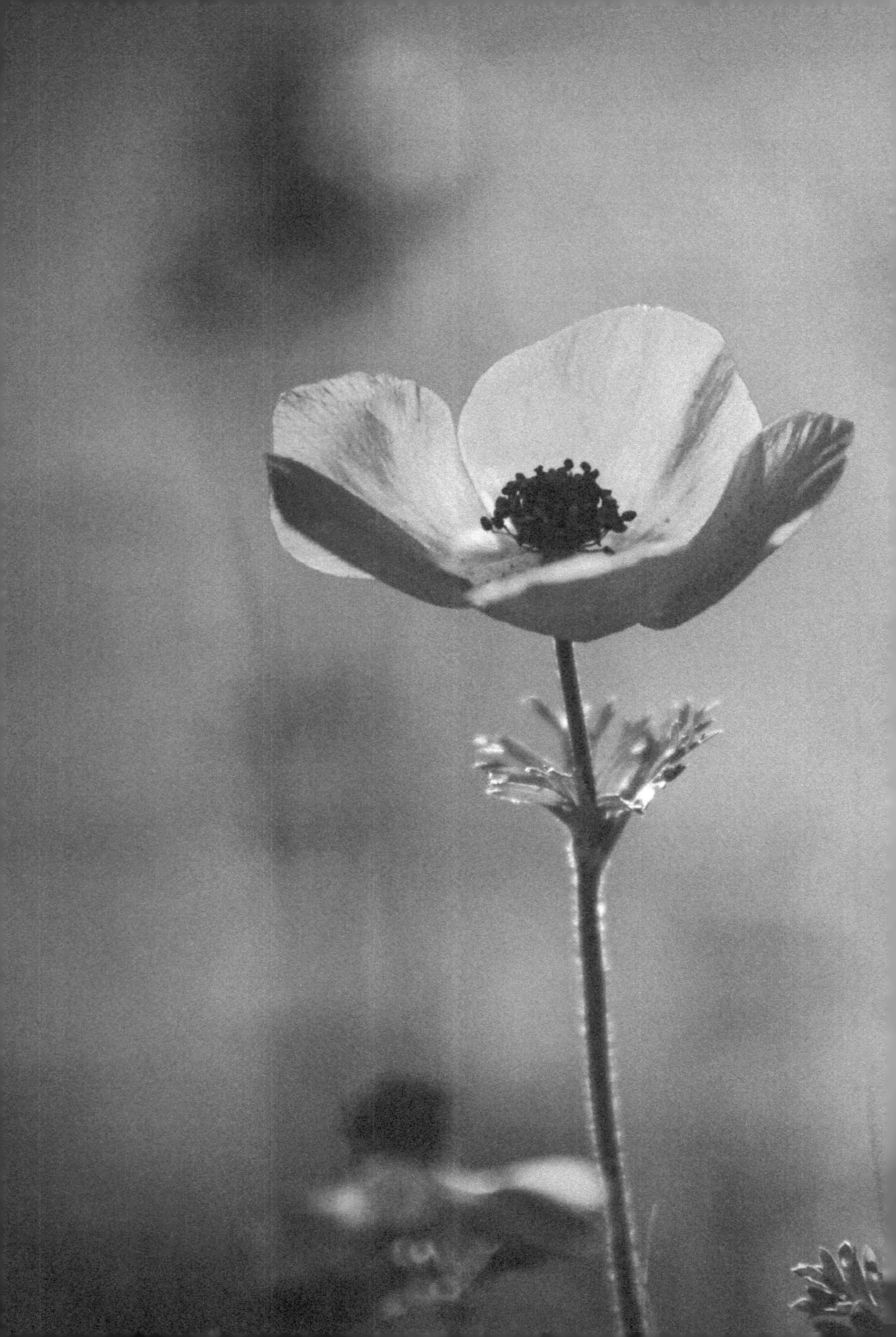

CHAPTER FIFTEEN
CHAOS

Fury boiled close to the surface as Malice's words hit me, the promise of violence singing in my blood. This was what I was made for.

"Where?" I snarled, not allowing Merri another inch for her bratty behavior. I grabbed her by the elbow and forced her behind the shield of my body.

"Upstairs. Third-floor balcony."

Almost as if we'd summoned them, five winged bastards stormed down the staircase Grim and Merri had just used.

"How the fuck did they get in?" Grim's voice was cold as steel, threatening retribution for Malice's security system failing.

I pushed forward, leveling my gaze on Sin. The how didn't matter right now. Only neutralizing the threat. "Stay with her. Do not let her out of your sight." Then I looked to Malice. "You too. Grim, you're with me."

Grim's answering smile was pure death. Appropriate, really, given who he was.

"They won't get past me," he promised.

Not for the first time, I was thankful he was on my team.

Death and War always walked side by side into battle. We'd decimate these intruders and use their ashes as fertilizer for Grim's precious plants.

"Ah, look, they sent *grandpère* to welcome us. *Comme c'est... délicieux.*" The first of what I assumed to be pride demons—based on the black feathered wings and celestial perfection of his face—crooned in a French accent.

My gaze flicked to Grim's. This was worse than we thought. "The Prince."

"Our master didn't mention the horsemen. She must be very special indeed." This came from a second demon, his Russian accent thick and laced with smug assurance. "I see the fear in your eyes, mighty warrior. Our master wants what you have." His comrades' chuckles filled the room as they stood in wait. "Give her to us, and we'll make this a swift and painless end for you."

Grim released a deep growl as he removed his gloves and dropped them on the polished marble floor. Closing the distance between him and the Russian demon, he sneered, "Unfortunately for you, I won't do the same."

My smirk couldn't be contained as Grim wrapped his bare hand around the demon's throat. Watching the light leave their eyes was always my favorite part of witnessing Grim use his power. I could've done with more combat leading up to the main event, but in cases such as these, we didn't have time to pussyfoot around.

The demon clutched his throat, and his eyes flew wide open as he gasped and wheezed dramatically. "Not... the hand... of death." He carried on with his over-the-top spectacle for a few more seconds before breaking off in a dark chuckle. "Do you mind? I've got a date later and don't want to bruise."

Grim looked down at his hands in confusion, letting go with a rasped, "What?"

The first demon grinned. "One must have a soul to be reaped, Grimsby. Or has it been so long since you've come across our kind that you've forgotten the rules?"

Truth be told, we hadn't encountered a Knight before; the apocalypse had never gotten far enough for one to rise. Upon the release of one of the seven Princes of hell, so too would their Knights—soulless beings bound in servitude to their prince. Together, the Princes and Knights formed the Army of the Apocalypse, with Lucifer at the helm. Technically, my brothers and I were supposed to have a place amongst their ranks, but when we chose to stand against Lucifer and protect Merri, we'd dropped that mantle.

If Grim's death touch wouldn't fell these enemies, it was down to me and my weapons. Calling upon my power, I first attempted to manifest the shield of War, but instead of the red-and-black plated armor I donned when striding through battlefields, nothing materialized.

I was still weakened from my time as Hel's battery.

"Fucking Hel and her fucking ritual," I grumbled before switching tactics. I'd been a Spartan before I was a horseman. Fought battles wearing nothing but the blood of my enemies. All I needed was a blade.

This time when I called on my power, twin blades formed in my hands.

The demons weren't laughing anymore when I loosed a battle cry and charged forward. I dispatched Frenchie with a single slice through his neck. His head rolled down the stairs with a satisfying plop.

"Who's next?" I asked, glory surging through my veins as I charged up the next couple of steps to one of the three possibilities, trusting Grim to handle himself with the Russian asshole.

Two females attempted to lunge at me simultaneously, one from each side. They snarled and hissed, claws bared and fangs on display.

I easily dodged them, whirling around and slashing each of them across their faces before crouching down and driving my blades up and through their chins on my ascent.

"Not so pretty now, are you?" I gloated, pulling my blades free and watching their bodies drop.

The last demon tried to run, no longer feeling so confident about a face-off with me.

I let him get to the top of the stairs before throwing my sword like a lance and pinning him through the heart. The tip of the blade sank into the wall behind him, holding him there like a grisly showpiece. Who said art wasn't fun?

Perhaps I should pin them all up and display them like the insects they were.

Grim had the Russian on the floor, blood bubbling up from the demon's lips as his chest was slowly crushed under Death's boot.

"We... will... never... stop," the demon said through choked gasps. "The... whore... belongs... to him."

Rage turned my vision red, and with a fierce bellow, I stalked to where Grim had him held immobile. In one smooth move, my sword sank through his skull and straight into the marble beneath.

Grim swore. "Did you really have to ruin the marble? Now I'm going to have to replace the entire floor."

I rolled my eyes. "Sorry. I'll try to be more careful the next time I'm saving your life."

"Saving my life? The fucker was already dead."

"You better than anyone should appreciate the difference between dead and dying. He was *mostly* dead, at best."

The demon's body turned to ash, revealing my sword, coated in blood and buried at least two inches deep into the stone. I didn't want to think about why my reaction to the asshole's words was so strong, only that I was doing my duty and protecting our charge. It definitely wasn't him calling her a whore that lit such a powerful fire within me.

Grim stood to his full height, raking a hand through his silver hair before turning to me, a retort on the tip of his tongue. But the soft ding of the elevator arriving on our floor stopped us both as we watched the doors open, revealing a lone black feather.

"There was another one," I said, heart pounding as I raced to the staircase and leapt over the railing, landing in a crouch on the bottom floor.

Merri

S**in's arm** was an iron bar across my chest as he pushed me deeper into the room and farther from the conflict we could hear in the hall. For the second time tonight, it felt like the world flipped on its axis. One moment I'm deep in Operation Make The Horsemen My Bitches, and the next we're in the middle of—I shit you not—a break-in.

The brush of Sin's warmth across my tits had me fighting the urge to punch him in the kidney even as the contact sent shivers down my spine. Now was not the time to lust after the sexy incubus. It was a simple biological response to his magic. Nothing more.

"Stay put. We'll handle this," he said softly, his attention locked on the direction Chaos and Grim had disappeared.

I opened my mouth to argue the *don't worry your pretty little head* of it all, but decided against it.

"Good girl. Just like I like you, mouth shut, eyes open," Malice muttered.

Oh, he was in for it. I was going to make his life a living hell once we were done fighting to stay alive.

Chaos's resonant rumble filtered to us, stopping any other conversation. "The Prince."

My brows furrowed in pure confusion. There was a prince? That was new.

"Already?" Sin asked, but Malice stopped him with a harried, "Shh."

A guttural male voice I didn't recognize joined in. "That's right. I see the fear in your eyes, mighty warrior. Our master wants what you have."

Me? Oh fuck. It was me, wasn't it?

Goddammit. I just wanted to live in my little bubble and cam in peace.

But I guess Lilith knew what she was talking about when she sent me here. She'd seen this coming. Which also meant all the alpha male posturing these guys had been doing wasn't just an act. I really was in danger.

Shit.

Apprehension raced through my veins like lightning, making me tingle in a very uncomfortable way. I took a few steps back, and then a couple more for good measure, until I was practically pressed into the far corner of the room.

"Why are they talking this out? What the fuck is Grim doing? He should have killed them all by now," Sin asked Malice, his stance still tensed and ready to defend his territory.

"I don't think he can."

A look of confusion flickered across Sin's face before he seemed to cotton on to whatever Malice was hinting at.

"You think they're Knights?" Sin asked, voice laced with disbelief.

"Where a Prince goes, they follow."

"Fuck," Sin hissed. "How do they know we have her?"

Malice shook his head.

Before they could continue, a wall-rattling bellow came from the hall, followed by the unmistakable sounds of fighting.

Call me a damsel, but I pressed my back against the wall and prayed for this to be over. I had nothing I could use to defend myself except a lamp and maybe a book from the shelf nearby. I supposed I could try and lust everyone into submission, but now seemed like a terrible time to attempt weaponizing my succubus power. I needed focus and control for that, and in my first true life-and-death situation, I had neither of those things.

A hysterical laugh escaped, and I slapped a hand over my mouth, not wanting to draw any attention to my little corner of the room. I needn't have worried. The boys were too busy with their whispered confab about mysterious Knights and Princes, and the other two were balls deep in battle.

A tickle of wind across my neck had me turning my attention toward the bookcase to my right just as the soft, sweet voice whispered my name.

"Merri. Come. I'll keep you safe."

I spun around, a scream poised on my lips, but the second my eyes met the deep brown ones of the woman hidden within a secret doorway, every ounce of apprehension leached away as a sense of warmth and security wove itself around me.

She was beautiful. No, angelic.

"Come, my dear. Come with me."

Her gaze held me in a vortex of such peace and promised nothing else existed. There wasn't even a choice. I went. All I wanted was to be wrapped up in the comfort of her.

I followed her down a spiral staircase that spilled us out of another hidden door and into the butler's pantry downstairs. The passageway must've been used by staff once upon a time.

The angel smiled at me, her eyes shining with pride. "Such a beautiful girl, you are. Let me take care of you. I'm sure this has been a trying time."

She stepped close, taking my hands before putting my wrists together in front of me. I glanced down at the feel of corded rope sliding along my skin.

"Ah, ah, ah, keep your eyes on mine, sweetheart. That's it. I've got you."

Yes, she had me. She'd take me away from all of this. I'd be happier with her. Safe.

"Merri!" Chaos's roar snapped me out of the creature's spell, making me take one quick step back before he tackled her to the floor.

Before I could do more than draw in a shuddering breath, he'd grabbed the woman by the face and snapped her neck.

I had to blink a couple of times, my brain failing to fully process what was happening.

Chaos hadn't just snapped her neck. He'd torn her head clean off.

He was still holding it while her body was slack and spurting oil-like ichor.

Then, chest heaving, he turned his gaze on me. Fury blazed in his eyes as he stood, dropped the head, and stalked to me.

"What in God's name possessed you to go with her, you stupid little fool? Do you have no sense of self-preservation? Are you auditioning for the role of helpless idiot?" He wasn't simply chastising me; he was yelling at me like he was a drill sergeant and I was in boot camp.

"I . . ." I began, but honestly had no response that would suffice. I understood why he'd think so, how my wandering off with her had looked. He didn't know about the thrall. That I hadn't been in control of my mind or my body.

"It's our job to protect you, and yet you run off with the first demon you see? Do you think this is a game? That everything we've told you has just been an elaborate ruse? What the fuck is wrong with you? I should . . ." He raked a hand through his hair and let out a frustrated growl. "Fuck, Merri, I don't know what to do with you."

I hated myself for the whimper that escaped along with a single tear.

He continued walking forward, sending me back a few steps until my shoulders hit the pantry door. Chaos was a breath away from me, his hulking frame dwarfing me, the heat of his rage radiating off him.

"If anything had happened to you . . ."

These weren't the sweet words of a lover, but they were filled with a confused sort of anguish. For some inexplicable reason, my life mattered to him. *I* mattered to him.

I just wished someone would tell me why.

How had I ended up in the middle of this? Why was I the one the demons were after?

"Chaos," I whispered, but anything I'd been about to say was cut off when he roughly took my face between his hands, and his lips crashed down on mine.

Heat shot through my body, but there was hardly time to register it. Almost as soon as it began, the kiss ended. Chaos backed away as though I was a snake who'd bitten him, that disdain I knew so well banked in his eyes.

I was still buzzing from the electrifying sensation of his mouth on mine, fingers lifted to brush my undeniably bruised lips.

We were going to have to talk about this. There was no way the man could kiss me like that and expect me to forget it ever happened. I stepped away from the door and opened my mouth to do just that, but we were no longer alone.

"Chaos," Malice called, the sound of multiple sets of footsteps accompanying him. "Merri's missing!"

The man in question glared down at me, his meaning clear. He didn't want me to say a word about what had just transpired between us.

I gave a little nod to show I understood.

He held my gaze for a beat longer and then backed away, calling out to the others as he did. "I've got her."

Those words weren't spoken with the relief of a man who'd rescued his charge. They were filled with an anger I couldn't understand. Chaos had me, that much was true, but he sure wasn't happy about it.

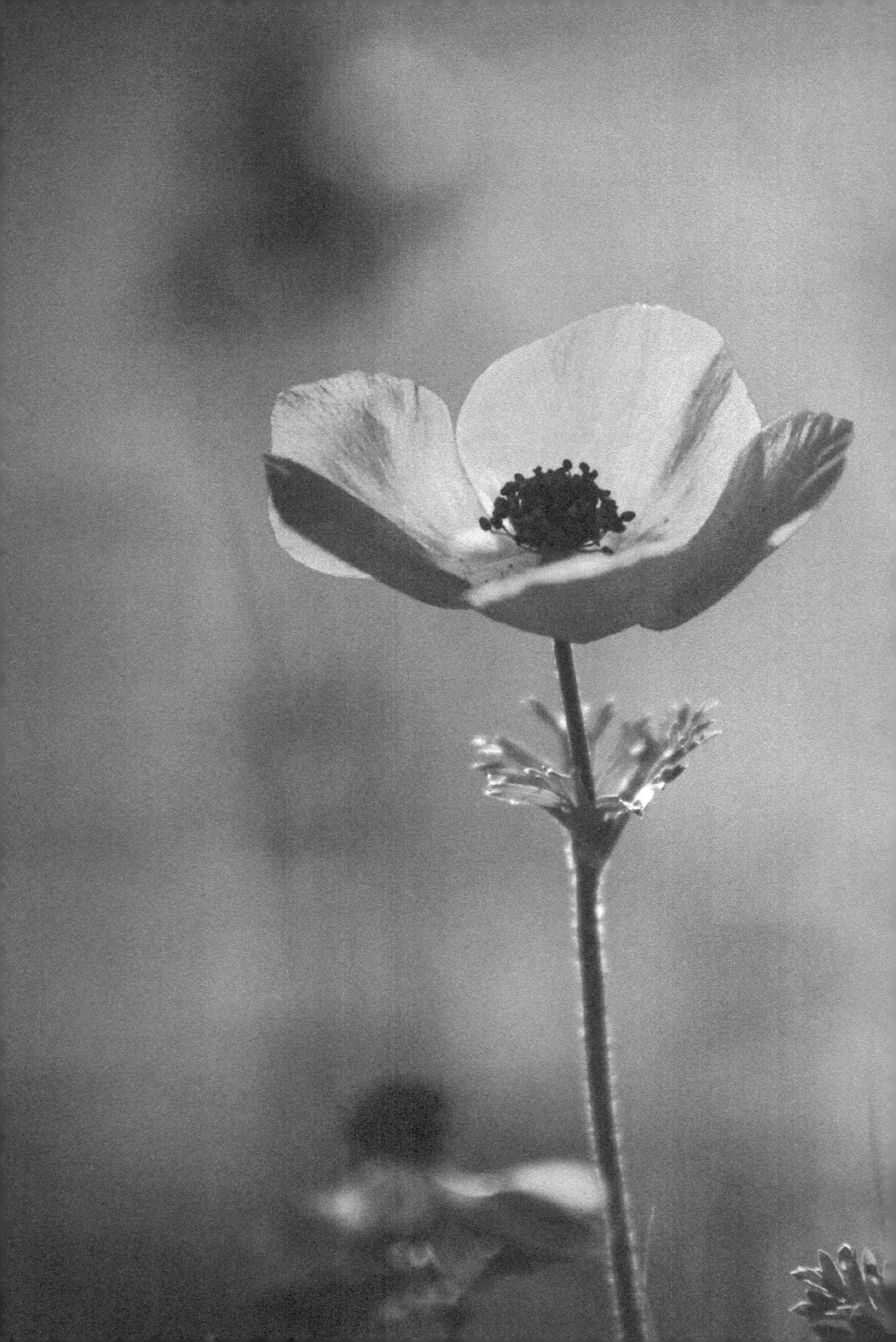

CHAPTER SIXTEEN

MALICE

Chaos's words lifted a weight from my chest as they registered, but I needed to see with my own eyes. If anything happened to her, we'd lose. I never took a loss well. Not once.

Clearly.

It's the entire reason we were in this fucking mess in the first place.

Grim and Sinclair were hot on my heels as we raced down the stairs and skidded into the kitchen.

I noted the piles of once-demon ash beside a fuming Chaos and how pale Merri's face was as she stood in shocked silence a little ways behind him. This had been too close of a call. We'd nearly lost her, and Chaos was the only reason she was still with us.

Sin and I'd had one fucking job.

Her.

Despite his ability to sense the emotions of others, Sin barreled forward, completely unaware or uncaring of the volcano about to erupt. Part of me wanted to sit back and watch the carnage about to unfold. Sin was the youngest of us, the cockiest too. He thought he could charm his way into anyone's good graces. Not this time.

"I wouldn't—" I started, but Chaos snarled as Sin closed the distance between them on his way to Merri.

The crack of a fist meeting Sin's nose echoed through the kitchen, accompanied by Sin's cry of pain.

"You were supposed to watch her," Chaos roared, rearing back to deliver another punch.

Blood poured from Sin's crushed nose as he braced for another blow, but Chaos stopped as Merri touched the warrior's elbow and begged, "Please, stop. Don't hit him again. It's not his fault. I slipped away when the angel beckoned. I couldn't stop myself. I was trapped in its thrall."

A shudder ran through Chaos before he knocked away her touch. "That was no angel. It was a pride demon."

"Knight, technically," Sin corrected, proving he'd learned absolutely nothing about squaring off against an enraged War.

Chaos growled at him. "If you want to keep your nose on your face, I suggest you shut the fuck up. Actually, why don't you take Merri back to her room and stay fucking put while the grown-ups figure out how the hell any of this happened."

Sin wiped his bleeding nose with his sleeve and sniffed before locking eyes with Merri. "Come on, kitten. We're in trouble."

Surprisingly, Merri didn't argue. She was still pale and looked shaken. Hopefully she didn't die of shock before the night was over. That would really be salt in the wound of this attack.

Prickling awareness made the hairs on the back of my neck rise as soon as Sin was out of the hot seat. Here it came. I had a lot to answer for, questions I'd been asking myself the moment the demons breached our walls. I stiffened and turned around to find Grim standing a fair distance from me, arms crossed, jaw set, eyes boring into me.

"Explain."

The one word carried the promise of endless pain and suffering if my answer wasn't what he wanted to hear.

Chaos settled in, still fuming as he leaned against the island.

I cleared my throat, suffering none of the same illusions as Sin.

"I'm not sure what you want me to say. Our security system can't account for winged demons dropping onto your balcony."

"That seems like one hell of an oversight," Chaos muttered.

I threw my hands up in the air. "What do you want me to say? It's not like they set off any of the proximity alarms until after they were already breaking the door. We didn't get advance warning like we would have if it was a helicopter or something. No one would have been able to prevent this."

"How did they find us?" Grim demanded.

"Well, you live in a great bloody penthouse, Grimsby. Not exactly subtle."

"Protected by wards that conceal my identity. To the rest of the world, I'm a reclusive billionaire, not a horseman of the apocalypse. And no one knows we have her."

"But you've lived here for decades," I pointed out. "And there are many who do know who you are and where you reside. It's an open secret. Anyone could have outed you for the right price."

"I don't think it was *us* they found. He was surprised we were here, remember?" Chaos said, his eyes finding Grim's.

"So they managed to track down Merri," I mused.

"Fine, but only Lilith and her pet know where Merri is. So how did *they* find out?" Grim pressed.

"Loose lips sink ships." Even as I said the words, I knew they weren't true.

"Lilith can't be bought. She's unflappable," Chaos added with a shake of his head. "It had to be something else."

"There's only one option. Merri's camming site. It's her only link to the outside."

"I thought you said you took precautions that would make her untraceable," Grim accused.

I shrugged. "If you know where to look, nothing is truly untraceable." It was a blow to my ego, but it was the truth.

"Fine. The camming is out."

I shook my head at Grim's heavy-handed ultimatum. "That's not an option. Merri has to feed."

His stare was icy as he focused on Chaos. "Yes. She does. Which brings us to a bigger issue. If the Princes are already being released, time is of the essence. We don't have the luxury of a slow courting process to make her love you. The clock is ticking. Lucifer nearly took her from us in a matter of days. We cannot afford to waste any more time. Breed her."

Chaos straightened and scowled at both of us. "I'm not taking something she's not willing to give."

Dark laughter left Grim as he adjusted the cuffs of his sleeves. "Then you and Sin better get to work and do whatever it takes to ensure she gives everything to you. I don't care how you do it. Make her want you. Get it done."

Grim stormed from the room, and Chaos looked at me. "Has he met her? No one can make that girl do anything. She's as stubborn as he is."

I snickered, giving his arm a pat as he brushed past me. "Better you than me."

He cocked an eyebrow at that. "You're not as impervious as you pretend to be, brother. I saw your face and heard your fear. You care for her."

"I could say the same about you."

"I do not."

I mutely raised a brow, matching his expression. "Methinks the lady doth protest too much."

"Fuck you, Malice."

"I think you mean fuck *her*. And if you're lucky, Sin will have already gotten the job done while we were down here arguing. Nice work, by the way."

Confusion swept across his features.

"You punching him and then sending the two of them off together so she could care for his wound. Brilliant."

A scowl marred his brow before he wiped his expression clean. "Yeah. Whatever. Clean up this mess, will you?" He gestured with his head toward the ash on the floor. "Since it is your fault and all."

He left me there, staring at the pile of demon remains, but I didn't mind. I had far more to think about than how to breed Merri. We'd never be successful if the Knights were able to get to us. Granted, they hadn't realized who they were up against, which worked out in our favor since I knew we were all still weakened by Helene's ritual. Thankfully they'd all been decimated this time, but what would happen when more followed in their wake? Surely her location was now known. Wasn't it? I needed to overhaul the security measures in this place, perhaps find a coven willing to work with us on setting more powerful and demon-proof wards. Before all that, I'd build Merri a server even I couldn't hack into. It would at least buy us time if not hide her entirely.

We still had one ace up our sleeve. No one else knew Merri had the power of the four horsemen behind her.

Yet.

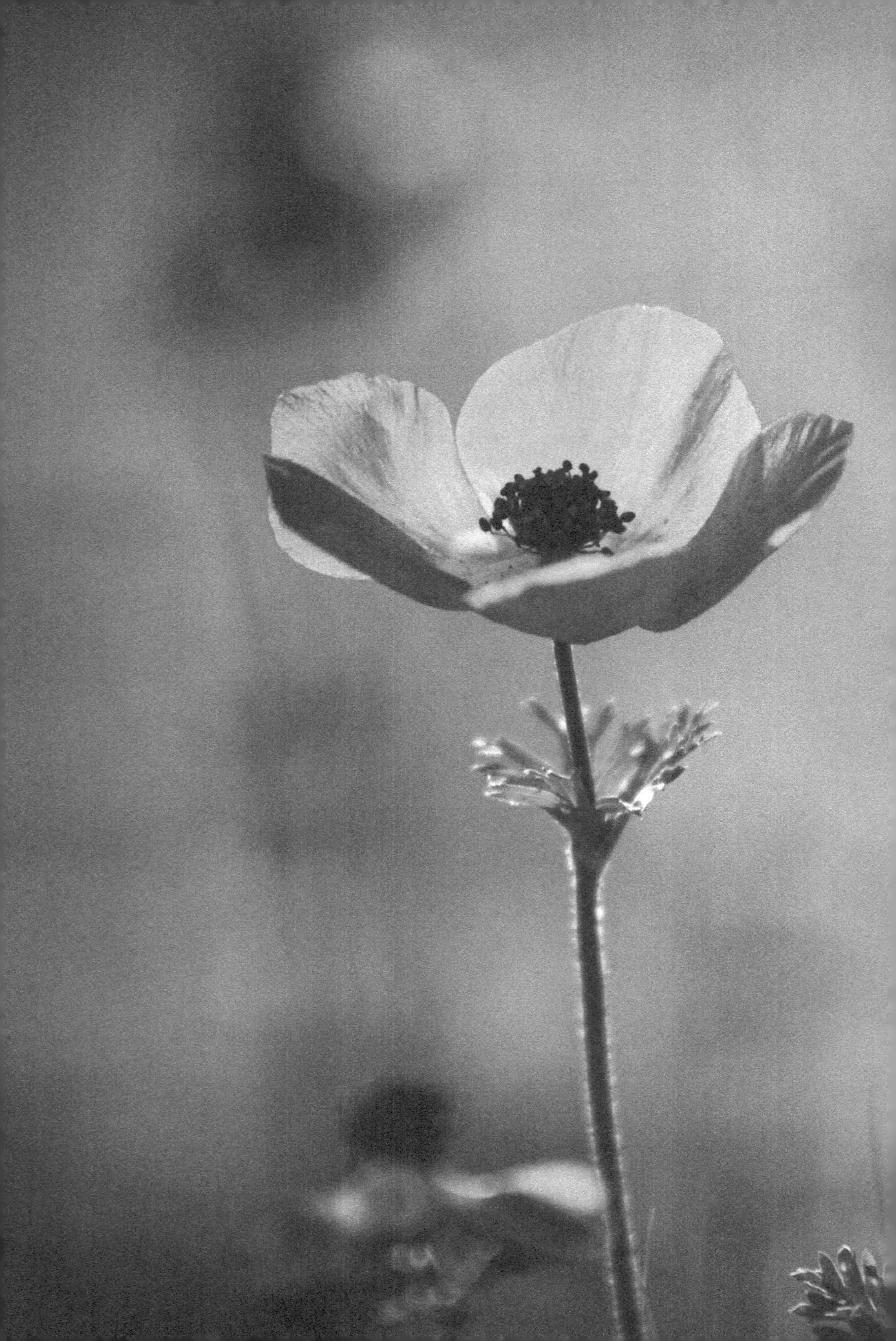

CHAPTER SEVENTEEN

SIN

Merri was uncharacteristically quiet as we made our way to my room. I'd expected a full-on rant from our resident brat over needing a babysitter, but she was still incredibly rattled from tonight's attack. The energy coming from her twisted my gut uncomfortably. This wasn't her usual level of frustration or irritation mixed with hunger. All I felt was shock and unease.

Opening my door, I gestured for her to enter my domain without words. She didn't need me to flirt and seduce right now. Merri needed a friend. Could I be one? I'd never tried. Nothing like jumping straight into the deep end to find out.

"Are you . . . okay?" I finally asked.

Merri blinked at me and raised a brow.

"Right. Stupid question," I muttered.

"I feel like I should be asking you that," she said, either not hearing me or choosing to ignore my words. "You're still dripping blood."

Fuck me. In all my concern for her, I'd forgotten about my destroyed nose. What was wrong with me? My face was my moneymaker. I needed to be beautiful so I could feed.

Well, to be fair, it didn't matter what I looked like. My incubus charm could turn me into a walking wet dream no matter what my physical features were, but it was always easier to lure in prey when you had what I'd once heard Lilith refer to as "pretty privilege."

"Sit down, Sin. You're bleeding all over the place." Merri snapped into caretaker mode, latching onto the role like it was a life preserver as she rushed into my attached bathroom.

I did as she said, taking off my bloodied shirt and balling it up before using the fabric to stop the bleeding. Dammit, that one was a favorite of mine. I'd finally worn it enough it was perfectly broken in.

"You don't have to—" I started before she forced my head back and shoved a wad of toilet paper against my nose. "Ouch, kitten. I'm gonna heal on my own. You don't have to make it hurt worse in the meantime."

"Incubi don't have healing..."

"Horseman. Basically a god," I said, all smug and proud. I even cocked a brow for good measure.

She didn't crack a smile, roll her eyes, or even give an indignant huff.

"What's got you so shaken up?" I asked, not really understanding why someone like her would be affected by a handful of demons. Okay, technically they were Knights, which made them like uber demons, but still. She lived at *Iniquity* with Lilith, of all creatures. The original demon herself. It can't possibly have been her first rodeo. While a sanctuary, surely a fight or two had broken out during her time there.

"If Chaos hadn't found me..."

"But he did. And you're safe."

Merri gave me a look before softly admitting, "I don't think I ever realized what it was like. Being *un*safe, I mean. I've always been the thing people were afraid of. I was the monster who'd suck your soul out of your body and leave you nothing more than a husk. Something to be feared and never trusted. I..." She let out a heavy breath and shook her head, as if at a loss for words. "You all kept telling me I was in danger, but I don't think I truly understood what that meant. Not until tonight. Not until I realized I could fall victim to the same sort of power I employ."

I wanted to touch her so badly. Comfort her and make sure she knew she wasn't in danger right now. My hand twitched with the effort to keep from doing just that. She'd think I was trying something because all I was to her—or anyone really—was sex.

"Merri—"

"I know you four aren't telling me everything," she said, but it wasn't an accusation so much as a statement of fact. "Tonight was about whatever my aunt's involved in, wasn't it? The apocalypse?"

I kept my face as expressionless as I was able, knowing I wasn't allowed to reveal the more intimate details of the role she played in said apocalypse.

"Sin, please? I need more than what you guys have given me. A fucking angel just tried to kidnap me."

"Knight."

"Exactly. Not just a regular demon. A Knight who serves some kind of Prince. This has to do with the end times, and they want me. You said so yourself. But why? As blackmail or revenge or something? A way to get back at my aunt for what she did?"

"Yes." No one said I couldn't tell her when she was right about something. And I didn't technically answer all her questions, I was simply agreeing with the "or something." She could assume what she liked.

Scoffing, she rolled her eyes. "Yes to which one? Why are you being so cagey?"

"Look, sweet cheeks, you're smart. You'll figure this out on your own, and honestly, the info I have is only gonna be provided to you on a need-to-know basis. For your own good."

"Yeah, okay. Because you, who have known me for just over a week and have spoken to me on barely more than a surface level, are clearly an expert on what's good for me."

The return of her attitude was a relief, and if I'm being honest, a bit of a turn-on. I shifted, using my discarded shirt to hide my semi. I may not be the most self-aware of the horseman, but I was pretty sure she wasn't going to appreciate looking over and seeing a tent in my pants when she was giving me what for.

What could I say? I liked a challenge. It was rare to find one in my —for lack of a better word—profession.

"Go on, then. Tell me something that's not surface-level about you. You think I don't know what's good for you? Prove me wrong."

She crossed her arms under her perfect tits and scowled. If she wasn't careful, I'd wipe that expression off her face with my fucking mouth.

No.

No, Sinclair. We are digging deeper than surface level. We are getting to know each other. Learning about our vulnerabilities and stuff.

The possibility of getting to know more about the woman in front of me sent a little flutter off in my belly. Completely unused to the sensation, I thought it might be indigestion. A little heartburn after all the stress of the attack. Then I realized I was actually excited.

The realization was so unsettling I immediately told myself it was only because getting to know her better would help me with our mission.

"You first," she snapped, hitting me with her vibrant blue gaze.

Me?

For as much as I was used to being the center of attention, no one ever asked me about . . . me. They wanted to know about my rock star persona. Not *me*.

"Uh . . . well."

"Are you seriously trying to tell me you *don't* want to talk about yourself?" One perfectly shaped russet brow arched.

"Well, I mean . . . sure. But there's so much to say, it's hard to narrow it down."

"Uh huh."

"I've lived for—" Not wanting to date myself, I kept it vague. "A long time. You might need to narrow the scope a bit for me. What do you want to know?" I pat the blanket next to me, silently bidding her to sit.

She pursed her lips and sat down next to me on the edge of the bed. "Okay, let's start with something basic. What was your childhood li—wait. Did you even have a childhood? I can't imagine horsemen babies or little kids. You guys probably just popped into existence. Boom, hot men here to ruin the world."

"You think I'm hot?"

"Sin," she groaned. "If you're not going to be serious, then I'm not going to waste my time."

"I was just kidding. Sorry." Loosing a heavy sigh, I flopped back on the bed, arms flung out on either side of me.

Of all the questions she could ask, she went with that one. The mythology of the horsemen was a secret. I didn't know of anyone outside our foursome who knew the truth of it. Could I trust Merri? *Should* I?

My internal debate lasted all of ten seconds.

If the truth would help me save the universe, then I had to risk it, didn't I?

I gripped the back of her shirt and tugged hard, pulling her down to join me on the bed. She let out an adorable little squeak of protest, but I stopped her when I began speaking.

"I wasn't always a horseman."

"No?"

"Nope. I was just a regular human man. An actor and musician who wanted to be loved by everyone on the planet."

"How'd that pan out for you?" she asked, turning her head to look at me.

"Well, as an actor, I was B-list at best. I had some success but never a real breakout moment. It's part of what led me down this path." One of my hands fisted into the blanket as century-old emotion knotted in my stomach. "I hungered for more. Nothing was enough to fill the emptiness inside me. I knew I was destined for greatness, and I wanted more. One night I was approached in my dressing room by a man. I thought he might be an agent or studio exec, ready to offer me my big break. In some ways, that's exactly what he was there to do, but definitely not in the way I'd expected."

She rolled on her side so she was facing me, her face inches from mine. "What happened?"

"He said I'd be irresistible, known and respected the world over. Revered—though not by my current name. If I'd simply agree to take over for him."

Her eyes widened. "He was a horseman?"

"Yes. Famine." I offered her a wry smile. "He recognized a bit of himself in my endless craving for more."

Her eyes widened with the knowledge I'd just offered, but she remained silent as I continued.

"There was no dramatic ritual, if that's what you're wondering. It was all shockingly boring if I'm being honest. He looked me in the eye, asked me if this was what I truly wanted, and we shook hands." I reached out and tucked a lock of her hair behind her ear. I couldn't fucking help myself. "I woke up in this very penthouse, surrounded by those other three fuckers."

She hummed softly. "It's ironic."

"What is?"

"You wanted to be loved by everyone. Instead you're lusted after and feared."

Letting out a bitter laugh, I turned my head away from her. "No one can love a horseman. I gave up on that a long time ago. And to be fair, my predecessor never promised me love. The rest of what he offered all came to pass, just maybe not in the way I'd thought." I thought back to the first time my incubus gift appeared and chuckled. What a night that had been.

Merri didn't try to placate me with meaningless words. Instead she shocked the hell out of me by taking my hand and weaving her fingers through mine in a silent show of support. "And the others, did they all inherit the mantle as well?"

"No. Only Chaos. As far as I know, Malice and Grim are the originals. And before you ask, I have absolutely no idea how they manifested in the world. Neither of them talk about it."

"My money is on fully grown hot guy manifestation."

I grinned and elbowed her gently. "See, you do want us."

"Want is very different from trust."

"We are here to protect you. You're safe with us."

"But you're not safe with me, Sin."

I frowned at her words. "I'm a horseman of the apocalypse, Merri. And an incubus."

She shook her head. "You don't understand. My hunger is insatiable."

"Hellloooo, Famine," I waved a hand in the air and pointed at myself. "If anyone can understand endless hunger, I'm pretty sure it's me."

"I killed the one man I'd ever loved."

It was all starting to come together. This sweet succubus was traumatized by her past. Who among us, really?

"He was human?"

"Yes. I thought I was too, at the time. We were kids, really. In high school."

With the memories of my own first night as an incubus fresh in my mind, she didn't have to say anything else. I had a very clear picture of what happened.

"It doesn't have to be that way every time, kitten. I promise."

Tears filled her eyes. "How can you promise that? Lilith kept me locked away because I'm so powerful. She knew it was the only way to keep everyone safe."

"Are you sure that's why she did it? Or was it because it's what *you* needed to feel safe?"

She blinked at me, her long, wet eyelashes sticking together. "What do you mean?"

"Well, you were scared. Grieving for the boy you'd lost." I refused to refer to a teenager as a man on principle. "Terrified of your own power. She offered stability. Safety. The certainty that it wouldn't happen again under her watch. She gave you a place to recover and find yourself again."

Merri hummed. "I never thought of it that way."

I squeezed her hand. "See, I'm pretty smart. And if I'm right about that, then it stands to reason I'm right about other things too."

Merri's gaze went unfocused as she considered my earlier reassurances. "I guess you might be right. When Chaos kissed me earlier, I didn't feed from him at all."

My whole body stiffened. Chaos fucking *kissed* her? Mr. I Only Growl At Her In Passing went straight in for the kiss while I'm over here opening my chest and spilling my secrets?

"I . . . that's . . . uh, great?" I finally spluttered.

"It was the first time anyone has kissed me since . . ."

I could tell there was more she wanted to say, could sense the confusion and sadness the admission caused her. I wondered if she was picking up on the rampant jealousy currently raging through me. Maybe I could distract her with another truth bomb.

"Closing yourself off from people isn't the answer, kitten. Not for your succubus nature or your heart." I was still holding her hand, my thumb rubbing small circles on her skin. "How you've survived this long is a miracle. You need physical contact. Camming won't cut it."

"You said it yourself, I've survived this long."

"Surviving isn't living, Merri. And I think we both know that it's not enough. The celibacy thing is not going to work. You've been camming every day, sometimes twice a day, and you're still starving. Sooner or later, your succubus is going to demand more."

I knew I'd ruined the moment as soon as she released my hand and sat up. That wasn't what she wanted to hear, even if it was true. Actually, more than likely *because* it was true.

"I'll make do," she said, her voice detached and cold. Then she stood and walked to my door, muttering on her way out, "I always do."

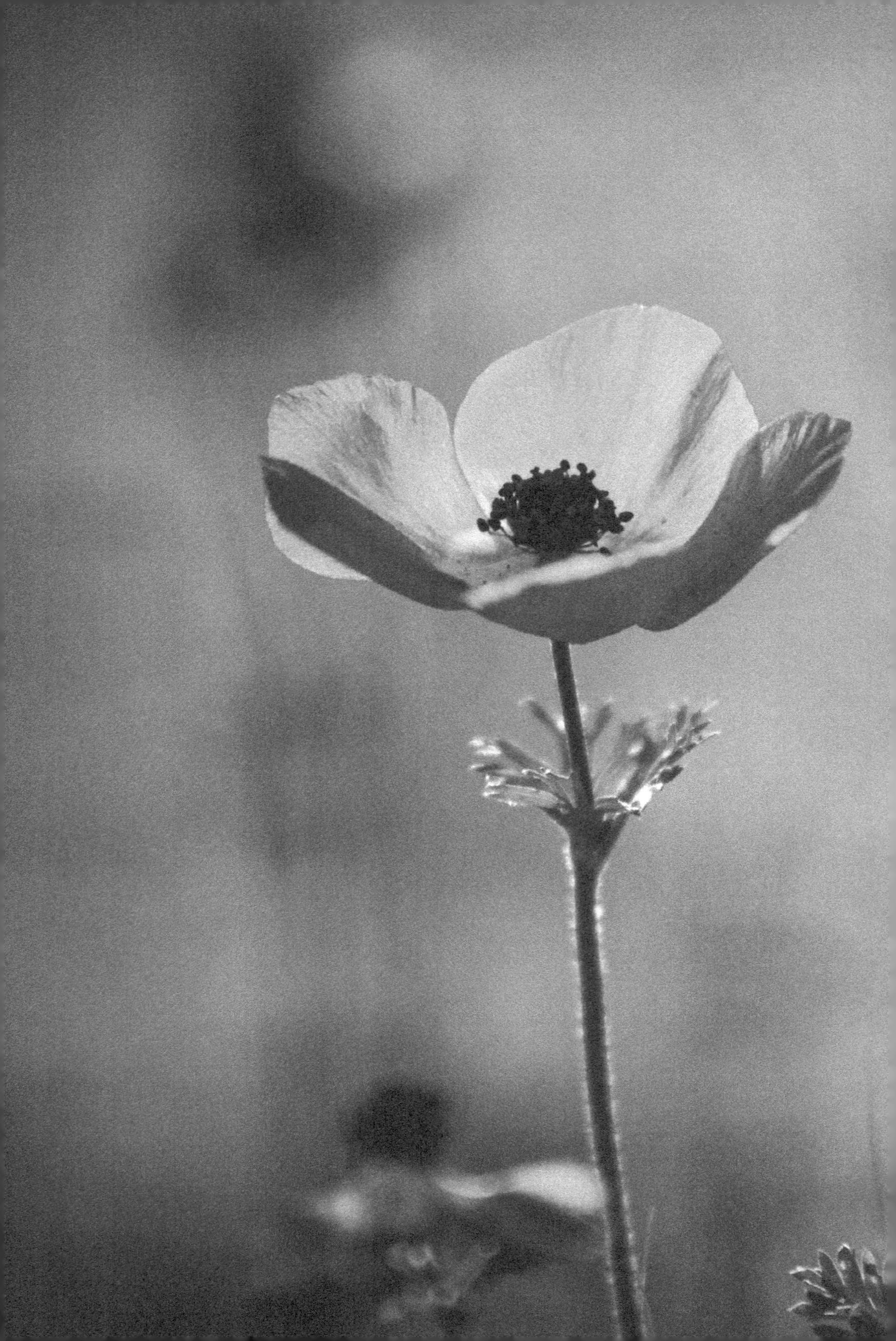

CHAPTER
EIGHTEEN
GRIM

"Fucking ungrateful, entitled pricks, the lot of them," I grumbled, my annoyance swelling.

The decanter in my hand was woefully empty as I took the elevator down to the bottom floor to my bespoke wine cellar. I'd crafted an entire corner specifically to house my collection of Brimstone whiskey and now that my brothers were here, my stores were rapidly depleting. I was going to have to call Hades and ask for another shipment at this rate.

"The least they could do is refill the decanter after they empty it, but noooo. Would serve them all right if I cut them off. Bloody parasites."

It wasn't like they didn't know where the cellar was. They'd left nothing more than a few drops in the crystal container this time. No excuse for bad manners. I'd have to teach them a thing or two if they were going to live in polite society. Clearly the years of rock stardom had only made Sin worse, and Chaos? Well, who knew what he'd been up to. War was never civilized.

Malice was only slightly more tolerable, though I suppose the years of living on his own had taught him a thing or two about picking up after himself. So there was that, at least.

My grumbling continued as I reached the large wooden door, its pointed arch and oversized iron handle all that was left of the Bavarian castle I once called home. Ah, the good old days. Back when all I had to worry about was being the first to successfully kick off the apocalypse. Now, strangely, I was supposed to stop it.

One constant I'd banked on in my long life was my purpose. The other was that I bring death to all things. Now, for the first time, both of those constants had been tested. No wonder I was feeling so out of sorts.

Stalking down the rows of expensive wines from across the world, I zeroed in on my goal—the beautiful bottles of amber liquid nestled in a special case. Perhaps I should get a lock to keep Sin out. He knew exactly where to come to find the precious commodity, and eventually he would have done exactly that. Selecting one, I uncorked it and refilled the decanter, my nose picking up on the distinctive notes of brimstone and hellfire mixed with peat.

More than ready to enjoy a glass, I returned the bottle to its resting spot and turned, only to stop dead. A splash of familiar flaming hair peeked out from around the corner, spilling across the floor in a way that felt unnatural. Instinct screamed at me to go to her, and the sight that greeted me when I rounded the tall wine rack had all my senses on alert. Merri wasn't supposed to be in here, but more than that, she shouldn't be curled up on her side like a child hiding from a monster.

"Wildflower?" I called, forgetting myself as I used my secret nickname for her.

When she didn't so much as stir, I set the decanter down and crouched in front of her. I'd been alone, so I hadn't bothered with my gloves, which meant I couldn't even give her a shake.

"Merri," I tried again, louder this time.

Her skin was deathly pale, dark circles ringing her eyes, but she blinked and finally focused on me. "Hi, Daddy," she whispered. "I didn't think anyone would find me here. No cameras."

The instant her eyes locked on mine, I was nearly knocked over by the wave of lust that accompanied them. Her power was unchecked, searching and needy. I scrambled away from her.

"Control yourself," I snapped, terrified of what might happen in my ungloved state.

"I'm trying," she said, her voice wobbling. "It's been so hard."

She could say that again. I wasn't a stranger to arousal, but the reaction my body had to her was painful and immediate.

Slowly pushing herself up to a seated position, she rested her head in her hands and let out a soft, defeated sigh. "I'm starving. Sin was right. The camming was barely keeping me going, and without it..."

Fuck.

This was my fault.

It had been three days since the attack. Three days since my edict against Merri's sole energy source.

She continued with the most pathetic look on her face. "You guys don't even jerk off. At least when I was at *Iniquity,* I could snack on the surplus sexual energy from patrons. This is like living in a convent. Except a convent is probably more horny. You know the nuns are getting off to thoughts of hot priests."

I would have laughed if she didn't sound so forlorn. And frankly, she looked terrible. I'd seen hospice patients who looked healthier.

"Come on, wildflower. You can't be down here. Let's get you to your room and sort you out."

She stared at me in shock for a heartbeat before nodding and reaching for me. I was at a loss for all of two seconds, knowing the last thing I could do was give her my hand. Pulling myself together, I offered my fabric-covered elbow instead, fighting a groan as the heat of her palm radiated through my shirt.

"I'm not contagious, you know. And I might be desperate, but I already swore not to feed from the unwilling," she muttered, her steps unsteady as I led her from the little room.

"It's not me I'm protecting. It's you."

"Ah, the classic it's not you, it's me speech," she mused with a raspy bark of laughter.

"I'm glad you see things my way." I hated the way her words affected me, making me wish things were different, that *I* was different.

It had been ages since I'd let myself fall into the deep pit of yearning for casual affection and physical contact. Hel had all but burned it out of me after that absolute shitshow of a relationship. Or so I'd thought. Until Merri showed up and sent my carefully contained life tits up.

I stared down at the crown of her head, at a complete loss as she snuggled into my arm like a kitten.

Fuck.

I couldn't give her anything she wanted or needed. All I could do was hurt her.

Punching the elevator button, I waited none too patiently for the car to descend so I could get her safely tucked into her room and away from me. Forgetting my gloves was a mistake I wouldn't make twice. As Merri had proven once again, just because I planned on spending a night alone didn't mean I was going to get my wish. She had a way of turning up at the most inconvenient and unexpected times.

"Finally," I growled when the elevator chimed its arrival and the door slid smoothly open.

I charged forward, causing Merri to stumble in my haste. If I were anything other than the literal hand of death, I would've caught her. Instead I stiffened and prayed she'd right herself without me helping. So much for chivalry.

Her grip on my arm tightened, and she sagged even harder against me.

"Mmm," she hummed, "you smell good."

My eyebrows flew up in shock. I couldn't recall a single time in my existence that someone remarked upon my scent. Death wasn't exactly known for its subtle or pleasant aroma.

"Do I?" I murmured, tamping down the urge to ask her what I smelled like.

"Mmhmm. You smell like . . . like you were rolling around in the dirt."

A sharp bark of laughter escaped before I could stop it. "What?"

"Yeah. Like fall. Leaves and rain." She pressed her nose to my chest and took a deep inhale. "Damp earth. Crisp air." I could hear the smile in her voice. "Makes me want to curl up in a blanket and crack open a book. Take a nap . . ."

I wasn't sure how to feel about any of that. Was it a good thing to have a scent that made a woman want to fall asleep? Better than running away in horror, I supposed.

With the way she was pressed against me in this tiny box, I couldn't help but breathe in her scent as well, and I had to admit, sleep was the furthest thing from my mind.

The sweet vanilla smell had my mouth watering, but once I let myself sink into the complexity of the fragrance, I realized she was everything I loved. The slight bitterness of coffee gave her a dark note I hadn't expected, but then there was the warmth and familiarity of bourbon blending with the two, all layered with just a hint of spicy jasmine. She was delectable, and my body fucking recognized and responded to her without my permission.

If she got any closer to me, she'd feel exactly how hard being around her was for me.

I was so high off her, I'd have sworn I downed the entire decanter of whiskey, except I hadn't had a single drop. This buzzing, swimming feeling in my head was all her.

I opened my mouth, not entirely sure what I was about to say—warn her away, perhaps, or maybe beg her for more—I was an absolute tangle of conflicted urges. Before I could do any of that, her knees gave out, and she slid down my side.

Fear punched through the sensual haze I'd been lost in, and I reacted on pure instinct. Instead of reaching for her, I jerked my arms away, terrified she might accidentally brush against my skin in her fall.

"Merri," I called, crouching down beside her crumpled form.

With careful hands, I shook her shoulder in an attempt to bring her around. The oversized shirt she wore did nothing to cover her legs, making it impossible for me to safely pick her up.

"Wake up, wildflower. I need you to walk for me."

She was breathing, that much I could tell, but her eyes didn't open at my urging.

Fuck.

The elevator finished its ascent, the door barely more than a crack open before I started bellowing. "Malice! Get your arse over here right now!"

The fucker didn't show for what felt like an eternity as I reached out and pressed the button that would hold the elevator door open. I'd have called for the others, but they were both out taking care of the demands of their power tonight. Malice was the only other person here.

"Mal! I need your help! Do you hear me, you wanker?"

Slow, heavy steps echoed from down the hall, Malice's irritated grumbling unmistakable.

"Hurry the fuck up," I barked.

"What is it now? Can't a man shower in fucking peace?" He rounded the corner, hair dripping, a towel in one hand, a pair of joggers haphazardly pulled on by the look of them.

"It's Merri—"

But I could tell from the way the blood drained from his face that further explanation wasn't necessary.

"Jesus fucking Christ, Grimsby. Did you kill her already?"

"Me? What? No!"

The words exploded out of me. Apparently I did need to explain after all.

"She looks dead."

"She's starving. I found her in the wine cellar, nearly unconscious. She collapsed on our way to her room."

"Well, pick her up, you twat."

I held up my bare hands. "Can't. Not without killing her. It has to be you."

He could not have looked more put out. "Fuck's sake," he grumbled, dropping the towel and pushing into the small space to scoop Merri up.

I followed him out of the elevator, panic giving my voice an edge as I pressed, "She needs to feed, Malice. She's fading fast."

"I told you she needed her fucking cam work. You feed her."

"It can't be me. I'm not safe."

"So get Sin or Chaos. They both volunteered."

"They aren't back yet, and"—I risked a glance at Merri's face, her lips pale and bloodless, complexion waxy and drawn—"I don't think we can wait."

Mal let out a woeful sigh and rolled his eyes before looking down at her. I saw the flicker of concern cross his face, but as fast as it appeared, he schooled his expression back into the indifferent, stony facade he usually wore. "Fine. Just this once."

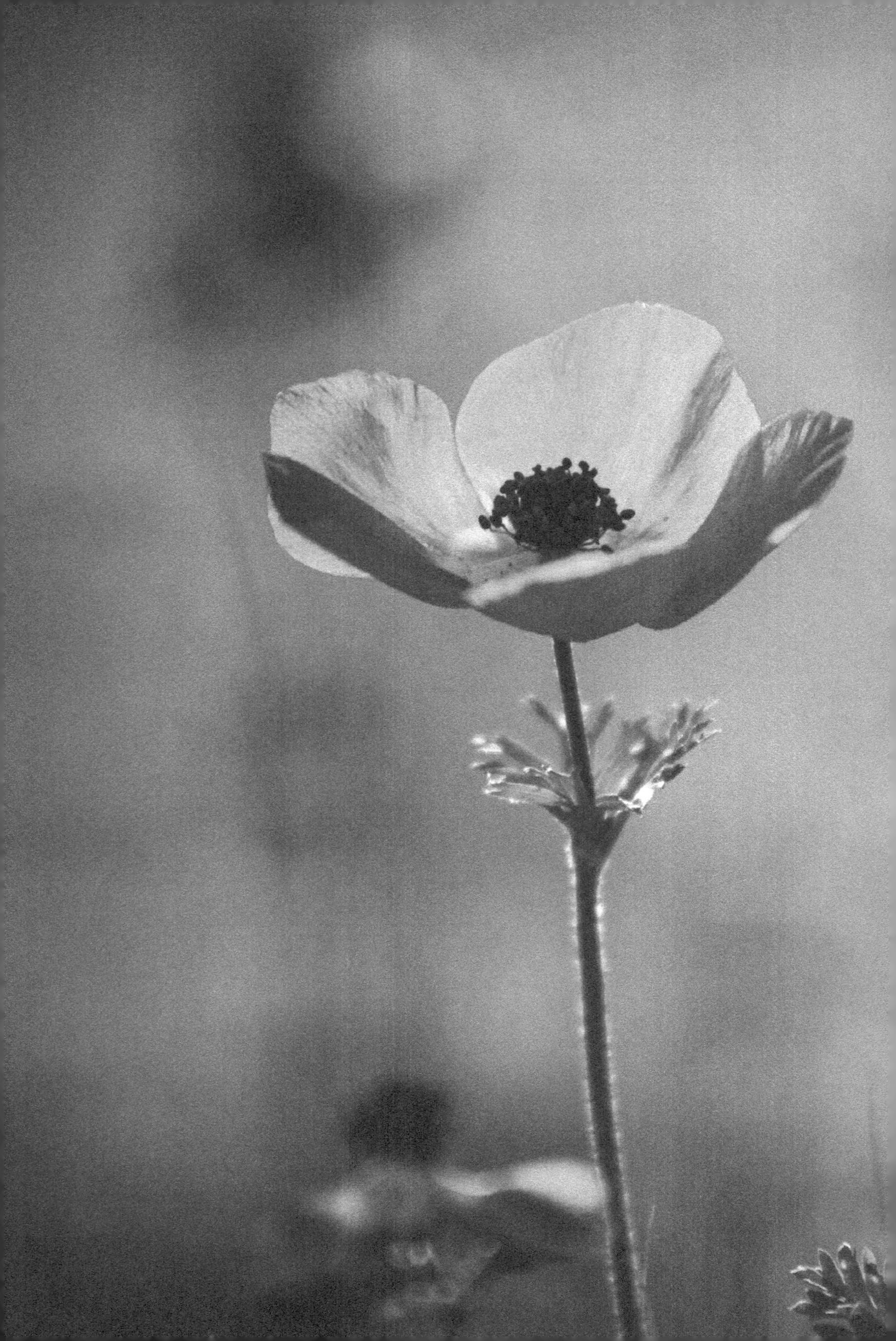

CHAPTER NINETEEN

MERRI

The room was swaying gently. Why was it swaying? Was I on a boat? How the fuck did that happen?

"It can't be me. I'm not safe." The smoky velvet-coated voice reverberated from within the firm male chest my head rested against. He didn't sound pleased. In fact, Malice sounded like he was... mocking Grim.

What had happened from stepping into the elevator to now?

And why did it seem like it had been a game of musical Brits? I started off with one and woke up with the other.

"Bloody hell," he continued, still either unaware or uncaring that I'd come to. "Haven't had a wank in centuries, and now I have to do it with a fucking audience. What a show it'll be, all ten fucking seconds of it."

That got my attention.

Wide awake now, my eyes snapped open. "Wait, *what*?"

"Oh, nice to see you awake, sleeping beauty." If one could major in sarcasm, Malice would surely have his PhD.

He kicked open my bedroom door and carried me into the room before unceremoniously depositing me on my bed.

"Let's get this over with. I have things to do this evening."

I pushed myself up to my elbows, which was harder done than said. My head was swimming and my body felt like it had been filled with lead. "Get *what* over with, Malice? What exactly do you think is going on here?"

He stood before me, bare-chested, beautiful, and glaring. God almighty, I've said it before, I'll say it again. It was really unfair for the horsemen of the apocalypse to be so pretty. I squinted, trying to parse out which one he was supposed to be. Now that I knew Sin was Famine, and I could only assume, given his aversion to touching me, that Grim had to be Death, and Chaos was a walking war machine so that one was basically a gimme—I shuddered, recalling the way he'd ripped that demon's head off—so that only left . . .

"Pestilence."

He blinked, then smirked and held his arms out on either side of his body before taking a bow. "In the flesh."

"Definitely too pretty."

"Not always. You should see what I can do with a plague."

"No thanks. I think I'll pass."

Huffing, he pulled my desk chair around and sat, legs spread, six-pack rippling, one hand on his waistband. "It's been ages. This won't take long. Do you need a bib or something?"

My eyes went wide. Was he talking about feeding me?

For someone offering to rub one out, he sure didn't seem, well, excited. My eyes dropped to his lap, and my brow hitched up at the complete lack of notable interest. Gray sweatpants showed everything, and that was not an eager bulge. That was a sleepy bulge.

"It doesn't work that way. You actually have to, you know, want it."

He rolled his eyes. "I'm a male, hellcat. I pretty much always want it."

"And yet you haven't done it in centuries? Sounds like you don't want it that badly."

A flicker of discomfort flashed across his face. "I have my reasons."

"I'm sure you do. But I'm not going to feed off someone who isn't willing. It would be like eating potato chips when what I really need is a nice juicy steak."

The discomfort in his eyes was replaced by confusion, and I felt compelled to elaborate.

"Potato chips are great, but they don't actually nourish you. It's empty calories, you know? It won't fill me up. So if your goal is to feed me, well, I hate to break it to you, but that's not going to get the job done."

A muscle in his jaw flexed before he locked eyes with me. "What do I need to do, then?"

God, he hated me. He hated everything about being here right now. I'd felt more sexual excitement at the gynecologist's office. The only emotion I could glean from him was mild disgust. This was never going to work.

"Get me someone else. Sin or Chaos."

He shook his head and leaned back in the chair. "No can do. Sorry to disappoint, but I'm the only option. They're both out."

Out? Those fuckers got to go out while I was locked up in here? Fucking double standards.

"Where's Grim?"

"If you think I'm unwilling . . ." He chuckled darkly. "Grim isn't going to be any help."

"Well, this isn't going to work for me. You can barely tolerate me." I gestured to his lap. "Your dick isn't even hard."

He shifted in his seat, and I swear it was like I'd summoned a monster because just the mention of his dick had it . . . inflating.

"Jesus Christ, do you have an air compressor attached to that thing?"

"See? I'll make it work."

He didn't get it. Hard or flaccid, if he wasn't fully invested, he wouldn't enjoy it. And if *he* didn't enjoy it, I'd get nothing out of it.

This wasn't just about the mechanical act of getting off. This was about pleasure. True pleasure. Mind-melting, toe-curling pleasure. The kind you could only find when you lost yourself to the moment completely. Right now, Malice looked like he was bracing himself for a boring business meeting, not like he was in desperate need of release. All this would give him was an unsatisfying orgasm. I needed something like what I'd had with OriginalSin during our private cam session. That had been the last time I'd fed and been sated for longer than a few hours.

"Look, just forget it," I muttered, flopping back on the bed. I'd rather starve to death than have to explain this to him. I closed my eyes, exhaustion seeping into every cell of my being. Maybe I'd just waste away and become one with this duvet.

Malice loosed a heavy sigh that I could relate to in the depths of my soul. Then he stood, or I gathered as much from the creak of the chair and the soft pad of his footsteps. I opened my eyes when the bed dipped as he sat gingerly beside me, his hand hovering over my knee for a beat before he finally allowed it to rest on my skin.

"I know I'm a cranky, insufferable arsehole. I can't help it. It's who I've been for centuries. But I do really want to help you right now. I just . . ." He dragged a hand through his hair and heaved another long-suffering sigh. "I don't know how to make this better for you."

Propping myself on my elbows once more, I stared at him, the contact of his palm on my bare knee only serving to amp up my appetite. It was like holding a plate of freshly baked cookies under a starving person's nose but not allowing them a taste.

"You tell me you're willing, but all I'm picking up from you is how uncomfortable you are. Maybe if there was something else, hell, even your hate might help because hate fucks serve a very important purpose, but this"—I gestured to him—"indifference isn't going to cut it."

"You're only feeling what I allow you to feel, hellcat. I've got such high walls up I'm basically trapped in a tower of my own making."

"Well, Rapunzel, then I think you know what you need to do."

He closed his eyes and tightened his hold on my knee. "Hang on. It's been a long time since I've even attempted this. It might—"

All at once, I was flooded with a tidal wave of emotion from him. I couldn't contain the gasp as fear, betrayal, loss, hurt, and, most of all, deep aching sadness hit me.

Oh.

Oh.

He was a broken, broken boy. And there was no word for how much that called to me.

"Mal," I whispered, reaching out for him without even realizing it.

His eyes found mine, reflecting all that I was feeling. "Do you understand now?"

I nodded.

"It's not that I don't want you, Merri. But the last time I allowed anyone behind these walls, they . . ." He shook his head, not ready to bare anymore of himself to me.

He didn't need to. I felt it to my core.

"Please don't pity me. That will make this even more difficult," he rasped. "Give me something to focus on, something to help me forget her betrayal."

It might have been the wrong move, but I needed him to see that affection didn't have to come with a price. He deserved to receive tenderness just like everyone else. Coming to my knees, I closed the distance between us and reached for him, my fingers trailing along the side of his cheek.

"You don't have t—" he began, but I stopped him with a gentle press of my lips to his.

∽

Malice

SHE WAS FUCKING KISSING ME. Bloody hell, I didn't even remember what to do. My hands just sort of fluttered around her face like drunken butterflies.

"There it is," she whispered against my lips, her eyes fucking luminous as they blinked open.

Her gaze trailed down my chest to the more than obvious and insistent erection tenting my joggers. Now there was no denying how much I desired her. Not with my walls down and the taste of her lips lingering on mine.

"I can work with this," she said, her voice still dropped in a sultry whisper.

Oh fuck yes. Please work it.

But I quickly realized she had no intention of touching me. More's the pity.

"What do you want me to do, Mal?" she asked, backing away and sitting on her heels.

"What do I want *you* to do? This is all for you. What should I be doing?"

Her lashes fluttered as she cast her gaze down at her hands, a hint of pink creeping up her cheeks. "I didn't expect you to want to hand over control. You don't seem like the type."

"I'm not. But this is a very different situation. Believe me, Merri, if we were doing this for any reason other than seeing to your hunger, I would already have you exactly where I want you."

She raised a brow at that, an emotion I didn't have a chance to name flashing across her face. It was then I realized that Merri was as complex a creature as I was. Just because she was built for sex in every sense of the word didn't mean she was solely her inner demon. In the short time we'd all known her, Merri had proven she contained multitudes. I think she wanted to feel desired and cherished for who she was beyond her succubus nature, much as anyone else would.

"You can feel my desire for you. I let down my walls. But that's as far as this goes between us. I can give you this and only this. Do you understand? It's all I have." My voice was low and careful. It had to be. Boundaries existed for a reason, and I was lowering mine in order to help her, but I couldn't afford to demolish them completely. The kiss already had me reeling. I needed to reclaim some sense of control.

Her expression shuttered, and she nodded. "Just a transaction. Nothing more than a live-action cam session. Got it."

The tiniest flicker of guilt flashed in me, but I snuffed it out before it could catch fire. She understood, and that's all I asked of her.

"You should sit over there if this is a cam session. Put some distance between us."

Swallowing through a tight throat, I forced myself to my feet and followed her suggestion. It was wise to get away from her soft skin and lush curves. Less temptation.

"Like this?" I asked and sat back in the same chair, though now it was positioned facing the end of the bed, my legs spread wide.

"That'll do," she said, her voice clipped and professional.

Already, I was mourning the loss of the tenderness it had held when she held my face between her hands. If I hadn't been staring at her so unashamedly, I would have missed the tiny furrow between her brows as she closed her eyes. But then, as though a weight had been lifted, some of the sadness I carried seemed to vanish.

She let out a shuddering sigh, a lone tear slipping down her cheek before her lids lifted and those beautiful eyes found mine.

"Did you just..." I couldn't complete the question, too in awe of what had just happened.

Merri nodded. "It was getting in the way."

No fucking kidding. I'd carried the weight of that with me for centuries, and just as easily as tossing a napkin in the bin, she'd taken it from me. I think I could love her for that alone.

If I was capable of love.

Which I wasn't.

"No wonder people are so addicted to your kind. Who needs drugs when you have a succubus?"

She laughed, but it was hollow. "And I'm just as deadly."

"Who among us?"

She smiled slightly when she took my meaning and dipped her chin as if ceding the point. Then she cleared her throat and shifted on her knees, back to business once more. "I need you to tell me how you want this to go, Mal. I want to do what you like to make sure this is good for you."

God's teeth, why did those words wrap around my blackened heart and feel so fucking good?

My throat was so tight I had to clear it before I could get a word out. "Anything . . . anything you do will turn me on. Stop toying with me. You can sense it from here."

Her cheeks flushed, and I could see her nostrils flare as she inhaled, drawing my lust into herself. I thought that was going to be it, but as she exhaled, she sent that lust back tenfold.

"Fuck," I grunted, my cock so hard it physically ached.

"If you won't give me specifics, I'll just have to improvise," she murmured, lying back against her pillows and shimmying out of her little sleep shorts.

My hands were balled up so tight my knuckles hurt from the pressure, but if I touched myself, this would be over. A small part of my brain whispered that reaching my peak was exactly what I was supposed to be doing, but the rest of me—the innately selfish part—wanted to savor this moment. Who knew when or if I'd ever get another one.

"You don't have to worry about lasting with me," she promised, her fingers trailing seductively over her breasts on their journey down to her belly. "Your pleasure is my five-course meal. So however you need it, Malice, take it."

She was more dangerous than I'd given her credit for. If I were a weaker man, I'd have already been balls deep inside her, pledging my loyalty for all time. Her power filled the room, thickening the air and drawing me farther into the haze of lust she created.

"Touch yourself, hellcat. I want to hear what you sound like."

It was so easy to forget that Merri was no blushing virgin. She may look as innocent as the cliché girl next door, but she was pure siren when she obeyed my command without delay. "Like this?" she asked, sliding her fingers through her slick folds. "Or like this?"

This time she sank two fingers inside herself, her back arching slightly and her words cutting off on a soft gasp.

"Don't fucking fake it," I snapped, knowing she was putting on a show. "Play with your clit until you're dripping on the bed. If I'm going to come, so the fuck are you."

This time, the gasp was real. She looked at me, and her eyes flared with a desire that matched my own.

"You can't come if you don't even take yourself out of those sweats," she challenged.

Oh, I probably could at this point, but I didn't want that. If I was finally about to break my self-inflicted celibacy, then I was going to fucking do it right.

I reached down, taking myself in hand over the top of the cloth, squeezing the base of my cock and noting the way she stared at me while I did. I couldn't help my smug grin. Merri was the one who was used to putting on a show, but she didn't know what to do with herself when she was on the receiving end of one.

Another punch of lust swept through the room, this one significantly stronger than the last. I couldn't help but wonder if that was because it was real. *Her* lust, not just her using her succubus power to manipulate my own.

Precum leaked from my dick, leaving a damp spot on the gray fabric. Fuck it. I shoved the waistband down and freed my throbbing length, letting her see exactly what she was doing to me.

"Show me how you like to be touched," she rasped.

"You first."

Her eyes lifted to meet mine, a slight challenge in them, but it seemed that, for once, she was too desperate to play any games. She wanted what I was offering. Badly.

Parting her thighs wider, she trailed her fingertip over her clit, dragging a moan from her at the contact.

"Keep going," I urged, my voice rough with my own pent-up need.

She worked her clit faster, her back arching and hips rolling in time with the movements. The perfume of her arousal filled the space, making my cock pulse in my grip. I squeezed hard around the base, working to stave off the threatening climax.

Not yet.

Not until I see her come.

"Oh fuck."

"Come for me," I rasped. "I won't give you what you need until you do."

I could see the conflict on her face, and I knew from previous discussions with Sin that succubi and incubi could have trouble reaching orgasm before their partners. Many of them needed their partner's release to authentically achieve their own. It wasn't impossible, but it was difficult.

"Please," she whimpered, her hand moving in tight circles as she chased the pleasure she so clearly wanted.

"Yes." It was barely a whisper as I stood and crossed the room, not stopping until I stood at the end of the bed.

"Malice?"

My little succubus nearly stopped what she was doing when she realized I'd changed positions, but her gaze went to my straining cock, and the focus on our shared goal returned.

"Are you ready?" I asked, giving myself a careful stroke. My eyes rolled back in my head, a soft grunt escaping at the sensation pulsing through me.

"Beyond."

Me too, hellcat. Me fucking too.

"Don't hold back," I ordered, giving myself another cursory

stroke. Her eyes were locked on the movements, memorizing them as if there was going to be some kind of test once this was over. I shifted, planting my feet wider apart and reaching down with my other hand to give my balls a squeeze.

Merri moaned, her cheeks stained red with her arousal. "More," she begged.

Breaking my no-contact rule, I reached for her, snagging her by the ankles and yanking until she was nearly flush with my thighs, that pretty pussy so close all I had to do was notch myself at her entrance.

"Finish yourself off, Merri. Right fucking now. I can't wait any longer."

Her breath hitched, and her fingers moved fast and hard, eyes never leaving my cock as I stroked in earnest. The climax hit me hard enough that I had to brace myself with my free hand on her thigh, the euphoria buckling my knees and erupting from me in powerful waves I had no desire to stop. I'd have been embarrassed at how fast it happened, but Merri's cries of my fucking name shut that down before it could take hold.

"Give it to me, hellcat. You got my orgasm. Now give me yours."

Her eyes lifted and held mine as she did just that. The sight of her finding her pleasure was a beauty so perfect it cut straight through me. I'd never known intimacy like it, and despite all my claims of keeping up boundaries, I knew she'd just knocked each and every one of them down.

I came again, the pleasure so sharp it bordered on painful as stripes of my cum joined the evidence of my first orgasm on her thighs. All it would take was my fingers pushing my seed inside her to beat Sin and Chaos to the task we'd been assigned. That thought terrified me as much as it thrilled me.

Backing up, I put my dick away and raised my mental barriers so fast there was no way she didn't feel it. There was no question as to if she'd fed. I could feel my essence leaving my body as she'd done it.

Her skin was dewy and glowing, the dark circles under her eyes gone, her hair vibrant and shining.

Me, on the other hand? I hadn't been this weak since Hel's ritual. Truth be told, that ritual was probably the reason this was hitting me so hard. I hadn't had a chance to test my powers the way the others had, but I knew I was far from my physical peak. My limbs were heavy and sluggish, eyelids drooping. Instead of retreating to my room, I fell onto the bed and succumbed to sleep.

The last thing I registered before fully losing consciousness was the brush of Merri's lips across my forehead and her softly whispered, "Thank you."

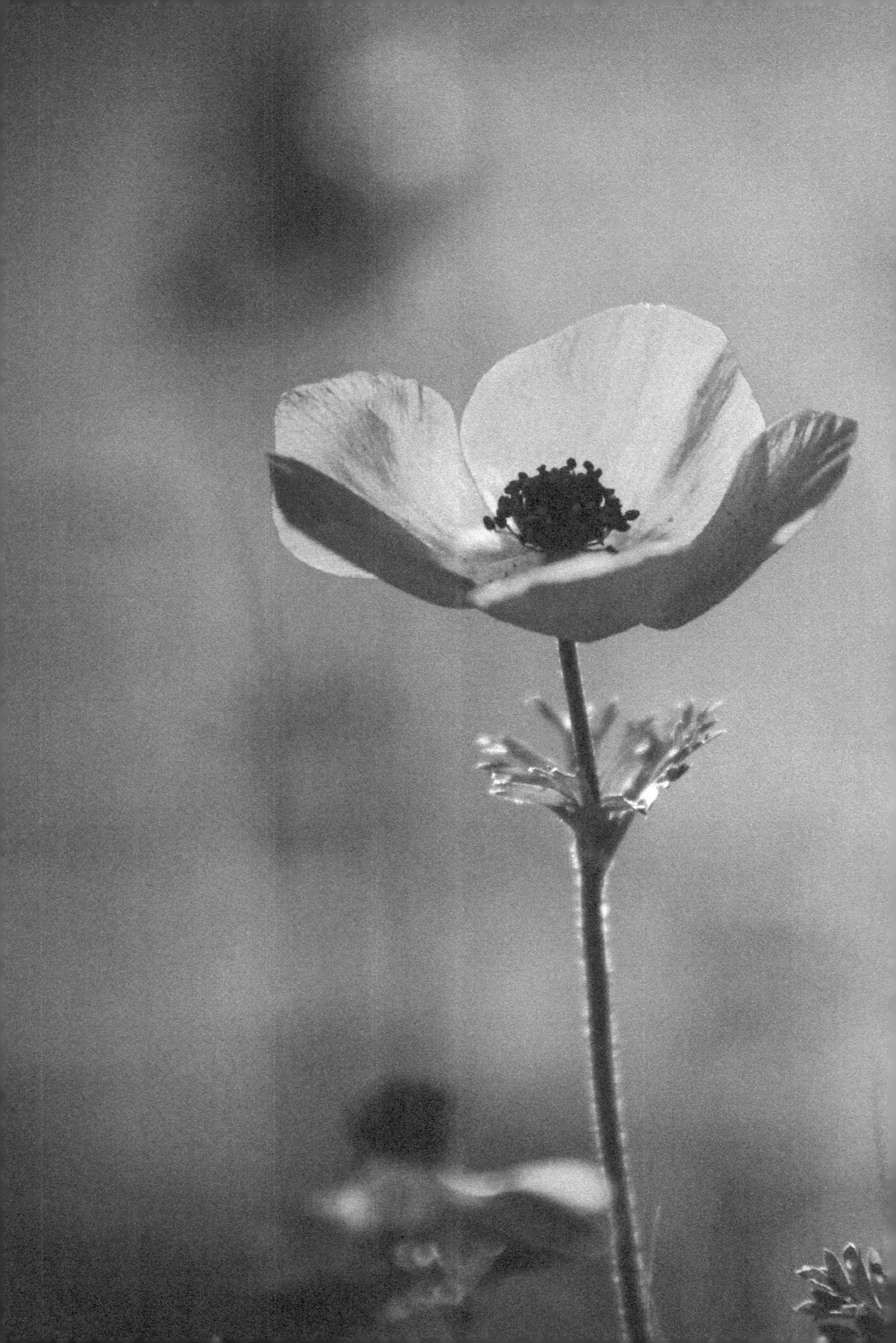

CHAPTER TWENTY

MERRI

The singing in my blood as Malice's lust-filled energy pulsed through me sent me into a euphoric haze I hadn't experienced, maybe ever. Feeding in person, in the same room, while touching each other was something I'd avoided for so long. I hadn't associated it with anything other than death and heartbreak.

Until now.

Rolling my head, I studied Malice's form. He was turned away from me, sprawled on his stomach with his face toward the door.

"I'm not sure what the appropriate etiquette is here. Should I thank you, or . . ."

He didn't respond.

Oh no.

Oh fuck.

I sat up, panic clawing away my afterglow.

"Mal," I whispered, giving his shoulder a shake. "Oh, please don't be dead."

A soft snore was his only response.

Oh, thank God.

I wasn't a two-time murderer, after all. Malice took a deep breath and rolled on his side, murmuring, "The virus's R_0 is seven. Brilliant, work, I know."

Was he dreaming about creating a plague?

"Um, have a nice blight, I guess," I mumbled, pressing a soft kiss to his forehead before swinging my legs off the other side of the bed so I could go clean myself up.

Malice's cum was sticky on my skin, and as much as part of me loved it, I knew I wouldn't if I walked around with him all over me. Cum was sexy for about two minutes. Then it cooled and congealed and got... weird.

I padded into my bathroom and turned on the faucet, my mind drifting as I waited for the water to warm up. Tonight had been a series of strange and unexpected events, first with the nearly starving thing, then the Grim coming to my rescue part, all to be followed up by a little mutual masturbation with good old Pestilence. I grimaced. No more referring to him by his horseman title. It was decidedly *unsexy*.

Jesus, he hadn't given me an STI when he came on me, had he?

Fuck, how would I even check for something like that? Supernaturals were immune as a rule, but he was sort of the most infectious person on the planet so...

The last thing I needed was some sort of super-herpes.

I bet there wasn't any kind of medication to help manage symptoms.

Shit, I needed to talk to Andi. I was spiraling. I could feel it coming.

Freshly cleaned, I came out of the bathroom and quickly changed into a pair of leggings and a cozy sweatshirt. Malice was still snoring and talking in his sleep, definitely down for the count. That was good. I needed to use this to my advantage because he wouldn't like what I was about to do.

Andi was the only person I could share any of this with. While she may not be a supernatural, she'd still understand what I was feeling right now and help ground me. She'd had all the sex, multiple times compared to my one-and-done status. I clearly wasn't prepared for what being intimate with someone in real life would do to me. Physically or mentally.

Was this PTSD?

Fuck, I needed my phone. All it took was a little cum, and I was a disaster. Go figure. Lilith would die of laughter if she could see me now.

With the softest steps known to man, I crept out of my room and down the hall to Mal's lair. Grim was probably locked in his tower with his plants and storm clouds, for which I was incredibly thankful in this moment. But Sin and Chaos could return at any time, if they hadn't already. The last thing I needed was for one or more of the Grumpy Gang to find me somewhere I didn't belong.

I paused outside his room so I could take a centering breath. Technically I wasn't breaking and entering since the door was already cracked open. So why did I feel like I was about to set off an alarm that would have the horseman running my way prepared for battle in under a second?

Because you know he wouldn't want you snooping around, and after everything he just shared with you, it feels like a major violation of his trust?

I scowled at that pesky inner voice, muttering, "Shut up. I'm just reclaiming what belongs to me. In and out. Easy peasy."

Clearly I wasn't buying what I was selling because my hand was totally trembling as I pushed Mal's door the rest of the way open and stepped inside. I hadn't been in here before, and I barely knew the man, but somehow this room felt like *him*. For starters, his cologne or natural musk or whatever it was filled the air. Right now, all that served to do was make my body react to memories of his ragged breaths and the way he'd grunted as he spilled his seed all over me.

Down, girl.

The room itself was pretty sterile, which was hilarious, all things considered. The bedding was a blend of navy and gray. The wooden bedframe was the same deep color as his desk, which housed a couple of computer monitors, both of them currently dark. Aside from the impressive display of tech, this could've been a dorm room for all the personality it didn't have.

Understanding how private and locked down Malice was, the lack of personality made sense. There was nothing here anyone could use against him. No photos, no trinkets, no potential weakness to exploit.

That worked in my favor. It simply meant fewer places to hide things, like pilfered phones.

Yanking open his desk drawers, I rifled through each one, finding nothing more than pens, sticky notes, a few random cables that must've gone to his electronics, and a headset or three. Boring, and not at all what I wanted.

With a huff, I spun around and eyed his closet, thinking that maybe there might be a secret stash or safe of some kind hidden at the back. I opened the door, and another wave of his scent accosted me. I had to ignore the flutters it set off in my lower belly.

Not the time, Meredith.

A cursory search revealed nothing beyond a startling amount of flannel and dark hoodies. Maybe when this was over, he'd let me take him shopping for a wardrobe refresh?

I shook my head. Once this was over, he'd be long gone. They'd be rid of me.

"If I were a sneaky horseman of the apocalypse, where would I hide my captive's phone?" I murmured, narrowing my eyes as I scanned the room.

All that remained were the bed and a nightstand. The nightstand was way too obvious. He definitely wouldn't hide a contraband item there. But maybe under the bed?

Dropping to my knees, I crouched low so I could peer under the footboard. Besides a few stray dust bunnies, there was nothing to find.

Under the mattress, then?

I was more than a little sweaty and breathing hard when I

finished checking under both the box spring and the king-size pillow-topped mattress. Hell, I even stuck my hands inside the pillowcases to make sure he hadn't squirreled it away in there.

Nothing.

Sighing, I sat down on the bed in defeat before making a last-ditch effort and pulling open the nightstand drawer. And there it was, plugged in and everything.

Well, fuck. I wasn't sure what that said about Malice and his thoughts about me. Was he not worried about me finding my phone? Did he think I didn't have the lady balls to try? Or was I supposed to find it?

My hand hovered over the slim device, wondering if this was some sort of trap.

Didn't matter. If it was, there's not much more these men could take from me anyway. I'd rather risk it so I could talk to Andi than fear the repercussions. Better to beg forgiveness than ask permission.

Snatching the phone, I unplugged it and tapped the screen, surprised when it woke up and I saw the passcode had been disabled. Had he been snooping? Of fucking course he had.

I sighed, knowing there wasn't a whole lot to find. I kept all my X-rated content on my computer. My phone was strictly for chatting with the handful of friends I'd managed to keep over the years and Lilith. Not really titillating stuff.

I tapped open my messaging app, my eyes widening when I saw that there were multiple threads that showed activity within the last few days. And I didn't mean unread messages. I meant responses. From *me*.

"You sneaky shit," I growled, clicking open my thread with Andi.

> ANDI:
> Hello, gorgeous. I'm back, refreshed, and can't wait to hear how you've been doing.
>
> ANDI:
> um . . . j'scuse it's been hours. Where are you?

I rolled my eyes at her made-up French but kept reading as her messages continued.

> ANDI:
> Ma'am. Are you alive? You haven't logged into the site in days. Do I need to send out a search party?
>
> ANDI:
> I'd take your silence personally, except you haven't even seen my messages yet.
>
> ANDI:
> Merri, it's not funny. You don't have your location on. I can't even find you if you've been abducted and murdered.
>
> ME:
> I'm fine. Just need some space.

Anger simmered in my veins upon seeing the reply I most definitely did not send. If this jerk cost me the only close friend I had, I was going to tear him a new asshole.

Panic clutched my chest as I realized if he had access to my phone, that meant he might have done irreparable damage to my client list as well. Even though Andi said I hadn't logged into the site, there was still the possibility Malice had opened my private message app linked to that account. Sure, I had it hidden in a special secret folder on my phone, but he'd already hacked me.

I couldn't afford to alienate any of my regulars. Even though I wasn't allowed to cam currently, eventually I'd go back, and I needed them to be there when I did. It was quite literally a matter of life and death. I had to be able to feed regularly. Who knew how long Malice's top-up would last? I couldn't count on the boys to see to me, and I'd barely made it three days without my camming.

Frantic, I opened the app and logged in, sagging in relief as I saw all of my messages appeared unread.

SIN

There were two from OriginalSin. Just flirty notes that suggested we schedule another session. But ShyGuy25 was more insistent.

> SHYGUY25:
>
> Good morning, beautiful. Hope you have a great day!
>
> SHYGUY25:
>
> You didn't have a stream tonight. Hope you're feeling okay. Would it be stalkery if I said I missed you?

I usually replied to him rapidly when he reached out. Whether I wanted to admit it or not, I enjoyed his attention. Guilt gnawed at me for my silence, even though it hadn't been intentional on my part.

> SHYGUY25:
>
> Merri, are you okay? Did I do something to upset you?
>
> SHYGUY25:
>
> It's been days. I'm getting worried. If I said something that made you uncomfortable, I'm really sorry.

It was the last one, though, that really got to me.

> SHYGUY25:
>
> Okay, I get it. You don't want to talk to me. I'll stop messaging you. But I really do hope you're okay.

Oh, fuck. Poor Cole. He didn't deserve this. He was kind and caring, and in another life, if we'd met in person and I wasn't a man-eating succubus, I'd definitely have given him a chance.

> **MERRI-GO-ROUND:**
> I'm so sorry, Cole. I'm here. I was super sick with food poisoning and couldn't get out of bed.

I was such a fucking liar, but what else could I say? I've been taken by the four horsemen and am being held hostage while they protect me from some big bad who wants to use me to get back at my aunt for trying to ruin the apocalypse. It was a little wordy.

There was no icon next to his name to show he was online, but I was still disappointed when my message remained unread.

I still needed to set things right with Andi, though, so I closed out of the app and returned to my text messages. I was about to type out a reply when I realized that this was not a text situation. This was a hit-the-call-button situation.

My heart lodged itself in my throat as I listened to the rings.

"Please, please, please," I chanted, about to give up hope when the fifth ring was interrupted by Andi's dry, unamused voice.

"Does this mean you've gotten enough space?"

"Andi," I breathed, my relief that she'd answered so intense I was lightheaded.

"I was worried about you, you know? And then *that's* how you respond? You need space."

I could hear the air quotes on the last word in her tone. "I'm sorry. Really. I didn't mean to hurt your feelings, I just..."

Once again, I couldn't reveal the actual truth, and I was pretty sure the food poisoning excuse was out, so all I could do was stay as close as possible to the truth and apologize. Even though I wasn't the one to do it, she still had gotten hurt. And for that, I really was sorry.

"I'm really sorry. There was a break-in at my place and I had to lay low for a few days. I wasn't allowed to talk to anyone while they were... investigating."

"Oh my God! Are you okay? Did they hurt you?"

"No, no. I'm fine. Promise. Just some damage to the place. And with what we do, I had to make sure there weren't any rogue clients after me."

I squeezed my eyes shut, hating the lies pouring out of my mouth even though they weren't that far from the truth.

"Ugh, fucking stalkers. I get it. I had one once. He thought he was God's gift to the world. Do you need somewhere to stay? I can make up my couch."

"No, I'm okay. Staying with some local friends for the time being." Andi didn't know I was in London and now didn't really seem like the time to mention it.

"Are they hot friends? Male friends? Big, strong, strapping protective types?"

If we were on a video call—which she *loathed*—I knew I'd see her brows waggling.

I let out a little laugh. "How did you know?"

"Because the first thing I'd do after a break-in is find myself a bodyguard or two."

I almost said, *how about four*, but heavy footsteps in the hall stopped me. "Oh, call waiting! It might be the investigator. Call you later!"

Hanging up before she could get another word out, I shoved my phone into the pocket of my hoodie and stood, trying and failing to look innocent as the door swung open.

Chaos stood in the doorway, a scowl on his ruggedly handsome face. I was so busted. But at least it wasn't Malice staring me down right now.

The horseman crossed his arms over his chest and leveled his gaze on me. "Start talking, Red."

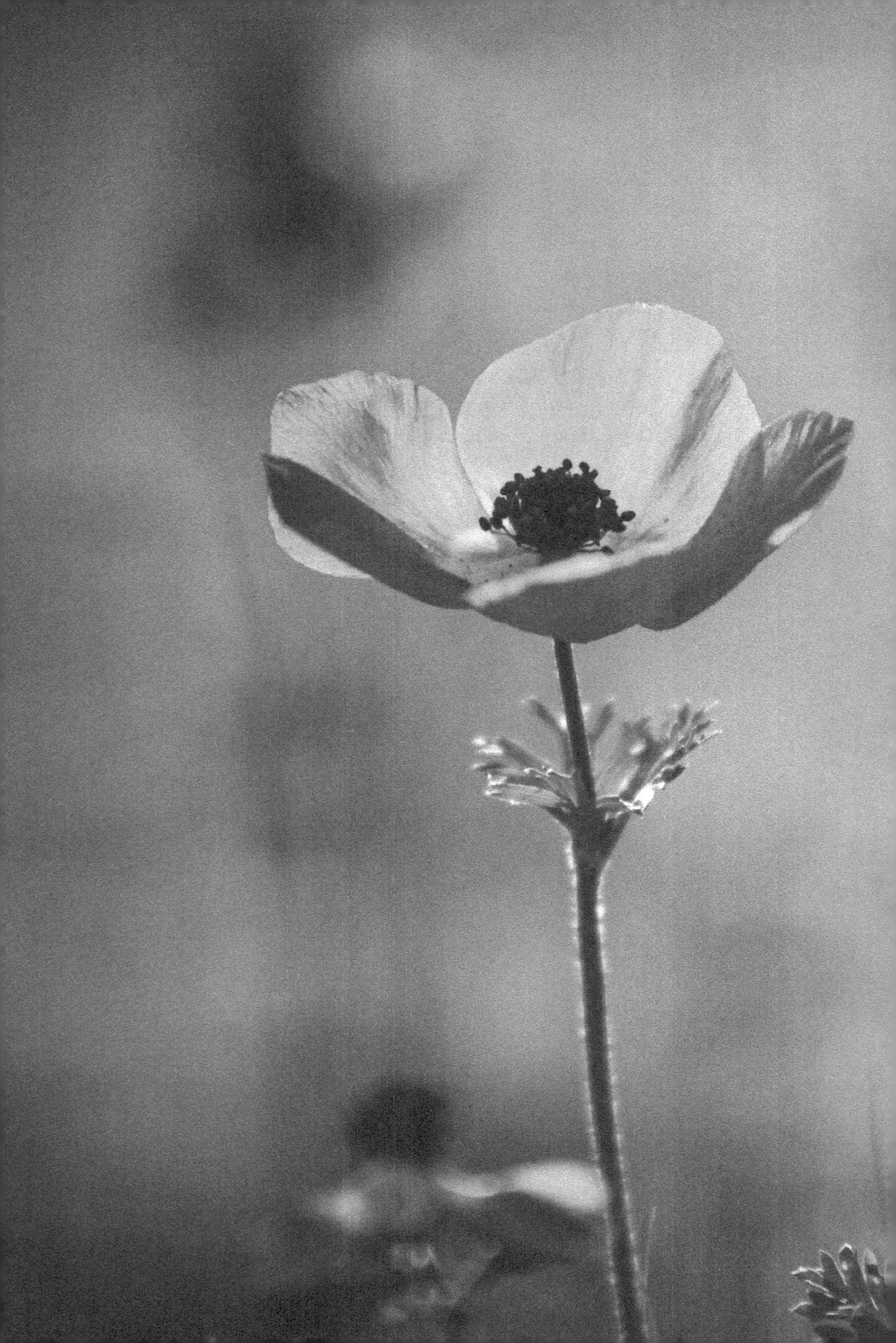

CHAPTER
TWENTY-ONE
CHAOS

It had been far too long since I'd felt this degree of calm deep in my bones. I'd pummeled more than my share of opponents tonight, finally releasing all that pent-up violence within me, and it was good. Real fucking good, if I was being honest. For the first time in who knows how long, it felt like I could breathe easy.

I shifted my duffel bag, hoisting it up higher on my shoulder as I prowled through the foyer, eager for a shower and my bed. I might actually sleep tonight. What a novel concept. It had been nothing but fitful nights filled with restless limbs, tangled sheets, and racing thoughts.

As I rounded the corner and headed into the hallway that housed our rooms, I paused outside Sin's door, listening for signs he'd returned. Nothing hinted at his presence. If he was home, there'd be some music blasting, or he'd be playing one of his many instruments to pass the time. Merri's room was next, and I tried to ignore my body's need to peek inside and check on her. She hadn't looked well when I saw her last. Grim's no-camming rule hit her harder than I think any of us were prepared for.

I didn't hear anything coming from her room either, so I assumed she'd gone to bed early. Imagine my surprise then when I heard the soft murmur of her voice coming from Malice's room.

A low, rumbling growl built in my throat. Jealousy burned through me, unwelcome and unbidden. I had absolutely no excuse for it. Not one I was willing to admit to, anyway.

"What happened to that adamant insistence you weren't going to get involved?" I grumbled under my breath. "Such a fucking hypocrite. You've got the self-control of a sailor in port, Malice."

Her laughter floated through the wood, and I reacted without thinking, opening the door and bracing myself to find the two of them making the beast with two backs. I couldn't be held responsible for what I did to Malice, but I was pretty sure it would end in me turning his face into nothing but meat once my rage took hold.

I never had been good at sharing my toys. Or my weapons, for that matter.

Fists clenched, I stood in the doorway, fully prepared to make Malice feel my wrath. Instead I found myself equally charmed and intrigued. Merri stood beside Mal's bed, fully clothed, hands in the pocket of her hoodie, eyes wide, and looking guilty as hell.

"Start talking, Red."

"It's not what it looks like," she said.

"It never is."

"I was bored."

"So you decided to go snooping?"

She winced and took her plump bottom lip between her teeth. "Kind of?"

"Find anything good in here? Mal's not known for having much of an attachment to material belongings."

"So I've learned," she said with a heavy sigh as she walked around the bed and came closer.

Narrowing my eyes at her, I asked, "What have you done with Malice? There's no scenario in existence where he'd leave you to your own devices in his domain."

"He's having a nap."

I glanced at the obviously empty bed. "I find that hard to believe. Malice doesn't nap."

"Don't know what to tell ya, big guy. He does now."

"Where?" I demanded, knowing I'd have seen him if he'd been sprawled out on one of the big couches in the front room.

"Erm, my bed?"

"Are you asking me?"

"No?"

I couldn't help but laugh, even if the thought of him in her bed made zero sense. "Why is he in your bed and not his own, Red?"

She shrugged, trying to brush past me, but I caught her by the arm.

"Don't ignore my question."

"That's where he fell asleep. I wasn't going to kick him out."

"But why was he there in the first place?"

I appreciated nothing about the jealousy twisting in my gut. There was only one reason Malice would be in her room, and I hated it. I hated it because even though I hadn't made any moves myself, he wasn't supposed to be the one to seduce her.

"Well . . . I'm a little fuzzy on the specifics."

"What?" I all but shouted. If Mal had taken advantage of her, I'd have his head on a pike faster than Vesuvius wiped out Pompeii.

"No, no, nothing bad. I've been starving since the attack, and, um . . . he helped me."

My eyes narrowed once more as I took her in. She clearly wasn't starving now. In fact, she was luminous. Everything about her seemed to glow. Her hair had an extra sheen, her eyes filled with inner light, her skin radiant and youthful. Merri had always been beautiful. No one could argue that, but now? She was breathtaking.

"I see."

"You're mad."

"No."

"Your jaw is clenched."

"It's always like this."

She raised a skeptical brow. "You know how when a woman says she's fine and she's never actually fine? That's you right now."

"It never should've gotten to this point. You shouldn't ever be unclear about the details of your feeds."

"If it makes you feel better, that part is crystal clear. It was the before times. There was a cellar and Daddy Death and passing out in an elevator...I think?"

No. That didn't make me feel a damn bit better. Also, *Daddy Death*? Grim was in on this bullshit too? Fuck me.

"Merri, if you are in need, you have a responsibility to ask us for assistance."

"When the fuck am I supposed to do that? You avoid me at every turn, Mal ignores me, and Grim won't even touch me. All I have is Sin, and he wasn't here. Neither were you, in case you forgot. Apparently I have to be on death's door—or in his wine cellar—for any of you to help me."

Had it really been that bad? Was I off releasing my pent-up violence while Merri had been nearly starved to death?

What kind of protector was I?

One who nearly let her get taken by a Knight. One who couldn't recognize her suffering. One who didn't deserve a moment of her time.

That stopped now.

"Go get changed."

Her eyes widened at my abrupt shift in topic. "What? What's wrong with what I'm wearing?"

"We're going to the gym. Meet me down there in two minutes."

"But I—"

"Two minutes, Red. No arguing."

I didn't give her any room to fight me on this. Turning away from her, I strode back down the hall and took the stairs, heading for the gym.

Merri was going to learn something useful tonight. And I was going to teach her.

Tension built in my muscles as I awaited her arrival, the clock on the wall ticking down the seconds until she was officially late. If I had to, I'd toss her over my shoulder and haul her to the gym myself, but I wanted to see if she'd heed my command.

Ten seconds past my time limit, she stepped into the room, her long hair up in a high ponytail, body now clad in a matching set of skintight baby-pink workout clothes. Fuck. She couldn't help herself. The woman was my every fantasy come to life.

"Okay, big guy, I'm here. What do you want from me?" she asked, hands on her hips.

"You need to learn how to defend yourself. You were completely vulnerable during the attack, unable to fight or resist the thrall of the Knight. I can't do anything about the latter, but I certainly can help amend the former."

A slight smirk tugged at her lips. "You want to teach me how to fight?"

"Yes."

"Can I have a sword?"

My expression fell flat. "No. No weapons."

"But..."

"Aside from the danger of putting a blade in the hands of someone who can barely throw a punch, you are unlikely to be armed during any attack unless you make a point to be at all times. You need to be able to use your body to defend yourself before anything else. It is the first and only weapon you can count on."

"Not true."

"How do you figure?"

"Well, I'm a succubus. That comes with its own arsenal, doesn't it?"

I shook my head, not remotely about to entertain the thought of her unleashing her sexual wiles on me. "You were the first to admit you don't have a good sense of control of your power. We're sticking to the basics." I pointed down at the mat in front of me. "Get your ass over here."

She did as I asked—okay, demanded—but she muttered under her breath the entire way. "Isn't that the whole point of practice? To get better at something?"

Ignoring her attitude, I positioned myself in front of her. "Let's begin."

We went through the requisite moves all people should know to counter an advancing attacker. She did quite well, especially when learning how to break a hold from behind, but now it was time to test what she learned, a.k.a. employ the element of surprise.

"See? I told you I was a quick study," she said, pride suffusing her tone. "Now can I have a—" Her words cut off with a shriek as I tackled her to the mat, pinning her smaller body under mine.

"What was that?" I rasped, my lips at her ear. "Not so confident now, are you?"

"You cheated," she grunted, the breath mostly knocked out of her.

I pushed up a little, my eyes finding hers. Before I could come back with a snide retort, I noticed the way her body felt beneath mine. Soft to my hardness, sweet and supple while I was rough and rugged. I breathed in the faint scent of her perfume as the reminder of how kissing her had felt took over every other thought I had. Without conscious thought, I pressed my hips into her, making us both groan at the friction.

Fuck, I wanted to kiss her again. No, I wanted to drive inside her and make her whimper my name. I could. We weren't separated by much more than a few layers of fabric. If she'd let me, all it would take was a few tugs until we were bare.

I rocked into her again, wondering how attached she was to her pants. Maybe I'd just rip them open and spare the effort of pulling them off.

Her lips curled up in a wicked grin as she arched her back, pressing her perfect breasts into my chest.

I dipped down, my lips less than an inch from hers when it hit me. She'd played me. The second our eyes had locked, she'd hypnotized me with some succubus spell.

"You little..." I growled. "Now who's cheating?"

Rolling her hips, she gave me a soft moan that I felt all the way to my cock. "You started it. Now we're even."

I couldn't argue her logic, so I went on the defensive instead. "Do you think an attacker will fight fair? You'll be lucky if they even announce their presence."

She wriggled under me again, reminding me that I was still absently grinding my cock against her.

"Fuck," I barked, pushing myself up and off her.

I needed distance, or I was liable to fall deeper under her spell and let her feed as deeply as she required. Would it be so bad? There were far worse ways to go. I'd witnessed them on the battlefield.

"What now, big guy?" she asked, jumping to her feet. "We gonna go another round or two?"

There was no missing the sexual innuendo layered in her words. Or the way her lips curled up as she took in my response to them.

"No. You're clearly not ready for more intermediate work. Your form is all wrong, and you're weak as hell." I pointed to the punching bag in the corner. "Go spend some time on that."

"Fine. But I'd better not catch you checking out my ass while I work out this... tension."

Heaving a sigh, I turned away from her. Just the mention of her ass had my eyes desperate for the sight. As her soft grunts and the sound of her punches landing filled the space, I ran a hand over my face and worked to regain control of my aroused body.

My mind drifted back to how I felt coming home tonight. I shook my head and swallowed back a groan. So much for feeling relaxed.

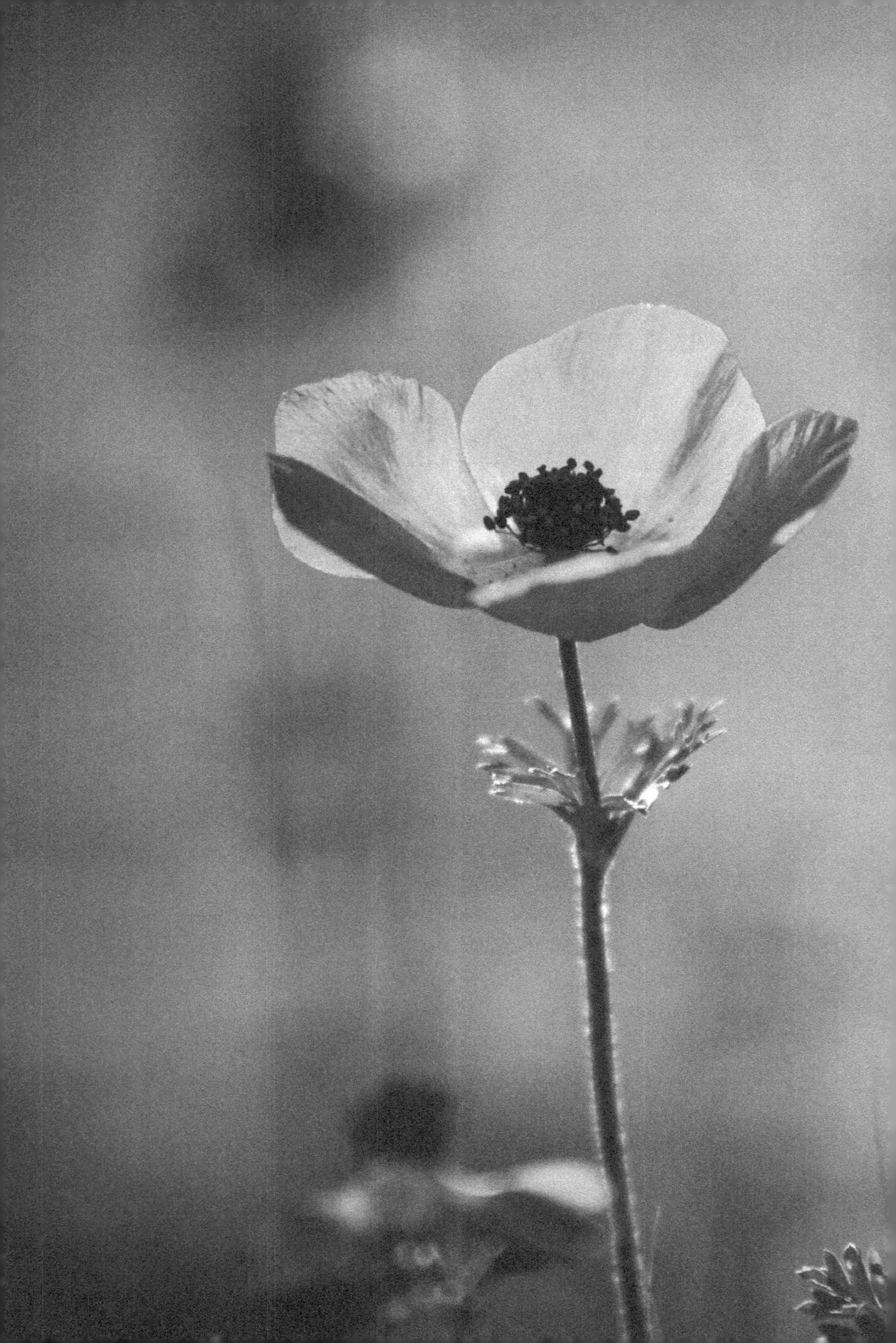

CHAPTER TWENTY-TWO

SIN

Have you ever been so hungry your stomach ached? That was me right now. I was starved beyond reason. Desperate to feed. The only place I could safely do that was within the walls of *Iniquity*.

Lust was thick in the air, potent and all-consuming, but I forced myself to hold off. Lilith was very clear that she didn't want to share her source, and I wasn't stupid enough to try and steal a piece of metaphorical bacon off her plate. Besides it being hers to take when she wanted, the rules of this club revolved around consent. The patrons consented to her feeding, they consented to whatever acts they committed, and most importantly, they hadn't consented to me taking a damn thing from them. If I did, I'd be on my ass in the street so fast I wouldn't know what had happened.

As if mere thought could summon her, Lilith appeared beside my corner booth. It was dark up here, but there was enough light on the dance floor below that I could still make her out easily enough. She was dressed in a black leather gown, her tits nearly spilling out of the exaggerated W of the neckline. Her dark hair was down tonight in loose curls that reminded me of the starlets I once knew. And, as always, her lips were blood red.

"Famine. To what do I owe the pleasure?"

The words were casually offered, but there was nothing casual about them.

"Oh, you know me, Lil. I'm here for a good time, not a long time."

Anger flashed in her eyes and her fae prince companion took a seat across from me, the thin gold chain connecting them glittering every time he moved. "Speak to her like that again, and your time will be shorter than you know."

"You look like absolute shit, Sinclair," Lilith observed, ignoring her pet.

Taking my cue from her, I did the same. I knocked back the glass of bourbon I'd been nursing. "You think? I'm starving. You failed to mention that the little gift of yours is *celibate*." I practically hissed the word like it was something contagious.

Her expression shifted to an exaggerated mockery of innocence. "Oh, did I forget to share that bit of information? Forgive me. I thought, based on your reputation, it wouldn't be an issue."

"Well, it is," I said, very aware of the pout in my words.

Crombie snickered, his muttered, "Amateur," making me grind my teeth.

"What I'm not understanding is why you're here, in my club, attempting to feed off my patrons when you could find a willing meal on any street corner in London."

Why did the thought of seducing a random person off the street make my stomach churn? It was always strangers for me. I never needed a connection to feed. Hell, I didn't *want* one.

Instead of attempting to explain any of that, I went with the explanation I hoped would serve me best. "I thought you'd appreciate my discretion. Didn't want to draw too much attention to my whereabouts lest I accidentally get spotted with *you know who*."

Lilith's eyes flashed as she slid into the spot next to her companion, but I couldn't tell if it was with amusement or anger. "Is that so?"

I nodded.

"Then I suppose I have no choice but to extend you a very limited pass."

"Lilypad, surely he should be at home, fulfilling his duty?" Crombie murmured in her ear. "It's not our responsibility to be his babysitter. He's a grown horseman."

Lilith's eyes dropped down my body, and her lips twitched up in a smirk. "He certainly is."

Crombie snarled, and I would have sworn I heard thunder.

Lilith giggled and patted his knee. "I was simply agreeing with you, darling. No need to throw a tantrum. And besides, you just proved the point I was about to make. Just because a man is grown doesn't mean he won't find himself in need of a little TLC from time to time."

I wasn't sure if I should thank her for that one. It seemed like it might have been a thinly veiled insult. "I need my strength if I'm going to be at my best for her." That much was true. I didn't want them to know we'd already almost let her get taken by the Knights of Pride. Something told me Lilith would be a lot less accommodating if she found that out.

You're assuming she doesn't already know.

A little shiver shot down my spine at the thought. Lilith seemed to know everything, but since she hadn't brought it up, I sure as shit wasn't going to. I was afraid of very little—godlike being that I was—but this creature in front of me held one of those places, right next to facing my true death.

She met and held my stare, and while her lips were still curled in a playful smile, her voice was pure ice. "I'll let you feed from one of my girls. You can have your choice, but"—she held up a slender finger, the pointed tip of her nail stained black—"there's an expiration date on my generosity. Every second you are here is one less opportunity for you to accomplish our shared goal. I didn't work this hard for everything to all come crumbling down around me. Figure your shit out, Sinclair. Do what you were made for."

It took every ounce of bravado I possessed not to shrink into my seat as my fucking balls threatened to shrivel up under her glare.

"If it were up to me, she'd already be in the family way, Lil."

Her lip curled up in distaste at my use of her shortened name, and I swallowed, speaking quickly to distract her from my faux pas. "She's not interested in fucking any of us. I don't take what's not freely offered."

"Have you never heard of seduction?" Crombie crooned.

This motherfucker.

I glared at him.

"Of course I have," I snapped.

"Well, you can't be very good at it." He trailed his knuckles down Lilith's arm. "If you were, your little problem would already be solved."

"I'm the fucking king of seduction, you wingless firefly."

Lilith had to tug on the chain connecting Crombie to her to stop him from going for my throat at my insult.

Undeterred, I continued. "She wants love. She needs it." That was my takeaway from our little heart-to-heart the other night. It didn't seem pertinent to mention that she was also terrified she was going to kill anyone lucky enough to bury themselves inside her. That problem would be easily solved, the other matter...not so much.

"And?" Lilith prompted.

"That's not something any of us are capable of giving her."

One dark, perfectly shaped eyebrow lifted as she assessed me. "Aren't you?"

"What the hell do we know about love? We exist purely to raise chaos and destruction. We're the walking antithesis of love. I mean, come on, Grimsby can't even fucking touch her."

"Hmmm," she mused, but didn't elaborate. For some reason, that only made the urge to squirm in my seat stronger.

"Just let me feed and I'll get out of your hair, okay?"

Again with that twist of discomfort in my gut. I knew what I wanted, but Merri had to be willing and ready to be with me. Even if we were only feeding. With her camming situation off the table, that meant I couldn't participate any longer. We'd been explosive even though we weren't in the same room. I'd left our chat completely sated. Satisfied. Fulfilled. Without the ability to engage with her in that way, I needed to supplement. I didn't have to enjoy it, though.

Plenty of creatures fed themselves without particularly enjoying their meal. This would be like that. A dry, tasteless sandwich instead of a mouthwatering feast.

"Are you certain?" Lilith asked.

I nodded.

She slid out of the booth and rose to her full height, Crombie following immediately after. Her blue eyes sparkled as she leaned down and whispered, "As you wish, darling."

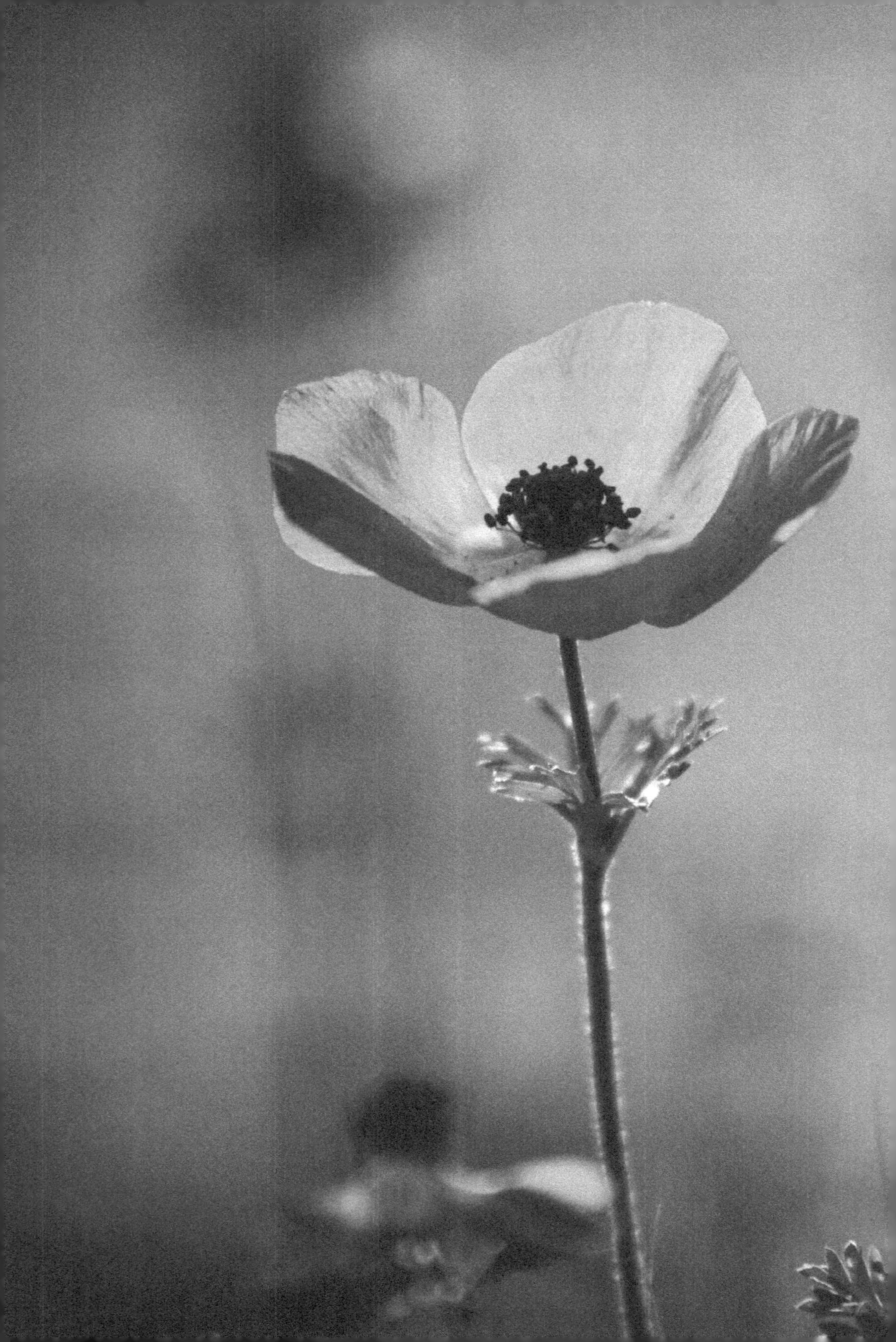

CHAPTER
TWENTY-THREE
MALICE

That sneaky little succubus had been in my room. I could smell it.

When I'd woken and she was gone, I thanked my lucky stars I didn't have to face up to what we'd done. I hadn't been so bloody vulnerable with anyone in centuries. I didn't like how raw I still felt about the whole thing. Or that part of me craved another round or ten.

This was why I hadn't wanted to get involved in the first place.

The rest of them didn't understand what it meant to have a woman crush you with her lies. To find out you had everything you wanted within your reach but were never given the chance to take it. Merri and her fucking womb were echoes of what Odette had used me for. Except this time I wouldn't be an unwitting sperm donor.

For just a moment, I'd thought maybe Merri was different. When she touched me so sweetly and refused to feed without my consent. But the first opportunity she'd had, the woman snuck into my room and rifled through my belongings.

She'd tried to disguise her pillaging, but I'd immediately spotted every item that was out of place. The slight dent in the pillow, the crease on the bedspread, the Post-its in a different position in the drawer. It was as obvious to me as if she'd spray-painted her name on the wall.

So what had all of that in her room been? A distraction? Her chance to get me out of the way?

Deep down, I knew it hadn't. There was no faking how ill she'd been, but knowing that did nothing to abate years' worth of anxious, intrusive thoughts.

I was only important to her when I was useful.

Anyone would have suited her needs.

She was going to use my vulnerabilities against me.

"Fucking hell."

Yanking open the drawer where I'd kept her cell phone, I stared at the cold, hard evidence right in front of me. All she'd wanted was her phone. Knocking me out with her feeding was a surefire way to keep me from stopping her.

Serves me right.

Feeling like a complete and utter knobhead, I spun out of the room and beelined for the bar cart in the main lounge. The only thing that would comfort me now was oblivion.

Not even turning on the lights, I made for the crystal decanter of Brimstone whiskey, pulling the stopper out and pouring myself a double—no, make that a triple.

"Good thing I went back and replenished our supply." Grim's deep voice startled me badly enough that I flinched, and some of the mind-numbing alcohol sloshed over the side of my glass.

"Motherfucker," I barked. "What the hell are you doing sitting in the shadows like that?"

"From the looks of it, the same as you," he said, holding up his own highball glass. "Cheers."

"Doubtful. You weren't the one who had to sacrifice your scruples tonight."

Not that it had taken much to convince me in the end. But who the hell wanted to be logical or fair when they were dead set on nursing a grudge?

"Oh yes, because it was such a hardship jerking yourself all over her. Fucking child," he grumbled.

"She sucked my soul out of my body through my dick, if you must know."

"Did she?"

I flopped into the chair opposite him and took a pull of the whiskey, relishing the way it burned. "Well, no. Not literally. But she might as well have. I see why Lilith kept her under lock and key. Merri is..."

Incandescent.

Captivating.

Mesmerizing.

Addictive.

"Potent," I finally said aloud.

"I'm sure that's why he wants her."

"She's the vessel. Pretty sure he'd want her if she had one tooth and was balding."

"Lucky for you, she's not."

I snorted, lifting my glass to my lips once more. "Lucky for us all."

"Mmm," Grim hummed, but I couldn't tell if it was in agreement.

Heavy footsteps in the hallway betrayed Chaos's presence before the rumble of him talking to himself reached my ears.

"Should've known better than to get a succubus under me. Of course she'd play a dirty fucking trick like that."

Grim opened his mouth to say something, but I held up a finger. I wanted to hear this.

"She used my own attraction to her against me. Tried to get me by the balls."

"Welcome to the club," I muttered, unable to stop the words from leaving my lips.

Grim raised a brow at me, his lips twitching with suppressed laughter.

The lights snapped on, leaving Grim and me to blink owlishly at the sudden shift.

"What the fuck is this? Book club for assholes?"

Grim looked around. "I see no books. Just alcohol and commiseration."

Chaos's brow raised at that. "Clearly you've never been to a book club." He stalked toward the cart and filled his own glass. "What are you commiserating about?"

"Do you really need to ask?" I countered.

"Don't see why you should be complaining," Chaos mumbled.

Oh, for fuck's sake. "You weren't here. Remember your little vanishing act so you could release your power? I would've gladly let you take this one for the team. Instead, I had to . . . let her in." I whispered the last part.

"Let her in? Like . . . your butt?" Sin's voice carried down the hall, stronger than it had been over the last few days.

I scoffed. "No. Not—What is wrong with you, Sinclair?"

He strode in, went straight for the decanter, and got himself a drink.

"We're going to need more whiskey," Grim said to himself.

"She's ruining everything," Sin answered.

The three of us exchanged looks before I sighed. "Fine, I'll ask. How is she ruining everything when you clearly just had a successful evening?"

He'd looked little better than a pile of three-day-old manure when he'd left this evening. Now he was the picture of health, all smoldering rockstar once more. Even with the chip on his shoulder.

"Because I couldn't enjoy it," he spluttered, his face twisted in confusion. "Like . . . at all. I think I'm obsessed with her. How did that happen? I don't get obsessed. They do."

"Trust me, you don't want her coming after you," Chaos said bitterly.

Sin's eyes narrowed, and he finally seemed to realize that the rest of us mirrored his mood. "What the fuck did I miss?"

"Hurricane Merri," I replied.

"You guys played with her without me?" The sulk in Sin's voice was damn near petulant. "That's not fair."

"She played with us. Well, from the sound of it, at least two of us." My traitor of a dick twitched at the memory of her whimpering my name as she writhed on her bed.

"Mal fed her while we were out."

Sin's gaze snapped to Chaos, absolute shock written all over his features. Then he turned on me.

"What happened to 'I'm never procreating again'?"

"You weren't here. Either of you," Grim said, surprising me by coming to my defense. "It was either Malice assist her or let her lapse into a coma."

"It was that bad?" Sin asked.

I nodded, remembering how poorly she'd been.

Grim shifted in his seat before clearing his throat. "She was starved. It's my fault. I took away her only source of sustenance."

"For good fucking reason."

Grim sighed, pinching the bridge of his nose. "Yes, but if this is the alternative, then we're going to have to figure out something else. We can hardly let her waste away before we accomplish our goal."

"I love that he says 'we' when he has no intention of participating," Sin said.

I rolled my eyes, ignoring him as usual. "I'm already working on a better firewall." It was far more complicated than that, but these three barely knew how to use their cell phones. It wasn't worth the breath to try and explain the nuanced details of my genius to them.

"And what if she needs to feed again before you have that up and running?" Chaos asked.

"She shouldn't. Most succubi and incubi only need to feed every week or so." Sin's brows were uncharacteristically furrowed.

"She's not most succubi." I said what he hadn't.

"So we don't know how often she'll need to feed?" Grim asked.

"You're saying she could need to take from one of us tomorrow? Or twice a day."

"That won't work. She drained me until I couldn't help but pass out."

Sin's frown deepened. "That's unusual. It must have been because she was so depleted."

"Or because he was," Chaos pointed out.

The four of us wore matching scowls at the reminder of Hel's trickery. When we got our hands on her, she was going to have one seriously bad day.

"Maybe a bit of both," I mused.

Sin nodded, though he still looked troubled.

"Where is she now?" Grim asked, his voice holding more than a hint of concern.

"Safely tucked away in her room. I took her to the gym for some self-defense training. Speaking of." His gaze shot to mine. "I thought you could help her learn how to shield her mind against thralls and compulsion. If we learned anything from the break-in, it's that she's severely lacking in those kinds of defenses."

Alarm shot through me at what he was implying. If I worked with her and taught her how to protect her psyche against these kinds of attacks, it would mean she and I would spend far too much time with our walls down. I'd have to see into her soul just as she'd see into mine.

But I was also the only one capable of teaching her. Shielding of that kind was sort of like building up an immunity, which, as an expert on spreading infection, was sort of my wheelhouse.

"Fine," I gritted out, already dreading it.

"Good. Malice will repair the firewall so Merri can get online and feed as well as teach her to protect her mind. Chaos will train her to defend herself physically."

Sin raised his glass. "I'll work on knocking her up. Grim will keep us lubricated with whiskey."

Grim rolled his eyes. "I will continue to keep my distance so I don't kill her."

"Annnd break," Sin said like we were a sports team about to return to the playing field.

"Why do we tolerate him?" I asked.

"Because we have to." Chaos sighed.

"Because you love me," Sin countered.

"He's not invited to the next book club," I said.

"Definitely not," Grim agreed.

"Book club?" Sin asked, confused.

The rest of us laughed, purposely keeping him out of the loop.

"You think this will become a regular thing, then?" Chaos asked.

"With Merri around? It's practically assured."

"To book club then?" Chaos said, holding up his glass.

"To book club," Grim and I said in unison.

Sin looked between the three of us, his frustration at being left out mounting. "What fucking book club?"

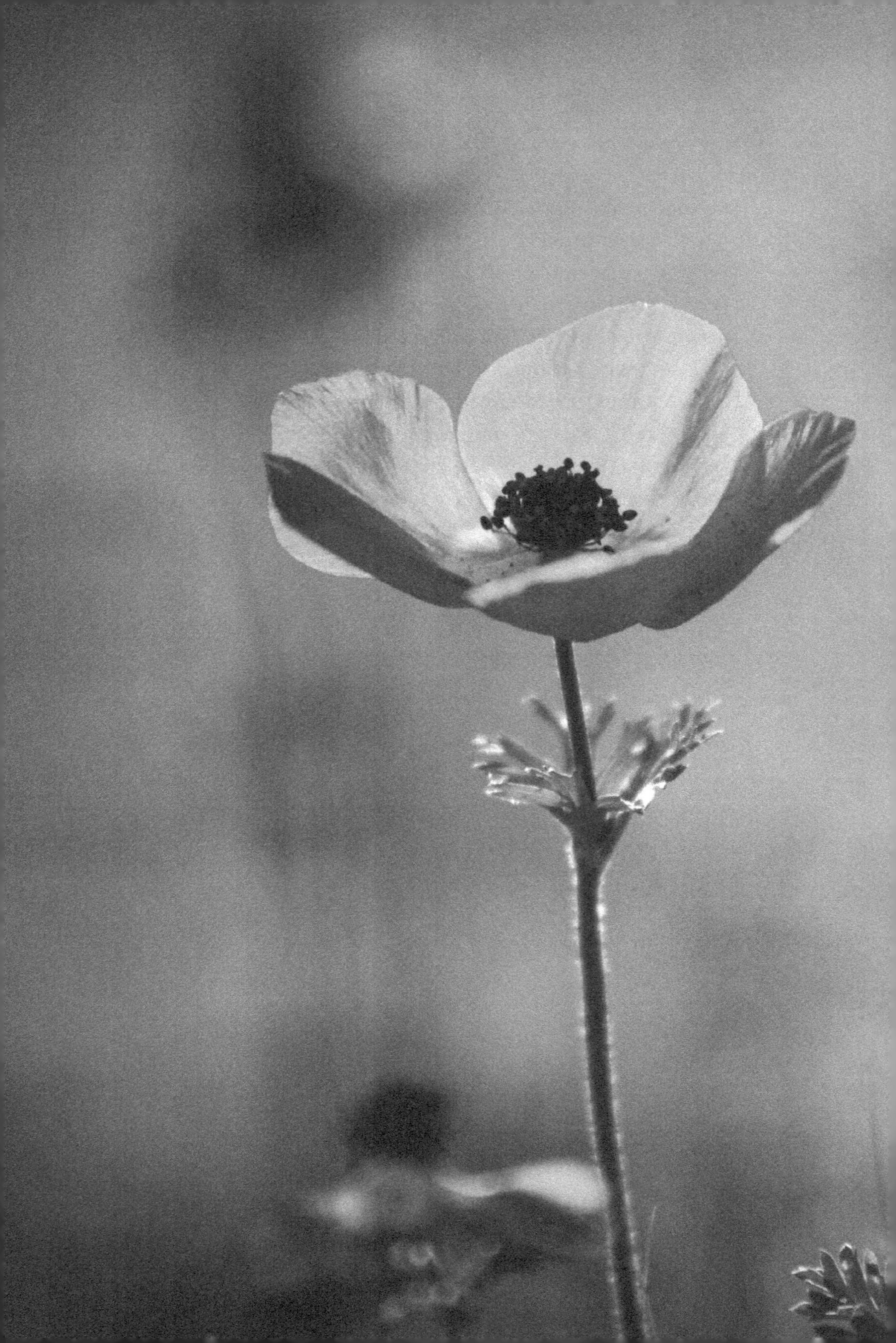

CHAPTER TWENTY-FOUR

MERRI

I tipped my head back, drinking in the salty sea air and the way the warm breeze caressed my skin. It was so good to be here, in my beautiful dream paradise, where I was safe and not being kidnapped by demons.

"Penny for your thoughts?"

My eyes snapped open, and a smile stretched across my face as I discovered my sexy dream man leaning over me.

"I wondered if you would be here."

"Miss me?"

"What would you say if I admitted I did?"

He brushed his knuckles across my cheek before he grabbed my hand and tugged me to standing. "Come on, let's have a sunset stroll. You can tell me all about what has you so tense."

"Is it that obvious?" I asked on a laugh.

He held his thumb and forefinger an inch apart. "Maybe just a little."

"And here I was thinking I was relaxed."

"Darling, your shoulders are so tight I'd wager even a deep tissue massage wouldn't unknot them."

"Deep tissue massages can be quite painful, you know."

"Not when I do them."

"Was that an offer?"

"Do you want it to be?"

Damn, my subconscious was a flirt.

I didn't answer him as we continued down the beach, our toes in the surf, fingers intertwined. Something else was weighing on my mind.

"Merri, I can feel you thinking. What's wrong?"

Apparently my subconscious decided I didn't need a sexy dream lover so much as a sexy dream therapist. Fair enough.

"Everything is so confusing right now. I feel like I can't breathe without doing something wrong."

"Because of them?" He stopped us and turned me to face him. "They have you trapped."

I wrinkled my nose as I considered the question. That was true to a point, but it was so much more complicated than that.

"I just feel so out of control of my own life. I mean, when the four horsemen show up and tell you they're kidnapping you for your own good, you don't exactly get a say in the matter."

Some unnamable emotion flickered in his eyes before he closed them and took a long, slow breath.

"I don't get a say in when I feed. I don't get a say in who I talk to. I don't even get a say in where I live. It's infuriating."

When he opened his eyes again, it was like he was staring straight into the depths of my soul. "So take back control."

"Wh-what?" I asked, laughing a little to disguise how off-center I felt.

"Take back control. It's your life. No one can tell you how to live. Nor should they."

"You say that like it's easy."

"It *is* easy. They only have control because you let them. So take. It. Back."

"B-but they're keeping me safe."

He shook his head, lips pressed into a thin line. "Are they?"

"They are the good guys."

"Ask yourself this question, Merri. Really think about it. They kidnapped you. They're mistreating you. Are they the heroes?"

He released my hand and stared intently into my eyes, one look conveying a truth I hadn't even let myself fully consider.

"Or are they the villains?"

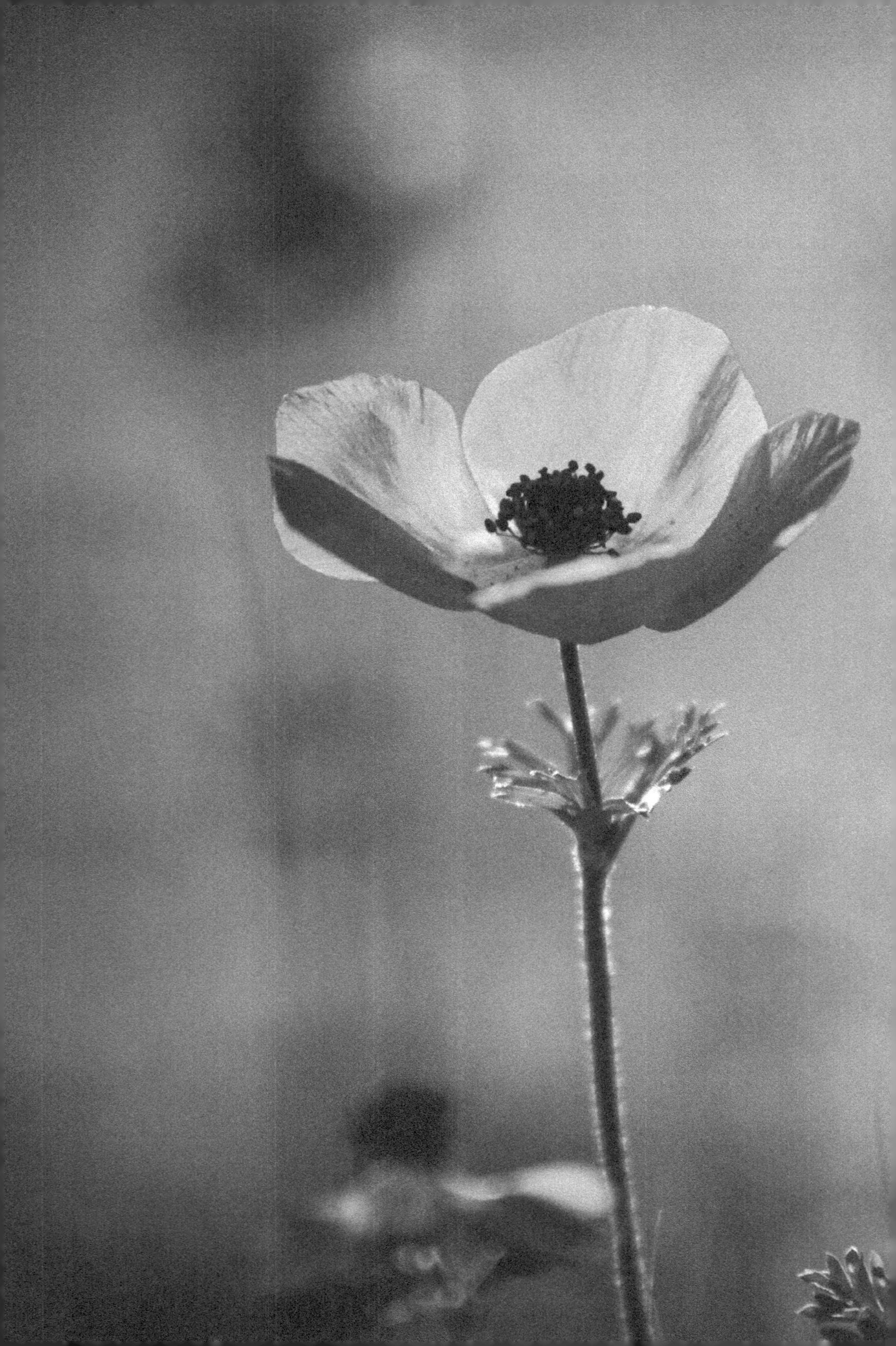

CHAPTER TWENTY-FIVE

MERRI

A girl could get used to the amenities in this penthouse. I may not have chosen to be stuck here and would rather be free to do whatever the fuck I wanted, but at least I had a steam sauna all to myself. I sat on the bench as steam filled the room, breathing in the slightly scented damp air and letting the heat permeate to my bones. Ever since my dream with mystery hot guy, I hadn't been able to get his words out of my head.

"Are they the villains?"

My knee-jerk response was no, of course not. Lilith would never intentionally put me in harm's way. She'd done nothing but protect me from the day she'd taken me under her wing.

But what if she was wrong about them? What if the horsemen couldn't actually be trusted? Were we both fools for thinking that they were capable of being protectors? I mean, the four horsemen of the apocalypse weren't exactly harbingers of glad tidings. They were foretold to bring about the literal end of the world. That didn't scream heroic.

I groaned and rested my head against the light gray tile. I was no closer to finding my answer now than I was two days ago. Which meant I just had to keep on trusting Lilith. Maybe these worries were nothing more than intrusive thoughts my subconscious brought to light via one very attractive manifestation.

The hiss of another batch of steam as it pumped into the room made me flinch, but I took another deep breath and forced myself to relax into my surroundings again. I needed this. I'd avoided every opportunity to be around any of the guys since my dream, and doing so had made me a ball of tension.

Not that I was going to be able to continue doing so for much longer. Already, my hunger was rearing its needy little head. Malice's gift had kept me sated far longer than my camming ever had, but it wasn't a permanent solution. Sooner rather than later, I was going to need to ask one of them to lend a helping hand—or penis, as the case may be.

A wave of longing crested within me as I recalled the shattered look in Malice's amethyst eyes as he found his release. The man had given me so much more than an orgasm to feed from. He'd let me behind walls no one had ever breached. It was satisfying in a way I couldn't fully describe, but if ever there was proof that not all orgasms were created the same, his was certainly it.

And fuck did the greedy bitch inside me want to experience it all over again.

Feeling a little lightheaded from the heat, I forced myself to stand. The second I was upright, the ground lurched beneath me, and I shot my arm out, trying to catch myself on the wall.

"Whoa!"

I stood frozen, heart racing as I tried to figure out what the hell that had been. Just when I'd sensed it was safe to move, the ground trembled again.

And this time, it didn't stop.

Another scream was torn from my throat as I tried to keep myself from slipping and sliding on the slick floor. Were we having a fucking earthquake in London?

It'll be over soon.

What was I supposed to do again? Stop, drop, and roll?
No, you idiot. That's only if you're on fire.
Get in the damn doorway.

Easier said than done, given that I could hardly keep myself upright.

With a shaking hand, I wiped at the steam-coated door, a terrified squeak leaving me as I watched the door of the spa room swing wildly and the water of the hot tub slosh up and over the ledge. The ground was literally rolling.

Oh my God, is this ever going to stop?

An ominous cracking sound echoed off the walls as tiles began raining from the ceiling. Here I was, naked, sweaty, and about to die in a steam room. I needed out of this tomb before my death became a reality.

The trembling seemed to be dying down, so I used the extra stability as my opportunity to open the door. Before I could turn the handle, a large shudder jerked beneath my feet, sending the shelving unit filled with towels and other tchotchkes crashing down and blocking my escape. The only thing that kept me upright was my death grip on the handle.

"Fuck, no!" I shouted, panic creeping up my throat as I shoved at the door.

Nothing. Not even a little movement.

I couldn't stay in here. Not with the steam still filling the room and the temperature rising. Surely someone was nearby. They'd let me out.

"Help! Please, somebody, help me!" I screamed, pounding on the glass in hopes one of them would hear me.

The shaking finally stopped, but I wasn't confident it would stay that way. I'd seen *San Andreas*. I knew about aftershocks.

When no one immediately came for me, I stumbled back, intent on running and breaking through the glass or something. Using my body as a battering ram was better than nothing. Seriously, it wasn't a well-thought-out plan. I just needed out of here.

Instead of a brilliant action-star moment, I slipped and went down hard. Pain burst across my hip and side, and by the grace of God, I just barely managed to keep my head from slamming onto the floor. The last thing I needed was a concussion or to lose consciousness while in here.

On shaky legs, I attempted to get to my feet, head swimming as the steam continued to billow in, the temperature rising to 140 degrees and climbing. The digital thermometer on the wall was flashing red. Red was bad. I'd already been in here too long by the time I'd decided to leave, but now I was in the danger zone, even for a supernatural creature.

I might be a succubus, but our kind was more human than most.

As soon as I put weight on my hip, I knew it was a lost cause. Agony ripped through me, and I fell to the floor again. Dragging myself to the door, I banged and screamed in desperate hope someone would find me. No one heard me. I shouted until my throat was raw, hitting the door over and over until I finally gave up. I pressed my cheek to the smooth surface, breathing heavily in the thick, hot air, knowing it was no use.

"Fuck," I whispered, my voice ragged.

Of all the ways I thought I might die, trapped in a steam sauna hadn't even made the top one hundred.

※

Chaos

Sweat trickled down my forehead, and my arms shook as I placed the fifteen-hundred-pound barbell on its rack with a grunt. The metal groaned in protest, but I knew it could handle the weight. I regularly benched this much, not that you'd ever see my name in the Guinness Book of World Records. The pathetic human who held that title only lifted 1401 pounds. But they had so little. I wasn't going to take that away from him.

I'd only just sat up, towel in my hand so I could wipe the sweat from my brow, when the ground jerked beneath me.

"What the hell?"

I'd lived through my fair share of earthquakes, but never in London. It was about as unexpected as tits on a mouse. Or at least it was until you remembered that the end of days had begun. When faced with that eventuality, earthquakes were the least of our worries.

The mirrored wall on one side of the gym shattered from the force of the rattling. Racks of weights crashed all around me, and glass fell to the floor in deadly shards.

"Motherfucker!" I shouted, rushing to the doorway and waiting out the quake.

This wasn't normal by any stretch of the imagination, which meant one thing. Another Prince had been released and brought a new wave of destruction with him. I would bet everything I owned that this was far from the worst of it.

When the shaking finally died down, I carefully made my way down the hall, intent on finding the others. The penthouse had seen better days, and I could already hear Grim's cursing as he tallied up the damage.

Malice's indignant shouts rang out from the stairwell. "I told you we needed to mount the shelves in my room to the wall, Grimsby! Now my computer is ruined, and it's going to take weeks to rebuild. You can kiss Merri's fancy firewall goodbye."

Oh shit. Where the fuck *was* Merri?

My brothers and I were practically indestructible, but she was much more fragile than we were. She could easily be a casualty of the quake.

"Where is Merri?" I hollered, hoping one of them had eyes on her.

Footsteps on the stairs announced Malice before he came into view. "I thought she was with you, training."

I shook my head. She'd been avoiding me for days. "No. I thought you had her."

"Fuck. I'll look upstairs, you check down here. She can't be far."

Spinning around, I jogged back down the corridor, peeking my head into the pool room and finding nothing. I was just about to make for the kitchen when I heard a muffled shout coming from the direction of the spa.

Apprehension zinged through me, starting in my heart, which I really didn't want to acknowledge. I raced to the door and pushed into the room that housed a couple of massage tables along with the hot tub, cold plunge, and steam sauna. Water coated almost every inch of the floor, with sodden towels and broken bottles strewn about. The marble statue of Poseidon that Grim had unironically purchased centuries ago was now nothing but rubble spread across the floor. The god's face was at the bottom of the cold pool.

Not lingering to consider the hidden meaning behind that, I didn't stop moving until I was standing in front of the steam room. Merri was a lump on the other side. Her long hair sticking to her face and torso where it had escaped from her hair tie.

"I'm trapped!" she shouted, though her voice was hoarse.

My heart gave another clench when I realized she'd been screaming for a while.

Springing into action, I hauled the shelves away from the door and tossed them aside, desperate to get to her. I yanked the door so hard it came off its hinges, and clouds of steam billowed out, hitting me in the face, the heat nearly painful.

Merri toppled forward, landing on her hands without the glass to support her weight.

"Shit, sorry." I crouched down, picking her up without thinking, though I immediately realized my mistake.

She was completely naked.

And now all those curves I tried so hard to ignore were pressed against my shirtless skin.

"I . . . thought . . . I was . . . going to die . . . in there," she said through panting breaths, her cheeks red, body covered in sweat, eyes glassy and almost feverish.

"I've got you, Red."

I carried her to the first available surface, which was a massage table, and sat her down, hoping she would cool off before damage was done. Her hip and side sported a deep purpling mark that had nothing to do with the heat.

"What happened here?" I asked, gesturing to the injury.

"I fell."

"I'm sorry none of us were here." The guilt of knowing she'd been so close to me and still in peril gnawed at my gut.

"It's o . . . kay," she panted, still breathing hard.

She needed water, but I didn't want to leave her on her own to go get some. She also needed a shirt. It was taking everything in me to ignore the rosy buds of her nipples or the sweet flare of her hips.

I could blame her allure on her being a succubus all I liked, but the truth was, she was nothing more than a vulnerable woman at the moment, and I was the pervert lusting after her. Merri's power wasn't in play here. I wanted her. I'd been afraid for her. Those emotions were all mine.

"Did you find her?" Sin skidded into the room, worry written all over his face as he scanned the debris left by the earthquake. "Fuck. What a mess." His eyes alighted on Merri, and the man immediately tugged off his tank top. "What happened?"

"She was trapped in the steam room," I explained, already stepping back and allowing him to claim my place in front of her.

He draped the loose cotton over her head, concealing the body my fingers were itching to explore. But the arm holes were low cut, meaning more than enough temptation remained.

I had to get the fuck away from her. Before I did something incredibly stupid.

"She needs water and rest. Take care of her," I grunted, not letting my eyes meet hers before I turned away and stalked out of there.

This was getting out of hand. I knew bringing her here was a bad idea, but I never expected it would be because I'd want something more with her. We were supposed to breed her to save the world. Full stop. She wasn't supposed to mean anything.

She wasn't supposed to be . . . mine.

I stumbled as the word floated through my mind, denial hot on its heels. I shoved down the rightness of it. The relief and primal possession that surged through me at the mere suggestion that I might keep her.

No.

No.

Merri was a job. That was all she could ever be.

I wasn't a man who could offer a future to anyone. Fuck, I wasn't even a man. Not anymore.

I was War.

Fucking horseman of the apocalypse.

And it was time I started acting like it.

OPERATION PFFN SUPER SECRET VIDEO CORRESPONDENCE: #3

Static screen blinks to life. Asher Henry sits and rests his elbows on his knees, then leans closer to the camera.

<<static>>
<<clothes rustling>>
<<paper rustling>>

Asher: All right, I'm gonna skip the pleasantries and just dive in. We've got a lot of information to go over and people these days have the attention span of a gnat.

Asher sits back on the couch and runs a hand over his face.

<<clothes rustling>>
<<couch spring squeaking>>

Asher: I sent Remi out on an errand so I could get through this without interruption, but since he is one of said gnats, I also have some pre-recorded stuff to share so I can keep my portion to a minimum. I hope you're sitting down wherever you are because this isn't going to be easy to hear, but it's not going to do you any good to sugarcoat it, so let's just hit the highlights.

Photo of a massive crater in the earth appears on screen.

Asher: You know what that crater used to be? Mount fucking Everest. The news is saying it imploded due to its core eroding without our knowledge. That's a bunch of bullshit. That mountain collapsed and caused a planet-wide 9.5 earthquake. And do you know why? Ding ding, the apocalypse. In case you haven't received our earlier communications, I won't assume that you're up to date on all the important details. If you are, skip ahead a bit; otherwise let me fill you in. The world is ending. The seven Princes of hell are being released on some sort of unknown timer, although given that there was only a week between the first and the second, seven days is our current theory.

Asher glances off-screen and shakes his head.

Asher: *dark chuckle* Asher, you might ask. How do you know this was the second Prince? Well, viewer, I know because we have our own personal alert system by way of the sexy Irish priest my partner can't stop flirting with. Caleb confirmed that as soon as the earthquake hit, his scar lit up like a Fourth of July fireworks show.

Asher frowns.

Asher: Well, not like actual fireworks because there was only the burning, not the light. You know what I mean. His alarm went off, which means we're one step closer to this hellscape becoming permanent. So, if you're seeing this, welcome to the apocalypse. I'm glad you're not dead yet. Let's keep it that way, yeah?

<<claps hands together>>

Asher: Which brings me to the main point of today's video. My friends and I have been trying to find the answers all of us will need to ride this fucker out. If there's even a way to do that. But instead of sitting here recapping hours of brainstorming sessions like some kind of two-bit anchorman, I thought I would just let you see for yourselves.

<<static>>

Video changes to show a living room with the entire wall covered in papers and red string. Gavin Donoghue walks in frame and stands at the center.

<<footsteps>>

Kingston Farrell joins the rest of the group, who are seated and looking at Gavin.

Kingston: *clears throat* Uh, Gavin? Are you finally going to explain why the entire living room wall is covered in papers and red strings? It looks like a crazy murder board in here.

Gavin: What an astute observation, Kingston. Did you come up with that all on your own?

Kingston: I've watched CSI.

Gavin: What an asset you are.

Kingston sits up straighter in his seat and preens.

Kingston: Thank you for noticing.

Gavin rolls his eyes and walks to the far end of the wall.

Gavin: *huffs out a breath* Is everyone here?

Asher: Yup, everyone but Remi and the girls are accounted for.

Alek: I can't believe he actually agreed to sit this out. Based on the way he took over those other updates, I thought for sure he'd attempt to run this one as well.

Asher: I bribed him with sex.

Tor: Smart move.

Asher: I know my audience.

Noah Blackthorne leans forward in his chair.

Thorne: Carry on, Donoghue. What is all this?

Gavin: This is a timeline of the apocalypse. We started here, at Blackwood, when Death made her final move. Thanks to the intel Tor and the others provided, we know that some sort of portal opened, which kicked everything off.

Pan: *obnoxiously clears his throat*

Gavin: I was getting to you.

Pan: Well, hurry up, then. Give credit where it's due.

Gavin: *huffs in annoyance* Thanks to Pan, we now know that the portal was actually Lucifer being released from his prison. Which started the timer on the seven other prisons.

Gavin points down the timeline at two other pieces of paper.

Gavin: As of this morning, the second Prince has been released, and mass destruction hit the world. Tsunamis followed the earthquake, flooding, cities were leveled, fires, death. It's only going to get worse. And the demons who've begun crawling out of the bowels of hell are ready to take out every living thing in their path.

Ben: Th-the h-humans don't s-stand a ch-chance.

<<loud sexual moan>>

Everyone stops and looks around in confusion.

<<loud sexual moan>>
<<loud sexual moan>>

Pan: Oh! That's my phone.

Ben: Does R-Rosie know y-you used h-her v-voice like th-that?

Pan: Of course she does, Bentley. Consent is a very important part of a healthy relationship.

Pan taps screen and accepts phone call.

Pan: Auntie Lilith, thanks for getting—yes, they're all here. *slight pause* Of course, I'll put you on speaker.

Lilith: Time is of the essence, pets, so I'll get to the point. It is of the utmost importance that you prepare for what's to come. Every single player will need to be on the board when we reach the final battle. Every. Single. One. Gather your army. You're going to need it.

<<beat of dead air>>

Pan: Auntie Lilith?

Kingston: Did she just hang up on you?

Hades: She hasn't changed a bit.

Kai: Is it just me, or was that not very helpful?

Alek: Oh, I dunno, she told us we'd need an army. That sounded like helpful advice to me.

Hook: Did someone say army? I'm the head of quite an impressive armada. If anyone knows how to gather and lead the troops, it is I—

Hades: Don't you dare fuckin' say it. Everyone already knows who you are.

Hook: —Captain Hook. You know, you're the god of the underworld. If I was the god of the underworld, I would introduce myself as Lord Hades everywhere I went.

Hades: We should have left you in Faerie.

Kai: The Shadow Court would've banned me for life.

Caleb: Gentlemen, Hook is right. He is skilled in this area. We should defer to his expertise.

Alek and **Tor** let out twin grunts of outrage.

Kingston: *voice low* It's okay, buddy. He didn't mean that you weren't.

Alek: I'm the son of Odin's chosen warrior, for fuck's sake.

Kingston: And we're all very impressed with you.

Caleb shakes his head, ignoring them completely.

Caleb: We should heed Lilith's advice. If that's all she said, it's because it's all she could say. So that means we need to come together and rally our forces. Kai, will the Shadow Court fight at your side?

Kai nods.

Kai: Aye. If our world ends, so does theirs. I can contact Jensen and beg their aid.

Tor: Our father will call every warrior in Novasgard to defend our cause.

Alek: Yes, all we need do is ask.

Thorne: The Blackthorne vampires are ready and waiting. We will call all the families together and enlist their strongest fighters.

Kingston: And you already know the pack is on standby. I can have most of the wolves in North America here by the end of the week. Just say the word.

Caleb turns his focus to Hades.

Caleb: And you, Hades?

Hades scowls.

Hades: And me, what?

Hook: *cough* Suchaprick. *cough*

Hades: It's not like I can get any of my family on board here. The gods don't care if this world ends. We are infinite. We'll simply rebuild and perhaps be able to get some more worshippers out of this.

Kai looks at him, shocked.

Kai: So you're willing to let everyone here die? Even our mate?

Hades: Did I say that, dragon? No. Don't put words in my mouth. I will do everything possible to defend Dahlia. My brethren won't.

Gavin: That sounds like a matter for another time. What about the horsemen?

Hades: What about them?

Gavin: You said they were there with you? At the ritual?

Gavin points to a piece of paper on the wall and nods to himself.

Gavin: Yes, I have it right here. They were essential to Hel's opening the portal. Do you think they might be of some assistance? Either in stopping this or perhaps providing some useful information?

Kingston shifts in his seat.

<<rustle of fabric>>

Kingston: *laughs* Yeah, that sounds like a solid plan. Which one of us is going to call them up? Excuse me, Mr. Horseman, can you help us *stop* the world from ending? I know it's your entire reason for existing, but we'd really like it to not happen.

Hades: Well . . . actually, it's not the stupidest plan I've ever heard. They're fiercely competitive, and they have one hell of a bone to pick with Helene right now. It wouldn't surprise me if they'd be open to some kind of alliance.

Kingston: So we stop this apocalypse so they can start a different one.

Hades shrugs.

Hades: You got a better idea?

Asher: Okay, so we reach out to the horsemen. How the fuck are we going to get ahold of them? Gabriel has gone MIA.

Hades: Leave it to me.

Asher: You know them or something?

Hades: We have semi-regular poker games.

Thorne: *chuckling* Semi-regular? Do you pop over there every third Friday or something?

Hades: More like every quarter century or so.

Kingston: Hey, Daddy G!

Gavin and Caleb both turn to him, then scowl.

Asher: *snickers* Wrong daddy, Count Chocula. Wait till Remi hears about this.

Gavin: *groans*

Caleb: What do you want, Kingston?

Kingston: Did you hear what he said? You're not the oldest guy in the room anymore!

Caleb: I'll thank you to shut your mouth, Mr. Farrell.

Thorne: *snorts* Good luck with that. If you crack the code, will you give it to me? I've been trying to shut him up since the day we met.

Tor stands and walks to the display.

<<chair squeak>>
<<footsteps>>

Tor: We're forgetting a key part of this strategy. Lilith said we needed to get all the players on the board. As we can see here...

Tor points to the display.

Alek: There are only three sets of us here. But we don't know who the fourth group is.

Hook: Care to elaborate? For the rest of us who don't share twin brains.

Ben: I s-see. E-each horsewoman h-had a child. W-we're all c-connected s-somehow.

Kai: So you're saying Famine has spawn of her own in play?

Thorne: How can you be sure? Death won. What need is there of a fourth group?

Alek: She would have been prepared for her turn.

Asher: Pan and I are living proof of that. Our bitch of a mom made two so her plan could be played out.

Alek: See? It stands to reason there's a kid out there somewhere, likely as tangled up in this as the rest of us.

Tor: Exactly.

Tor nods and slaps his hand across the crude illustration of Famine on the board.

<<hand smacking paper>>

Tor: We need to find out who this one is and find the final players.

<<static>>

Asher reappears on the screen.

Asher: You still with me? I know that was a lot. Trust me, I sat through that meeting live. We were all reeling as much as I'm sure you probably are. And like us, I'm sure you are left with more questions than answers. But that's why we're sending out the puffin signal. If you received this, we need your help. Not just with the final battle but in figuring out who the final players are. Not only could they be in grave danger, but if my suspicion is right, then they might just be the key to saving us all.

<<knock on the door>>

Asher: Fuck, I've pushed my luck far enough for one day. Time to go. Keep an eye out for my next correspondence. And if you need a safe place to hide, the coordinates to our location are heading your way in a separate message.

Asher gives a two fingered salute and the screen goes black.

<<static>>

End of transmission.

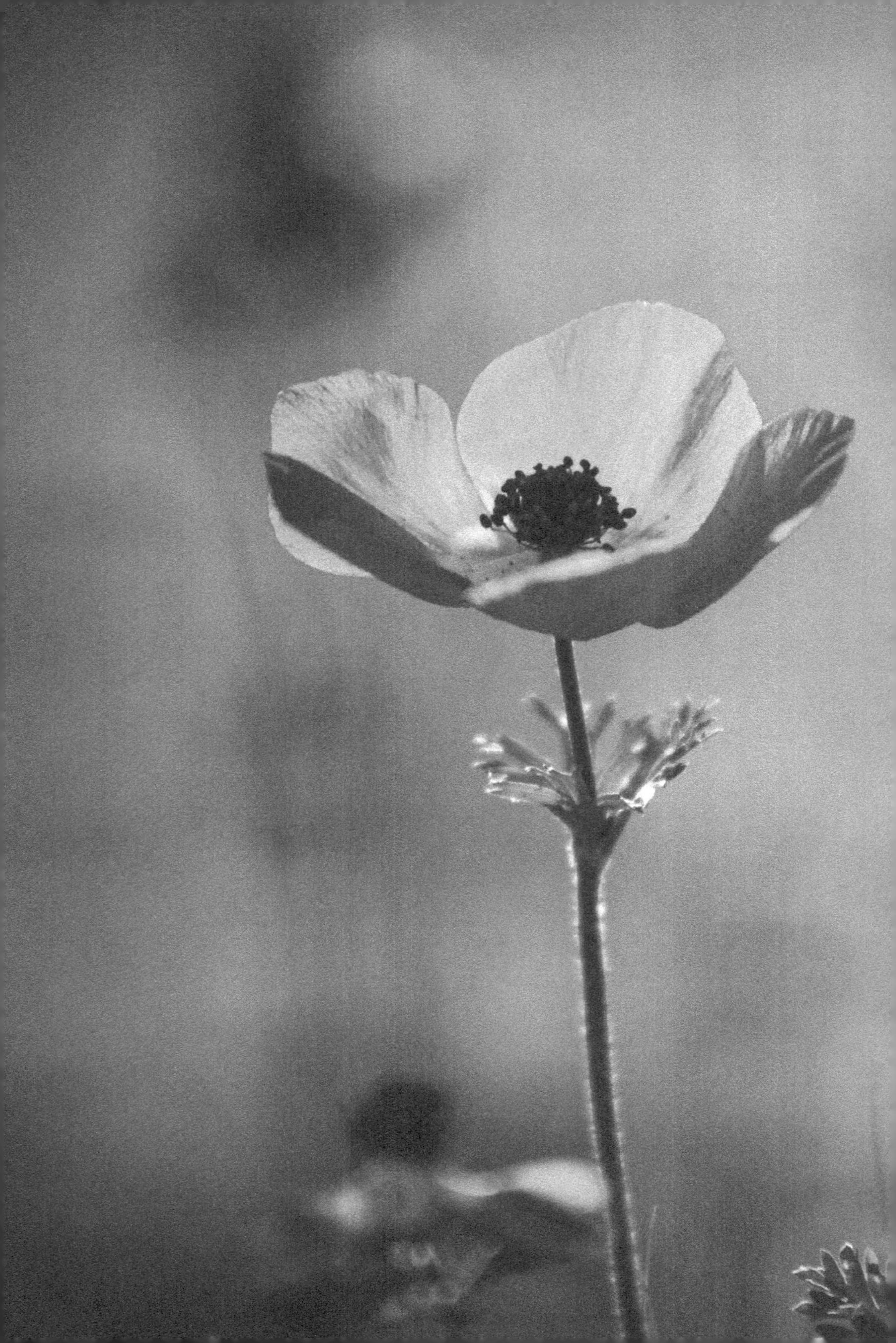

CHAPTER TWENTY-SIX

MERRI

I paced outside of Chaos's room, fingers knotting in the strings of my hoodie as I chastised myself.

"If you're not feeling brazen enough to waltz right in, then just knock on the door, Meredith. Jesus."

The latest round of WWLD—What Would Lilith Do—had led me here. Outside of Chaos's door, attempting to find the courage to thank him for saving me from a rather tragic end. My memory of the immediate aftermath of the earthquake was a little spotty, but one thing I knew for sure: if Chaos hadn't got me out, I would have died in that steam room.

He deserved a thank you, at the very least. If he liked me more, I would have even considered hugging him, but since he kissed me in the kitchen, the man had been filled with horny fury. I thought he'd finally reached his breaking point during our training session, but he had the self-control of a saint. Or maybe a eunuch. If I hadn't felt the proof of his arousal, I would have thought for sure he was a dickless wonder. But nope. His trouser snake was a solid nine inches, at least. And I'd never wanted to be a snake charmer more in my life.

Arousal curled low in my belly at the memory of him on top of me, rocking his hips. God, these men brought out desires I hadn't let myself entertain since Jimmy.

Shaking my head, I took a steadying breath and just bit the fucking bullet. Three sharp raps on the wood later, I was standing there, holding that breath I took and waiting for Chaos to answer.

Silence was all I got for my trouble.

I knocked again.

He still didn't answer me.

Was he ignoring me? Or had he gone somewhere?

I reached out and turned the knob, cracking the door open just enough for me to call out, "Hello? Chaos?"

The lack of response, along with the darkness, gave me my answer. No one was home.

I bit down on my lower lip, wondering where he snuck off to. I hadn't seen him in the main room or the kitchen, so he must be in the gym.

To be fair, Chaos was just about always in the gym, so I probably should have started my search for him down there.

With butterflies dancing in my belly, I headed for the staircase that would lead me down to the remnants of the gym. The penthouse had taken a beating in the earthquake, but at least the walls were still standing.

I hadn't been back down to this floor since it happened, and I was mentally bracing for the carnage. The last time I'd seen it, chunks of the ceiling and walls had littered the hallway, but I needn't have bothered. It was miraculously cleared. If not for the cracks in the plaster, I wouldn't have even known there'd been any damage. While I'd been holed up in my room recovering, the guys had been busy restoring the place to rights.

I kept my footsteps light as I crept to the gym, but once again, Chaos was nowhere to be found. He'd been here though, of that I was sure. Not only could I smell his spicy cologne, but all the equipment had been reset, and the broken bits of mirror swept and disposed of.

He had to be here somewhere. I hadn't heard the elevator or anyone moving around, for that matter. Grim had locked himself in his office. Malice was up to his eyeballs in trying to rebuild his destroyed computer. Sin... well, Sin had been keeping a close watch on me until I told him I was taking a nap.

This was like a game of hide-and-seek, except Chaos didn't know I was it.

Maybe he was working on the spa room. There'd been so much damage to the tiles and the steam sauna. I was sure that kind of repair work took a lot more time and effort. Unbidden, an image of Chaos wearing a pair of low-slung jeans, work boots, and a tool belt came to mind. Mmm. Yes, please. Maybe he'd get hot and have to pull his T-shirt over his head before he tucked it into his belt. The man had a back on him that would make anyone take a second or third look.

Oh my God, Merri. What is wrong with you? Are you in heat or something?

Shaking away the lust, I resumed my search only to spot my prey with a bag slung over his shoulder in front of the elevator. I opened my mouth to call his name, only to watch him walk into the car and smack a button. I peeked up at the numbers above the door to figure out where he was heading, my eyebrows flying up when it showed him going down.

Down?

Was that asshole leaving?

No fucking fair.

They said I wasn't a prisoner, but no one ever invited me out. They said they needed to protect me, but they wouldn't let me do anything with them outside of these walls.

Well, fuck that.

My subconscious was right. I needed to take charge of my destiny, and part of that included making my own decisions.

I was only trapped here if I continued to allow it.

It was time for my first field trip.

Knowing I'd never catch Chaos if I waited for the private elevator to return, I spun around and headed for the stairwell. These were the back stairs that acted as an emergency or second exit. If I took these down a few floors, I could grab one of the building's main elevators and hopefully meet Chaos on the ground floor. Also, bonus, no one would be the wiser.

I zipped up my sweatshirt and tucked my hair into the dark fabric of the hood, thankful I'd planned on using the treadmill after my chat with Chaos so I was already fully dressed with tennis shoes on and everything. I even had my phone—which I hadn't let out of my sight since I recovered it—in case I got lost.

Fully aware my plan was half a plan at best and that it fully hinged on speed, I didn't waste a second. I wasn't trying to win any prizes for strategy, just flex my independence a little. Besides, how mad could the Grump Squad get if I was technically still with one of them?

And if I wasn't safe with Chaos, then there was no point in them protecting me at all. He was *the* horseman War. The toughest of tough motherfuckers. Besides, the plan was to meet him in the lobby, not leave the building.

I told myself all of this as I raced down five flights of stairs before bursting through the door and calling an elevator. If I lost him, I wasn't quite sure how I'd get back into the penthouse. I didn't exactly have a key.

The elevator door opened immediately, and I thanked my lucky stars it had been close to this floor as I got in and punched the button labeled LOBBY.

"Please don't already be gone," I murmured.

I drummed my fingers on my thigh, absentmindedly grooving to the soft Muzak that pumped through the speakers. I didn't get to hear enough of the song to be sure, but it sounded like it might be a jazzy version of "Don't Fear the Reaper."

Then again, maybe I was projecting.

As soon as the doors slid open, I was out of there, glancing around in search of my target. The man in question strode with purpose right out the front door, leaving me in his very handsome dust.

"Fuck," I muttered, debating for all of a heartbeat whether to keep following him.

It wasn't much of a debate. I couldn't get back into the penthouse without him.

"In for a penny . . ." I said beneath my breath as I sprinted through the super upscale lobby to the front door. I made it outside just as Chaos closed the door of a cab. Thankfully this fancy building had a taxi stand, and there was another car idling just behind it.

Yanking the door open, I threw myself inside and shouted, "Follow that cab!" at the driver.

"Yes, miss." The driver's shoulders shook as he very clearly attempted to keep in his laughter.

I chuckled to myself. This was the most ridiculous thing I'd ever done. And, if I was being honest, probably the most fun. Even if it was also spontaneous and likely short-sighted.

As we wound through the streets of London, I was finally able to take in the landscape of the city with new, post-apocalyptic eyes. Piles of rubble littered the sidewalks and street corners. The remnants of Big Ben stood like a ghost in an eerily orange sky. Smoke wafted up to join the clouds from nearly every direction.

"Shame, innit? To see our city in such a state?" The cabbie's voice was tinged with a deep sadness. "It hasn't looked like this since the blitz. Me mum told me stories of how the walls came down around her while the bombs fell. It's only by the grace of God that she survived."

I made a soft sound of assent as I continued to drink in the destruction. London was barely recognizable. On almost every corner, there were groups of people with signs saying *Repent* or *The End Is Here*. I couldn't blame them for their assumptions—and, you know, they weren't wrong. More than one iconic bridge had collapsed, along with several famous landmarks. The London Eye was more of a crescent moon, with little sparks shooting off the metal railing every now and then. Many of the small mom-and-pop stores were closed, the doors and windows that weren't barricaded with wood broken and clearly looted. And while a few of the larger chain stores remained open, they appeared to have been nearly wiped out.

Given the state of things, I was shocked traffic was flowing as steadily as it was. Then again, most cars seemed to be fleeing in the opposite direction. That was, out of the city. Not to mention I had a strong suspicion there'd been some supernatural intervention when it came to clearing the main streets. I couldn't prove it, mind you, but the fact that I was in a cab chasing after Chaos sort of spoke for itself.

"Are you sure you don't want me to take you to the airport? Or maybe the train station, miss? You should get out of here. Go to the country where it's safe. We're overrun with looters and criminals, not to mention the religious zealots. It's not a good idea to wander around anymore."

As the cabbie continued trying to convince me to run for my life, I trained my focus on the taillights of the taxi Chaos was in. They were stopping.

"Stop here!" I shouted. "I have to get out."

The man did as I asked, his old face lined with worry as I bounced in my seat, anxious energy coursing through me while I waited for the payment to go through.

Handing me back my phone, he warned, "Be careful, miss. A girl like you out on her own isn't safe."

"Don't worry about me," I said with a bravado I didn't exactly feel as I shoved the door open and prepared to bolt. I'd known things were bad; the earthquake was a pretty big indicator, but seeing the reality of it was a shock to the system. "Drive safe!" I called behind me as I jumped out of his car, just barely catching sight of Chaos as he turned down an alley.

I was no longer chasing Chaos in a silly attempt to prove my autonomy. Now I wanted to glue myself to his side to make sure we both stayed safe.

Rounding the corner of the alley, I spotted Chaos as he walked past a mountain of a man who had to be part ogre and through a nondescript door that could have been the back entrance to a butcher shop for all I knew.

"What the hell are you up to?"

This better not be some sort of drug deal. Or worse, a kinky sex club.

I would so tell Lilith he was cheating on *Iniquity* if it was.

Well, the only way to find out was to get past that guard, and since I didn't have a wad of cash on me, the only way to do that was to put my skills to the test. I stood up straight, strode up to him with the confidence of Lilith, and looked him dead in the eyes.

He crossed his arms over his chest and frowned down at me from his towering height.

"Sorry, love. You're not on the list."

"Oh, are you sure? Check again."

The ogre didn't even blink, so I stepped closer and sent my power right into him. His mouth fell open, eyes glazing over and pupils dilating.

"Let me in, and I'll make all your dreams come true," I murmured seductively.

He couldn't move fast enough.

"Y-yes. Of c-course," he stuttered, his eyes closing halfway as I sauntered past him. "I'll do anything you want, pretty lady."

I winked and blew him a kiss. "You better rest up. You're looking a little sleepy."

The ogre yawned. "G-good idea. I need to be ready for you."

A laugh was my only answer as I waggled my fingers at him in a little wave and followed the sound of a roaring crowd deeper into the building. Feeling incredibly proud of myself, I took the stairs waiting for me at the end of the little hall two at a time.

"All right, Chaos, time to uncover your secrets."

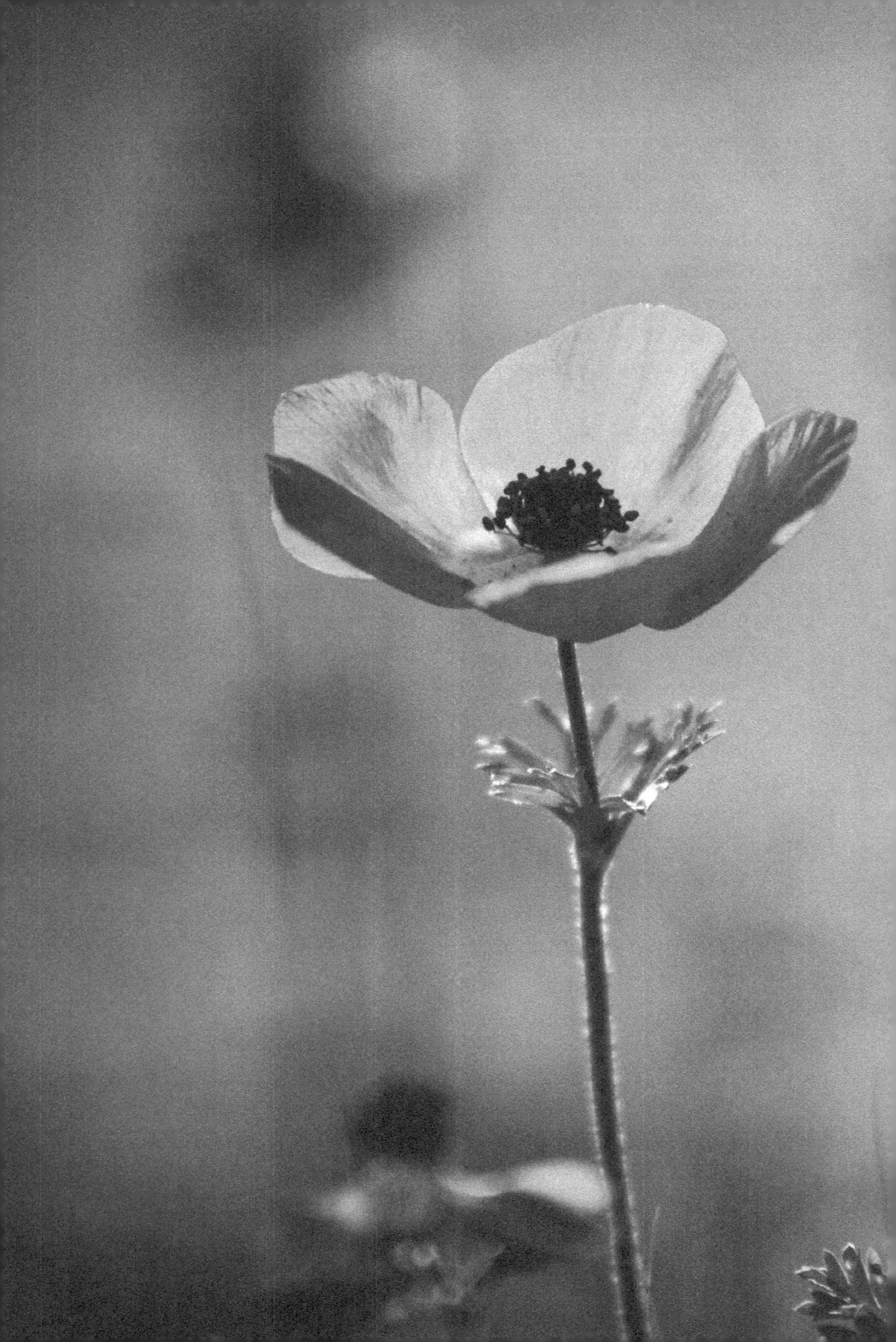

CHAPTER
TWENTY-SEVEN
CHAOS

Warm air hung thick in the depths of Max's—an invite-only gambling and fighting hall—the musky scents of shifters mixed with the coppery tang of blood and heady aroma of dark fae magic. No humans darkened the doorstep of Max's. Ever. In fact, I had it on good authority Max set a ward on the entrance to repel anyone without supernatural blood.

I cracked my neck as I stood in the back, waiting for the announcer to call my name. I was cutting it close tonight, arriving with mere minutes to spare before my scheduled fight. I was the headliner, and to say the promoter had been practically shitting bricks by the time I finally arrived was not that much of an exaggeration.

I couldn't blame him. There was no scenario in my mind where Charlie hadn't banked on my odds of winning being so high I was a sure thing. If I didn't show, he'd stand to lose more money than God.

He was right. I was a sure thing. Even though tonight felt . . . different. Off. Exceedingly tense.

From my view in the fighter's tunnel, I could see the dimly lit crowd crammed into risers like sardines as they waited for the main event. The pit sat empty, a lone spotlight beaming dead center. As soon as my opponent and I took our places, the lights would go up, casting us in sharp relief so the spectators could get what they paid for. Blood, violence, destruction. Maybe death.

There was a reason this place was such a well-kept secret. The things that happened here were not for the light of day. Or for the morally inclined. It was absolutely perfect for the likes of me.

I bounced on the balls of my feet and shook out my arms, attempting to keep my muscles warm and loose. Being amped up before a fight was nothing new to me, but tonight everything just felt . . . more. I could only assume it was due to the excess tension in the air. Likely a result of the earthquake just a couple of days prior.

The denizens of this underground world weren't about to let a little something like the looming apocalypse keep them from their revelry. If anything, it only seemed to ignite their craving for dark and dangerous misdeeds.

I certainly understood the mindset. What better than a brush with death to remind you that you were still alive? These creatures held to the ideal if you can't beat 'em, join 'em. I had no doubt when the time came to join Lucifer's ranks, they'd all jump at the chance. Angels, they were not.

"All right, you fiends. Are you ready for some bloodshed?" the announcer called, his thick accent betraying his Welsh roots.

The roar of the crowd made my ears ring, reminding me of my time spent in the fighting pits in my former life. Except then, I at least had a weapon and shield. Now it was bare skin, fists, and brute force. Which I had in spades.

The audience began chanting my name, stretching it out into three syllables and stomping their feet rhythmically in a way that made the floor shake.

"Air-is-ton! Air-is-ton!"

The announcer introduced my opponent, which was met by a wave of boos. No one was here for him. They wanted me.

The pulse of power within me was strong enough that I couldn't stand still. If I didn't release some of it, I'd kill the Minotaur I was set to fight with one punch. Closing my eyes, I unzipped my hoodie and placed the hood over my head to drown out my surroundings. Then I let my power spill from within, just enough to keep from losing control. The crowd's reaction was immediate. The already frenzied audience's shouts rose to a fever pitch, their lust for blood unparalleled.

"And though he needs no introduction, let's welcome our reigning champ back to the pit: Ariston the Destroyer."

Stalking down the tunnel, I kept my gaze trained on the cement floor in front of me before taking the few steps down into the pit. They didn't get to see any reaction from me. I never acknowledged them in any of my fights. I was here for one purpose and one purpose only. Expel my rage and continue on my way.

The Minotaur waited for me, all snorts and heavy breathing, slime dripping out of his nostrils and down the piercing through his septum. His horns were stained red, eyes blazing with fury. But it was the scars that decorated his arms that caught my eye. Brands, perhaps? They were strategically placed and reminded me of runes. They also looked fresh and painful.

If it had been some sort of attempt to strengthen him for the match, it wasn't going to do him any good. All it would serve to do was offer me a prime target as I took his ass out.

Not that I needed one.

I was War.

Period.

He could try all he liked, but he had no chance.

Lowering my hood, I slipped the sweatshirt off and dropped it over the ropes that denoted our fighting ring. Another ripple of power flowed out of me and into the crowd. If they were wild before, they were feral now.

The Minotaur pawed one cloven hoof, huffing in warning as he lowered his head and aimed his horns at me.

A soft feminine gasp pulled my attention away from the beast before me, abject shock hitting me full force as my gaze connected with Merri's brilliant blue eyes.

Before I could do a damn thing about her being out of the penthouse, alone, fucking unguarded, the bell rang, and the Minotaur charged. As eager as I'd been for this fight, all I wanted now was for it to be over. I had to get her out of here. Merri was a lamb in a den of wolves. There was no way she'd escape it unscathed.

Planting my feet, I met the Minotaur's charge head-on, arm cocked back and ready to swing. I hit him across the side of his face hard enough that I felt his jaw shatter and heard the snap of his neck before he fell to the ground. With only one hit available to me, I had to pour all of my power into it, sending a shockwave of violence through the room.

The crowd roared, their shock and fury palpable. They'd come for a show and while I'd technically delivered, most only felt disappointment. I'd robbed them of their bloodbath, even as I gifted them a corpse.

"And the winner, in . . . ten seconds. Ariston the Destroyer!" the announcer said, trying to save some of the energy in the pit.

He failed.

Anger was written on their faces. Arguing broke out amongst them as they jeered and booed. We were trapped in a tinderbox, and I'd just lit the fuse.

Without a second thought, I jumped over the ropes and into the crowd, my focus locked on the woman who hadn't so much as blinked since she spotted me. I was Moses parting the damn sea as I stalked straight toward her.

"Chao—"

Her utterance of my name cut off as I grabbed her none too gently by the nape and directed her up the stairs and back into the alley outside. What was it about this woman that could get me so heated? She spun me up, sent my blood boiling, and I'd had enough of it.

"What the hell were you thinking?" I bellowed, chest heaving as I crowded her against the brick wall. "Is this all some fucking joke to you? Do you care that little about your life, or are you just seeing how far you can push us before we fucking snap and forget that we're supposed to be the ones protecting you?"

Challenge flashed in her eyes as an angry flush crept up her cheeks. She opened her mouth to likely tell me to go to hell, but I didn't give her the opportunity. My palm encircled her delicate throat as I stared daggers at her, anger, fear, frustration, and most confusing of all, desire rushing through my veins.

Before I could stop myself, my lips crashed down onto hers. I couldn't go another second without feeling her kiss. Now that I'd had it once, the memory lay in wait in the back of my mind every moment of every day. She was an addiction I'd never expected to be vulnerable to. But just one taste of her, and I was hooked.

Instead of shoving me away, Merri pulled me closer, a soft whimper escaping her as she reached up to weave her fingers through my hair and hold me in place. I took the opportunity of her parted lips to slide my tongue inside her mouth, deepening our kiss. Fuck, I wanted her.

No, I *needed* her.

Bending my knees slightly, I grasped her around the thigh with my free hand and pulled her up. She wrapped her legs around me, locking our bodies together and pressing the rigid length of my cock against her center. The way she moaned into my mouth as she rolled her hips in search of the friction my steel-hard erection provided pulled a groan of pleasure from me in return. If only she was wearing a skirt, I could tug her panties to the side and drive into her.

But I wasn't so lucky.

A pointed cough to my left had me pulling away from her, though I kept her pressed up against the wall and shielded her with my body so I could assess the threat.

Waiting for us both at the other end of the alley were three very familiar, very pissed-off horsemen.

"Fuck."

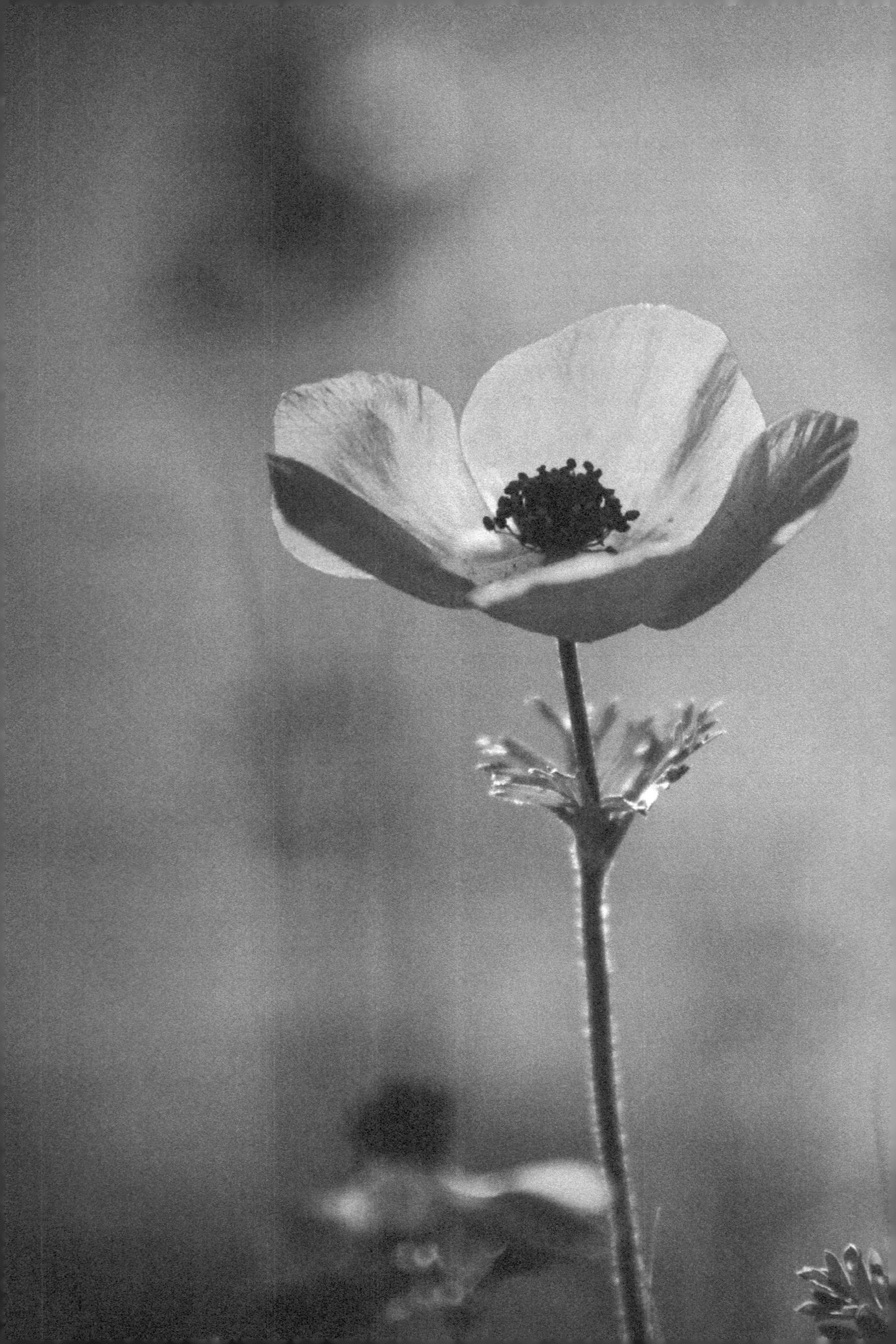

Chapter
Twenty-Eight
Grim

"Where have you got off to, wildflower?" I murmured, stalking through the halls after finding Merri's room empty.

The cameras we used to keep tabs on our little captive had been down since the earthquake. Malice was doing everything he could to get them back online as fast as possible, but without his computer, we were flying blind.

All her usual haunts were empty, and with each one I checked, my ire mounted.

One tiny succubus should not be wreaking this much havoc on my life.

"Fucking Lilith."

As I shoved through the gym door, I had a scolding poised on the tip of my tongue. She shouldn't wander around without us knowing her plans. It was risky enough when the cameras had been working and we could keep an eye on her. But even then, the last time she did that, she nearly steamed herself to death.

But as with every other room, no one was there. Not even a wisp of perfume lingered as evidence of her presence.

"Fucking hell."

It should not be this difficult to locate a single woman. The penthouse was large, but it wasn't unending. Where the hell could she be?

Deciding this was no longer solely my responsibility, I took the stairs two at a time and bellowed for my brothers. If my day had to be interrupted with this nonsense, so did theirs.

"All right, all right, keep your shirt on, old man. I was taking a nap and having the nicest dream," Sin drawled as he padded down the hall, sleep rumpled and groggy.

"How nice you were able to take a nap while the rest of us continue to work on getting this place up to scratch again," Malice groused, joining us in the hallway.

Sin squinted at him, annoyance coloring his expression. "What do you want me to do, Mal? Fuck the holes in the wall? I'm not exactly built for repair work. Though I do have a great handyman outfit at the ready for when roleplay requires."

"Are you fucking serious?" Mal asked.

"Yes. He is." The sigh in my words had to betray my irritation, but Sin just grinned at us both.

"As a heart attack. I have a whole costume box. Construction worker, fireman, police officer, and my favorite . . . cowboy." He waggled his brows. "Oh! And how could I forget my priest costume? That one is a frequent flier."

"I'm surprised you didn't say pilot," Mal muttered.

"Oh, he's a frequent flier too."

"I fucking despise you."

"Right back atcha, wankstain."

"Wankstain?"

"I keep a running list of all the insults you hurl at me so I can use them back."

"Fuck's sake, will you two stop squabbling like a couple of children and focus for one damned second? I can't find Merri."

That shut Sin up quicker than I'd expected. He was coming to care for her. I could see it in his eyes. Good. That was good. He had a job to do, and I gathered it would be easier if he fell for her.

"Where is she?" he asked.

"I don't bloody know. That's why I called you two out of your rooms. I think she's gone."

"Gone where? Perhaps she just nipped to the loo?" Sin asked, adopting a fake British accent. He withered under Malice's and my twin glares. "What? I was feeling left out. You two sound all posh and cultured. I was just trying to fit in."

"No," Mal said.

"But I just sound so stupid. Did she go to the baaaathroom?" he put such emphasis on his American accent I nearly cracked a smile. "See? Stupid."

"If it walks like a duck and it quacks like a duck . . ." Mal said, brows lifted.

"How do we find her?" I barked, tired of their shenanigans. "Mal, what can you do? You said she's got some kind of tracker. Did you implant it when she was sleeping?"

Malice looked at me as if I'd just insinuated he'd performed a heinous offense. "No, I did not implant anything inside her whilst she was sleeping, Grimsby. Who the fuck do you think I am?"

I cocked a brow in answer.

He rolled his eyes, ignoring my silent dig. "She did steal her phone back. I can track that. The satellites haven't fallen from the sky—"

"Yet," Sin supplied helpfully.

"—so the GPS should still be working."

"Should?" I grumbled.

"Well, we haven't checked, now have we?" Mal pulled his own phone from his pocket and tapped the screen a few times. "Ah, there you are, ma petite. What in God's name are you doing in a place like . . . ooooh. She's safe."

"How do you know that?" If my fists were clenched any harder, my knuckles would've cracked.

"She's with Chaos."

"Wait, he took her out on a date?" Sin asked, his jealousy evident.

"No, fuckwit. Does that sound remotely like something Chaos would do?" Mal countered.

"So why is she . . . ohhhh. Bad girl, kitten. Sneaking out without permission."

"If he doesn't know she's there, she isn't safe at all. Get your things. We're going to find our girl," I said, stalking down the hall and toward the elevator.

"Our girl?" Sin asked in a loud whisper.

"Guess he's not as impassive as he pretends."

"Wait, was that him being impassive?"

"Just get your shit, Sinclair."

I heaved a sigh and squeezed the bridge of my nose. Maybe the end of the world wouldn't be so bad if it would save me from a lifetime spent with these bellends.

***

Fifteen minutes later, the three of us stood at the mouth of the alley that led to Max's. Honestly, I don't know what I expected, but finding Chaos practically devouring her up against the wall was not it.

Malice let out a low whistle while Sin complained, "Why is everyone getting some except for me? Don't look at me like that. You know I'm right. I'm the sex machine, Chaos is the war machine, Grim is the death machine, and you . . . well, I guess you're the snot machine."

Chaos was so lost in Merri he didn't even hear the conversation taking place, which only pissed me off more. We could be anyone. Lucifer's minions were legion. They could show up anywhere at any time, as they'd fucking proven a week ago when they broke into my fucking penthouse. Sure, he was blocking her with his body, but they were vicious. The damage they could do was very real.

She let out a soft moan and dug her fingers deeper into his hair as he began rocking his hips into her.

"That's it," I growled. "This has gone on long enough."

Mal stepped forward. "Allow me."

Then he cleared his throat loud enough to make Chaos stop, his body stiffening before he pulled his lips away from our charge and looked over his shoulder at us.

"Fuck."

"Oh please, don't stop on our account. It was just getting good," Sin said.

Malice glared at him. "That's enough out of you."

"You're such a prude."

"Excuse the hell out of me for not wanting to watch them fornicate in a fucking alley."

"Fornicate? How old are you? Also, you are Pestilence. Since when are you prissy about a little dirt? Germs are supposed to be your thing."

In a voice almost too soft to hear, Malice muttered, "She deserves better."

Chaos placed Merri back on the ground and turned to face us, the flush on his cheeks and the raging tent in his shorts making it all too clear how unhappy he was with our interruption.

"What are you doing here?"

I strode down the alley, eyes locked on Merri, where she peeked around Chaos. "Shouldn't I be asking *you* that?"

"Don't be mad at him. It's not his fault."

"Oh, trust me, wildflower. I know exactly who deserves all my blame."

Merri winced, but I continued speaking. Some of my anger had waned now that I could see for myself she was unharmed, but the threat to her safety remained.

"We need to get you out of sight. There are too many creatures looking for you. What the hell were you thinking, running off like that?" I scolded.

"You said I wasn't a prisoner."

I gritted my teeth against the wave of frustration that accompanied her argument. "You aren't. But that doesn't mean you're not in danger. Bloody hell, Merri, you were almost kidnapped a week ago. What more is it going to take for you to believe the threat is real?"

"You're right. I'm sorry."

My mouth snapped shut at the unexpected apology. I was so used to her stubbornness that I wasn't prepared for her to be agreeable.

"If it makes you feel any better, I never planned on leaving the building. I thought I'd catch him in the lobby, and then I didn't, and I don't have a key, so I couldn't go back up to the penthouse, and I just sort of figured I would be safer with him than on my own, so I just kept chasing him."

Her ramble was adorably earnest, and I found myself relaxing further.

"Why were you following me in the first place?" Chaos asked.

A fierce blush stained her cheeks as she looked at him. "To tell you thank you for saving me."

I could feel the wind leave our collective sails at that. It was hard to stay mad at someone who was being so sincerely vulnerable. Sort of like scolding a puppy.

"Can we continue this conversation somewhere less . . . outside?" Sin asked, his shoulders tight and gaze darting from side to side. "I can feel the angry energy coming from Max's. What happened in there?"

Chaos shrugged. "I ended the fight in one punch."

"Ah, yes. That will do it." Mal jerked his head toward the street. "Let's get a taxi back. We can discuss the dos and don'ts of excursions in the future, Merri."

As we stood on the pavement waiting for a taxi, I finally let the rest of my tension bleed out. She was safe and back where she belonged—with us.

Merri was less relaxed, caged as she was by the four of us. I could tell she was waiting for the other shoe to drop, that she knew us well enough by now to know that she hadn't heard the end of this. If I was a kinder man, I might try and assuage her fears, but where was the fun in that?

She had to learn her lesson somehow.

When the taxi arrived, Merri was the first to scramble in, seating herself as far away from me as possible. It stung to know I repelled her so, but it was for the best. Death wasn't typically welcomed with open arms.

After everyone was settled, I took my place and told the cabbie where to take us. From my vantage point, I could already make out the building that housed my penthouse. I took a risk and glanced at Merri, her beauty calling to me even though it shouldn't.

Without any warning, a deafening boom rattled the windows and caused the taxi to swerve.

"Christ, not another one!" the driver cried.

"That wasn't an earthquake," Chaos replied, his tone ominous.

My focus went to where we were headed, the top three floors of the building now engulfed in flames, black smoke curling high into the sky.

"What was it?" Merri asked, craning her neck to see around one of us and out the window.

"My fucking penthouse."

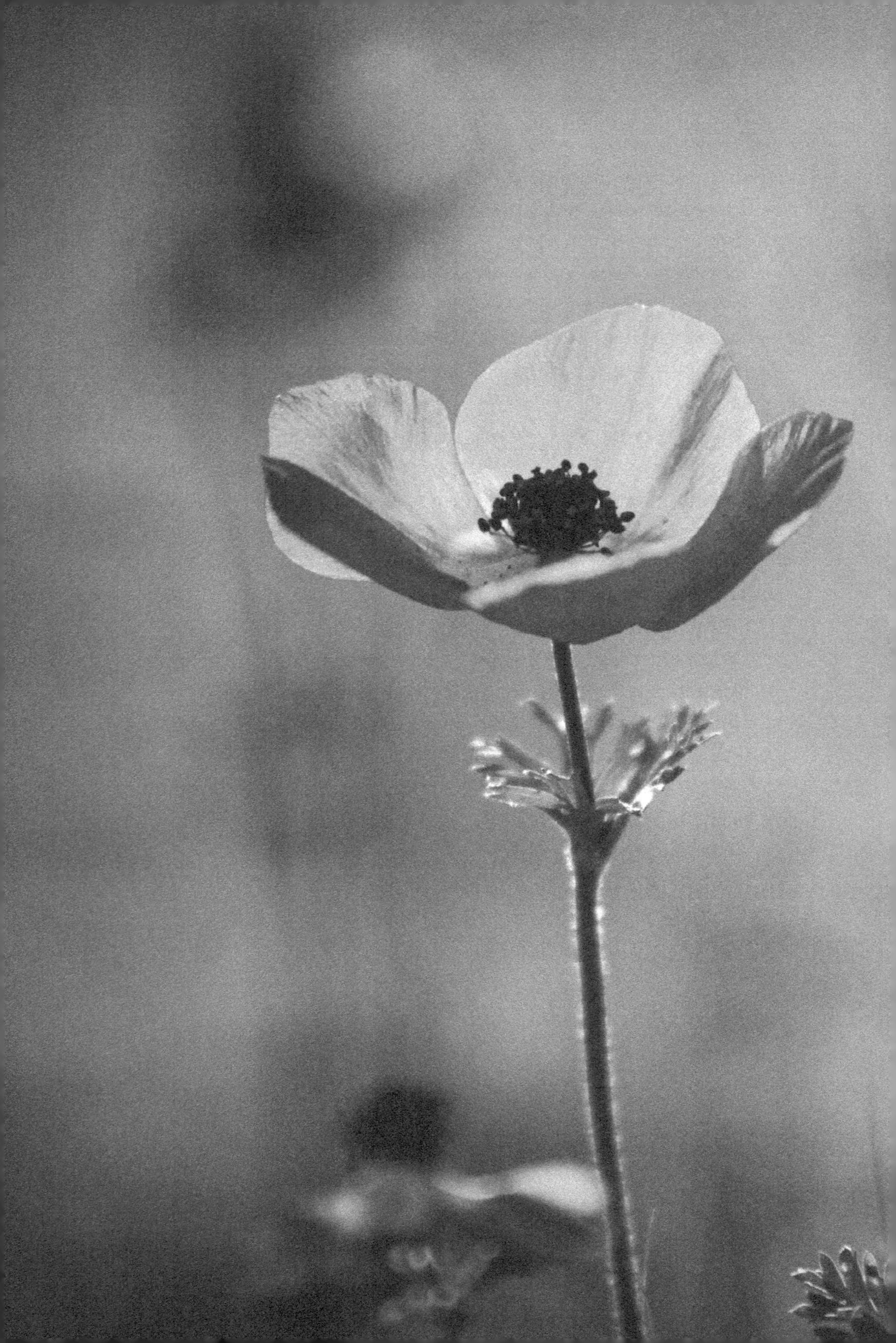

CHAPTER TWENTY-NINE

MALICE

Grim was right. His penthouse was engulfed in flames, the ash raining down on us from where our cabbie had dropped us off across the street. Flashing blue lights reflected off the nearby buildings and the firefighters standing nearby were debating the best way to douse the fire safely. Grimsby was speaking with the police while the rest of us waited off to the side and tried to figure out what our play was.

"Did you hear that?" Sin asked, blatantly eavesdropping on Grim's conversation. "They're saying it was a gas leak."

"That's no fucking gas leak," Chaos muttered.

"His poor plants." Merri's words were so soft I was sure they weren't meant for our ears, so I didn't say anything.

"Plants?" Sin asked, taken aback. "What about all our stuff? I had so many vintage records stored there. Oh man, and my guitar! I'll never be able to get another one like that."

"You can buy a guitar at any pawn shop," I deadpanned.

"Not one played by Hendrix. Not unless Daddy Death over there can raise him from the ground."

"So check out some auctions. There are lots of other dead musicians with memorabilia you can hunt down. It's not like you can't afford it."

"The world is ending, Malice. You think I have time to go to a fucking auction?"

I shrugged. "What else are you going to do? Your sole purpose was to end the world, and that was already taken care of, so the way I see it, you have nothing but time on your hands."

"That is not my sole purpose, and you know it."

"Don't see you doing anything about your *other* purpose, so it might as well be."

Grim's form cast an ominous shadow as he strode back to us, his expression well . . . grim as he shook his head. "It's a total loss. We're not getting back in there. They say it's a gas leak, but—"

"Envy."

"Pardon?" Grim asked.

"It was demons. Specifically, envy demons. I can sense them."

"More Knights?" Chaos asked, hand brushing over his stubbled jawline.

"Has to be."

"So the earthquake . . ." Sin trailed off.

"Another Prince was released. The timing is too perfect for this not to be connected," I confirmed.

"Why do they keep going after you guys?" Merri asked, her blue eyes bright and so fucking naive.

"They're not after us, Red. That pride bitch wasn't trying to steal you from us just to make us angry. They want you."

All the color drained from her face. "They . . . they're the ones trying to get back at Lilith for interfering with the"—she glanced around at all the bystanders and dropped her voice—"you know what?"

Fuck. I wasn't sure of the right way to proceed with this conversation. Letting her assume this was about Lilith was misleading, but at the same time, as long as she knew she was the target, where was the harm? If she knew the full truth, that Lucifer needed to use her as his vessel—as his breeder—to birth the antichrist and bring about the complete destruction of the mortal realm as she knew it, I had no doubt it would traumatize her. How could it not?

Before I could offer an answer, Grim beat me to it.

"We need to get out of the open. Come with me."

He didn't even wait for us to respond. Grim made a beeline for the entrance to the underground garage, and we followed like fucking lemmings. But the sight of all those cars had me concocting a plan for all of us to escape so we could reconvene somewhere no one would find us. At the very least, it should buy us some time against future attacks.

Grim walked to a biometric scanner on the wall and pressed his thumb to the screen. A hidden panel opened with a soft whir, revealing rows of car keys. He grumbled something under his breath before selecting a key fob and pointing it at a shiny black Range Rover.

"Are you secretly a superhero or something?"

Grimsby stared at her until she squirmed.

"Right. Horseman. So, supervillain, then."

He grunted before walking to the SUV. "Get in. All of you."

"Where are we going?" Sin asked, opening the back door and gesturing for Merri to crawl into the far back before him.

"I have no fucking clue, but we need to get away from here."

"I have a place we can go," I offered. "It's a safe house of sorts. Not too far, but not close enough for them to track us down."

Grim tossed me the keys. "Let's go."

I caught them one-handed, already moving toward the driver's side. I winced, thinking about what might await us. Hopefully Christian had been earning his wages. If not, there'd be hell to pay.

Unless he'd died or something.

Hmm.

As far as I knew, the monthly wire transfers were still going through as scheduled. So he was probably alive.

Probably.

Guess we were about to find out.

∼

"Are we there yet?" Sin whined.

Chaos reached back and smacked him. "So help me if you ask that one more fucking time."

Sin pouted and rubbed the side of his head, careful not to move too much and jostle the sleeping succubus curled up against him. "But he said it wasn't far. We've been driving for eight fucking hours. Eight hours is far. The last time I traveled in a moving vehicle for this long, it was a tour bus. With a whole ass bedroom. Not squeezed in the back of this clown car like a fucking sardine."

"From my vantage point, you look more comfortable than the rest of us," Chaos snarled, looking over his shoulder at the man in question.

Was that jealousy in his voice?

"We're almost there," I said, clocking the sign I'd been looking for and turning onto the road that would eventually take us to the gate.

I loved it here and hadn't been back in far too long. Isolated, remote, on a small island in France, this home offered every comfort I needed with none of the annoying people I was forced to encounter in a city. As we drove down the road covered by a canopy of trees that would be strikingly beautiful in the summer and fall, I wondered if Merri would be as pleased with what I had to offer as she was with Grim's penthouse. She may have pretended to be unaffected, but she took advantage of every amenity there.

"Wake up, kitten. Mal says we're almost there," Sin murmured.

My gaze flicked to the rearview mirror, and I watched her as she stirred. As we breached the canopy cover, I smiled to myself when the château came into view and my hellcat gasped.

"Where are we?" she breathed.

"Don't get too excited. He's probably taking us to the groundskeeper's shack," Chaos said.

"I can't believe you still have this place." Grim turned his silver eyes on me, a curious expression on his face.

He was the only one of my brothers who'd ever spent time here, and that had been centuries ago.

"Call me sentimental."

"Did you win this place in a bet or something?" Sin asked, craning his neck around to take in more of the sprawling estate.

"Or something," I muttered, recalling the day I'd first set foot on the property and decided I had to own it. After suffering from a short but deadly battle with an unexpected illness, the original owner had transferred the title over to me.

I pulled to a stop in front of the main entrance and just sat for a moment, taking it all in.

"You said a safe house." Merri's tone was almost accusatory.

"Yes."

"This is a castle."

"It's a château."

"Which means castle."

I fought a grin. "Technically it means 'large French country house *or* castle'."

She rolled her eyes.

The others were already attempting to climb out, but my attention was pulled to the man coming around the side of the house. Ah, so he wasn't dead then. Splendid.

"Who the fuck is that?" Chaos growled, his whole body stiffening next to the car.

"It's Christian. The groundskeeper. He's one of mine, don't worry."

"A groundskeeper? This is totally not a safe house," Merri grumbled, climbing out after Sin.

"Monsieur Laurent?" Christian questioned as he approached, speaking to me in French. "I recognize you from your picture."

"Call me Mal. You look just like your grandfather," I replied in perfect French.

"Did you know him? How is that possible? You can't be much older than me."

Fuck. I'd forgotten myself for a moment. "There's a photo of him in one of my other familial estates."

"Ah, very good. Shall I show you inside?"

I nodded and gestured for him to lead the way.

Merri rushed over to me, her voice low. "You speak French?"

"Clearly," I answered, lips twitching with amusement. Dropping my voice and switching back to French, I asked, "Does that turn you on, hellcat?"

When Merri's only response was a blush, I chuckled. I'd take that as a yes.

"So that's a yes to the French, then," Merri whispered.

"We all speak it," Grim added.

"Not me. I only speak French kissing," Sin said with a wink.

Chaos shoved him. "Jesus. It's a wonder you ever get laid. Seriously. Your game is so fucking weak."

"As far as I can tell, neither one of us has gotten laid in a long fucking time. Your game is as weak as mine."

Chaos's gaze lingered on Merri. "Don't be so sure about that."

Christian pushed open the heavy arched door, and we followed him inside the château. "My apologies for not having everything ready for you, Monsieur. I was not aware you were coming or that you would be bringing guests. I will have supplies for you within a few hours. How long will you be staying?"

"It's not a problem. We will be staying indefinitely. Our lodgings were destroyed in the earthquake."

Christian nodded. "I understand. We were lucky here. The improvements your father insisted upon were fortuitous indeed. They kept the structure of the château strong and aside from a few broken windows and an unfortunately unlucky chandelier, the estate escaped unscathed."

"My father was a very wise man indeed."

Christian gestured to the left. "The main salon is aired and cleaned per your usual requirements. There are also a few snacks and some wine in the kitchen. The rooms will need to be prepared, but I will do that now so that you may clean up and rest. Is there anything specific you'd like for dinner?"

I looked to Merri and then realized she was following none of this. Switching back to English, I repeated the question for her.

"Oh, um, anything will be fine. I'm not picky."

Christian's eyes widened as it dawned on him that Merri didn't speak a lick of French. "My apologies, mademoiselle. I will speak only English from now on." He stepped forward and took her hand, dropping his head as he placed a kiss on her knuckles.

I thought Chaos was going to rip his head from his shoulders for touching her.

But it was Grim who growled, "That's enough."

"You have a most beautiful daughter, sir," Christian said to Grim, a dazed expression on his face.

"Tone it down, kitten. You're gonna get the guy killed." Sin's voice was full of humor as he pulled her away from the unfortunately smitten groundskeeper.

Merri blushed. "Sorry. I blame the French."

"So do everyone else," I muttered.

"Is this beautiful creature spoken for by any of you?" Christian asked, taking a step toward her, fully enraptured by Merri.

Even as I hated the attention he was giving her, I couldn't blame him. The succubus was captivating. It was her literal nature. Still, best I remove temptation before one of my brothers decided my groundskeeper had outlived his usefulness.

"Yes," snarled Grim, clearly put out at being referred to as Merri's father.

Christian's face paled as he finally realized his faux pas. "Erm..."

Grim began slowly removing his leather gloves as he took a step toward Christian. Well, fuck. This just went from bad to worse.

"How about we all take a walk and stretch our legs while Christian gets those rooms ready," I suggested, taking Merri by the elbow and hauling her back toward the door. "Come on, Grimsby, I think you'll really love what I've done with the gardens."

With a final scowl in Christian's direction, Grim trailed after us, and we all left my groundskeeper blissfully unaware of his painfully close brush with Death.

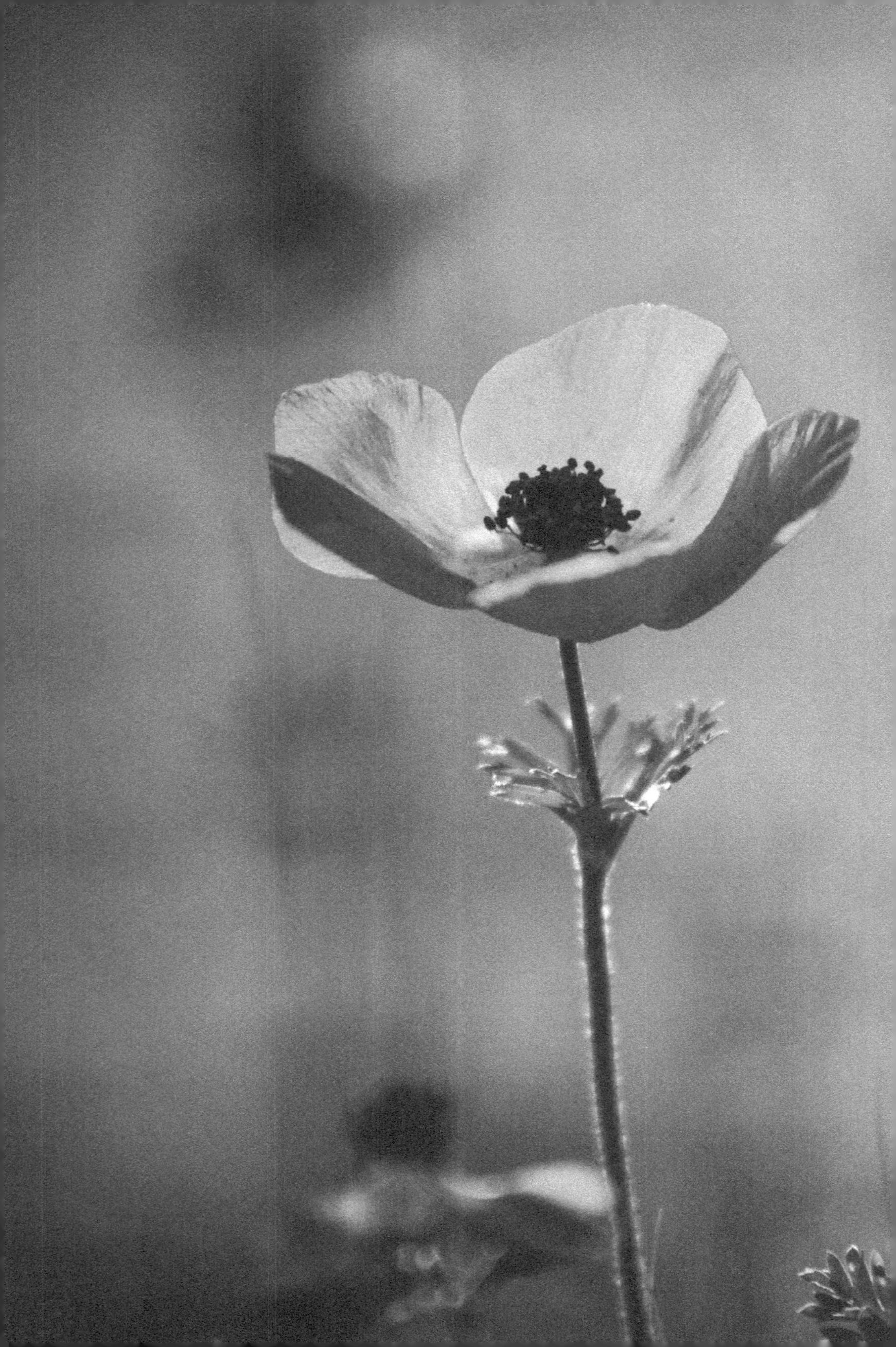

CHAPTER
THIRTY
SIN

This house was not without its problems. Drafty, old as fuck, more than likely haunted, and built like a maze. I couldn't find my way around to save my damn life. If it weren't for the unmistakable scent of coffee calling to me like a siren called a sailor to his death, I'd probably still be lost in some random corridor. I'd found the billiards room, though, so it wasn't all downside.

"Who does an incubus gotta fuck around here to get some coffee?" I called as I stumbled my way into the kitchen. "Oh, Christian. My bad." I gave the groundskeeper a sheepish grin.

Christian slid a full cup of freshly brewed liquid gold across the massive stone island between us. "There you are. No fucking required."

"You sure?" I asked with a little wink, figuring if he was comfortable enough to joke about it, so was I.

"Positive."

"Your loss. I'm delicious."

I brought the mug to my lips and closed my eyes as the rich flavor of the coffee coated my tongue. "I take it back. *This* is delicious. I'm trash."

Christian chuckled and turned back to whatever he was doing as I made love to my coffee.

Glancing around the enormous kitchen, I looked for any clue my comrades were up and about. Grimsby barely slept, so I was certain the grumpy fuck would be here somewhere.

"Where is everyone, Chris?" I asked.

He stiffened at the nickname. "So far, the only one I've encountered is Mademoiselle Merri. She opted to take her coffee in the morning room."

Pretentious fuck.

I wasn't sure if I was referring to Malice or Christian, but a morning room? Come the fuck on. What douchebag had so many rooms in their house they had to keep track of them by the time of day?

"And where can I find that oh-so-special-it-has-its-own-name room?"

The groundskeeper smirked. "It's just across the foyer on the east side. It will be the one with all the beautiful sunlight streaming in the windows."

Ah, because morning. Now it wasn't as pretentious, I guessed.

"Thanks."

Christian tipped his head. "My pleasure."

"So is this going to be a regular thing? Coffee with Christian?"

He chuckled. "Non. I was just putting away the last of the supplies. Per Monsieur Laurent's directions, I will return to my cottage unless summoned so that you may have your privacy."

"I see. Well, in that case, it was nice meeting you. Now, if you'll excuse me, I have to see a pretty redhead about my morning smooch."

His brows raised, but he stayed silent.

That's right, Frenchie, she's not just Grim's.

Without further ado, I spun around and headed off in the direction he'd indicated. It wasn't that hard to find the room after all. I just followed the scent of Merri. We'd spent enough time around each other now that it was easy for me to pick out the distinct notes of her natural perfume.

The pocket doors that led into the morning room were mostly open, affording me a perfect view of her as she sat on a tufted sofa in a beam of sunlight. If I didn't know she was a succubus, I'd have mistaken her for an angel, or maybe a fae. Her coffee sat untouched on a small round end table within arm's reach.

"It's a shame to waste good coffee, kitten," I said, stepping into the room as I spoke.

She jumped, so lost in her thoughts she hadn't heard my approach. Eyes wild and hand pressed against her chest, she gaped at me. "Sin, Jesus. You startled me."

"I see that."

She stuck her tongue out, and suddenly all I could do was think about sucking on it. The image sent a wave of need straight to my dick, which was now very obviously thickening in my jeans. Fuck, she was the most arousing creature I'd ever known.

Merri sucked in a deep breath, her eyes darkening as she caught the unmistakable rush of lust. Now that I was standing in front of her and could really take in her appearance, it was so obvious how badly she needed to feed.

She would be stunning no matter what state she was in, but I couldn't help but notice the smudges beneath her eyes, the dull quality of her hair, or the paleness of her lips. If she'd been a painting, I'd say that she'd been bleached by the sun. The life was just sort of draining out of her.

"How long has it been since you fed?"

She stiffened at the accusation in my voice. "Um, not since Malice. Well, I got a little hit off of Chaos, but it wasn't exactly filling."

"We need to get you taken care of. A hungry succubus is dangerous."

Her gaze flicked away from me, shame washing over her face. "You don't have to remind me. I already know."

"Already know what?" Malice said from the door.

"Ah, perfect timing, Mal. Our little sex demon needs you to get her camming situation handled ASAP. Where are we at with that?"

Merri sat up a little straighter, hope in her eyes.

"It's all ready to go. I just came from delivering my spare laptop to your room, hellcat. You can log in whenever you like, and there's no way you'll be traced."

He's said something similar before, but it seemed counterproductive to point it out. Merri needed access to her website unless, of course, she wanted to begin regularly feeding on the four of us, but even though things had started to shift, she clearly still wasn't comfortable enough to come out and ask us. Until she was, she needed an alternative that would keep all of us safe.

Chaos came barreling into the room, his eyes a little wild, expression frantic as he zeroed in on Merri. "There she is. Fuck, Malice, why is your house so large? How can we keep her safe if every inch of this place is like a game of hide-and-seek?"

Oh, Chaos. You're just as much of a goner for her as I am.

Malice raised an eyebrow. "And where exactly do you think she'd run off to?"

Chaos shrugged. "I dunno. That's sort of the entire point."

"We're on an island with only one access road, not to mention the gate surrounding the property. Even if someone swam their way to shore, no one is sneaking up on us here. She's as safe as we can make her, Chaos."

"That's what you said about my penthouse. Now it's gone." Grim's deep voice rumbled through the room as he joined us.

"To be fair, you were the one who said your penthouse was safe. I simply said it was as safe as I could make it. Had you left it up to a vote, I'd have suggested the château sooner."

"This isn't a democracy."

"Can we not make Daddy angry this early in the morning?" I asked in a weak attempt to lighten the mood.

"Merri needs to feed. I can feel it," Chaos said, abruptly turning the ship around.

"Yes, we've established that. She's all set." Malice sighed and rolled his eyes as he turned his focus back to the woman in question. "You shouldn't have any trouble. If you do, you know how to find me."

"Do I? Is there some special Pestilence signal I should flash into the night sky or something?"

The corner of Malice's lip twitched up in the semblance of a smile. "Just call out my name."

"So she'll be camming?" Chaos asked, his expression unreadable but his disappointment palpable.

My, how things had changed. Just a couple of weeks ago, you couldn't have paid the guy to fuck Merri, but now he was all but foaming at the mouth to volunteer. Glancing around the room, I realized it was the same for all of us. Without even trying—and despite our best efforts—she'd managed to wrap each and every one of us around her little finger.

"Don't sound so sad, Chaos. She puts on one hell of a show."

"How do you . . ." Merri's eyes flew wide. "OriginalSin. I should have fucking known!"

I could have reacted one of two ways. Tried to hide the truth or owned up to it. Honesty was always the best policy.

Slipping into the southern accent I gave my persona, I smirked. "In the flesh, darlin'. I have to admit, I've been missing your outfit of the day posts. And that private session we had was"—I sucked in a sharp breath and let my eyes flutter closed—"fucking perfect."

She gaped at me, her pouty lips opening and closing like a fish. "How . . . I . . . but . . ." She finally gave up trying to form a coherent sentence and just shook her head. Then something else seemed to occur to her because she scowled and cast a squinty-eyed glare at the rest of us. "Who else has been spying on me?"

"I mean, is it technically spying when it's on the internet?"

"Malice!"

He held up his hands. "That wasn't an admission of guilt, just an honest question."

"Your whole platform is based on anonymity, kitten. I was protecting my identity and feeding you at the same time." I knew she wasn't really that mad at me. If anything, I'd bet she was annoyed she hadn't figured it out based on my handle alone.

"Ugh, fine. But you didn't have to give me a fake-real name, *Emmett*."

"Who said it was fake?"

She blinked at me, and I used her surprise to distract her further.

"Besides, if you think the expression 'Death is always watching' didn't stem from somewhere, then you aren't paying attention. Not a single one of us is innocent here."

Grim's brows pulled together as he straightened his shoulders. "Leave me out of your nonsense, Sin."

"But throwing you under the bus is so much fun."

Grim glared at me. "It seems you have the matter well in hand. I'll be in the garden."

He left before any of us could reply.

Merri took that opportunity to get to her feet. She swayed slightly, and I swear to God, all three of us moved at once to help her steady herself.

"I'm okay," she protested.

"No, you're not," Chaos said, gripping her bicep.

"I will be."

Chaos, Malice, and I all exchanged worried glances. Our dynamic with Merri had changed so dramatically since we'd almost lost her twice now. Each one of us seemed more devoted to our cause, but it was more than that. We weren't just interested in fucking her.

I knew I really liked her now. I more than liked her, if I was being honest with myself. I *cared* about Merri. The thought of something happening to her made me ragey. I could only imagine what it did to Chaos. He'd run in here like the house was on fire when he thought she might have disappeared right under his nose. Chaos never worried about people like that. And Malice . . . Well, his heart may as well have been carved out of ice, he was so cold and indifferent most of the time. Still, even he was drawn to her warmth. She'd thawed him in a matter of weeks.

And that didn't account for the changes in Grim. He was about as cuddly as the thorns on one of his prized rose bushes, and yet he followed her around like a sunflower chasing the sun. He was as obsessed with her as the rest of us. Even if he wasn't prepared to admit it.

Poor girl.

If she'd thought we were insufferable when we were trying to keep her at a distance, she was in for one hell of an awakening now that she had our joint attention.

"I'll be in my room. Thank you for your help, Mal. I'm sure after a session, I'll feel a lot better."

We watched her go, all of us quiet until she was out of sight.

My gaze slid to Malice. "Sooo, do we all get our own laptops, or are we all piling in your room?"

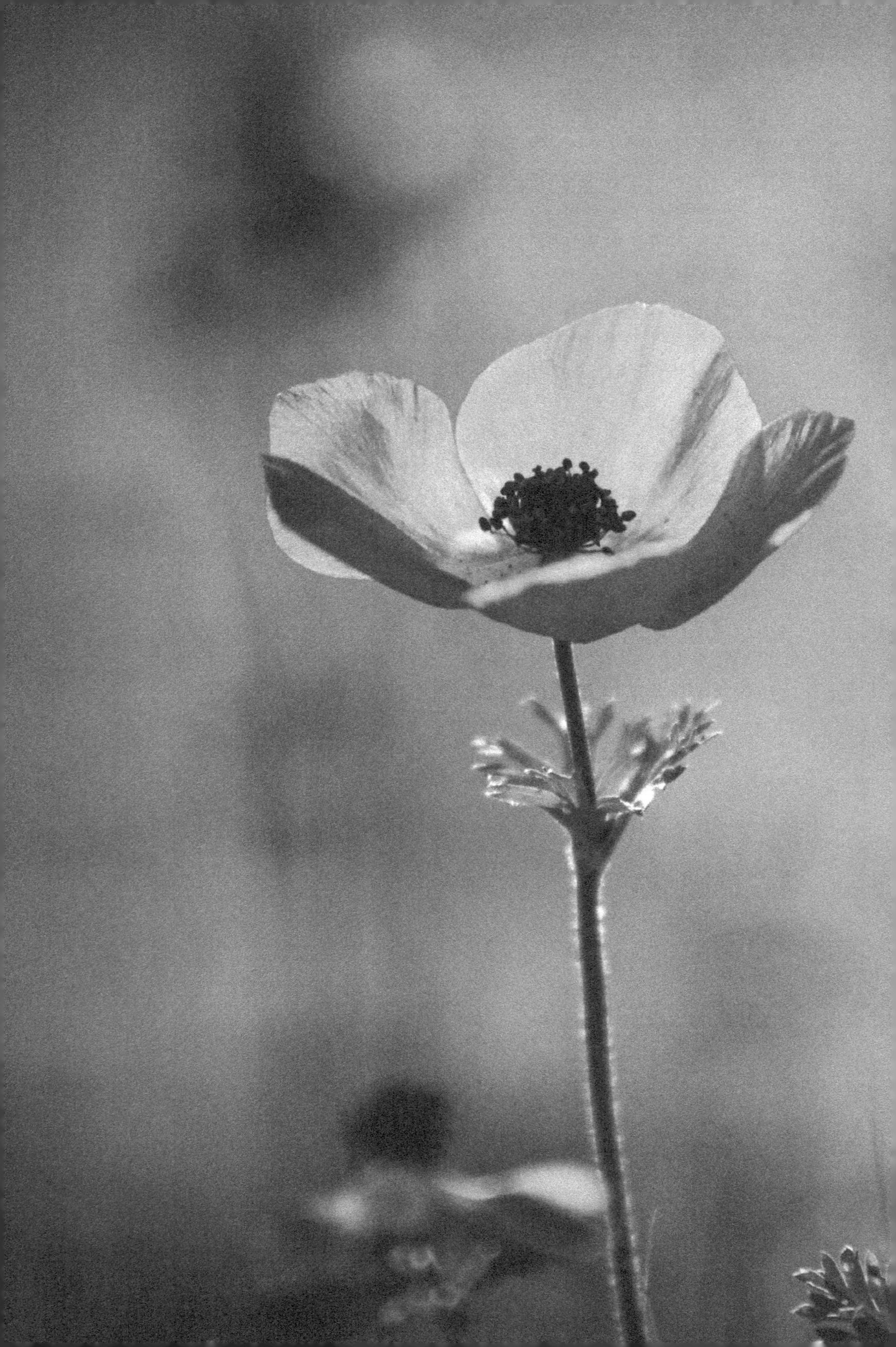

CHAPTER
THIRTY-ONE
MERRI

True to his word, Malice had left a laptop on my bed for me. The sleek, modern device felt completely out of place in a room that looked like it belonged in a museum or maybe a period piece like *Bridgerton*. Part of me wanted to flounce around in a fluffy dress and wig and say *Let them eat cake*, even if that was historically inaccurate.

I shook my head as my gaze wandered back over to the crackling fireplace and what I was pretty sure was an honest-to-God Degas. Like a real one, not a print. I had never been anywhere this sumptuous in my life. I was a little afraid I might break something irreplaceable. Even the bed was gilt and opulent. Four-poster, king-sized, and like sleeping on a fucking cloud. With the rain beating against the window and the wind howling, I had half a mind to burrow beneath these covers and stay here. Hell, I was pretty sure the apocalypse could take out everything but this island, and I'd be fine as long as I could stay on this bed.

A ping pulled me back to my laptop, the incoming notification alerting me that Andi was online and had sent me a message.

PRETTYPENNY:

Baby girl! Tell me your presence online means you're all up and running again.

Oh, God, where to begin? And how much could I even share?

MERRI-GO-ROUND:

Finally looks that way. It was touch and go there for a while.

PRETTYPENNY:

Was it the quake? I lost my internet connection for a hot fucking minute over here too.

Even though it was Andi, I decided to keep my response vague. Mostly because of the numerous warnings from Sin and Malice that I could not share any personal—or potentially personal—details while online. It wasn't Andi I was worried about, but if people decided to go after her in an attempt to get to me, I didn't want her to know anything that could put her at risk.

MERRI-GO-ROUND:

It did a lot of damage to the place I was staying.

PRETTYPENNY:

Did you have to find somewhere else to stay?

Fuck.

MERRI-GO-ROUND:

You could say that. I'm sort of doing the digital nomad thing for now.

I winced at the lie but figured if it kept us both safe, she'd ultimately understand and forgive me for it.

> **PRETTYPENNY:**
> You can always come stay with me if you need to. My couch is your couch.

> **MERRI-GO-ROUND:**
> You're sweet. I think I'm all set for now, but I will let you know if that changes.

> **PRETTYPENNY:**
> Still shacking up with the hot brute squad? I don't blame you for choosing them over me. In times like these, it helps to have someone watching your back.

A wave of hunger made my vision blur, and I had to close my eyes against the accompanying dizzy spell.

> **MERRI-GO-ROUND:**
> I hate to cut our chat short, but I need to get set up for my live.

> **PRETTYPENNY:**
> Can I make a suggestion?

> **MERRI-GO-ROUND:**
> For my live? Sure.

It wasn't unusual for Andi to offer advice on what kind of content I might want to consider for my site, but it had been a while since she'd offered.

> **PRETTYPENNY:**
> Check in on ShyGuy. I've seen the comments on your feed wondering about you and when you were coming back. He's one of your regulars, right? It seems like he might really be missing out on the "girlfriend experience," and I'd hate for you to lose the steady income stream if he has to find it somewhere else.

Guilt twisted in my gut. Cole probably thought I'd abandoned him.

The rest of them were regulars on lots of profiles. They didn't have strong attachments, just a strong urge to get off. Cole wanted the companionship his severe agoraphobia wouldn't allow him to go out and find.

MERRI-GO-ROUND:
I'll send him a video message free of charge.

PRETTYPENNY:
Perfect. Exactly what I would have done. Ah, they grow up so fast.

MERRI-GO-ROUND:
Thanks, Mom. 😊

PRETTYPENNY:
I prefer Mommy, thank you.

MERRI-GO-ROUND:
Of course you do, you skank.

PRETTYPENNY:
You know it! But also, is that any way to talk to your mother?!? Don't make me ground you! Now go do your chores, or you can't have any dessert. And by dessert, I mean your hot brute squad.

Why did my cheeks burn with embarrassment?

MERRI-GO-ROUND:
It's not even like that . . .

PRETTYPENNY:
Suuuuuuuure.

Rolling my eyes, I closed out of our chat and clicked on Cole's username. He'd been so happy after I'd sent my last message and had resumed his regular check-ins, even though I hadn't been able to reply to most of them.

Deciding that Andi was right and I needed to amp up the "girlfriend experience" a.k.a. making sure he felt valued and like this wasn't just transactional, I rearranged myself on the bed. Instead of lying back on the pillows, I twisted my body around and laid on my stomach, giving my shirt a tug so my cleavage was practically spilling out of the soft gray V-neck. Then I fluffed up my hair so it looked like we'd just been rolling around the bed together. Checking my appearance in my webcam, I pinched my cheeks and bit my lower lip a little so I was flushed and pouty.

There we go.

One girlfriend coming up in three...

Two...

One.

"Hey, handsome. I've been missing my favorite guy, so I wanted to check in with you." Did I make my voice a little breathless? Yes. Did I bat my lashes at the camera and amp up the sweet and tender expression on my face? You betcha. Could you see the tops of my nipples because my neckline was so low? Damn straight.

"Are you around for a chat? I'd love to hear how you're doing. It's been way too long, and I really miss your voice. Let me know when you can, okay, handsome?" I blew a kiss into the camera. "Hope to talk soon."

I barely hit send before a reply came in. I laughed, mentally making a note to do something similar for 1N3V1T@BL3. I definitely owed my newest subscriber some personalized content.

SHYGUY25:

Yes.

SHYGUY25:

Hell yes.

SHYGUY25:

Always yes for you.

MERRI-GO-ROUND:

Video?

SHYGUY25:

Is that even a question?

My smile was genuine as I sent him a video chat request. I wondered fleetingly if today would be the day he finally let me see him, but when the black screen appeared next to my video feed, my question was answered. One day. I was sure of it.

"You look so beautiful, Merri," he said, his voice soft and earnest. "I was worried about you."

"I'm sorry. It's been . . ." I shook my head as I trailed off.

"I get it. Same here. I can't believe that earthquake. Things are getting really intense out there."

"Are you staying safe? Do you have everything you need?" I asked, suddenly worried about my little shut-in, locked away all by himself.

"Not gonna lie, knowing you care makes me feel good."

"Of course I care. You're special to me, Cole."

"Am I?" The way he asked, like it meant the world to him to hear that, warmed my heart, but it also reminded me why I pulled away in the first place. Feelings were involved on his side, and I was not in a place where I could reciprocate them even if I wanted to. Even assuming the connection between us was genuine, Cole had no idea I was a succubus, and I had no intention of ever having a Jimmy 2.0.

"What's that look on your face, Merri? Are you okay?" Concern laced Cole's voice, which prompted me to take a glance at myself in the camera.

He was right. My expression had gone vacant. Fuck, I was hungry.

I got on my knees and pouted into the camera. "I just missed you. I miss what we share together. The way you make me feel."

"God, I've missed you too. I've been out of my mind with worry that something terrible happened to you. Not knowing where you were, that you were safe, it was awful. I just wanted to take care of you."

"That's because you are a good man, Cole."

I pulled my T-shirt over my head, wanting to redirect this conversation to something a lot sexier. I needed his mind—more specifically, his lust—in the game. If I didn't feed soon, I would be right back where I was when Grim found me in the wine cellar.

"D-do you want me to request a session?"

"What?" I rasped, reaching behind my back and unhooking my bra.

"I'm not paying for this right now. Shouldn't we—"

"Consider this my gift to you. For being so good to me."

My bra fell free, baring my breasts to the cool air in the room. Even with the fire burning in the hearth, this old home was drafty, and one glance outside told me the storm was still raging. Wind, rain, and now lightning flashing in the sky made this moment somehow even more intimate.

His soft hitched breath carried over the speakers of my computer and practically caressed my needy skin. "Fuck, baby. Touch yourself for me."

Replicating the feeling, I trailed my fingers down my chest, eyes falling closed as I pretended they belonged to someone else. But when the image came to mind, it wasn't Cole I was thinking of. It was Sin. Maybe that's because I didn't know what Cole looked like. Or maybe it was because I'd just learned that Sin had tricked me, and we'd been in a very similar situation to this one with explosively satisfying results.

It was because I was hungry and needed relief.

That was all it was.

It definitely wasn't because I was already addicted to one of the four men sharing this castle with me.

One. Ha.

I was such a fucking liar.

A thin tendril of lust curled through the room, all of it coming from Cole, but it wasn't enough by a long shot.

"Are you touching yourself, Cole? Make yourself feel good. Please? I need it."

"Merri," he whispered, his voice laced with desire.

Another little shiver of his lust raced across my skin, but it only seemed to ramp up my appetite. I was pretty sure this was what it felt like to be starving in a restaurant but stuck waiting for your table. I could smell how delicious and satisfying the meal was about to be, but I wasn't actually able to eat any of it yet.

"Ungh." His groan was drawn out and sexier than it had any right to be. "I bet you taste as sweet as you look, baby."

I let my hand travel down between my thighs, knowing he'd need a little more inspiration to help him get there. This didn't need to be a lengthy session; I just needed him to come.

"Oh, Cole. I'm so wet for you."

He groaned again, his panted breaths coming closer together as he worked himself over. "Yeah, you are. Fuck. It's been too long. I'm close."

"How close?" I breathed, desperate to feed.

"Too close. Goddamn, baby. I'm . . ."

"Come on, Cole. Give it to me."

"Yes, I'll give y—" His pleasure-filled words cut off as a wall-rattling clap of thunder exploded overhead, and the power went out and with it, the Wi-Fi.

"No!" I shouted, slamming the laptop lid down. "Motherfucker!"

Malice had better fix this right fucking now. A girl could only take so much deprivation. I got to my feet and instantly regretted it as my head swam and the floor tilted.

"Merri?" Sin asked, pushing my door open and inviting himself inside just in time to watch my graceless fall to the floor. "Fuck!"

He scooped me into his lap, brushing my hair away from my face and looking down into my eyes.

"Wh-what are you doing here?" I asked, my voice weak as the starvation got the better of me.

He shrugged. "I was sort of holed up outside your door waiting to see if you'd have any leftovers."

Of fucking course he had. I couldn't even be mad at the guy. He needed to feed just as much as I did. Although he was not in nearly as bad of shape as I was.

"Come on, kitten. Let's go find the others."

A weak moan of protest was all I could manage.

"Power's out, and you're starving. It's us or . . ."

There was no "or." I wasn't going to make it without feeding.

He ran a soothing hand down my spine. "It'll be okay, kitten. We're going to take care of you."

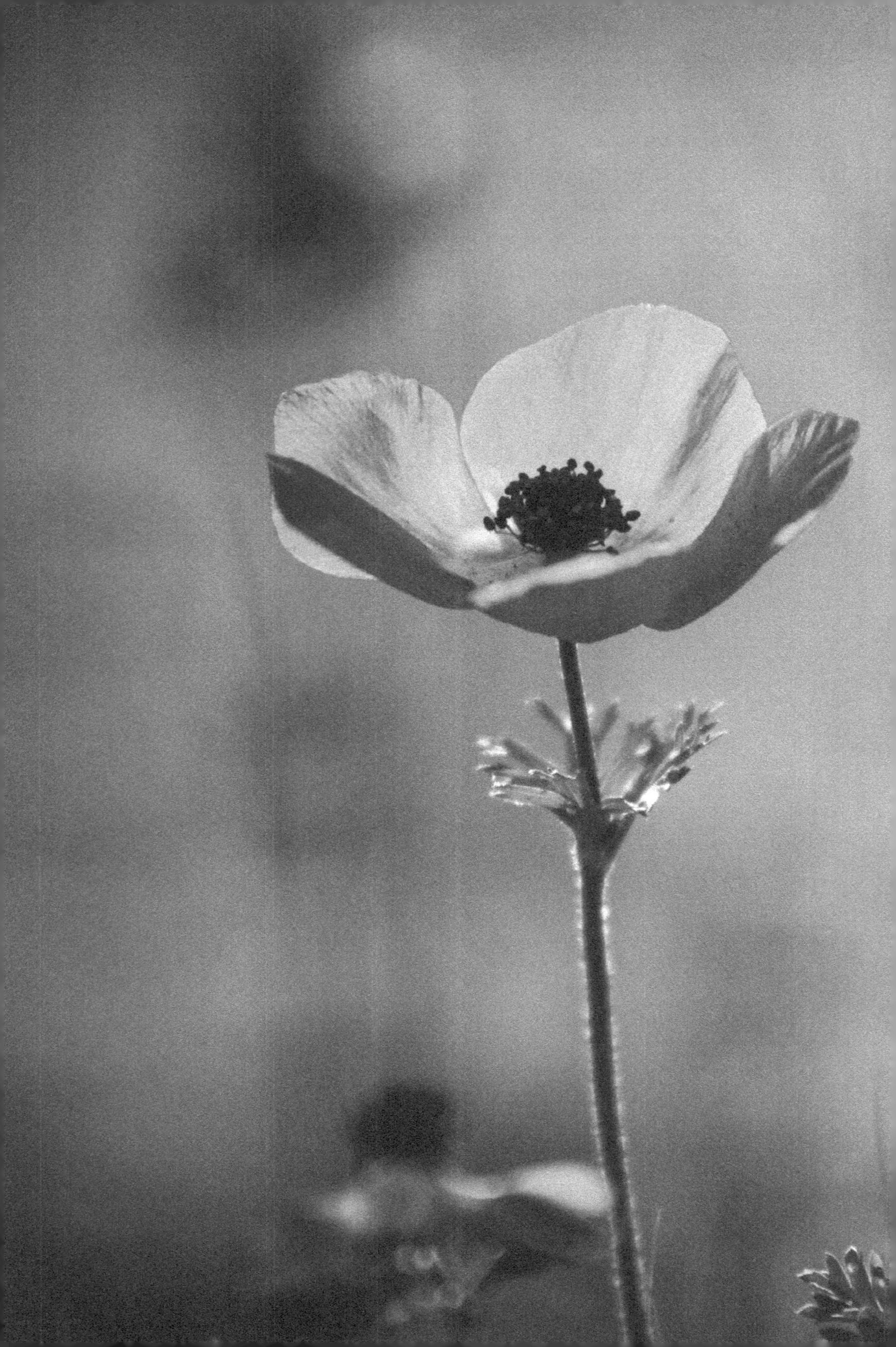

CHAPTER
THIRTY-TWO
GRIM

"Chaos! Malice! Grimsby! Get in here! I need your help!" Sin's voice ricocheted down the hall, tearing my focus from the candles I was lighting in the parlor.

I turned toward the sound just as he kicked open the door and came stumbling in with a barely conscious Merri in his arms. She was naked from the waist up, her long hair covering most of her delectable curves.

"Oh good, you're already here."

"What happened?"

I don't know why I bothered asking the question; it was obvious enough. I'd seen her in a near enough state barely a week ago. She must not have been able to feed before the power went out. I could feel that same tug to be close to her. I hadn't understood or maybe even clocked it at the time, but looking back, I'd definitely felt it. Her inner demon was trying to lure potential targets. An internal fail-safe to protect her from starvation.

Chaos barreled into the room like an angry bull, all grunts and growls as he watched Sin lay Merri down on a chaise longue, her red tresses spilling across the silver fabric reminiscent of blood in the dim light.

"What the fuck did you do to her, Sinclair?"

Sin stepped back away from her, his hands held up in supplication. "It wasn't me. She was trying to feed, and the power went out."

The light of Malice's torch preceded his entrance into the room. "Is everyth—oh, bloody hell, not again," he said, taking in Merri and immediately piecing together what had happened.

"Is this a true storm, or an attack?" Chaos asked, moving to the window and lifting the curtain to peer out into the night. As if on cue, thunder boomed, and a bright flash of light streaked across the clouds.

"Does it fucking matter? Either way, Merri needs us," Sin practically snarled.

Chaos dropped the heavy fabric. "Of course it matters. We need to know if demons are about to break through the windows. Unless you'd rather not take any precaution and be caught with your literal pants down, Sinclair."

Malice sent his focus outward before saying, "Just a storm. Although it's less clear if it's a side effect of the apocalypse or truly natural."

"And they say global warming is fake," Sin muttered, turning his attention back to Merri.

No one seemed to notice as I backed slowly away from the tableaux the three of them created. Or so I thought until Sin called my name.

"Where do you think you're going?"

"You know I can't be a part of this. You three have things well in hand."

"You're not getting out of it this time, Grimsby. You don't have to touch her, but you need to participate. It will be safer for all of us."

"What do you mean?" Chaos asked, gaze sharpening on Sin's face.

"She's gone too long without again." Sin shot a pointed glare at me. "It's neither safe nor smart to let her drain one of us in order to charge her battery. Think of her like a bear who didn't eat enough before hibernation and woke up early, ravenous, blowing through any available food source in order to survive."

"She's a . . . bear?" I asked slowly, trying to make sense of his ramble.

"No. But I see what he's saying," Chaos said, already taking off his shirt. "Scarcity breeds desperation."

"He's right. She nearly put me in a coma because her need to replenish her energy was so great the last time." Malice pulled up a chair and sat only a few feet from Merri. "All of us together give her a supply she won't drain. More of us equals a bigger pool to draw from. Less risk all around."

Ah. That made sense.

I scowled at Sin. "Why didn't you just say that in the first place?"

"Pretty sure I did. Not my fault you don't understand metaphor, Grimsby."

"Piss off."

Didn't they understand how dangerous I was to her? Could she feed off of me safely? Or would my darkness corrupt her simply by taking my energy as sustenance? I was the personification of death. How could anything about me nourish instead of destroy?

Sin finally seemed to register my internal debate. He brushed Merri's hair away from her forehead before whispering instructions to her. "Get comfortable." Then he came to me. Keeping his voice low, he met my stare straight on. "You're not going to hurt her, Grim."

"How can you know that?"

"For one thing, the three of us won't let you. For another, Hades fucks without killing all the time. If he can do it, so can you. You don't own the market on death magic."

"Hades doesn't kill everything he touches."

"You're not going to touch her."

I was ashamed of the tightness in my chest at the thought. "But—"

Sin reached out and grabbed my shoulder, the heat of his palm radiating through the fabric of my shirt and startling me. Touches were few and far between with the four of us. We kept to ourselves, and they certainly gave me a wide berth, but right now, this bit of connection grounded me.

"For once, we aren't the bad guys, Grim. Lilith came to us so we could save her. You and I both know she would never risk Merri's safety by doing so if she thought we would do more harm than good. Feeding her is part of that."

He was right. In all my years, I'd never once been charged with saving anyone. But that was exactly what I wanted to do for Merri. I wanted to save her as many times as she needed me.

Heaving a sigh, I nodded before unbuttoning the cuffs of both of my sleeves and rolling them up. "Fine. Where do you want me?"

"You can sit anywhere you're comfortable," Merri answered, her voice raspy with exhaustion. "I don't even need to be able to see you if you don't want me to. But it will work best if you're in the room."

"I don't mind you watching."

I was startled by my admission, but the way her eyes seemed to flicker with interest was enough to soothe any embarrassment my vulnerability caused.

"How come that line never works when I say it?" Sin asked, choosing a spot that allowed him to touch Merri.

"Because we don't like you?" Malice offered.

"Because she's prettier than you are," Chaos said right on his heels.

Sin pouted and rubbed at his chest. "Ouch, guys."

Merri lifted her hand and gently touched Sin's thigh. "I think you're pretty."

"Yeah?"

"So pretty, Sinclair."

His smile was shockingly tender as he brushed his thumb over her lower lip. "They're right, though. I'm nowhere near as pretty as you."

She smiled, but it was weak and sent a bolt of worry through me.

"How do we start?" Chaos asked, his dark brows pulled together as he watched Sin flirt.

I didn't blame him. Her attention was like the sun shining on you. Pure and beautiful, filled with warmth none of us thought we'd ever find.

"Well, first, I'm going to give our girl a little boost."

"A boost?" Merri asked, her eyes locked on his as he leaned down.

"Uh huh. Just consider me a shot of espresso, kitten. I'll perk you right up."

"Idiot," Malice muttered.

Merri's lips twitched with laughter a second before Sin teased her with the merest hint of a kiss and then replaced his mouth with his thumb. He dragged her lower lip down as he pressed his thumb inside with a whispered command. "Suck."

Her moan of approval as she obeyed had my cock jerking to attention. Fuck, but she was magnificent. And she hadn't even done anything.

"It's her arousal," Malice explained, his face carefully blank, although his body betrayed how rigidly he was fighting for control.

"I felt it last time," Chaos added, his voice low so as not to distract her from what Sin was doing. "It was like getting punched in the dick with lust."

Malice nodded his agreement. "She's hardwired to make sure we want to play with her."

"I don't need any interference to make me want to play. The last time she didn't use a hint of her power, and I was ready to take her against the alley wall."

"This isn't just her being a succubus?" I asked, somehow needing to know I wasn't the only one feeling helplessly drawn to our charge.

"Not for me," Chaos said.

"Me either," Malice muttered, though he seemed far more put out by the admission.

"Fuck." I said it under my breath, but they all heard me.

Sin pulled his finger free with an approving hum and got on his knees next to the chaise. "Do you want me to touch you or keep my hands to myself?"

"I need you to take charge. You understand me better than anyone else in this room."

He smirked. "Fuck yes, I do. Hips up, kitten. I can't go another minute without showing them your pretty pussy."

She let out a breathy whimper as she lifted her hips so he could tug her sweats down her toned legs. Jesus fucking Christ, the way her body returned to an effortlessly sensual position after she was bare had my cock throbbing. The flickering firelight mixed with the soft amber glow from the candles I'd lit made all of her curves appear even more mouthwatering.

Merri didn't have to try to be seductive. She simply was. It was as natural to her as breathing.

"Fuck," Chaos grunted, taking a seat on the sofa and palming his straining dick.

My body echoed the sentiment. I couldn't remember a time I'd ever felt this primed. And when Merri whimpered as Sin brushed her hair behind her shoulders and exposed her bare breasts, I had to adjust in my seat to relieve some of the tension in my trousers. I'd positioned myself directly across from Merri but farther back than the others. It was darker here, and I felt safer tucked into the shadows.

Malice prowled around a writing desk, moving toward the fireplace. I glanced his way, wondering where the fuck he was going, when I realized he'd moved only so he could get a better view. Positioned as he was before, Sin was blocking almost everything worth seeing.

Sin moved just enough to the side and dropped to his knees that our view suddenly improved dramatically.

"Spread your thighs, pretty girl. Let them see how wet you are," Sin whispered against her collarbone as he kissed his way down to her breast.

Her back arched and her legs spread wide as Sin sucked one nipple into his mouth. Her thighs glistened with arousal, the slick evidence of her need perfuming the room and making my mouth water. Sin slipped two fingers inside her and began a slow pump of his hand, causing her to whimper.

I squeezed my trouser-covered thigh hard enough my knuckles popped, but God help me, I stayed in my chair. Chaos let out a low groan and freed his dick from his joggers but wasn't working it yet. The soft hiss of a zipper was my only clue that Malice was doing the same.

"Oh God," Merri moaned, writhing against his touch.

"How are you doing, kitten?" Sin asked, nibbling his way up her neck.

"I need . . ."

"Tell us, baby. We are here to give you every fucking thing you want," he encouraged when she faltered.

"I need more from them."

Sin smirked as he leaned up and glanced over his shoulder. "You heard her, boys. Stroke 'em if you got 'em."

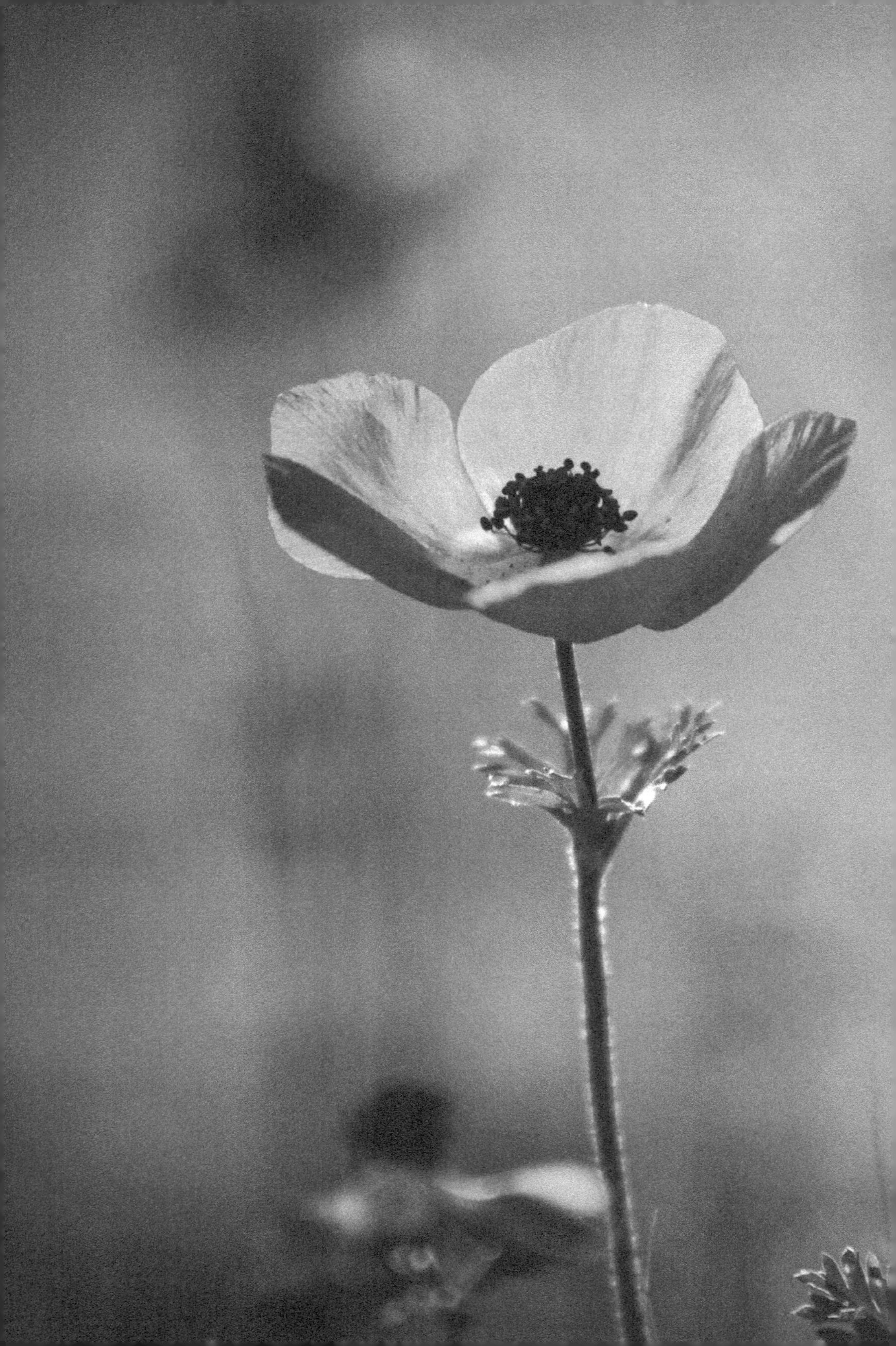

CHAPTER
THIRTY-THREE
CHAOS

I'd never been jealous of Sinclair, not until Merri crashed into our lives. Now if I gave myself free rein to move out of my chair, I knew I'd throw him across the room so I could take his place and be the one who dragged those noises from her.

I didn't have much interest in knocking her up, at least not in the primal sense. But uncovering the mystery of what her perfect fucking cunt felt like wrapped around my dick? That was my new purpose in life. I'd spent my existence either fucking or fighting, and if I was being honest, fighting was getting old.

Sitting here, dick straining and leaking precum, I couldn't think of a single valid argument for keeping my distance. Originally I told myself it was because Sin would take care of it, and I wasn't about to fuck some girl just because Grim told me I had to. My dick, my choice. Next it was because the way I felt when I was around her freaked me the fuck out. I wasn't about to be the latest stallion in a succubus's overflowing stable. But then I'd gotten my first taste of her, and now all I wanted was more.

So when Sin's smirked command came, I didn't need to be told twice. I palmed my erection and stroked slowly. A hiss of pleasure escaped as tingles ran down my thighs.

"Make her moan for us, Sin."

Grim's directive shocked me, the tension in his voice matching his posture. He hadn't joined us, his cock still begging for attention as it strained against his pants. His fuckin' loss. If I worried too much about what he was doing, I was going to miss out on the best show of my life. And frankly, that was not an option.

"Fuck, yes, please," Merri moaned.

The sounds she made were as much torture as they were music to my ears. My cock would have been in the torture camp at the moment. Sin used his thumb to rub tight circles on her clit as he did something with his fingers that made her arch her back, nipples furled into tight buds.

"Gods," I groaned, using the pad of my thumb to spread a drop of precum across the head of my dick, mimicking what Sin was doing to Merri's needy little clit. "Fuck," I grunted, hips thrusting to meet my strokes. It was nowhere close to what I wanted, but watching her chase her own climax was enough to have me panting.

Grim's breaths were shaky, but the stubborn ass remained stoic. I didn't know how he could do it. Her scent blossomed in the air, lust heady and thick, and as we all watched on, her pallor grew rosy and the luster returned to her hair.

Merri was feeding.

Once I noticed the shift, I could feel the subtle pull on me as she fed. It wasn't an obvious thing, like someone nipping at your ear. It was more like the lapping of a wave against your feet, and as the water receded back into the ocean, it took a little bit of you with it.

A pearl of precum beaded to the surface, and I was so close to reaching my release it was embarrassing. I'd barely gotten started, but the sight of Merri being pleasured turned me on more than I ever expected. Sin had explained how his incubus powers worked more than once, usually as a prelude to trying to get one of us to let him feed, so I knew that Merri's arousal was akin to a spider's web. And the more worked up she got, the better it felt for all of us. It was the sexiest parasitic relationship I could imagine. With the way I was feeling right now, I didn't even care if she ate my head when she was done with me. I just wanted to exist in this forever.

And that's what made her arguably the most dangerous creature in the room.

"Please, please, please," she whispered, rocking her hips against Sin's palm.

"Yes, baby. Let go. I'll give you as many as you want."

I hadn't really heard Sin work, but I had to admit, when he turned it on, he was a master of seduction. Go fucking figure. Guess he was the man for the job after all. I'd bang one of the horsewomen before ever admitting that to him, though.

Malice had been incredibly quiet through all of this, but I saw him prowling toward her, his eyes trained on her face, hand moving over his cock in long steady strokes.

I didn't have time to worry about whatever he murmured as he positioned himself near her head because her whole body tightened and Sin grunted, "Fuck yes, give it to me."

Merri's climax moved through her body in an almost perceptible wave. She came so prettily, her back arching, a pink flush spreading up her chest and neck as a plaintive moan ripped from her throat. I'd been close before this, but when I caught sight of her toes curling into the chaise, I was done for.

Everything that had been building gathered into a brilliant explosion of bliss as I reached my climax. Coming with Merri was a bit like getting swept up in a supernova. I was no longer in control of my body; I was simply along for the ride. I was also pretty sure I roared out my release, but I couldn't hear anything other than her. I couldn't see anything other than her. Every part of me was linked to her.

And it was in the middle of that storm that clarity struck with the brilliance of a bolt of lightning.

I was so completely fucked.

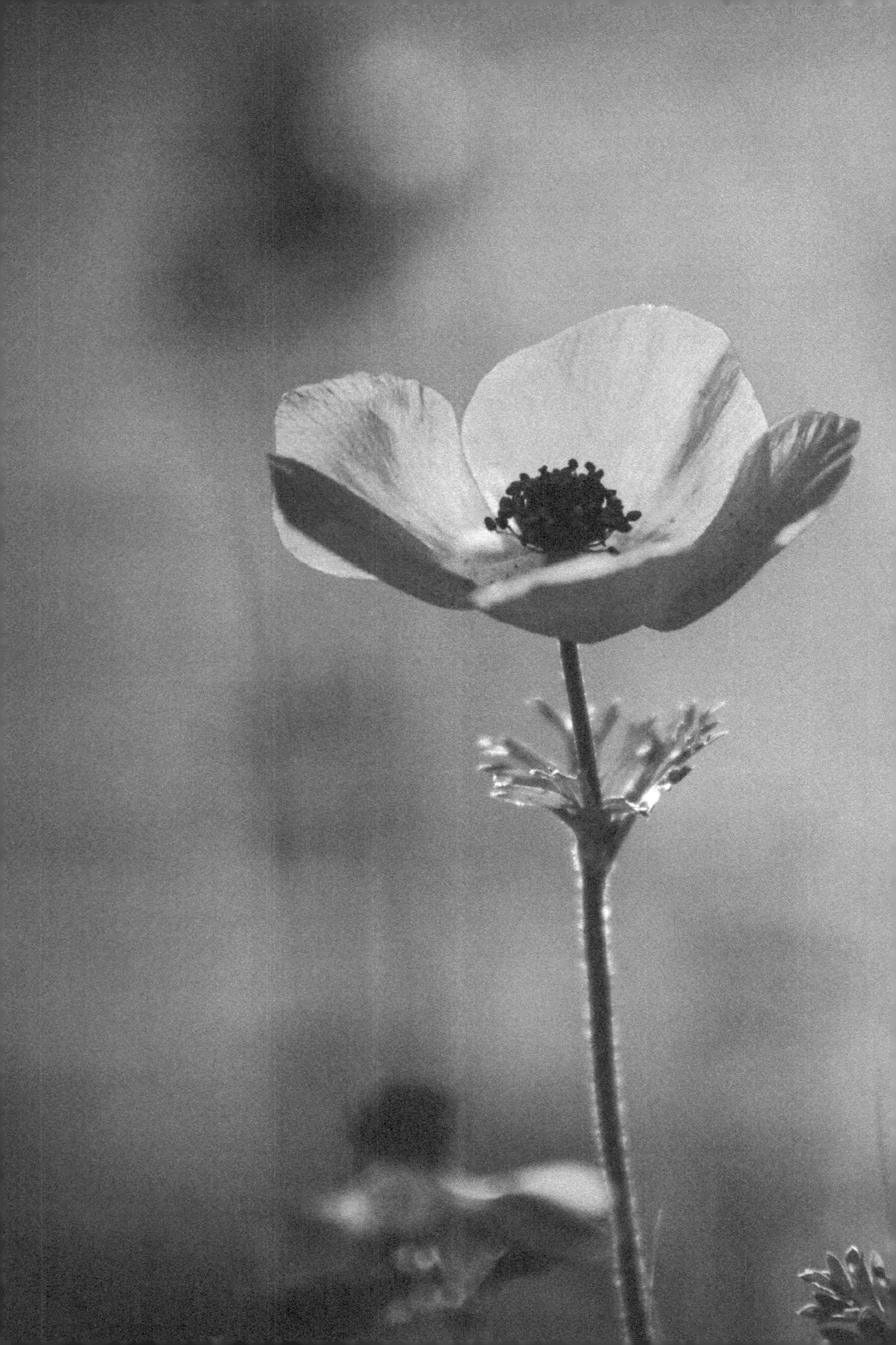

CHAPTER
THIRTY-FOUR
MALICE

Merri feeding was one of the most satisfying things I'd ever witnessed, and that was saying something. I designed complex viruses out of nothing. I brought down entire civilizations with nothing but a simple sneeze. I was feared by all and embraced by none. But watching this woman blossom and open for us, feeling her as she took down my walls with nothing but a softly uttered plea, was more powerful than anything I'd ever created.

We'd done this dance before, her and I. So I already knew that she'd need to be able to tap into my emotions for this to work. I didn't think I'd ever be comfortable sharing them with my brothers, but whether it had been earned or not, she'd shown me I'd be safe with her. At least in this.

It was always possible she'd turn around and use it against me later when she'd gotten what she needed from me. That certainly had been my experience with past partners, but the train had already left the station, and there was no stopping it now.

I couldn't resist touching her, not when her breasts were on offer and so close. Trailing my fingertip over the swell of one perfect globe,

I grinned at the way she arched into my touch. I circled the dusky bud of her nipple and then pinched her hard enough to elicit a soft cry.

Leaning my head down to put my mouth by her ear, I murmured, "Be a good girl and open your mouth, hellcat. I have something for you."

A barely discernible whimper escaped her as she obeyed, and my fist flew over my cock as I finally gave into the building pleasure. The first jet of my cum hit her bottom lip, the rest painting her tongue and chin. Using my thumb, I pushed my gift a little deeper into her mouth.

"Don't waste it."

Merri came with a cry, her body undulating as she rocked against Sin's hand. Chaos roared loud enough to rival the thunder outside, but I was too focused on the sight of my seed dripping from the side of her mouth.

"Swallow it. Put it where it belongs."

Her eyes fluttered open and found mine, her throat working beneath my hand as she did as I'd commanded. "Such a good girl."

I'd been so focused on her that I hadn't even noticed if or when the other two finished. Chaos obviously had, but I hadn't the foggiest what Grim and Sinclair had been doing at the end there.

"Is everyone okay?" Merri asked, sitting up and taking a long, slow breath.

She looked like her normal self again, all vibrance and vitality. The embodiment of health.

Sin caressed her thigh. "I think the real question is whether you're okay."

"You all took such good care of me. I'm so okay."

All of us? I risked a glance at Grim, who was standing now, hands balled into fists at his sides, a large damp splotch on his trousers. Chaos's chest was splattered in drying cum as well, and he snagged his shirt off the floor before he wiped up the evidence of what we'd done. It was less clear what Sin had done with his release. For all I knew, he could have finished in a Kleenex.

They should have been smarter, like me. I'd fed her in more ways than one.

"Thank you," she said, her expression as earnest as her voice. "I can't tell you how much I appreciate you doing that for me. Once we get the power back, I'll be better about managing my feeding."

"Or you could continue utilizing the resources at your disposal," Sin suggested.

Merri's eyes flicked from me to Grim, her cheeks a rosy pink. "I don't want to be a burden. You don't have—"

"If you finish that sentence, Red, I'm going to take you over my knee, and I promise you're not going to enjoy it."

Merri pressed her thighs together, visibly squirming.

"Don't be so sure about that," I murmured.

"Only a brat would enjoy making you do that. Is she a brat, Chaos?" Grim asked.

"Why are you asking a question you already know the answer to?"

Grim chuckled. "Just making sure we're all on the same page."

"I'm not always a brat," Merri said, a little pout in her voice.

"Okay, kitten," Sin said, giving her knee a pat.

"I'm not! You guys are just so . . ."

We all looked at her, but it was Sin who spoke first. "Dominant."

"Bossy," she corrected.

"And you are defiant. Stubborn. Petulant. The definition of a brat." Grim ran a hand through his hair as he assessed her.

"I don't know, sometimes she can be a good girl. I've seen it." I brushed my thumb over her lips once more because I just couldn't resist.

She blushed to the roots of her hair.

"Maybe all she needs is a little motivation," Chaos mused, studying her.

"You mean something like brats can play their games, but only good girls get to come?" I suggested.

Merri whimpered, a bolt of her lust punching through the room.

Sin's chuckle was low and warm. "Oh, she likes that."

"If you know what's good for you, wildflower, you'll live by that creed. Life will be much sweeter if you do."

"You guys, I'm disappointed. You're all forgetting how much fun it is to tame a brat. One of the best things in the world." Sin handed Merri his shirt and grinned like a mischievous cat as she slipped it over her head.

"I like wearing your clothes," Merri murmured, then let out an enormous yawn.

"Good. You can wear them until you're ready to take them off. Come on, kitten. It's time to tuck you into bed."

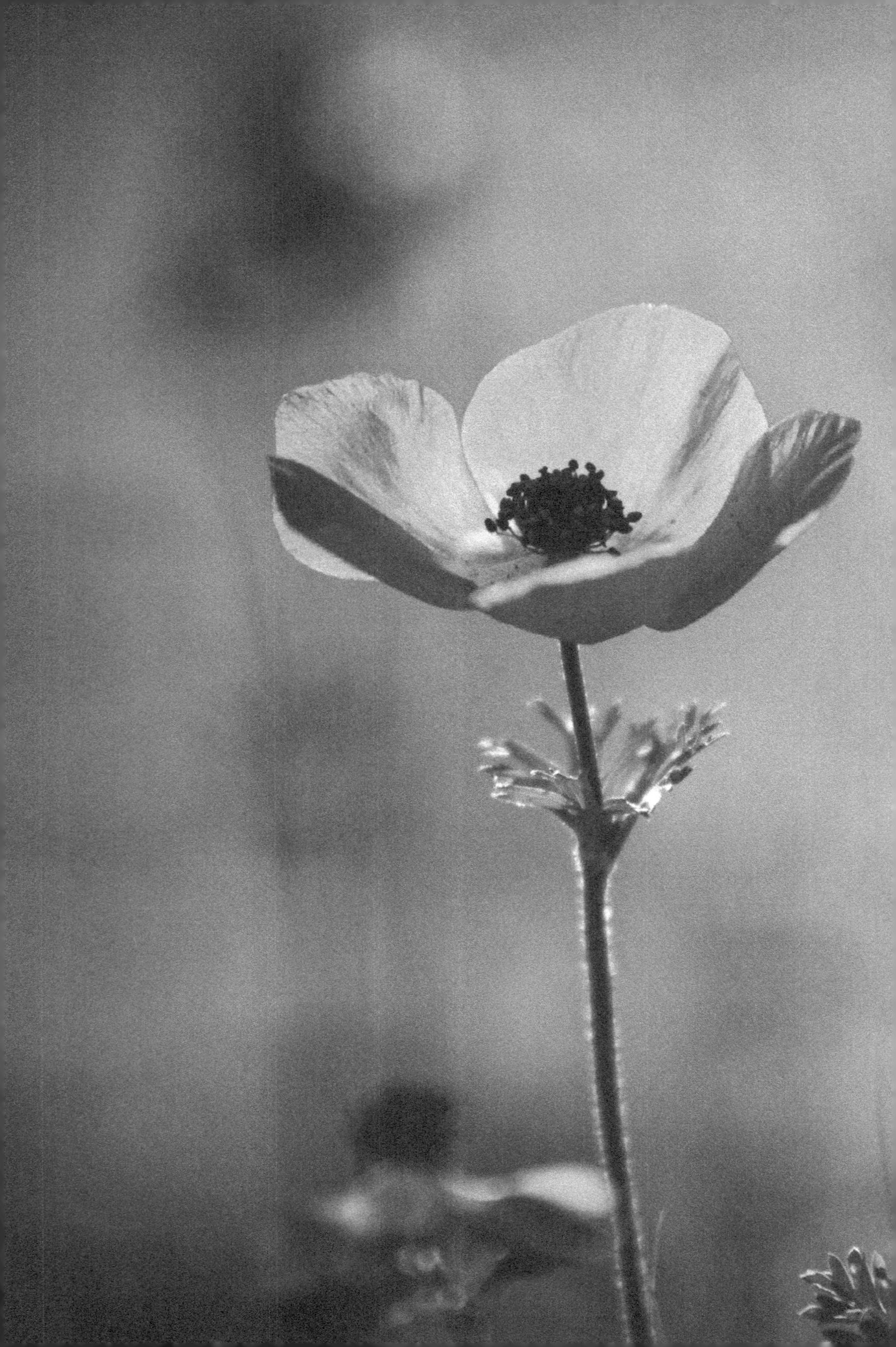

CHAPTER THIRTY-FIVE

SIN

"You really didn't have to carry me back to my room," Merri protested as I gently laid her down on her bed.

The storm was still raging outside, but the fire was going strong and cast more than enough light for us to see by.

"Pfft, as if I would miss out on an opportunity to hold you, kitten."

She nuzzled into my neck and inhaled, humming happily as she did. "You smell good."

"So do you. It's the pheromones. We're the same. Drawn to each other."

"Why don't our kind usually mate with each other, then?"

"We're a selfish breed by nature. Easily bored and prone to a wandering eye. We're not like other species who are predisposed to finding their perfect sexual match. Our females aren't overly fertile, and the males can mate with humans, so it's not a matter of repopulating like it is for so many others. We're mostly immortal and, well..." I shrugged, feeling like I was getting lost in the weeds.

"Do you have a wandering eye?" she asked, playing coy, but there was enough vulnerability hidden in the words that I knew she was worried about my answer.

"I've been known to," I admitted, reaching out and tucking a lock of hair behind her ear. "But recently, my gaze has been firmly fixed in one direction. I'm not a born incubus, though, so you can't measure me by normal standards."

"That's right. You were a Hollywood fuckboy before it was cool."

I chuckled and pressed a kiss into her hair. "Yes. But I'm turning over a new leaf. Being a fuckboy has really lost its charm."

She rolled her eyes as I walked into her bedroom. "You have such a way with words."

Fatigue sat on my shoulders with every step I took, but I didn't let her see past my mask of confidence as I deposited her on the soft bed. "Get under the covers, sweetheart. You're due a nice long nap after such a big meal. I'll see you tomorrow."

She grabbed my arm, holding me in place. "Wait, you didn't . . ." Her eyes scanned mine and then dipped lower as she studied my face. "You didn't feed with me."

"I know better than to steal food off someone else's plate, kitten. That meal was for you."

"But you're hungry."

I was starving, actually. Sitting there next to her, taking care of her as she and the others found their climax . . . It had been my own personal version of hell keeping myself from sampling any of it. It was a bit like standing in front of a buffet but not allowing yourself a single bite.

I shrugged. "I'll live."

"Sin," she chastised.

"I'm fine, Merri."

"Please let me help you? I know you've gone out and fed since I came to you guys, but you can't do that here. I'm all you have, and I'm offering." She reached for me and slid her palm up my bare stomach. "I want to give this to you."

I caught her by the wrist, lifting her hand and bringing it to my mouth so I could press my lips over her pulse. "You don't owe me anything, Merri. Just because we fed you doesn't mean you have to return the favor."

"What part of 'I want to' did you miss?"

Fuck me sideways, she was a goddamn dream. "Are you still wet for me, baby?"

"Why don't you find out for yourself?"

My cock gave a happy twitch at her teasing offer. "You want my fingers between your legs again."

"And?"

I chuckled as the brat reared her head. "You're insatiable."

"So are you."

My grin was wholly unrepentant. "Damn straight. I can go all night and well into the morning and still come back for more."

"Promises, promises."

Who knew flirting could be so much fun? Usually it was a means to an end, but with Merri, it was enough all on its own.

"It's more than a promise. It's a guarantee. You and I may never leave this bed if we're not careful."

"Mmm, I don't hate the sound of that. Me and this bed already have a bit of a thing going, but I suppose you could join us."

"Sharing is caring, huh?"

"Maybe. With the right person."

I crawled onto the bed, fitting myself between her thighs and hovering over her so our faces were close enough I could kiss her if I wanted. And I wanted. I wanted so fucking bad. I'd stolen a kiss from her earlier, but this was different. A kiss from an incubus was a tool used to gain trust and mesmerize prey. I never used it to my advantage because, for me, this was intimate. It was a privilege. This meant I was vulnerable to her, that *I* trusted *her*. Kisses held power.

Until Merri, I never kissed on the mouth.

I was basically the male version of Julia Roberts in Pretty Woman.

"You know," I murmured, preparing to shoot my shot. "This is sort of like our first date."

"Is it? Why, Emmett, you move so quickly, taking me to bed on our first date."

"Technically it's you taking me to bed. You shameless hussy."

She grinned, reaching up and threading her fingers in my hair. "No one is forcing you to stay. You can leave any time you want."

I dropped my weight on top of her until she was basically a human pancake. "Not a fucking chance. I finally got an invite to join you in bed. You're never getting rid of me now."

Her body trembled with laughter beneath mine. "Oh no. Whatever shall I do?"

"How about you let me taste you and make you come on my tongue?"

She quirked a brow. "I thought this was supposed to be about you."

"Making you come *is* about me. You know the score, baby girl. Your pleasure is mine."

In answer, she parted her thighs a little wider. "Well then, you'd better get to work . . . Emmett."

I winked at her as I scooted down the bed until my face was right between those lush thighs. "Whatever you say, darlin'." Gripping her by the backs of her knees, I spread her legs until her beautiful pussy was open and ready for me.

Her breath hitched, the sound pulling my gaze from the work of art in front of me and up her body to meet her eyes. Surprisingly, they were filled with apprehension. I cocked a questioning brow, waiting for her to elaborate.

"Go easy on me, Sin. It's my first time."

I laughed and bit down on the soft flesh of her inner thigh.

"I'm serious."

"What? You're not a virgin. You told me—"

"He never did this. No one has."

Oh. Fuck. Yes.

"Oh, kitten. You better grab onto the headboard. I'm about to rock your world."

She tensed as I leaned forward, so I pressed a light kiss just above her swollen clit and whispered, "Close your eyes and trust me to make you feel good."

Then I dipped my head and dragged my nose up her slit, inhaling her perfume and committing it to memory. She whined and tried to wriggle away on instinct. We couldn't have that. My little succubus needed to learn how to take what I gave her.

Moving my hands to her hips, I held her in place and made the most of my time between her legs. I nibbled and kissed her everywhere but the one spot I knew she craved most. Sucking and tasting, teasing while also arousing her to the point of begging me for more.

Giving a woman head was much more involved than simply sucking her clit until she came. The pussy was a finely tuned instrument, and if you knew how to play it right, the music you could make together would be transcendent.

I waited until her moans were mostly pleas before I started to feed, knowing the sensation would send her skyrocketing. I couldn't contain my chuckle as she bucked and screamed my name, her fingers twisting and gripping my hair as she held me in place and writhed against my tongue.

"Sing for me, sweetheart. I want the others to hear you."

Her flavor flooded my mouth, sweet and a little salty, and distinctly mine. I'd taste her for hours after this, smell her on me, bask in the memory of being the first man to get this from her.

"You ready to come for me, Merri?"

"Yes. God, yes."

Finally, I gave her the attention she'd been waiting none too patiently for. Her clit was so swollen it looked painful, but that was the point. A skilled lover knew how to coax it out of its hiding place, to arouse her so much there was nothing she wanted more than your touch right. Fucking. There.

As my lips closed over her clit, I sank two fingers deep inside her and curled them up, pressing on just the right spot in time with my suction. She detonated in seconds, her slick sweetness coating my fingers and dripping onto the sheets.

My name was a breathless cry, and as she came apart, I drank deeply from the sexual tsunami she unleashed. I may not have fangs or an aversion to sunlight, but the way I fed wasn't all that different from a vampire. Merri's climax was so potent I felt lightheaded from the high of it. This one moment with her was enough to keep me nourished for weeks.

When she was boneless and sated and I was sure her orgasm had faded, I backed away from the cradle of her thighs. Sitting back on my heels, I gazed down at the beauty I'd claimed.

Skin glistening with a thin veil of pleasure-induced sweat. Hair a mass of red tangles, splayed out on the silk pillowcase. Eyes hooded. Lips swollen from biting them to stifle her cries. God, she was perfect.

"Look at you. Absolutely ruined," I breathed, proud as a fucking peacock.

She beamed up at me. "If I'd known what I was missing out on, I might have taken you up on your offer sooner."

I gave her my patented smolder. "You just let me know when you're ready for an encore, kitten."

"How about right now?"

"I mean, I'm always down to eat pussy."

"No, not that. I want more."

"More?"

She bit down on her bottom lip and nodded as she sat up. "More."

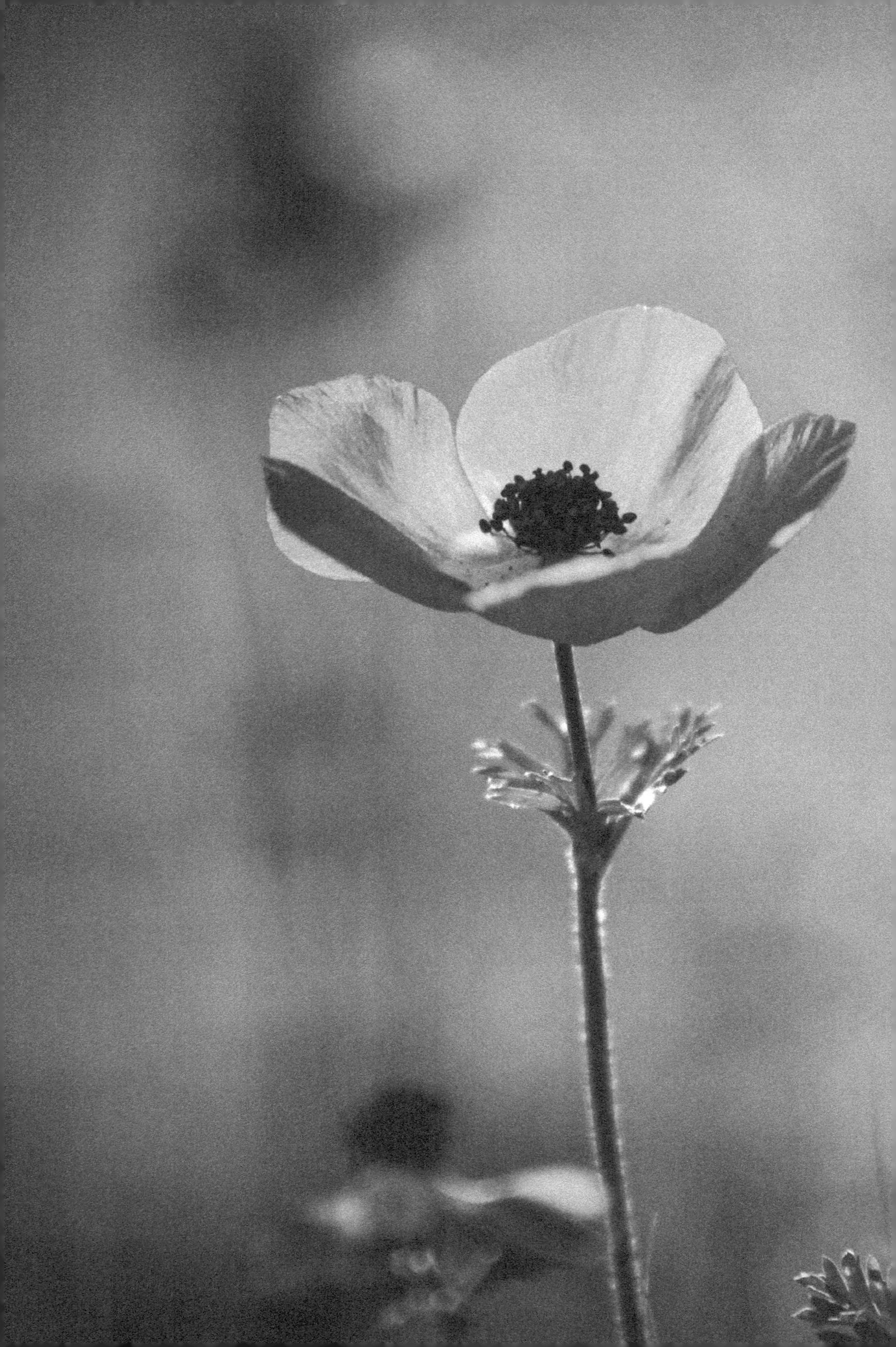

CHAPTER
THIRTY-SIX
MERRI

S in stared at me with something like awe written on his face. I knew this was the right decision. I'd never given oral sex to anyone. Jimmy and I had gone from kisses and heavy petting directly into the loss of our virginity with all the finesse of the inexperienced teens we'd been. Aside from practicing on a toy or two, these were uncharted waters. But Sin had proven he'd be the safest person for me to dive in with. Not only had he understood how to keep the others safe while I fed, he'd known exactly what I needed because he and I were the same. And not once had he pushed for more or tried to take advantage.

He also hadn't come.

His cock strained against the fabric of his sweats, a damp patch betraying how needy he was. I knew a man's tells, and this man's dick was telling on him in a big way. He needed release.

"So how should we do this? Personally, I've always loved The Way of the Hound. But I'm a fan of them all, really. Missionary. The Flea Bag. The Big Lebowski. Cowgirl. Reverse Cowgirl. The Praying Mantis, although that one can get a little messy and painful."

I gaped at him. "The . . . the . . . did you say The Way of the Hound?"

He nodded. "I've always felt doggy style was lacking in dignity."

"Wait. I meant . . . you want . . ."

Oh dear God.

I felt the color drain from my face as I realized his head had gone straight to intercourse while I'd been planning on a nice BJ.

"Don't you? You said . . . *more*." He lowered his voice for the last word, and I could see exactly why he'd thought I'd meant sex.

I swallowed, struggling to find my words.

"Hey," he murmured, reaching out to cup my cheek. "Where did you go?"

I blinked at him. "I . . . you know what happened the last time. I-I can't. I'll—"

Understanding washed across his face, and he immediately pulled me into a hug. "Hey, hey, shhh, it's all good, kitten. We don't have to do anything you don't want to. I'm happy just holding you. But just so you know, you don't have to worry about *that*. Nothing we do together will harm me. I'm Merri-proof. I promise."

"You don't know that." Tears sprang to my eyes at the thought of Sin meeting the same fate as Jimmy.

"Yeah, I do. Remember when I said we are the same? Remember how satisfying it was when we had our session together?"

I nodded, my stupid lower lip quivering.

"Baby, you won't hurt me. I'm your perfect match." He held my face between his hands, his eyes staring deep into mine. There was no trace of guile or deception there. Just raw honesty.

"You're sure?"

He nodded. "More positive than the Virgin Mary's pregnancy test."

I snickered. "That's pretty positive."

"Hand to God."

I canted my head to the side. "Are you allowed to say that? You know, being a horseman and all. Doesn't He work for the other side?"

"Shhh. Stop making so much sense. You said you want more. I need to know what that is. How can I give my girl everything she wants?"

I bit the inside of my cheek as I considered his words. I knew exactly what I wanted. I wanted to experience everything with him. He'd been one hundred percent right when he said that he would rock my world. Now that I knew what I'd been missing, I didn't want a single experience to pass me by.

"You swear I won't kill you?"

I could tell he was trying not to laugh, but he was determined to treat my fear as seriously as I was, and that meant more to me than anything else he could have done.

"Cross my heart," he said, drawing an X over the center of his chest.

"Then I want to do it. The hound's journey. The praying virgin. All of it. As long as it's with you."

The promise of rewriting my experience with sex, of taking something traumatic I'd carried with me for years and turning it into a new and beautiful thing, was too tempting to ignore. Sin was made for me. Just like he said. We were like two bookends, a matching set.

His smile stole my breath.

"I'm going to ask you a couple questions, okay?"

"Ooo-kay."

"Do you mind telling me how you and the other guy did things?"

"Why?"

"I want to make sure we start with something else. So we don't accidentally trigger you in the middle of the main event." He waggled his brows and made me laugh. "In all seriousness, this is a big step for you, and I want you to be comfortable and feel safe. You—" He swallowed whatever he'd been about to say. "Your experience matters to me. Can't ruin my satisfaction ranking, you know?"

My heart swelled with affection for this man who'd insisted he'd spent his life only taking and never giving. He'd given me so much in such a short time. Reaching down, I pulled the hem of his shirt up and lifted the fabric over my head. With a heated look, I dropped the fabric on the floor before rising to my knees so we were face-to-face.

"I don't want to be on my back, and I don't want it to be . . ." I wrinkled my nose, searching for the right word. "Sweet."

"So you don't want me to make slow, passionate love to you?"

"No?"

"Do you need me to fuck you, Merri? Hard and dirty, maybe a little rough, and a whole helluva lot of fun?"

Biting my lower lip, I nodded before reaching for the waistband of his pants and delving my hand inside. He groaned the instant my fingers brushed his hot, swollen length, tossing his head back with abandon.

"So good," he rasped.

"Yeah?"

"Fuck yeah."

His praise ignited my confidence, so I did it again, my grasp more firm this time.

Slick precum dripped from his tip, and I used it to my advantage, rolling my palm across the head and loving the way he rocked his hips forward.

"If you want me to come in your hand, don't stop."

"And if I'd rather you come inside me?"

"Then you'd better turn around and grab that headboard, baby."

My nipples tightened so much they ached. I did as he said, presenting my ass to him while I held on for dear life. To his credit, he didn't slam into me with no warning. His warm palm slid from the base of my spine all the way up to the nape of my neck before he twisted his fingers in my hair and pulled.

"The Way of the Hound, variation number one. One of my top three."

His thick cock nudged my pussy, but he didn't press inside yet.

"There's more than one variation?"

"Mmmhmm." He draped himself over me, his lips at my ear. "Variation two goes a little something like this." He released my hair and sank his teeth into the muscles connecting my shoulder to my neck. As he did, his crown breached my entrance, both sensations pulling a strangled gasp from me. "Both are winners."

"I can see why you think so," I panted. My body was still so turned on from what happened downstairs in the salon. I was pretty sure one swipe of his rough fingers over my clit would send me over the edge again.

He slowly pressed forward, his hand now wrapped around my throat. "And that's number three. I like them all, but I'm partial to the first one."

"What else do you like?" I asked. My eyes fluttered closed as he slowly worked just the tip of his thick cock in and out of me.

"Well, there's always the Sinner's Prayer," he murmured, taking my wrists one at a time and tugging until they were pressed together, his long fingers encircling them both. "Up straight, my good girl. Let me fuck you until you're praying to come around my cock."

"Yes," I agreed, knowing I was practically there already.

When he pulled all the way out and then filled me again in one smooth, hard thrust, I realized I was wrong.

I was Jon Snow.

I knew nothing.

Every brutal thrust pressed against that same spot he'd found earlier inside me. The room became nothing but the two of us, our bodies slapping together, my wetness dripping down my thighs, the headboard banging over and over on the wall. I was pretty sure some plaster dust floated down from the ceiling.

With every rock of his hips into me, I felt my control slipping further away. I was a puppet, and Sin was my master.

I didn't even realize I'd started chanting until his lips were at my ear again, his chuckle washing over me like a caress.

"Please, please, please," I begged.

"That sounds like a prayer to me."

His ragged breaths against my ear combined with the way he reached down and pressed on my lower belly as he drove into me sent me over the edge.

I came apart.

I came undone.

I came and came and came and didn't stop coming.

Tears streamed down my cheeks as Sin tensed and shuddered behind me, his desperate groan of my name letting me know he'd found his own pleasure, but this time inside me.

"Fuck, baby. You're squeezing me so good. Never want to leave you," he muttered, his words punctuated with heavy breaths.

I couldn't help myself. I was like a shark after the first hint of blood in the water. I fed without consciously choosing to feed. I fed as hard as I came, which is to say I couldn't stop. I was swept up in the sensation, gorging myself on his pleasure and floating in the beauty of what we'd created through the joining of our bodies.

He went limp behind me before finally rolling to his side, his cock slipping out of me and allowing me to fall into the soft mattress so I could catch my breath.

"Wow," I managed, tilting my head so I could glance at him beside me. "At the risk of stroking your ego, I think you undersold your talents, mister. That was even better than I'd expected."

I was already smiling, anticipating his smug comeback.

It never came.

"Sin?" I called, still smiling as I gave his shoulder a little shove.

No answer.

"Sinclair?"

I sat up and shook him, but he didn't respond. He didn't even blink.

"This isn't funny, Sin. Answer me." My voice was a reedy, tense thing.

But he didn't move. His chest didn't rise and fall. His pupils were blown, mouth slack, and I knew then and there I should never have trusted him.

A tear cascaded down my cheek as I stared at the evidence of what a monster I was.

"You fucking liar!" I screamed, my tears falling in earnest as I slammed my palm down on his chest. "You lied to me," I whispered, voice breaking. "You promised you wouldn't die, and you lied."

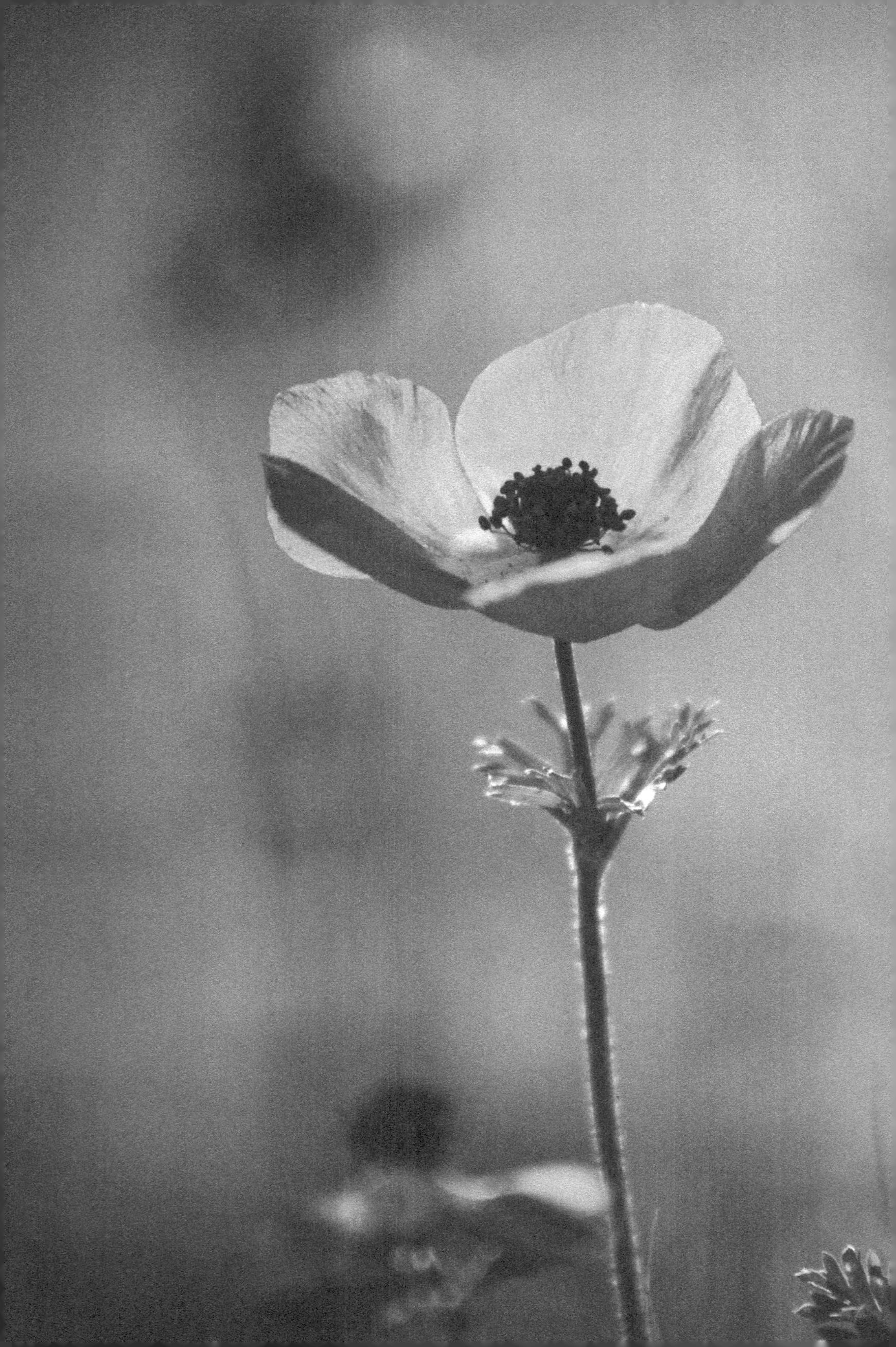

CHAPTER THIRTY-SEVEN
LUCIFER

"Wrong!"

Honestly, I didn't understand how any of these horsewomen were capable of tying their own shoes, not to mention starting the apocalypse.

"My king, I swear, I—"

I spun around, letting one of the poison-tipped daggers in my hand fly. This one nicked her ear, dark black blood splashing down her shoulder before joining the other drops on the floor.

"I care nothing for your promises. You have failed me at every turn. So I'm going to ask you one more time, you sniveling, worthless excuse of a demon. Where. Is. She?" I threw another dagger, this one sinking into her thigh. "Where is the wife you promised me?"

"The penthouse—"

"Is gone!" I roared, flinging my arm out to gesture to the two Princes standing at attention on the other side of the room. "You heard their reports as well as I. There weren't any bodies in the rubble, which means they escaped. Unless you're trying to tell me that my most loyal and devoted servants lied to me?"

Pride snarled and took one step forward before Envy stopped him with an arm across his chest.

"They've escaped with her. That's the only option. I'd feel it if she'd died," Famine spluttered like the weakling she was.

I threw the final dagger just for fun. This one hit her right in the tit.

She whimpered, her eyes shining with pain and fury, but there was a hint of relief in her eyes. Silly sausage. I was far from done with her.

"Oh no, Sabine. You don't get to play the victim here. You made me promises, and I fucking intend to collect," I said in a voice so soft it was little more than a whisper as I prowled closer to her.

Not even she was stupid enough to mistake the softer volume for the removal of a threat.

"Th-the dream walks."

"Yes, Sabine? Could you, in fact, be referring to the dream walks *I* had to initiate? The concept *I* came up with on my own? Oh please, do tell me what novel idea you think I should incorporate into my backup plan after you have failed me in every conceivable way, you stupid fucking cunt. I can't wait to hear this."

I pulled the daggers out one at a time, relishing her winces, especially on the last one, as I may have put a little too much mustard on my final throw. The blade was embedded in her spinal column. My aim could use a little work, if I was being honest.

She coughed up blood and dragged in a rattling breath. Oh, goody. I punctured a lung.

"Bring her into your dreams."

Her wounds began healing as I returned to my original place, then thought better of it and took two steps closer.

"Did I ask for your fucking help?!" I screamed, hurling a dagger and watching with no small amount of pride as it sank into her belly, just below her sternum.

She gasped like a fish, and I really wanted her to answer me. I was under no illusions about what I had and hadn't said. But we both knew if she tried to correct me, it would be the last thing she ever did.

"I . . . I . . ."

"I . . .I . . ." I mocked as I got in her face once more. "How about this, Sabine," I mused, voice turning conversational as I twirled one of the daggers and then slammed it straight into the center of her ribcage. I knew my grin was maniacal as I held her gaze. "How about you do your fucking job, or the next time I stab you, I don't remove the knife, and I leave you to hang over my throne as a warning to all others stupid enough to disappoint me?"

She made a gurgling sound.

"What was that?" I asked, cocking my head so my ear was at her lips.

"Y-yes, m-m-my lord."

"Great!" I chirped, snapping away from her with a bright smile. "So glad we're on the same page. Another fucking happy day here in hell."

Then I performed a tight about-face, hands in my pockets as I sauntered my way out of the room, softly singing under my breath, "Sweet dreams are made of me . . ."

The Mate Games: Apocalypse will continue with Chaos, coming soon. You can pre-order your copy here but while you wait, Lucifer wanted to make sure we offered you a little temptation.

You can download your copy of Grim's bonus scene at www.thematesgames.com/SinBonus or you can download it on audio and listen to it at www.thematesgames.com/SinAudioBonus

THE MATE GAMES UNIVERSE
BY K. LORAINE & MEG ANNE

WAR
Obsession

Rejection

Possession

Temptation

Devotion

PESTILENCE
Promised to the Night (Prequel Novella)

Deal with the Demon

Claimed by the Shifters

Captive of the Night

Lost to the Moon

DEATH
Haunting Beauty

Hunted Beast

Hateful Prince

Heartless Villain

APOCALYPSE

SIN

CHAOS

MALICE

GRIM

LUCIFER

MORE BY MEG & KIM

TWISTED CROSS RANCH
A DARK CONTEMPORARY COWBOY REVERSE HAREM

SINNER'S SECRET

CORRUPTOR'S CLAIM

DEADLY DEBT

ALSO BY MEG ANNE

BROTHERHOOD OF THE GUARDIANS/NOVASGARD VIKINGS

<u>UNDERCOVER MAGIC</u> (NORD & LINA)
A SEXY & SUSPENSEFUL FATED MATES PNR

HINT OF DANGER

FACE OF DANGER

WORLD OF DANGER

PROMISE OF DANGER

CALL OF DANGER

BOUND BY DANGER (QUINN & FINLEY)

∾

THE CHOSEN UNIVERSE

<u>THE CHOSEN</u>
A FATED MATES HIGH FANTASY ROMANCE

MOTHER OF SHADOWS

REIGN OF ASH

CROWN OF EMBERS

QUEEN OF LIGHT

THE CHOSEN BOXSET #1

THE CHOSEN BOXSET #2

The Keepers

A Guardian/Ward High Fantasy Romance

The Dreamer (A Keeper's Prequel)

The Keepers Legacy

The Keepers Retribution

The Keepers Vow

The Keepers Boxset

The Forsaken

A Rejected Mates/Enemies-To-Lovers Romantasy

Prisoner of Steel & Shadow

Queen of Whispers & Mist

Court of Death & Dreams

~

Standalones

My Soul To Take: A Forbidden Love Meets Fated Mates PNR

Also by K. Loraine

The Blackthorne Vampires
THE BLOOD TRILOGY
(Cashel & Olivia)

Blood Captive

Blood Traitor

Blood Heir

BLACKTHORNE BLOODLINES
(Lucas & Briar)

Midnight Prince

Midnight Hunger

∾

THE WATCHER SERIES

Waking the Watcher

Denying the Watcher

Releasing the Watcher

∾

THE SIREN COVEN

Eternal Desire (Shifter reluctant mates)

Cursed Heart (Hate to Lovers)

Broken Sword (MMF menage Arthurian)

∾

STANDALONES
Cursed (MFM Sleeping Beauty Retelling)

~

REVERSE HAREM STANDALONES
Their Vampire Princess (A Reverse Harem Romance)
All the Queen's Men (A Fae Reverse Harem Romance)

About Meg Anne

USA Today and international bestselling paranormal and fantasy romance author Meg Anne has always had stories running on a loop in her head. They started off as daydreams about how the evil queen (aka Mom) had her slaving away doing chores, and more recently shifted into creating backgrounds about the people stuck beside her during rush hour. The stories have always been there; they were just waiting for her to tell them.

Like any true SoCal native, Meg enjoys staying inside curled up with a good book and her fur babies . . . or maybe that's just her. You can convince Meg to buy just about anything if it's covered in glitter or rhinestones, or make her laugh by sharing your favorite bad joke. She also accepts bribes in the form of baked goods and Mexican food.

Meg is best known for her leading men #MenbyMeg, her inevitable cliffhangers, and making her readers laugh out loud, all of which started with the bestselling Chosen series.

About K. Loraine

USA Today Bestselling author Kim Loraine writes steamy contemporary and sexy paranormal romance. **You'll find her paranormal romances written under the name K. Loraine and her contemporaries as Kim Loraine.** Don't worry, you'll get the same level of swoon-worthy heroes, sassy heroines, and an eventual HEA.

When not writing, she's busy herding cats (raising kids), trying to keep her house sort of clean, and dreaming up ways for fictional couples to meet.